heroines...
confident heroes...
loves creating complicat...
She can be found @margotrad...
@margot_radcliffe on Instagram.

Ra...
heartwarmingly romantic...

Also by Radcliffe

Mr One-Night S...
Mr Temptation
Naughty or Nice
Getting Dirty
Losing Control
Unwrapping the Best Man
Our Little Secret

Also by Margot Radcliffe

Friends with Benefits
Sin City Seduction
Sinfully Yours
Bring the Heat

Discover more at millsandboon.co.uk

REAWAKENED

RACHAEL STEWART

FAST LANE

MARGOT RADCLIFFE

MILLS & BOON

First Published in Great Britain 2021
by Mills & Boon, an imprint of HarperCollins*Publishers*
1 London Bridge Street, London, SE1 9GF

Reawakened © 2021 Rachael Stewart

Fast Lane © 2021 Terra Rogerson

ISBN: 978-0-263-29798-0

MIX
Paper from
responsible sources
FSC® C007454

This book is produced from independently certified FSC™ paper
to ensure responsible forest management.
For more information visit www.harpercollins.co.uk/green.

Printed and bound in Spain
by CPI, Barcelona

REAWAKENED

RACHAEL STEWART

MILLS & BOON

To all the DAREdevils who loved DARE,
this one is for you!
It's been a blast, writing these super-hot tales,
and it's time to go out with a BANG!
Consider yourselves warned. ;-)

Much love,

Rachael xx

CHAPTER ONE

'To live is the rarest thing in the world.
Most people exist, that is all.'

—Oscar Wilde

Olivia

HOW RIGHT CAN one man be?

Wilde would definitely lump me in with the 'most'.

And do I care…?

I throw back a shot of vodka and wince into the mirror beyond the bar, my blue eyes sparking back at me as the answer burns with the alcohol.

I care.

And I'm doing what I can to make up for it. To make up for forty-five years of just existing. Of giving my all and coming out the other side, like this.

Don't get me wrong. I'm not bitter… *I'm not.*

I'm angry.

I'm angry that my husband of twenty years has gone. Taken away from me without any warning.

I'm angry that we spent our entire lives together dedicated to our work, to our charity, and we never found a balance.

I don't resent the work we did. Especially the help we gave those who needed it. Those without homes, without money, without family or support. Those living lives that we could barely bring ourselves to imagine.

Just existing isn't a choice for them; it's all they can do.

I had a choice, and I chose badly.

So no, I'm not bitter. I'm angry. Angry with myself for not living. Angry that we ploughed so much time into everything else that we never hopped off the treadmill long enough to actually live. Never saw the world with our eyes wide open. Had fun. Adventure.

Cue me. Now.

Sitting alone. Propping up the bar of the exclusive DareDevils club. The sultry beat to the music pumping through my veins, the soft white lights mixing with the vibrant strobes that work through the crowd, deepening the mood and highlighting the suspended dance cages above. Women and men locked within, their lithe bodies twisting and turning in movements that scream sex.

The same kind of allure thrums off the bodies below. People hanging out in varying states of dress. Subs crawling on leashes, led by their latex-clad Doms. Others, much like me, wearing club gear designed to entice, to seduce, to have the elusive fun I am so desperate for…

Hedonistic. Wild. Abandoned.

'Your room is ready for you, Sky.'

I swallow a surprised laugh at the young bartender before me. My pseudonym is something I came up with on the spot and having it repeated back to me triggers a little rush of embarrassment. I may be forty-five, yet something about this has me feeling childlike and foolish and way out of my comfort zone.

But then, isn't that the point?

I palm the cool bar-top with both hands like it will somehow steady me and return the bartender's smile that's so perfect I can easily believe him a model by day, a successful tip-gainer by night.

'Lead the way…'

Because, no matter how ridiculous or silly or foolish I feel, what lies in wait upstairs has not only the nerves but the anticipation clambering up my throat and I *need* this.

Another tick in the many, many boxes I have yet to fill…

Valentine

This bar is not my scene.

Not the mood, the people, the music…the blatant hunger.

It's carnal, animalistic, and the walls pulse with it.

Only I have no interest. For four years, I've been celibate. Four years avoiding anything close.

Yet here I am, and all for her.

Olivia Carmel.

The woman I'm supposed to help.

The woman whose PR image is going down the pan and taking her brand with it. And when I say brand I mean her company, her charity, her. All three. She's a celebrity entrepreneur, an icon, but since the death of her husband a year ago she's steadily gone off the rails and I've been sent to rein her back in.

To bring the Olivia the nation loves back.

To fix her.

I stroke my jaw as I watch her, my frown building, my curiosity too. She's all cool, suave and sophisticated against the seedy backdrop and I can't marry the two together. Not the venue and her. Not the tabloid gossip and her.

She's an enigma.

An enigma that's steadily pulling me out of my comfort zone.

I roll my shoulders beneath my tailored jacket and run a finger under my shirt collar, cock my head side to side. She's far, far from reach but her presence does something to me; it creeps beneath my skin, teasing, taunting, goading out the old me.

'Can I offer you another?'

I turn to my left, to a scantily clad waitress who I'm sure is offering more than the drink on her tray, and smile. It's tight and she backs up a step. *Easy.*

I'm six foot four and broad; a tight smile isn't

going to soften my look. Especially with the jagged scar through my eyebrow that looks like I spend too long inside a boxing ring when the truth is far simpler and comes with a dark tale of its own.

'No.' My voice is gravel thick, another side-effect of the same event, and it only makes her back up further. 'Thank you.'

My gratitude has her smile returning, her shoulders easing. 'No problem. Just wave me down if you change your mind.'

I nod and go back to Olivia.

She's perfectly poised on the bar stool. Her platinum blonde hair, smooth and sleek, snakes down her exposed spine in a ponytail that ends just above the low curve to her dress. Her eyes are all made up, the dark shade making her crystal-blue eyes strike out across the distance, her lips far more subtle in their blushing pink gloss.

The entire look is sexy, sultry, and so far removed from the polished businesswoman and wholesome charity organiser the press were once accustomed to.

She's not the official face of the charity any more; she stood down months ago when her wild behaviour first hit the tabloids. In all fairness to the press, they did cite mitigating circumstances. She'd recently lost her husband after all. But it wasn't long before they started putting the boot in anyway.

And I get her behaviour. I feel it. The ache of loss. The mark it leaves and the interminable chasm. I understand. And I know that's why Alan, my friend

and mentor, her chief operating officer, came to me
for help.

So that's why I'm here. To witness it for myself.
The truth. Not the persona the press now project, the
rumour mill doing its thing. I'm here to get a feel
for what lies ahead, to decide if it's worth the battle
that's bound to ensue and the raking over old wounds
that I seek to forget.

Is *she* worth it?

My head says yes. She doesn't deserve the hand
she's been dealt in life and the PR shitstorm brewing.
Not to mention the potentially grave consequences
if she takes it one wild step too far.

But my gut…that's a whole other ball game.

I'm too interested. Too intrigued. I feel it build
with the atmosphere as I wait for her next move.
Just how far does she partake in the illicit fun under
this roof? Is it natural curiosity that has her coming
here as an innocent bystander, an observer? Or is it
something more…is she seeking to indulge another
side to her?

A side I long ago denied myself…

I watch as she swirls the glass in her hand, her
eyes lost in the movement of the drink and then they
lift, pierce the mirror, pierce me.

My lungs still, my breath caught in some weird
suspended state…but she can't see me, I'm in the
shadows, and yet that feeling she sparks returns ten-
fold, stirring up something deep, long forgotten.

I shift in my seat, look away. It's time to go. I've
seen enough. She's nursed the same drink, not even

touching it until now. And, whatever she's here for, it doesn't matter; it's enough that she's crossed the threshold in the world of Public Relations. It isn't just some falsified rumour designed to discredit her.

I rise, turn to leave, but the bartender catches my eye as he pauses before her, says something that has her turning rigid. I can see her eyes dance in the mirror, see her cheeks streak with a flush of colour as she nods and then she's lowering herself from the stool. One long, creamy leg unfolding to reach the floor, followed by the other. Her red-soled black stilettos making her appear taller, all the more slender as she rises up...

Her dress, what there is of it, shimmers in the lights, the draping curve to its back sashaying as she turns and faces me head on, and I lose the ability to breathe once more. The dress ends mid-thigh, the high front and full-length sleeves contrasting with the skimpy rear, but the way it clings to her with that accentuating shimmer...

She's something else.

I force my eyes up, take in the sleek ponytail, blue eyes and alabaster skin and realise with a surge of heat inside just how much I'm attracted to her. And I haven't felt that kind of pull in so long.

I blame the alien environment, the carnal longing thrumming off the crowd. It's messing with my status quo. I haven't wanted anyone since Layla and no brief visit to a den of iniquity will change that. No matter what my reawakened body is trying to tell me.

I control *it*. Not the other way around.

I learned my lesson the hard way. And it really is time to leave.

I turn and smack into something.

'Shit!' it curses. Big brown eyes stare up at me as something cold and wet seeps through my shirt and glass shatters on the floor at our feet. It's the waitress from moments ago, her tray now devoid of drinks and stuck flat between us.

I step back. 'Apologies.'

'No, I'm sorry, I'll just…'

But I'm no longer listening. Every eye in the vicinity is now on me, on us.

Including hers. Olivia's.

Bollocks.

CHAPTER TWO

Olivia

I TURN TO follow the bartender as the sound of breaking glass snags my attention. A pretty brunette waitress is clutching a tray to her chest, her eyes wide as she blinks up, up and up at a man so broad and so tall he dwarfs everyone around him.

I watch as the girl blurts what must be an apology, watch her cheeks flush pink as she drops to the floor. And then his eyes flit in my direction, long enough for my heart to trip over itself, but not long enough that I get to drink my fill of his chiselled appeal.

It normally takes a good filter and camera angle to pull it off. But he's *au naturel* and I'm gawping, the new me eager to take in more…eager but he's not obliging. He's angled away now, crouching down to assist the waitress in the clean-up, and I'm left with the memory of the look he sent me. The slight flare to his eyes as they widened with…with what? Awareness, recognition…a mutual desire?

Because I don't know him. I'd remember if we'd

met before. He doesn't have a face or frame you could easily forget.

I watch as they pick at the glass, marvel at his profile. He's striking even from the side, all angular cheekbones, square jawline, and a curl in his dark overlong hair. The lights are too low to make out much more and I feel myself step closer, just a little, and sense the bartender pause as he realises I'm no longer following him.

'What's…' His voice trails off as he follows my line of sight and nods. 'Ah, I see. I can invite him to watch if you like. The viewing gallery is quite the experience and I'm sure he'll appreciate the time to dry off.'

My eyes snap to him, a quick shake of the head. *Good God, no.*

He gives a low chuckle. 'If you should change your mind…'

'Keep walking.'

I follow his chuckling form up the stairs and have the oddest feeling the stranger's eyes are back on me, making me regret my impulsive no. But can you imagine?

It's taken me three weeks just to get to this point, to have the courage to fill out the form, both asking for and consenting to what is to come, and I'm dizzy with it. To add him to the mix…

The heat blooms in my lower belly. I wet my lips.

'This is where I leave you. Second door on your left. Have fun.'

He's already heading back down the stairs.

'Ask him...' I blurt out before nerves get the better of me '...the guy downstairs.'

He smiles, gives a nod. 'Sure thing.'

And then he's gone and I take a breath, look to the door he pointed out. It's deep red and ornate, furnished with a knocker of a lion's head that would look more at home on the external door to a grand residence. I walk towards it, my heels too loud on the stone floor in spite of the music and chatter from below, and remind myself this is what I want.

This is what I came for. That after years of being the one to dominate in the bedroom, I get to experience the other side...

I rap the knocker once—*too hesitant*. Twice—*more determined*.

The voice of a woman on the other side reaches me, clipped, authoritarian. 'Come.'

Another breath and I push the door open, walk inside.

The walls of the room are much like the rest of the building: bare stone, raw, exposed. The earthy undertones adding to the primal energy that pumps through the heart of the club.

I scan the contraptions that line the walls, the shelves and hooks adorned with implements in all shapes and sizes. Some I can identify; some I can't even begin to label let alone imagine their usage.

I catch my gaping reflection in one of the many two-way mirrors separating the room from the viewing gallery and snap my mouth shut. Is someone watching me right now? Will *he* be there soon?

'Close the door.'

I jolt, squinting into the shadows as I seek her out even though I sense I'm alone, the tinny quality to her voice telling me it's being piped in.

Is *she* beyond one of the many mirrors, witnessing my hesitation?

My cheeks flush all over again—*a great start!*

I straighten my spine, lift my chin and close the door with far more confidence than I feel.

'Walk into the middle.'

The lighting changes, a soft spotlight illuminates a circle in the centre of the room and I walk towards it, stop when my feet are exactly central.

'Good, Little Kitten.'

A spike of something bolts through me. *Little Kitten?* Is that what I am to be called? Nathan and I never went as far as names in our bedroom games...

'You don't like it?'

I open my mouth, close it again.

'Well?'

'It's...it's not...' I suck in a breath for courage, let it leave with my verdict. 'It's unexpected.'

'I have a feeling there's much about tonight you will deem unexpected, Little Kitten, but from now on, when you speak, you will address me as Mistress. Is that understood?'

My body pulses with a frenetic kind of energy. I've never been spoken to like this. With Nathan I was the one with all the power, sexually; it was the one place I could take charge and I needed it. It gave our relationship balance in some twisted way.

But now he's gone I don't have that need. In fact, I'm craving the complete opposite.

I close my eyes, push him from my mind and the confusing spiral that was our life together. 'Yes.'

'Yes, what?'

'Yes. Mistress.'

'Better.' A mirror shifts in the wall, opening inwards, and she appears through it. The clip of her thigh-high boots as loud as the drum of my heart in my ears. Her hair, tied in a high ponytail, is as dark and as sleek as her zipped-up bodysuit. Her eye mask is studded and curves to a point either side of her jaw, leaving the bronzed skin of her chin and blood-red lips exposed.

She smiles, catlike, her eyes glittering in the low light as she takes me in. 'Now, undress, Little Kitten.'

What? No preamble? Just get naked...?

'I...'

My voice fails me as she walks towards an arrangement of whips, her fingers brushing slowly over them.

'I'm waiting, Kitten.' She doesn't even turn as she continues her perusal. 'And you really don't want to keep me waiting.'

She selects a riding crop and slowly turns to my immobile form.

I swallow. I know what I signed up for, but to strip, just like that...

'Disobedient Kittens will be punished.' She stalks towards me, circles me, a low undercurrent of warning in the soft purr of her voice. 'Especially when they have invited a guest to watch…and they are keeping him waiting too.'

My head whips around. *He's here!*

She laughs. 'You did invite him, did you not?'

'Yes.'

'Yes?'

'Yes.' Swallow. 'Mistress.'

'Well, be a good Little Kitten and do as you are told, let him see what you invited him to see.'

She glances towards a large mirror, its ornate gold-gilded edge at odds with the austere room, and smiles. That's where he is. *There.*

My body gives an excited shiver, my clit pulsing as I nervously wet my lips.

'We're waiting…' she murmurs from behind me, so very close to my ear.

I try to breathe, to quash the flutters rising up in my gut, and I sense her step back. In her place comes the riding crop, its cool leather brushing against my nape as she sweeps my ponytail aside, and my body shivers anew. Not with the cold, but with the thrill.

'Now…' she trails the leather down my spine, oh-so-softly '…strip.'

Valentine

Don't judge me. I'm already judging myself enough.

I was set on leaving. Just as soon as her legs disappeared up the stairs and I felt able. I say able because the moment her eyes connected with mine and I looked away I wanted to look back. Look back and stay fixed on her. Feeling trapped in a web of my own making.

Guilt that she should catch me here. Guilt that I'm scoping her out. Guilt that I feel more than is acceptable for a future professional relationship. Guilt that I should even want another woman.

Yeah, it's all guilt, my body goads me. The tension, the heat, telling me it runs darker and deeper than that, and my grip on the sill of the two-way mirror before me tightens. My eyes lost in the sight of her, watching the scene unfold, just as she invited me to.

Jesus H Christ.

I shouldn't be here.

But when the bartender reappeared and made a beeline straight for me to deliver her invitation, I followed him in some weird trance-like state. And when Electra, the woman now running the riding crop down Olivia's spine, opened a concealed door and pulled me into this room by the collar of my jacket, not once shrinking from my size, I was too stunned to speak, or back out, or do anything but follow her instruction:

Sit. Stay. Watch. Enjoy.

Like some obedient dog.

'Now strip.'

The command leaves her lips with the vaguest hint of warning and I watch Olivia, illuminated under the shaft of light, hesitate; her eyes connect with mine though she can't see me. She knows I'm here. Electra's made that clear. And I saw how it made her eyes flare, her throat bob and the quick flicker of her tongue over her lips as the idea brought with it an illicit buzz. A buzz I shouldn't feel, I shouldn't share.

Hell, I've gone without sex for four years. I've had zero interest, but this…it's not some tame encounter. It's dark, twisted and extreme. Profoundly erotic.

And she wants me here to watch.

No.

She wants some stranger in a bar to take on the role of voyeur. I could be anyone. Anyone at all. Some twisted fuck lying in wait. But I'm not. I'm no danger to her.

Someone else could be though.

And it's another sign that she needs my intervention.

The intervention Alan and the board have in mind to stabilise her, to bring back the old Olivia, the responsible one, the one millions of women look up to, admire, dream to emulate…

Electra flicks her wrist, the riding crop cracking over the curve of Olivia's clothed behind, and I flinch. The sound reverberates through the walls, through me, Olivia's surprised yelp carrying with it.

'I said…' the woman walks around to her front, pauses and steps wide '…undress.'

Olivia nods quickly, slipping the dress from her shoulders, shimmying it down, down and… I can't breathe. I can't look away.

One second she's clothed, the next she's all black lace lingerie and naked curves. Slender, curvaceous in one.

She straightens. The dress pooling at her feet and

her head turning to eye Electra as she waits for her next instruction.

'And the rest…'

Olivia eyes the tip of the riding crop that Electra is running through her fingers and swallows. 'Yes, Mistress.'

My gut clenches with need. The dormant sensation so fierce in its resurgence I can't draw breath, I can only watch as she slips the straps of her lace bodysuit down and her beautiful breasts spill free. Their pink hearts are puckered, tight with obvious arousal. And then she bends forward, hooking her fingers into the fabric at her hips and smooths it down her legs, unveiling her womanhood, all bare, naked, no hair…*fuck*.

She straightens and Electra lowers the riding crop to her inner thigh, pressing it into her skin as Electra's eyes take in the same exquisite sight, the hint of moisture glistening in the light. She slides the riding crop up, brushes it gently against her wet seam, and Olivia sways into the move, her teeth biting into her bottom lip, her body quivering.

'Very nice,' Electra murmurs, easing the riding crop back and forth, coating it with her need.

I watch the colour rise in Olivia's cheeks, see the blatant hunger in every tense muscle of her body as she clenches her fists at her sides and rides the leather.

'Enough.' Electra snaps the riding crop away. 'Pick up your clothing and place it on the table over there.' She points to a solid wood table that is bare save for a small box. 'There is something in the box I want you to wear.'

Olivia does as she's told and, hesitant, opens the lid of the box. Her eyes flit back to Electra.

'Put it on.'

She pulls it out. It's a headband with two soft black triangles. *What the fuck?*

She slips it on—cat ears. *Little Kitten.* I get it and, hell, it should look ridiculous. It should make me want to laugh. Instead, I'm enraptured, hooked on every instruction and Olivia's obedience. *The* Olivia Carmel—intelligent, stunningly sophisticated, empowered—willing to carry out every instruction Electra delivers.

'You can leave your shoes there too.'

'Yes, Mistress.'

She toes off one, then the other and looks back to Electra, the cat ears adorning her head, her eyes docile, her cheeks pink.

'Every good Little Kitten needs a collar; come and kneel before me and I will give you yours.'

Oh, God, I don't know how much more of this I can take. I shouldn't have come. I shouldn't have said yes. My body doesn't rule me, but right now I'm fixed in place. Immobilised with the heat coursing through my veins, surging south. Every one of my senses alive for the first time in too many years and killing off my trepidation, my moral code. All I can see is her. Her perfect body, naked, the cat-like ears only adding to her seductive pose as she kneels before Electra.

'Good, Little Kitten.' Electra touches the tip of the riding crop to Olivia's navel and her stomach contracts, her nipples tightening as her breasts lift with a sucked-in breath. 'Hands behind your back.'

Olivia obeys and slowly, so very slowly, Electra trails the crop up her chest, following the arch of her neck as she forces Olivia's chin to rise, her head tilting back. 'Stay.'

Olivia nods.

'Say, *Yes, Mistress*.'

She wets her lips, her response breathy. 'Yes, Mistress.'

'Better.' The room fills with the sharp click of Electra's heels as she walks to the hooks displaying various collars, leashes, restraints. She trails her red-tipped nails over them as she considers each, my cock swelling with every possibility. Dusty old fantasies colliding with the very new, very real...

'This one will do.' Electra plucks a black leather collar from a hook. Two chains fall from it, their clamp-ends clinking through the quiet. I see Olivia's eyes widen, her throat bob.

'Touch your breasts, Little Kitten, show me what they need.'

I quit breathing. I'm too enraptured by Olivia as she caresses herself, slow at first and then harder, more urgent as she loses herself in the sea of sensation. Plucking and rolling each flushed peak as her eyes stay hooked on Electra's heated gaze.

'Does that feel good?'

'Yes, Mistress.'

'Don't stop…'

Electra hooks the riding crop into her bodysuit and stands behind Olivia, her stance wide to accommodate Olivia's bent legs. She lowers the collar around Olivia's neck, frees her ponytail and flicks it over her shoulder before feeding the belt loop through. Tightening it and tightening it until Olivia's eyes flare up into Electra's. The two chains fall down her front, the clamps swinging by her navel.

'Now you can stop.'

She walks to her front, lifts one clamp and teases it around a puckered nipple, clamping it. Olivia rocks, her whimper escaping through her parted lips, her eyes all lustful and hooded. She repeats the move with the other, trapping it in the teeth of the clamp as Olivia cries out.

'Pleasure and pain,' Electra murmurs as she stands back to admire her handiwork. 'It's a satisfying mix.'

Olivia watches her, her nostrils flaring as she takes in air.

'I think we should see if your guest would like to join us.'

Olivia's eyes flit to the mirror, to me.

'What do you say, Little Kitten? I think you've behaved well enough to have a playmate.'

They're both looking towards me now and it wakes me from my stupor, a panicked sweat breaking out all over. I have to get out of here. *Now.*

This was a mistake. A huge, huge mistake.

The job, the favour, coming here…

Olivia Carmel may need rescuing but I'm not the one to do it.

I can't.

Olivia

Electra walks to the mirror she came through and my whole body is frozen in place. No, not quite frozen, because I'm overheating. I'm a hot mess inside, a lustful knot tightening and tightening and promising a climax so forceful that I want it just as much as I want to delay it. To prolong the delirium for as long as possible.

She presses a button in the wall and the mirror shifts; my heart leaps into my throat. The stranger, the one I invited, with the dark good looks, the intense gaze; he's…

Gone.

I see it in Electra's frown and then she walks inside the room and there's no sound. No voices.

Oh, God. What am I even doing?

I see my reflection in the mirrors and I don't even recognise myself in the shameless, wanton woman looking back at me. It shocks me to the core. I can't do this.

When he was there, watching, I was high on it. High on the thrill, the letting go, the idea of someone getting off on this as much as me, but he's gone and I'm…

'It seems your little friend has left us to it, Kitten.'

She's coming back into the room and I'm already at the table, about to scoop up my things.

'What are you doing?'

I spin to face her, my hands clutching my clothing to my chest. 'I'm sorry… I…I think I need to go.'

She folds her arms, purses her lips and narrows her eyes on me. 'Are you sure about that?'

'I'm…I'm…'

'We don't need your playmate for this…and you only need to use the safe word and I'll let you go.'

CHAPTER THREE

Two weeks later
Valentine

I WANT TO throw my phone at the wall when the alarm wakes me. I'm not ready to be awake. Two weeks of barely sleeping, and when I do sleep my dreams are lurid, wild, my body making up for four years' abstinence as it replays that night two weeks ago. A mixture of the real tangled up with my own vivid imaginings that make Olivia an almost permanent fixture in my head.

I unravel myself from the sheets that cling to my sweat-drenched skin. I have to shake this and soon. I may not be the one who changes the bedsheets, but it hardly feels fair, my housekeeper having to do it on a daily basis. She thinks I'm sick. I'm nowhere close.

Unless you count the fact that my obsession is somewhat twisted: *Olivia, the submissive.*

My body fires, determined to punish me for my celibacy, and in the most extreme way possible. I fight the image, the heat back, but my feet still drag as I make my way to the kitchen.

Caffeine—that's what you need. Caffeine and the gym.

It's my usual routine: up at five-thirty, coffee, gym, I leave, housekeeper arrives. Though lately she's here before I go, with concern shining in her wise old eyes.

I load up the coffee machine, set it to go and stalk to the floor-to-ceiling glass that overlooks the Thames and find my mind wandering. Already back to her. Proving my point, but I can't stop the thoughts.

Is she also awake, somewhere in the city? Looking out over a similar view? Is she happy? Content? Still searching for the elusive fix that will make everything feel better?

I push my fingers through my hair, shake it out and stretch. Try to banish her from my mind. I said no to the board, to my mentor. She will be someone else's problem. Someone else can fix her. Someone who can be trusted to control their basic instincts where she's concerned, instincts I thought long-since dead.

'Turn on the TV.'

The penthouse comes alive, the TV blaring to life with the news channel, though my focus remains inward. I'll go at it hard in the gym, up my reps, my run, anything to burn—

'Sources say the Bugatti Olivia Carmel was

driving struck the central reservation of the M40 at around four this morning...'

The fine hairs on my neck, my arms prick up, goosebumps forming with the sickening roll in my gut. I grab the remote, turn up the volume.

'...it's believed she was travelling alone to her home on the outskirts of Oxford when the crash happened.'

Camera footage fills the screen of a crumpled vehicle being pulled out of a ditch. There are police cars, floodlights, a fire engine, an ambulance...

'She is said to be in a stable condition. The police haven't confirmed whether she was driving under the influence but, in light of recent events, it does add to the growing concern around the successful entrepreneur following the sudden death of her husband and business partner, Nathan Carmel, just over a year ago.'

I toss the remote onto the sofa, turn away from the screen. *'Shit. Shit. Shit.'*

My curse is overtaken by the sharp shrill of my mobile ringing. I stride back to the bedroom and snatch it up, knowing who it is before I see his name on the display. I swipe to answer and raise it to my ear.

'Alan,' I snap out tightly.

'Valentine, I'm so glad I've caught you. I'm sorry to ring this early, but there's been a...a development. It's Olivia—'

'I've seen. It's all over the news.'

'Yes.' His sigh reaches down the phone, twisting

up my gut as the guilt swells. I close my eyes, try to shut it down. 'The press were there in an instant; it's like they know just where to be at the wrong moment... Well, I guess it's the right one for them.'

I murmur a nonsensical response.

'We need you, Valentine. *She* needs you.'

My eyes open wide. No. 'She needs someone else.'

'You're the best in the business. You understand what she's going through. And with the reputation of your PR company, plus the way this is heading, she won't be able to refuse your aid.'

She will when she sees me is my instinctive response. It was dark in the club, but I don't doubt for a second that she'll recognise me.

And the things I've seen, the things she *asked* me to witness...

'Valentine, you there? Val—'

'I'm here.'

'Please. I wouldn't ask if it wasn't important. Do you remember what you were like four years ago?'

My eyes close of their own volition this time, my mind transported back to that bleak morning in his office. I was broken, defeated, a mess.

'I'm sorry. I don't want to dredge up the past, but I need you to see you're the right person to turn her around.'

'You should get a psychologist, a counsellor.'

'Because they worked so well for you.'

He's right. They didn't stand a chance.

'And we've tried; she won't accept either.'

'This is different. She's different.'

'It's not, and you know it. You're making excuses, and I understand why, but…'

'You understand, and yet you're asking anyway?'

'Look, I know it brings back painful memories, but I wouldn't ask if it wasn't…if it wasn't a last resort.'

I blow out a breath. He wouldn't be asking if he knew of our little encounter though.

'And I trust you, Valentine. I know you can get through to her.'

'But…' I break off. What can I possibly say to refuse him? I can't tell him the truth, that I messed up big time. Once, by going to the club. Twice, by accepting her invitation. Thrice, by running like some scared and inexperienced teenager.

'I'm just asking you to at least try…for me.'

I swallow, my fist pulsing around the phone. I want to say it's not fair to put that on me. But that in itself isn't fair. I owe him.

'Valentine?'

'Okay.' It comes out gruff, barely audible. 'But if she's not on board, I walk.'

'Of course. That's all I ask.'

I grip the phone tighter, reiterating, 'I'm not forcing her to accept my help.'

Because the second she sees me I know she's going to baulk, and then what?

'Agreed. I'll be in touch to set up a meeting.'

'Okay.'

'Speak soon and…thanks, Valentine.'

'No problem.' It comes out quiet, born of habit, and I cut the call with a stifled curse.

I toss the phone on the bed and return to the living room just in time to catch a parting camera shot of the wreckage and a photo taken at a recent gala event. She's stunning. Her skin glowing pearlescent under the lights of the cameras, her hair in a loose updo, her dress a slinky red number, but her smile... it's haunted, strained, and I feel a punch to the gut so strong. I know that look. I wore it.

And I know Alan is right; I do get it and I can help her.

Not that she'll want me to. Not when she recognises who I am.

And I'll cross that bridge when I come to it, because one thing's for sure: she may baulk, but I can't walk away.

Olivia

'You can forget pretending to be asleep, Liv, and open your eyes!'

I grimace at my sister's pissed-off tone and tentatively open one eyelid, wincing as the bright lights of the hospital room sear my brain. 'Do you have to shout?'

'Shout? I want to do more than shout. I want to shake some bloody sense into you. What were you doing, driving at four in the morning?'

'I wanted to get out of the city.'

'At *four* in the morning?'

'I couldn't sleep.'

'So you took your shiny new toy out for a spin in the torrential rain and drove it into a ditch? Great way to wake you up.'

'I didn't do it intentionally.'

'Didn't do it…' She shakes her head in despair.

'Please, just calm down.'

'*Calm?* Are you serious? What's going on, Liv? Is it some weird midlife crisis? Is it Nathan, because seriously, sis, there's enjoying your freedom and then there's—'

'*Please, Fee.*' I wince as my head pounds in time to her words; the mention of Nathan and her very vocal expression of how messed up our relationship was making my stomach roll. I don't have the strength to defend him, to defend 'us', not right now.

'I'm sorry, but it's madness. Think about how Mum felt seeing it on the news before anyone had a chance to call her.'

'Mum?' I go to sit up and groan as pain shoots up my spine and my entire body seems to go into spasm. I collapse back, grateful for the plush pillow beneath me. 'Is she here?'

'No.' She softens her voice and leans in to press a soothing hand to my shoulder. 'I told her she didn't need to travel the length of the country to check on you because I was closer, and you were fine.'

'And I *am* fine.'

'Aye, you look it too.'

I roll my head to her, my smile small. 'Cheers, little sister, I love you too.'

'Just telling it how it is.'

'And I just need a decent sleep in my own bed.'

'Well, that's not happening until the doctors have all their test results back and they know you're okay.'

'I *am* okay.'

'Will you stop it?'

'Stop what?'

'Putting a brave face on everything!'

I close my eyes again, try to lose myself in the darkness that beckons. A brave face? It doesn't feel so very brave. Not really.

CHAPTER FOUR

Olivia

MY FACE IS feeling even less brave two weeks later as I sit in the boardroom with a less than impressed board around me. The glass table at which we sit reflects the view through the Georgian windows, damp and dreary, the perfect weather to match my mood.

When Nathan and I purchased the inner London townhouse and converted it into offices it was an exciting new venture, an investment, an opportunity. Bright, optimistic, happy.

Now I wish we'd fitted it out with splashes of colour—pinks, oranges, anything but chilling monochrome. Not even the verdant vibe of the strategically spaced plants can lift it.

I reach for my water glass and take a sip, feel the weighty silence settle around me, inside me.

I should have listened to my sister when she suggested I take a few weeks off. But, in my experience, being on holiday leads to too much thinking time, too much restless energy and a need to kill it off with something. Anything.

All of which would only land me back in this exact position.

'So, you understand, Olivia,' Alan, my chief operating officer, stresses, 'this is ultimately for the good of the charity.'

'Let me get this straight. I'm being given a babysitter for the good of the charity I am no longer the face of?' I try to keep my voice level as my fingers drum the glass table top.

'He's not a babysitter. His PR company is the best in the business. They'll fix this media blip and have everything smoothed over in no time.'

Anger spikes in my bloodstream, my teeth gritting. *Breathe. Just breathe.* 'It doesn't need smoothing over.'

'It does, Olivia, and you know it.'

Alan morphs into my late father now, his condescension cutting deep, and I bite my tongue on the 'Bullshit' that wants to escape. I eye them all—Susan, Peter, James, Scott and…Alan—take in their grave expressions and count to ten.

'I disagree.' Calm and controlled once more, I fix my focus on Alan, the man who's leading this little intervention. 'I stepped down months ago. I am not—'

'It doesn't matter that you've stepped down; you're still involved,' he interjects, giving me no quarter. 'It's *still* your charity as far as the public are concerned—the press, the investors, those that matter. It's for the good of the company too; you must be able to see that. *Nathan* would want you to see that.'

It's a low blow, bringing Nathan into this, and he knows it. I see it in the compassion that glistens in his otherwise stoic and weathered face. See it reflected in the eyes of the other board members as they all look to me, waiting for me to acquiesce, and I breathe through the flash of hurt, of anger, of… feeling cornered.

'You make it sound like I don't have a choice,' I say, fisting my palms on the table top as the fight burns ever brighter inside me.

'You don't.'

Valentine

I can be patient. I've spent years dealing with demanding celebs, aristocrats with over-inflated egos, politicians with crazy schedules and even crazier personal lives. It's the nature of the PR beast. They're the people who need their images fixing on a daily basis. And they're the people most likely to keep you waiting.

I can take it up to a point, but I don't pander to the theatrics. It's what made me good at it. Well respected. The man to call.

And now I run the company. I don't get dragged into the day-to-day grind. I spend more time wining and dining, reaping the rewards of a hard-earned career, all at twenty-nine.

But here I am, doing the job again. Waiting for the

first face-to-face confrontation with Olivia, and that patience I mentioned—it's wearing thin.

I sit in the reception of their converted Georgian townhouse, not your typical headquarters for a world-renowned logistics firm, but something tells me that has more to do with its founders: Olivia and her late husband, Nathan. And it can't be easy for her, walking through these doors every day and having that constant reminder of something she shared with the man she loved for over two decades.

Layla and I didn't even manage to get one decade together…but we lived enough for two.

My skin prickles, the cold sweat instant. She'd still be here if we'd lived a quieter life, toned it down, less parties, less—

'Do I have to remind you who founded this firm?' Olivia's elevated voice breaches the boardroom door, a welcome distraction from where my thoughts are heading.

The receptionist at the stark white high-fronted desk eyes the door, her brows raised, her cheeks pinking up. She clears her throat and looks to me, her polite smile so very forced.

'Can I get you another coffee while you wait, Mr Boretti?'

'I'm good, thank you.'

'I'm sure they'll be ready for you very soon.' She goes back to her screen but I don't miss the way her eyes flit to me beneath her lashes, part interest, part curiosity, and it provokes guilt. Guilt because I'm in some way prepared for what's happening beyond that door, what's about to happen when I walk in there, whereas Olivia...

And I've had time to come to terms with all I saw, but still it taunts me. She taunts me. On her knees, naked, a collar, clamps...

I run a finger under my own collar and shift in my seat as the receptionist's phone rings loud in the strained quiet. One ring and she already has it lifted to her ear. 'Yes, I'll send him straight through.'

She beams at me as she replaces the receiver. 'They're ready for you now. I'll take you through.'

She stands and smooths down her black skirt; her blouse is white and crease-free, not a hair out of place. She's almost too perfect and so very in keeping with the monochrome office. I look around me, glimpse others working in very similar attire that smacks of a very specific dress code policy.

'Here we are.' She pushes open the door and gestures for me to enter. I almost wish she'd announce me so I can avoid doing it for myself. Like it somehow incriminates me more than I already have myself. And even the thought itself irritates. I never shy away from confrontation and I certainly don't need someone else to announce me, and I'm here pro bono; it's not like they're paying me to do a job. It's a favour to a friend, to Alan.

But it's the guilt that's doing it. I never should've walked up those blasted stairs.

'Valentine, it's so good to see you.' I look from the receptionist to see Alan striding towards me beaming, blocking my view of the others still seated at the table.

He offers out his hand, which I take, and clasps my elbow as he gives it a hearty shake. 'Thank you for coming.'

'It's a pleasure.' I give him a grim smile as he steps aside and gestures to the room.

'We're all aware of your various accolades, of course, and we're confident you're going to do a great job.'

I wince internally. Not the best way to pitch me. And in front of the entire board. Not just Olivia. My eyes sweep over them, take in their smiles, which all show varying degrees of wariness, and I curse my naivety. I expected Alan to exercise a little more tact, to be more discreet. Instead it's an us-against-her situation and it couldn't make my position any pricklier than it already is.

'You?' It pierces the air, breathless, high-pitched, and every head turns to look at Olivia as she braces herself in the leather high-backed seat at the head of the table, her knuckles white as she grips the armrests. Her ponytail is as sleek as it was in the club, her crystal-blue eyes glaring despite the softer shade of eyeshadow. Not her lips though; they're blood-red, just as Electra's were.

Shit.

I meet her gaze head-on and force back the memories determined to fog up my brain.

'Sorry…do you know each other?' Alan's head

whips back and forth between us, his surprise as obvious as Olivia's shock.

She's pale, so very pale against the white of her dress that I actually think she's on the verge of blue.

'Not as such,' I say slowly, giving her time to recover. Maybe I should have pre-warned her, done anything but turn up like this. But then where would I even start? *Hey, you know the other week in the club where I witnessed you...yeah...like that, well, I'm the one the board are bringing in to put an end to said that.*

Her throat bobs and she blinks, her eyes flashing as her cheeks rapidly regain their colour.

'No, we don't know each other.' Her cool tone is at odds with the heat now flaring in her face as she uncrosses her legs and turns in her seat. She rises to walk towards me and I fight and fail to keep my eyes locked on hers. They fall to the strappy red skyscraper heels on her feet that are far too bold and daring against the bland backdrop. Not to mention a marked contrast to the white dress that fits her like a second skin, its bold asymmetric collar different, unique.

The entire ensemble is something only a confident woman would try to carry off...and she's definitely confident. None of the edgy nervousness I witnessed at the club. This is her true domain, her company, and she's showing me she's in control. Like a lioness looking after her cubs, priming for a fight.

She offers out her hand, her chin lifting so that

her eyes reach mine. Even in those heels I have several inches on her statuesque height.

'Valentine...*really*?' Her eyes flash with challenge, or is that...amusement? I take hold of her hand, barely aware of the contact until I feel her grip tighten with her shake and I have the oddest urge to pull her closer. 'I think you're the first Valentine I've ever met; your parents must be old romantics.'

She's overly at ease now. Her tease is bordering on flirtatious and I can feel the crease forming between my brows. I smooth it out with a forced smile as I question whether I imagined the explosive *'You?'*, the pallor...

Maybe she *doesn't* remember me. It was dark. It was late.

'You could say that.'

'And you, Mr Boretti... *Valentine*...' She drawls out my forename, the tease building in her voice, and I hear Alan cough to my left. Is it a sign of his own discomfort, or is it a veiled warning to Olivia to put the knives, or the flirting, away? I'm buggered if I know.

'Are you an old romantic too?' she purrs, Alan's cough not even earning the briefest of looks from her. 'Come to fix the reputation of a woman who has to be, what, nearly twice your age and should know better?'

'Really, Olivia.' Alan bristles. 'That's not...it's not...'

I'm used to my age being an issue among those

who don't know me, but being underestimated nearly always works in my favour. I don't like how she uses it now though.

'What, Alan? What is it?' she throws at him.

'I think what he's trying to say is that I'm here to look at the PR for the entire company, the charity too. Getting the right message out there is key.'

Her smile is saccharine-sweet. 'It is, isn't it? Reputations are so fragile in today's world, where social media helps spread the word faster than one can...'

She rakes her eyes over my entirety and doesn't finish. And I wait for it, wait and wait...

'Well, anyway, since it's not just me you're here to fix, I have some place else I need to be, so if you want to discuss strategy with Susan, our director of sales and marketing, I can get on with some actual work and we can talk later.'

'Olivia, I hoped—'

She cuts Alan off with a tight smile. 'Alan will make sure you have my PA's details, won't you? That way, a mutually agreeable time can be arranged.'

Alan gives a resigned nod.

'Excellent. It's a pleasure to meet you, Mr Boretti.'

And that's it, she's gone, and I'm left with five board members all looking at me with expressions as bulldozed as I feel.

And shouldn't it be the other way around?

Shouldn't she be the one left floundering, wondering what the fuck she's got herself into?

Olivia

This isn't happening. It's like some weird dream.

I walk through the office not really seeing anyone, my hand still warm from his touch, my pulse skittering and my cheeks… God, do they burn!

I need to get some air. Some air and some conviction that it's not him. That, no matter how similar he looks, it can't be. It just *can't*.

Pippa, my PA, is making a beeline for me through the open-plan office and I wave her away. I don't trust my voice, or my ability to keep a lid on the fire inside. I'm angry. No, I'm more than angry; I'm bloody livid.

Fixing the company's image, the charity's even, is one thing; fixing mine… I flick my ponytail over my shoulder and hold my head high. I won't let them do this to me. I won't let the office see me like this either. Just a few more steps and I'll be in the outer foyer, another few and I'll be in the crisp cold air and the…*rain*.

I grimace and detour to my office, pull my fierce-red coat off its stand and shrug it on, belt it tight and move before anyone else can try to talk to me.

How could they? How could Alan? And of all the people to get in…this man who looks so much like the one I saw four weeks ago.

Looks like? It is him and you know it.

My gut knows it. My wounded ego knows it.

My hypersensitive, pebble-like nipples know it!

Fuck.

'I beg your pardon?'

Jennings, our doorman-cum-security guard, frowns at me and I plaster on a smile. 'Sorry, thinking aloud.'

His frown deepens, his eyes not missing a trick. 'You okay, Ms Carmel?'

He's always addressed me as Ms so it doesn't sting with my widow status, but my smile still feels shaky.

'Absolutely. Fine and dandy. Just need to get out and stretch my legs.'

He reaches behind him and pulls a guest umbrella from the pot by the door. 'In that case, you best take this.'

'Thank you, Jennings.' My smile eases with his thoughtful gesture and a part of me feels desperate to spill all. I've known him for as long as we've owned the building, Nathan and I, and that's too many years to count.

And the truth is, I don't have a confidant that I can offload on. I won't even spill all to my sister, Fee. Nathan was my ear and he was enough. But I don't have him any more…

And that'll teach me for making my husband and our business my all.

Now that he's gone, there are a lot of things I don't have and many that I do. Money is the biggest thing. I have more money than I know what to do with. His life insurance, our company, our success, it's given me plenty.

But there's a huge gaping hole that I just can't fill. And each time I seek to, I end up in trouble. The Bugatti and the crash. The free-climbing incident last month where I narrowly escaped being impaled on a rock. The product launch party where my loose tongue lost us an important investor. The charity ball fiasco in which my dazzling red dress left a little too much exposed.

Is it any wonder the board want to fix me? I shake my head, my ponytail flicking with it.

Screw it, screw it all!

Life's too short. Every one of those incidents was about living by that motto and making the most of life. I won't go back to how things were.

I stride outside, the umbrella tight in my grip as I remember the one scenario the board doesn't know about… Valentine Boretti, on the other hand…he was there, until he ran.

And his swift departure brought a premature end to the entire experience. Not that he could know that…

Is it really him?

He didn't look as young in the club. But then it was dark and, if I'm honest, I wasn't exactly in tune with much else that night. I was set on letting go, losing my inhibitions. Going wild.

I feel my pulse pick up as I remember it all too vividly. Replay it in quick succession and then remember him not twenty minutes ago as he took my hand in his.

The carefully groomed hair with its definite curl, the square cut to his jaw, his clean-shaven skin, full lips, chiselled cheekbones and his eyes…they were so dark that night, dark and intense. This afternoon I could take in their vivid blue, but it wasn't just the colour on display, it was the past too, the memory of what he witnessed as they seemed to project that wild heat back at me, right there in the boardroom.

And he's a *man-child*.

A man-child with an ego the size of Narcissus, quite clearly.

He's young, he's in PR, and he doesn't just walk the talk, he struts it. Slick and confident in his vibrant blue suit, his perfect hair that took time to sculpt, those eyes so sharp and astute and in command. There's a slash through one brow that tells of some misadventure long ago and instead of damaging his flawless exterior, it adds to it. Making him roguish and charming and disarming in one.

And his voice…even now it shivers through me. Deep, raspy, practically hoarse. Who even *talks* like that but an aged smoker? Which really should make it a turn-off, not an almighty, knicker-wetting turn-on!

And, to cap it all off, I want to feast over the whole damn package when he's already rejected me. Rejected me when I was at my most vulnerable, most exposed— *Bloody hell*, I was naked and chained, for fuck's sake!

Not that I can blame him for the latter. I put myself in that position on my knees, wanton, willing, teetering on the edge of climax.

I swallow past the wedge of humiliation as I navigate the pavement outside, careful to avoid the pooling water in my heels. Heels that match the vibrant

red of my trench coat and lippy. An attempt at inject-
ing colour into the grey office that has always been
just that—grey, uniform, orderly, pristine. It was how
we wanted it and it's never bothered me before, but
this last year… I don't know. I want to change it. I
want to change it all. I have no one to please, to acquiesce to, but myself now.

Unless you count the board, of course, and they
can take—

'Olivia!'

I stumble and curse, one foot landing squarely
in a puddle, sending mucky water right up my legs.
Dammit!

I don't want to look behind me. In fact I don't
seem able to do much under the influence of my
name being called in that gravel-like tone.

I can hear his hurried footfall on the pavement,
catching me up, and I close my eyes, take a breath.

Valentine Boretti isn't running away now. He's
chasing me down.

Could this day get any worse?

CHAPTER FIVE

Valentine

'I'M SORRY, I didn't mean to startle you.'

Her ponytail sashays down her back as she shakes her head to the heavens and gives a high-pitched laugh. 'Really?'

'Yes, really.'

She lifts one leg to eye her splashed calf and assess the damage, and I force my eyes up to the tip of her umbrella. This woman and her extremities do things to me that I need to have under control.

'You could have fooled me.'

It comes out under her breath, but I hear it, every grumbled syllable. And I know she's not referring to the puddle incident; she's referring to the whole damn lot. Today, four weeks ago. Any doubt that she remembers me departs with the fresh weight in my gut.

'Look, can we talk?'

She's busy eyeing her other calf now and I don't want to look at her angled leg with the strips of red that start at her ankle and work their way down her foot, the daring colour and height of the stiletto heel sparking a fire that contends with the heavy guilt.

'Talk?'

Her prompt comes out sharp and I realise her eyes are on me now, and I'm…I'm staring. *Shit.* I clear my throat, snap my eyes up to scan the street in search of shelter. The rain already has my suit turning navy, my hair starting to drip.

'Yes,' I say, squinting against the rain as I look back at her. 'Please.'

'I told you, talk to my PA and we can arrange—'

'No.' I frown as I cut her off. 'I want to talk off the clock, away from the office.'

She eyes me as though seeing me for the first time. 'Now?'

'Yes.'

'You realise you're getting soaked?'

'Am I?'

'Your locks aren't going to look quite so perky if you stay out here much longer.'

I feel the oddest impulse to laugh. 'Like your legs?'

She purses her lips, her eyes narrowing. *Clearly a tease too far…*

'Are you trying to wind me up more?'

'No.' I blow out a breath. 'I'm trying to fix things so that we can have a positive start to our working relationship.'

The high-pitched laugh returns, her brows arching over her eyes that sparkle and blaze and bring back that crazy fire deep within.

'A *positive* start?'

'Yes.'

'You have to be joking!'

The wind picks up, whipping the rain into my face, and I duck beneath her umbrella, my only thought to escape it. Big mistake.

She scurries back, losing her footing on those silly, impractical heels— *Now you say silly, but what you really mean is...*

'Careful!' I clutch her elbow to steady her and quit the inner spiel that really isn't helping.

'Don't you...' She snatches her arm back, glares up at me. 'A bit presumptuous, don't you think?'

She eyes the umbrella now shielding us both and I sense she's fighting the urge to move away fully and take it with her. 'Why would I share my umbrella with a man...a man...?'

'Olivia!' I blurt out, my exasperation getting the better of me. 'Will you stop behaving like a child and just listen to—?'

'*I'm* behaving like a child?' Her eyes widen into mine. '*Me?*'

Her laugh is even more manic. 'You just appeared in *my* boardroom, summoned by the board of *my* company, to effectively put me in my place, and still have the gall to tell me to stop behaving like a child when that's exactly how I'm being treated.'

I'm listening to her rant, I am, but seriously, the way her skin flushes and her lips move, that luscious red lipstick marrying so well with the flush to her cheeks and the over-bright blue gaze…it's hard, real hard, to focus on responding.

Not in a way that would improve matters, at any rate.

I take a deep breath, eye the passers-by that I sense are starting to hover at our little scene and give her a grim nod.

'I know we met under unusual circumstances…'

I watch her cheeks colour even further; her lashes flicker and her mouth opens as though she would say something but nothing comes out, other than the smallest of squeaks, and the foolish urge to kiss her intensifies.

I try and breathe through it, watch as a lock of her blonde hair makes a bid for freedom across her cheek and feel my fingers itch with the need to brush it behind her ear…

'It's funny you mention those circumstances—' she pierces my reverie with a scowl '—because I find it a huge coincidence that you were also in the club that night. And when I say huge, I mean it was no coincidence at all. Was it?'

Swallow. 'No.'

She startles, flustered. She clearly expected me to lie or to delay the truth at least.

'I went to see if the rumours about you were real.'

'The rumours?'

I feel the space around us closing in, too many people, too many ears. I don't want to air my would-be client's dirty laundry in a bustling city street.

'Can we do this somewhere private?'

'What?' She fists her free hand on her hip. 'So I can give you another show?'

I admire her strength, her candour, but it really doesn't help us get where we need to be—on the same page, starting afresh.

And I *really* don't need the very vivid reminder of the last show she put on for me either.

'You know that's not what I mean. I just want to clear the air where we can't be overheard and… apologise.'

She cocks her head to the side, her eyes narrowing. 'You're going to apologise?'

'Is that so hard to believe?'

Nothing. No response, just a cool stare.

'Look, there's a bar not far from here…' I rake my fingers through my hair as her brows twitch at the suggestion. 'If you'll just give me the opportunity to apologise and explain, hopefully we can put this behind us.'

'I wouldn't get your hopes up.'

She looks past me now, chewing the inside of her cheek if I'm not mistaken, and I wait. And wait.

The rain is easing, her expression not so much.

'No, not the pub.' Her eyes flit to mine. 'My place is around the corner; we can take this there.'

'Your place?' I don't want to come across as surprised as I feel, but hell, it's obvious. 'I'm not sure… I don't think…'

Now her eyes return and stay, their depths sparkling with what looks very much like amusement. 'Scared I'm going to eat you alive, Valentine?'

She does a little claw action with her free hand, sound effects to boot. *Fuck*. I loosen my tie.

'Jesus, don't worry.' She outright laughs now. 'You're far too young for me…and, if I'm honest, I've a feeling I'd break you.'

I swallow and wish I'd forgone the tie altogether this morning. This really isn't going the way I want it to. Not even close. Just like the night at DareDevils, she almost has me on the run again.

'Look, Valentine.' Her sharp prompt has my pulse jumping. 'Do you want to talk about this or not?'

'Yes.' It's abrupt, to the point. That's all I want to do. Talk about it, put it behind us. No more innuendo, suggestion, flirtation or whatever the hell this is.

'Then we do it in the privacy of my own home.'

She starts to move but I'm rooted. A private booth in a pub is still a public place; it would be easy to keep a lid on…on *this*. It would be safe, secure, known.

But her home…?

Olivia

I tell myself I don't care if he follows.

I tell myself it's probably better if he doesn't. I'm teetering on the edge of some emotional blowout and I'm not sure I want him witnessing it. No matter the role he's played in the way I feel.

I'm too fragile. It would be better to leave it a day

or two, give myself time to think through the board's request to effectively 'play nice' with him and then face off our encounter four weeks ago.

My stomach rolls as I once again replay all he bore witness to during our *accidental* meet-up. Only it was no accident... He was there to spy on me.

My chest tightens, the bloom of anger threatening to set my skin ablaze all over again, and I grit my teeth, keep on walking. At least the anger beats the feeling of humiliation though.

I don't turn around and he doesn't attempt to walk in step with me and seek shelter under the umbrella again.

Good. Let him get soaked. It's no more than he deserves.

I inwardly cringe at my petty behaviour. But is it petty? When all's said and done, don't I have a right to feel and act like this?

I lead the way in silence, hoping I can get a grip on my emotions before we reach my home, but I'm no calmer, no more in control as I push open the gate to my small front garden. I physically have to stop myself from letting it swing back on him, his taunt, *'Will you stop behaving like a child...?'* fresh in my ears.

'Thank you.'

I don't respond as I walk down the path, leaving him to close the gate. I'm too busy telling myself this is a bad idea. But it beats doing it in the office or the pub or any other public place.

I pull my keys from my bag, surprised at how steady my fingers are, and unlock the front door. I step inside and turn to shake the umbrella out, keeping my eyes fixed on it and not his approaching form.

'It's a nice garden you have here.'

I don't respond, just thrust the umbrella into the tall pewter vase beside the door and fight the ridiculous urge to laugh. *Small talk? Really?*

I keep my mouth clamped shut, untie my coat, which is a flourish of colour in the otherwise stark hallway, and hang it on the concrete coat stand Nathan paid an exorbitant amount for a few years back.

Valentine steps in and I shift away, tossing my bag on the concrete console table created by the same artist as the coat stand and catch a glimpse of myself in the mirror above. My heart jumps. I look alive, vibrant, my eyes glittering, my skin pink... I'm as incongruous as my coat. I falter a little, shake off the shock and keep moving, straight for the gleaming white kitchen and the wine cooler. I pull out a bottle, not caring which.

'Can I get you one?' I take a glass out of the cupboard and let my eyes drift to him as he walks in behind me. He looks awkward, young, so out of place. His golden skin, brilliant blue eyes and cobalt suit, all colour against the pale backdrop, and I have the intense desire to jump his bones on my pristine centre island.

I'm losing my mind, quite clearly.

I lift my brows to prompt an answer and catch the way he eyes the bottle in my hand. 'What—too early for you?'

I check the wrought-iron clock that Nathan insisted we purchase even though it dominates the pillar that separates the kitchen from the dining space and the hard-landscaped garden beyond and take in the time. It's long past noon, long past acceptable drinking time.

'I'm good, thank you.'

'Suit yourself.'

I pour a large glass, throw back a gulp and stare out at the garden and the rain creating ripples in the long, narrow pool that runs down its middle. I must have forgotten to put the cover across after this morning's swim. But now I appreciate it, the sight of the rain causing a dance of vanishing circles that mirror the uneasy ripples inside.

I fear what he has to say, but I know I have to listen. That for the good of my company, the charity, I have to.

I flick him a look. He's unmoving and soaked through; the hair that was so groomed in the boardroom has taken on a foppish edge, the shoulders of his blue suit dark where the rain has seeped in. It makes him appear less…less perfect, less in control.

More young. More vulnerable. More palatable…

I throw back more wine.

That's palatable! Not a man half your age. A young, rain-abused and wickedly handsome PR guru sent to whip you into bloody shape!

A cocktail of anger and guilt fizzes in my veins. But it's the guilt that's winning out. Guilt that I desire him. Guilt that he's in my marital home at my invitation. Guilt at his drowned rat state. Guilt that

I'm drinking when he's not. Guilt that I haven't offered him an alternative drink when the well-trained hostess in me says that I should. Hell, even Nathan would turn in his grave.

Nathan. Nathan. Nathan.

Why do I still feel like he's in the room with me, judging me, advising me?

More wine. Another breath. And why the hell isn't Valentine speaking…?

'You want to get started?' I bite out. 'I assume you're a busy man and, believe me, there are plenty of things I'd rather be doing.'

Things I'd rather be doing…like him.

Jesus.

Why can't I control this—my own mind, my own urges?

I've been set free. I *should* be able to live how I want. Instead, I can't even get a handle on my emotions. They've never been further out of my control. And this desire to lose myself in something crazy, something wild and daring and all-consuming, it's getting worse. Because Valentine…he represents all those juicy things.

I force myself to face him. The sooner we get this done, the sooner he leaves without me succumbing to the other ideas coming alive, ideas which start with me defiling him right here, right now.

'Well?' I prompt and he starts, waking up from some stupor that has me keen to work out where his head has been. Was it keeping mine company in the gutter? The thought tickles me, teasing at my lips, which aren't so keen to form a straight line any more.

'Okay.' He rakes a hand through his wet hair, rubs his other down his face before shoving both hands deep inside his trouser pockets. I don't want to notice how the move encourages his jacket to open up, his unveiled shirt to cling to his obviously trim torso, or the way he bites down on his lip as he contemplates what to say…

And I shouldn't want him, not now. Not now I know who he is and in the cold light of day can *see* just how young he is.

So young, so fit, so virile… My mouth dries against the Chardonnay as my imagination runs wild, fending off my better judgement, which seems to intervene less and less these days.

'Firstly, I *am* sorry.' The sincerity in his tone draws my eyes to his and I can see it. In the intensity of his gaze, the way his brows furrow and his eyes widen. 'The night we met, my intention was to see it for myself, that the rumour wasn't merely malicious gossip aimed to discredit you.'

I scoff into my glass as I raise it to my lips. 'You make it sound like I have a horde of enemies waiting in the wings to take me down. I'm not a celebrity, royalty, a politician, anyone of consequence—what does it matter what I do?'

'The board believes it matters and they're right. As for the charity, it doesn't have a new face to replace you. You've stood down, but people still regard you as the spokesperson, the front.'

I'm quiet. I don't want to go back to the way I was, but I also don't want the charity to suffer either.

'And you have to realise that you're in the public eye. You as an individual. You're an extremely successful businesswoman; lecturers talk about you, young women look up to you, they study you, they want to emulate you.'

Another scoff. I don't want to listen. I don't *want* to be that person. Not any more. I don't want young women to follow my path, to sacrifice everything like I did and for what—to be forty-five and alone, lost, soulless?

But how can I explain that to him? We're standing in my home, worth a fortune in itself. Not to mention the other properties I have all over the world. I have wealth. I have everything. And I'm quoting the tabloids now. Just last week an article used my possessions as a way to balance the loss of my husband: *Hey, it's okay. Yes, she lost her husband, her sweetheart for over two decades, but look at all she has accumulated in that time.*

They don't even know the half of it. No one does. No one knows what our relationship was like behind closed doors. Except maybe Fee. And though I disagree with her to an extent, because I loved Nathan, he was a good man, he had a good heart, even if he didn't always show it, even if he did control almost everything, even if he was more like my father than I ever could have realised…

I let him take over, I altered myself to please him and played my part, losing sight of myself in our marriage, coming out of it not knowing my own mind, how to live. Truly live.

And wealth… What's wealth when you have no one to share it with?

My skin prickles, goosebumps spreading top to toe as the chill inside blooms. I fold my arms across my middle, take a breath and focus on what he came here to discuss, feeling decidedly more comfortable with that side of the conversation. Because, truth is, I want to know what he was thinking, I want to know why he ventured up those stairs and then ran.

'Rewind to a month ago…' I force myself to meet his gaze and ignore the nervous fluttering in my chest. Hell, I can be as confident as they come but the problem is, he does something to me, he sets me on edge, he makes me feel nervous, he makes me feel…like a lust-struck teenager again.

'Okay.'

I see the tension pulse in his jaw, but his willingness to go there gives my confidence a much-needed boost.

'You say the reason you turned up that night was to establish the truth in the rumour. Well, you got the truth. I was there. So…why take me up on the invite? You could have said no and left, in order to stay professional, you *should* have said no and left. Then you wouldn't have this…messy predicament to deal with.'

He stares back at me. Long, torturous moments where I start to think he may run. Again. But then he sucks in a breath that makes his chest swell, his shoulders arch back and out it comes with a gust of air.

'Because I wasn't in my right mind.'

My brows draw together, the meaning of his words sparking many a dangerous and salacious thought. I could say I wasn't in my right mind too; I was wrapped up in a carnal fantasy that I wanted made real and he would have been the perfect finishing touch.

I take a much slower sip of my Chardonnay and lean my hip against the stainless-steel work surface that I'm so keen to ruin him over. 'How so?'

He swallows and it's audible. He really isn't so suave and sophisticated and in control now. In fact, he has the distinct look of prey about to be taken down by its predator and I laugh softly. Does that make me a true cougar?

Another sip of wine and the idea settles. The excitement of it, the thrill that he's here for the taking…the idea of work, the board, the company… it's all blurry as the undercurrent between us builds and we're reliving that night four weeks ago.

I wet my lips, take another sip of wine and eye him over the glass. 'Cat got your tongue…Valentine?'

'Are you trying to put me on edge…Olivia?'

My smile grows with his mimicked tease and I step closer to him.

'Tell me the truth. Why did you go up those stairs?'

His eyes trail down my front, so swift I could have missed it if I hadn't been watching him so intently.

Another step closer.

'I've already told you. I…' His voice trails off as his eyes fall to my lips and I realise I've wet them again. Unintentionally, of course. 'I…'

'You…?'

'I couldn't say no.'

'But you should have?' I push, starting to understand and feeling the thrill of it pulse through my veins.

'Yes.'

'Why? Do you have a girlfriend, a wife?'

Something flickers in his face, an expression I can't place.

'No.'

'Well, then…' Relief eases between my shoulders. I didn't know I cared so much, but of course I would when every thought running through my mind needs him to be very much free and single.

'My relationship status, or lack of, doesn't come into it. It's because of this job, because it gets in the way of what I'm here to do.'

I nod as I run one finger around the rim of my glass. 'And what exactly are you here to do?'

'To help. To help you, the company, the charity.'

I nod again and step even closer. I'm only a foot or two away now and I can smell his cologne twisted up in the rain, the outdoors.

'You want to help me?'

'Yes.'

I let my eyes travel down the length of him. Slow, sure…

'Tell me, Valentine, do you like what you see?'

I stroke my chest now, so softly I can barely feel the caress of my fingers as they trail between my breasts, over my stomach and smooth down my side. All the while his eyes follow their path, hooked, mesmerised.

'You're a very attractive woman, Olivia.'

I know he means it. His gravel-thick voice is tight with it.

'That's not an answer. Do *you* find me attractive?'

He swallows, his eyes flicker and I know he's fighting his own response.

'I could check myself.' I purposefully lower my gaze to where his shirt meets with his trousers, and lower still, to the obvious bulge thickening behind his zip. 'If you like?'

He steps back. 'Olivia…'

'Olivia…?' I purr, stepping forward.

'I should never have gone up those stairs. I'm sorry that I did. I'm sorry that it puts you in an awkward position now.'

'Puts *me* in an awkward position?' I purposefully eye his zip again. 'I think it perhaps puts you in a more awkward position. Tell me, Valentine, have you thought of it often since that night? Have you thought about all you witnessed? Me, on my knees, naked, chained…?'

I reach out to trail a finger down his chest and he grabs my hand. 'Don't.'

'Don't what? Tease you?'

His jaw pulses, his nostrils flare and his hand

flexes around mine, hot and strong, the physical touch as tantalising as an intended caress.

'But you left, Valentine, you ran out just as it was getting good… Just think what you missed out on.'

He releases my hand, drags in a breath as he backs up, but I'm not letting him get away this time. I have no idea where this confidence is coming from now but there's something about the wild look in his eye that reaffirms his rejection had nothing to do with not wanting me and everything to do with the job he'd been asked to do.

And yes, he deserves hell for spying on me, for watching me, for running…but maybe this is a kind of torture for him.

Whatever the case, I'm having too much fun teasing and tormenting to get all huffy and pissed off.

In fact, I think an outright seduction will go some way to blotting out our teeny tiny history and creating a new one.

Valentine

She's so close I can smell her perfume. I can see the tiny flecks of brown in her otherwise crystal-blue eyes. And I can sure as hell read the tease that's there.

It's nothing like the tease in the boardroom now. The gloves are off and she's going all in, and I really need to get the hell out of here before—

'What are you scared of, Valentine?'

'Stop. Just stop.' I hold a hand up to her and she steps into it, presses her chest up against my palm. *Fuck.* I haven't felt a woman since…

'I won't tell, if you won't?'

I shake my head. 'That's not how it works.'

She smiles, gives a soft laugh that has her body vibrating into my palm and I snap it away, fist it into a ball at my side but I can't seem to step away any further. I feel like I'm being drawn in, transfixed by her every movement as she sips at her wine, so cocksure, so hypnotic.

'I beg to differ. That's exactly how it works, and I'll be happy to show you, educate you even…'

'Educate me?' I sound as strangled as my dick as it strains against my clothing, my blood surging south as my heart pounds in my ears.

'I have many years on you, many years of experience I'd be willing to share. What you witnessed a month ago is nothing compared to…'

She reaches out, her hand resting against my chest before trailing lower. My torso contracts, my breath stalling… No, no, no. I grab her wrist, stop her before she can reach her target. Me. Four years of going without. Hard and oh, so willing.

'I came to apologise and clear the air.' The words hurry out. 'Nothing more.'

Her eyes blaze into mine. 'You sure about that?'

'Yes.'

'You don't want to see what you missed out on?'

I gulp in air.

'You don't want to…' she scrapes her teeth over her lower lip '…*fuck* me right now?'

Yes. God, yes. I do.

My hand pulses around her wrist as my mind vies for control over my body. Think about the job. Think about her state of mind. The real reason you've been brought in. She's using you in the same way she used that club, Electra, the Bugatti… She's using you to aid in her downfall. To feed the vicious cycle of grief she's trapped in.

'I'm not what you're looking for, Olivia.'

'Oh, I think you're *exactly* what I'm looking for.'

I shake my head. 'No, I'm not. And I'm flattered, believe me I'm flattered, but…'

She pales, her eyes widening into mine as they seem to tremble and probe in one. 'You're rejecting me…again?'

She backs up, snatches her hand away. 'God, what's wrong with me? I'm such a fool.'

'You're no fool. You're just…grieving.'

She's still backing away and I don't think she's even listening to me now.

'Consider your apology delivered. You can go.'

I flounder as she turns away, walking up to the sliding doors that lead out onto an enclosed garden that's like a mini oasis. Paradise in the heart of London. All hard landscaping with potted plants flourishing, a narrow pool with a stone waterfall and a glass sheltered bathing area set off to one side.

She watches the water, her gaze withdrawn, her arms folded across her middle. Her blood-red lips, nails, shoes the only colour in the room and at total odds with it. The observation is peculiar in both its presence and its timing. Why would I even pick up on it?

Perhaps because she doesn't seem to belong in this hard, contemporary shell. What I've seen of her is so vibrant, colourful, daring.

'I said you can go.'

Except I don't want to go. Not now. I don't want to leave her like this. Her bleak demeanour is all the more pronounced as she stands surrounded by luxury, the kind that speaks of her extreme success.

But I wonder at the cost.

This was her marital home; they lived here together for a long time. How can she walk within these four walls and not confront that loss daily? I upped and left the second I lost Layla. Anything to cut myself off from the past, start afresh and forget.

'Why do you live here?' I say into the strained quiet.

She stiffens so I know she hears me, but…nothing.

I walk up to her. 'I'm sorry, I don't even know why I said it.'

Only I do. But to an outsider it's the strangest question in the world. Why wouldn't you choose to live in such a glorious haven from the bustling city outside when you can afford to do so?

'And yet you asked it?' She looks at me, brows pinched together, her eyes seeing far too much, and I look away. What can I say to that?

I asked because when I was in her position I didn't have the courage to stay. I didn't have the strength to face my past, day in, day out, and be okay. I asked because I think she's mad to do so.

Does it make her stronger than me on some level? Stronger and yet more damaged, because all the adventure she's pursuing smacks of a downward spiral that I've been asked to bring to an end.

'You sure I can't get you a drink? You look like you need one as much as me now.'

I startle, aware that there's so much in my face, so much that I don't want her to see. 'I don't drink.'

'You don't drink…? What, ever?'

'No.'

'Okay.' She drawls it out and her eyes remain fixed on me, too curious, too aware. 'Care to talk about it?'

'About what?' I'm playing dumb, but getting that personal with her is a bad, bad move.

'Whatever's got you looking like that?'

'No.'

She makes a soft sigh into her glass and goes back to looking at the view outside. 'Well, that makes two of us.'

'Agreed.' Though I want her to talk about it. I want to know what she's thinking. I want to know what makes her tick. I want to help her, just as Alan and the board want me to help her. I want to get her back to how she was…

'But there are other things we could do…' Her

eyes slide to me and hell, if I don't let mine slide to her. 'Things far more fun.'

It's like being on a rollercoaster…no, the waltzer… the dizzying speed with which she flips from seductress, to spurned, to pained, to professional, and hell, I can't keep up and I know it's all part and parcel of where her head is at.

'Seriously, Olivia, you need to kill the innuendo. We're going to be working together.'

'But too much work makes Valentine a very, very, dull boy.'

She pouts at me and the two personas are merging. Olivia Carmel, the renowned businesswoman, philanthropist and icon. And the sexy, no-holds-barred woman who was on her knees, her nipples clamped, her skin flushed with lust.

'Spoilsport.' The tease erupts, her eyes burning into my lips and I force myself to stay on task.

'So, are we okay?'

She shakes her head, a smile dancing on her lips. 'Answer me one thing. Job aside, if you'd been at the club that night as just another party-goer, would you have joined us in that room?'

I swallow. I won't lie. 'Yes.'

Not that she can know the true significance. That it would have brought an end to four years of celibacy, of being content living that way.

Content?

I think about the last four weeks, the tangled bedsheets, the restless energy, the incessant thrum when I'm in her presence. It's hardly content.

'Then we're okay,' she murmurs.

I close my eyes briefly, calm the rush inside.

'Good.' Poker face on. 'So I can count on your cooperation from here on in?'

Her smile lifts to one side as her eyes sparkle. 'You can count on me not letting our first encounter get in the way of doing the right thing for the business and the charity.'

'What does that mean?'

'It means I'll listen to what you advise and make my own decision.'

'Right. Okay.' I think.

'But I'm no pushover, Valentine,' she carries on. 'You'll need to convince me that your way is the right way.'

'Fair enough.'

'And while you're at it, don't expect me to play fair.'

My frown is instant. 'What does that mean?'

'It means I want you, and when I want something these days, I stop at nothing until I get it.'

Shit. It shouldn't turn me on. My heart shouldn't be racing. My cock shouldn't twitch. 'I should go.'

Her mouth quirks at the corner. 'Running away again, Valentine?'

'If you want to see it that way.' I'm already heading for the door. 'We have a meeting first thing tomorrow. I'll present my PR strategy for the next few weeks then.'

'That quick, hey?'

'Yes.'

'Oh, goodie, I can't wait.'

Can't wait? Jesus.

My entire body is thrumming. Reawakened. Needy. Lustful. Taken over by her energy, her blatant desire—her, just her.

'Neither can I,' I say to her door as I let myself out.

Neither can I...

CHAPTER SIX

Olivia

'YOU'VE DONE WHAT?'

I stare at Valentine across my desk and blink once, twice for good measure, and still feel like I can't have heard him right. For twelve months I've been free and now my wings are being clipped. And all by some upstart who would've been in nappies while I was graduating with first class honours from Oxford.

'I've arranged a dinner for Thursday night. There are people I'd like you to meet, politicians who can add weight to your charity agenda, influential people who—'

'No, I got that, but Saturday, you said…?'

He flicks his navy tie out and settles back into his chair, too sure of himself and what he has to say. His pristine hair is combed back in what must be a blow-dried quiff. His face is closely shaven, not a blemish in sight, save for the scar through his eyebrow that makes me shiver with speculation, fascination. His chiselled jaw and prominent cheekbones all sculpted and golden, and his lips…

No, don't go there!

I drop my gaze to his clothing. The sharp cut to his charcoal-grey suit that highlights his broad shoulders, his crisp white shirt smooth as it runs over what are sure to be washboard abs. Is there not a millimetre that doesn't appeal? A millimetre of imperfection that I can focus on…my eyes flit to the scar again.

No. Not working. It only adds a bad boy vibe to his authoritarian air, and in *my* office, going over *my* schedule.

I have the ridiculous urge to climb over my desk and yank the navy flap of silk until he's an inch from my face, muss him up while I make it clear I won't be treated like this.

Not again.

'I said I've made arrangements for us to attend a football match, a corporate box affair. I think the French striker Louis Dubois and his wife are the perfect replacement for you. The charitable work they've already done abroad makes them the ideal candidates to—'

'I don't disagree with their suitability. What I'm arguing with is the timing, the fact that you've taken it upon yourself to cancel *my* plans with *my* PA behind *my* back and you've not even been here five minutes.'

'Twenty-four hours, if I want to be picky.'

My eyes flare at him.

'As for the timing,' he carries on regardless, 'their

calendars are tricky at best. They're flying in for the semi-final, so it's now or in a month or two, and you know it needs to be now.'

'And like I said to you yesterday, it's me you talk to, me you convince and gain agreement with, *before* you go anywhere near my PA and adjust my plans.'

'You had a track day planned; it was hardly critical, not to mention—'

'It's *my* track day.'

'There'll be other track days; there won't be another opportunity like this.'

'That's not the point, and you know it.'

He shifts in his seat. I'd like to think it's because he's uncomfortable, but he's been in my office for an hour taking me through his plans and not once has he acted out of place, on edge. If anything, he's in his element, telling me how this should all play out.

And yes, I'm impressed with the ideas he's put forward. So far, they've been sound, easy decisions to make, but now we're onto my diary, my free time and he's taking over, just like…just like Nathan.

'I spoke to Pippa and we agreed—'

'You and my PA agreed?' I splutter, choking on my rising anger. 'Have you heard yourself?'

'What I'm trying to say is, we talked through your Saturday plans and we agreed she would call you before firming anything up. When she couldn't reach you, we made an executive decision.'

'An executive decision about my Saturday, my free time? How utterly thoughtful of you.'

'Like I explained, time was of the essence.'

'I hardly think waiting a few hours for us to have this meeting would have hurt.'

'I didn't think it would be this much of an issue.'

'Well, bully for you!' I snap and then want to slap myself. Because I know I'm being juvenile, but hell, I've just escaped one controlling relationship to enter another. And not with a lover, a boyfriend, a husband or business partner, but a man employed by my board to fix me. And I'm angry. Hell, I'm angry.

'When I discussed it with Alan and Pippa it made sound business sense.'

His words make my blood boil further. Having him ignore my outburst is worse than an outright dismissal of it. He might as well have sat there and said, *Now, don't you think you're overreacting?* Or, worse, his line from yesterday afternoon: *'Will you stop behaving like a child?'*

I suck in a breath, let it out, slow and measured. 'You discussed it with them…what? Yesterday afternoon? The early hours of this morning?'

'After our talk at your place I came back to the office and, like I said, Pippa did try to call you.'

My cheeks colour. It was just a talk, not an attempted seduction on my part…and Pippa *did* call me. Only I let it ring out as I enjoyed another glass of white followed by another. All in aid of forgetting: Nathan, work, Valentine, our talk, my seduction…

I can almost hear the inner laughter and it's crippling me. *You tried to seduce him—he was having none of it.*

And why would he when he's nearly twenty years my junior?

You silly deluded fool.

'How old are you?' I blurt out over the inner monologue that stings far too much.

'I'm twenty-nine.' He waves an easy hand at me. 'Is that a problem?'

I shrug, my smile intended to be just as easy, just as self-assured. So I wasn't graduating, but I was definitely at Oxford when he was running about in nappies. 'I just wonder how much experience someone of your years can truly offer me.'

'And just like that, we're back to your experience?'

And instead of the heat of shame returning at the reminder of my 'failed seduction', I'm warming with something far more appealing and dangerous to the professional nature of this meeting.

I'm not the only one either. I swear I see it firing in the depths of his sharp blue gaze.

'My apologies; does the mere mention of my experience in the bedroom put you on edge?'

His eyes spark all the more and the desire to crawl over my desk and put it to the test burns deeper, stronger.

He clears his throat, his knuckles whitening around the arms of his chair and I know I have him backed into a corner and I've not even moved…yet.

And I did warn him. Yesterday. I made it clear I wanted him and that I always—*always*—get what I want. Now that Nathan is gone there's nothing stopping me in my quest for life, for fun, for anything but the stunted life I had before.

'Do you disagree with anything else I've proposed this morning?'

I know he's changing the subject. I also know his body isn't focusing on the tame words coming out of his mouth and the tell-tale tension in his gruff tone has a thrilling little shiver running through me, pushing me to goad him further.

'Disagree? No, I wouldn't say I disagree.'

I push myself out of my seat and walk around the desk. His eyes stay fixed on mine, never once shying away, to take in my open shirt collar…my open *red* shirt collar that matches the red soles to my black patent shoes. I've dared to wear red shoes to work, a red coat even, but that's as far as I've pushed the black and white dress code Nathan enforced many years ago. I'm truly pushing boundaries, breaking the company mould and antagonising the board while I'm at it. But then they made the first hostile move when they brought Valentine in…

Though, if I'm honest, his presence is exhilarating, especially when I hold the high ground. Quite literally now as I press my behind into the desk edge beside his chair and look down at him.

'The subtle tweaks to our corporate message that you've discussed with Susan are sound.'

I cross my legs at the ankle, pulling the fabric of my black pencil skirt taut around my thighs, and watch how he fights the urge to look his fill, his white-knuckled fist closest to me gripping the chair arm tighter as I take it all in.

'An introduction to the politicians involved with Scotland's plans to end homelessness in all its forms, with a view to achieving something similar in England. All sound.'

I fold my arms, pull my shoulders back, knowing full well it causes the red satin to strain across my chest, enhancing my cleavage and—*bull's-eye*. I catch the way his eyes dip, their subtle flare, the twitch to his jaw that tells me he has it clenched.

A smile nags at my lips with the growing sense of victory and I force them to straighten as I continue on, wanting to get my point across even as my body wants so much to provoke the tension in his.

'You see I have no problem with any of that. But when you want to make a change to my diary, it's me who does it. Is that understood?'

He doesn't move, doesn't blink. His eyes burn into mine, long and hard, and my pulse races away with itself. Does he know how hypnotic his eyes are? How the blue glitters in the overhead lights? Is he using their intensity now to put me on edge?

Of course he bloody is!

I try to breathe and the air seems to scrape through my lungs, every nerve-ending heightened as I try to stay in control. I wet my lips, lower my hands to the desk edge and grip it for support.

'Is that clear, Valentine?'

He blinks, his lips curving ever so slightly at the corners. 'Yes, consider yourself understood.'

I suppress the telling sigh of relief. 'Good.'

But neither of us move. Our eyes are locked in some silent battle. This close I can see the dark line that surrounds his irises, making his eyes appear bluer, more penetrating. I can see the hint of sheen where his lips meet; even in their grim line they're teasingly full. I can smell his cologne, fresh, tantalising, urging me to lean forward and breathe him in deep. His cleanshaven cheeks that make my palms itch to feel their softness before running my fingers through his hair and ruining its perfect form.

God, how I want to see him lose it, go wild, make him as imperfect as me.

To have the man who willingly walked up those stairs at my invitation that very first night at Dare-Devils to witness me with Electra. The man who I imagine to be so far removed from the one sitting in my office right now...though they are one and the same.

An idea starts to form. An idea that not only serves as payback, but gets him away from business, from the professional, the platonic. Gets him so very far away from here.

'Pippa!' I'm already heading for the door. I know she's heard me because she's now shuffling papers on the other side of the glass and trying to look busy when not two seconds ago her eyes were definitely on us. I yank open the door. 'Pippa, can you join us for a minute, please?'

'Of course.' She stands, her smile wary and with good reason. She can read me like an open book and is sure to have noticed the tension building this side of the glass.

'Is everything okay?' She enters the room, glancing between us.

'Yes, everything's fine,' I assure her. 'Have you rescheduled the track day I had planned for this Saturday?'

'No, I was going to ask you about an alternative date.'

I look back to Valentine, to his calm and composed exterior I'm so desperate to crack. 'Can you reschedule it for next weekend?'

'Of course.'

'And tell them I'm bringing a friend.'

'You are?' Her brow lifts to me in surprise and I feel a weird pang deep inside, tying up my tongue. I shouldn't be so surprised that she's surprised. It's not like I often bring a plus one to anything. My sister is often too busy with the kids and Nathan dominated my social diary just as much as my professional one.

I plaster on a smile, give a definite nod. 'Yes.'

'Very well.' I'm relieved she makes no further comment, relieved even more when she reminds me of my purpose by adding, 'Please can you send me their licence details? They like to have it all sorted up front.'

'Oh, yes.' My smile is easy now as I look back to Valentine and catch his eyes narrowing ever so slightly. *Oh, yes, Boretti, you're getting the gist of where this is heading...* 'I'll get those to you as soon as possible.'

'Great.'

'Fabulous.'

'Any other special requests?'

'No. Just make sure they have the fastest and the best available. I'll make it worth their while.'

'Sure.'

She heads back to her desk and I swing the door closed.

'There you go, Valentine, all's well.' I dust off my hands as I walk to my desk and sit back down. 'This weekend we do football, and next weekend we do supercars.'

I look to my computer screen as I move the mouse to wake it up.

'Hang on, Olivia, I haven't agreed to—'

'Tit for tat, Valentine. You want me there this weekend, you'll be with me *next* weekend.' I flick him a look. 'Then you can consider us even on the diary front.'

'Do you really think testing out supercars gives the right image so soon after your accident?'

I shake my head. 'Get over yourself, Valentine. It's a racetrack. It's safe and fun. And something tells me you're in dire need of the latter.'

'This isn't about me; it's about you. You need to change the narrative, Olivia. You need to show people you're as stable as you ever were and that all this—all this adrenaline-seeking craziness is over.'

My entire body stills, my stare as chilled as I feel. 'For your information, the car accident was just that, an accident. I aquaplaned and it could have happened to anyone, in any car. You can't control how the media interprets something.'

'No, but you can control the ingredients that make up the story and reduce the collateral damage.'

I study him for a long, intense second, his words merging with my sister Fee's. But I have no interest in changing how I choose to live my life now that it's my own. Not for anyone—or anything—else.

'Are we done here?'

'I don't know,' he says gravely. 'Are you taking on board what I'm saying?'

'Are you saying I need to live the life of a saint, regardless of what makes me happy?'

'I'm saying you just need to tone it down, at least until we have the charity front sorted. Take a back seat from the media. Don't give them cause to speculate about your mental health.'

I laugh now. Abrupt. Harsh.

'My mental health?'

He doesn't even flinch. Instead his eyes soften, a line forming between his brows, and I want to look away from the concern shining so clear in the pools of blue, do anything but drown in them. 'I'm serious, Olivia, you need to take better care of yourself.'

A weird pressure builds in my throat, closing it up, my eyes sting. I blink. I swallow. But it just keeps coming.

'There are people close to you who are concerned for your wellbeing. The press aside, it's time you started to listen to them.'

I scoff and push away from my desk, stalk to the

window and stare out. Anything to stop him witnessing the way his words strike through the very heart of me.

'Consider your point made. Are we done here?'

He's quiet. Too quiet.

I spin to face him, arms folded, back straight.

'I repeat.' Louder. Stronger. 'Are we done here?'

He shakes his head, his shoulders ever so slightly falling. 'For now.'

He rises out of his seat, bending to take up his laptop bag from the floor.

'I'll pick you up at seven-thirty for dinner, Thursday. Wear something…' His eyes trail over me as he straightens, their sudden heat making my skin prickle. Christ, even my nipples harden against the boning of my bra, eager for more than a look from him when not two seconds ago I was chilled to the core and eager for him to leave. 'Wear something conservative.'

'Conservative?' A laugh erupts, my mood shifting so quickly that I'm dizzy on it.

'It's just a standard request. Dress to suit the occasion.'

'Oh, right. A standard request. You say the same to all your clients, do you?'

He clears his throat.

'I tell you what,' I say. 'How about I send some pictures through of various possibilities? That way you can choose my entire outfit…all the way from the base layer up.'

He looks ready to choke over the suggestion. 'I don't think you need to go that far.'

I bite my lip, fighting back laughter. 'I don't know. I think it could be kind of fun.'

He shakes his head and strides for the door.

'Running away again, just as things were starting to get interesting?'

He reaches for the door handle and looks back at me over his shoulder. 'I'll see you Thursday.'

'You will.'

He pulls open the door.

'Oh, and, Valentine?'

He turns to me once more and I give him a smile so full of satisfaction his eyes are already narrowing before I even speak.

'Don't forget to send me your driving licence details…a scanned copy would be *just splendid*.'

CHAPTER SEVEN

Valentine

IT'S THURSDAY. Seven in the evening. And I'm early.

But as I stand before her garden gate, the idea of returning to the car and doing a few circuits of the block doesn't appeal. I want to know she's ready, or at least close. I want to know we have this in the bag, that tonight she will be the woman I've respected from afar for years, the woman who had it all under control and a firm handle on life.

Now I'm here I have time to hurry her along.

Now I'm here I can reassure myself we'll get to dinner as planned.

Now I'm here I can acclimatise to her appeal *before* I have to perform normally in front of others.

And there's the real reason I'm here. To get used to her.

Doesn't matter that I've seen her plenty over the last few days. That I should be used to dealing with her and keeping a lid on the chaos she inspires within.

She's a wild card and no amount of knowing it helps me when I'm in her presence. Her ability to say or do something that I least expect. To drag my thoughts into the gutter when I should be focusing on business. She's impossible to predict, impossible to prepare for, and by getting here early I get to adjust to her long before we meet with the people who could be pivotal in the future success of her charity.

I push open her garden gate and stride forward. Remind myself of why I'm here, and who she is, and what this isn't—a date.

I lift my hand to the heavy-weighted knocker and my hand stills. I'm back in the club. Electra's room. The door and the lion's head and the view I saw within.

It's like a switch turning on, sending my pulse into overdrive before I even cross the threshold. 'Fuck.'

'Is that any way to say hello?' Her disembodied voice greets me from nowhere and I glance to my left, my right—there's a security camera—and grimace.

'A frown too…that happy to be here, hey?'

I shake my head, my lips lifting a little. 'My apologies.'

'You're early though; surely that's contradictory in itself.'

I look into the camera. 'You going to let me in?'

'I don't know. You going to smile properly?'

Christ, I laugh. A real laugh. To hell with the tension, the chaos that led me here early, I'm laughing.

'Better.'

The intercom goes silent and a few seconds later the door opens. She peers up at me through the gap, her heavy-lashed eyes sparkling and curious. Her make-up is soft and subtle. Her hair is gathered at the nape, loose strands falling either side of her face. I lose my voice, my head. For a moment all I can think is how beautiful she is.

She smiles at me, her head cocking to the side. One freed lock of hair teases at the opening to her gold satin robe. A robe that does nothing to conceal her curves, the pointed peak to each breast, her slender waist and her legs…they're bare from the mid-thigh down, her feet too, her dainty toenails painted red. And even with the evidence of the evocative shade on her nails, she's less man-eater and more… sweet and cosy, girl-next-door, and damn if I don't want her more.

I swallow, snap my eyes back to hers.

'You look like you've seen a ghost.' Her voice is melodic—teasing and amused in one. 'I just have to throw some clothes on.'

She pushes the door wider as she turns away, her scent lifting on the air and making me close my eyes for the briefest of seconds. When I open them again, she's already halfway down the hall and heading for the kitchen, her bare feet padding along the marble tiles, her luscious body swaying with such provocation I'm convinced she does it on purpose. Though she can't know how the robe glints in the white light of the hallway and enshrouds her in a captivating hue, her hair neatly twisted and making my fingers itch to untangle it, bring the seductress back, the submissive…

Fuck. My fists flex at my sides. I clear my throat and shake my head, hoping it'll empty the inappropriate thoughts out.

'Sorry to be early.' I close the front door and follow her into the kitchen. 'But I'd rather be early than late for tonight's affair.'

She sends me a little smile over her shoulder. 'You worried about your time-keeping or mine?'

Her smile lifts further as she laughs and reaches up into a cupboard for some glasses. 'I get the impression that you're many things, but I never had sexist down as being one of them.'

'I'm not—'

'No?' She raises one perfectly arched brow at me.

I'm not. What I am is pre-warned by Alan that she may let me down because it wouldn't be the first time she's been late in recent months. But I don't want to go there.

I raise my palms in surrender. 'Force of habit.'

I'm relieved she's still smiling, taking more delight in winding me up, but I'm still on edge, so very on edge. My mind wandering to the last time we were in this space and she propositioned me.

'Can I get you a drink while you wait?' I'm about to answer when she adds, 'Oh, that's right, you don't drink. How about a tonic?'

'A tonic would be great, thank you.'

She fills two glasses with ice, the robe shifting

over her body and making me crave to feel it over her skin, to have her look at me like she did the last time. She chooses that exact moment to meet my eye and I swear she reads the whole darn lot. The teasing quirk to her lips confirms it. I rub the back of my neck, ease my open shirt collar away as her eyes fall to my lips, their depths just as distracted, just as heated, but then they're back on the drinks.

She pours gin over ice in one and it crackles and pops, the sound adding to the electrically charged tension in the air.

'Lime, lemon?' she says as she pours the tonic. 'A dash of pink peppercorn, juniper, cardamom…?'

'Just as it comes.'

She sprinkles over her own glass what I can only deem as garnish and closes the distance between us, offering one out to me. Her scent reaches with her hand and assails me once more. It's nice…too nice. I can't pinpoint a single scent within it, only that it appeals to me because it's all her and it's haunted me since that first face-to-face meeting in her boardroom. Only now it's fresher, stronger, not dulled by the office and the aircon and observers who will see too much.

'Cheers,' I say, taking the glass from her.

'Cheers.' She clinks hers against mine, her eyes watching me closely—too closely.

I take a sip of the cold, refreshing drink, hoping it will ease the dryness in my mouth as I search for something to say, anything to break the connection fizzing between us.

'You obviously know what you're doing.' I eye her glass and the bits floating around.

Her smile is quick, but her eyes tell me she sees my remark for what it is—a distraction.

'What can I say? I was once an exceptional hostess.'

'Once? Are you saying you're not any more?'

She shrugs, her eyes leaving mine, and I sense a chill coming over her. 'There's not so much a call for it.'

'Entertaining?'

She wets her lips and gives a little laugh, but it's sad. Lonely even. And I have to fight the temptation to reach for her, to make her look at me. 'I can't believe a woman like you no longer entertains.'

Her smile is small. 'Nathan was the socialite really. He was the one with all the friends.'

'And now…' I place my glass down on the stainless-steel centre island. 'When w—'

'Wait!'

She leans across the island and takes what looks like a concrete coaster from the middle, sets it down beside my glass and places it on top. 'Sorry, that's *my* force of habit. Nathan was a stickler for them.'

Not her, though. That much is clear. I'm starting to get the impression that this whole house, the office, it's all Nathan.

'When was the last time you had people around? *Your* friends?'

She frowns at me. 'Why does it matter?'

'I'm just curious.'

Her eyes search mine and she takes a shaky breath, starts to move away. 'And I should get ready. We don't want to be late, remember.'

I reach for her on impulse. 'Hang on.'

Her arm flexes beneath my touch, the warmth of her skin permeating my palm. I want to pull her to me, kiss the surprised look off her face. But I can do neither and what do I really have to say when all I want is her reassurance that she does have friends? That she does have people she can talk to. That her social circle didn't revolve entirely around Nathan and since he's gone is non-existent.

Do I really want to expose that vulnerability in her minutes before we head out to a crucial dinner?

Her lashes flicker as she looks up at me and something inside me pulses, squeezes, makes it hard to think.

'What, Valentine?' Her voice is soft, husky, her lips glossy from where she's wet them and Jesus, do I want to be the one wetting them.

'Just tell me, when was the last time you had people around?'

She shakes her head, her laugh brittle, and the vulnerability I spy in her almost breaks me. 'You're my PR advisor, not my counsellor, Boretti. I'm going to get ready.'

And with that she sweeps out of my grasp and leaves me standing there in a cloud of her perfume, knowing the answer as well as if she'd said it herself.

I turn away, my eyes sweeping around the room

and seeing it with fresh eyes. There's no vibrancy, no fire or spark, colour or warmth. There's no *her*.

The strange sensation in my gut swells and I lift my tonic, frown into it before throwing back a swig and wishing for the first time in a long time that it was something stronger.

Olivia

'When was the last time you had people around? Your friends?'

I close the bedroom door and lean back against it, take a breath.

What does it matter? Why do I let him get under my skin?

I'm fine. I'm more than fine.

Though I know the mantra is getting old.

I push away from the door and throw back a gulp of G&T, wincing as the ice-cold drink catches in my throat and my eyes water. It's just the drink, not the pang his words provoked.

I strip off my robe and toss it onto the bed. The guest bed. I haven't slept in the master room since Nathan passed and the clothes in this wardrobe are all new. As is the bedding and the accessories. My first attempt at making this house a home again.

I lift my bra, already laid out on the bed, and slip it on along with its matching thong, their colour the perfect match for the burgundy bodycon dress I've chosen to wear. I step into it and fasten it up the back. It's the first time I've worn it. Nathan would never have approved of the daring colour but as I turn to look in the mirrored door of the wardrobe I smile and smooth my hands down my hips. Turn this way and that.

It's perfect and it makes me feel good…except…

I frown as I feel the ridge of my thong through the slim-fitting fabric and eye the mirror closely.

Not so perfect.

I check the rear, the front again, do a little wriggle as I try to reposition the band and make it invisible.

Blasted VPL. It's not happening.

I look to the closed door, beyond which Valentine is waiting down the stairs, and ponder the idea of going to dinner with him and whoever else he has lined up minus my teeny tiny slip of a thong.

I mean, it's hardly covering much anyway, not really, and so…

Little flutters start to erupt deep inside me. It's not something I've ever done before but hey, it's another for the bucket list…

But it's crazy.

A good…seriously daring…weird kind of crazy.

And hell, it beats the way I felt when I first entered the bedroom. This brings back the thrill of being near Valentine again, of having his scent fill my kitchen and his eyes burn into mine.

I smile as I bend forward and part the slit that runs up one thigh, reaching beneath to tug off my thong. I've already forgone the tights, my legs are glossed and primed to be unveiled tonight. It seems my bare pussy is too… I can't quite quash the giddy and disbelieving laugh that erupts as I toss the strip of lace back onto the bed and smooth my dress back down. I eye the mirror— There. Perfect.

I slide my feet into my waiting shoes. They're classic black with killer heels, something Nathan *did* approve of, so walking in them is a breeze, and I lift my black clutch off the bed. It's already loaded up with my purse, lipstick and phone, and as I throw back more of my drink and walk downstairs I feel ready for anything.

'Valentine!' I call from the hallway, placing the half-finished drink on the console table—*sans coaster, how daring.* 'I'm good to go.'

He appears in the kitchen doorway and my breath stutters. I'm fully aware of how he looks, I saw him not fifteen minutes ago, but seeing him again…he's just lethal. Lethal to my sanity, my neglected libido, everything.

And I'd feel foolish for my sudden immobilisation if it wasn't for the fact that I get the distinct impression he's suffering too.

'You look…' he breaks off, his fingers upsetting his well-coiffed hair so that my fingers no longer have to, though the fantasy of it persists '…great.'

'Thank you.'

He doesn't move and I play with the clutch in my hand. 'So…should we…you know…go?'

He snaps into action, so quickly I have to swallow another impulsive laugh. Because, truth is, I'm not amused by his temporary stupor, I'm flattered, more flattered than is safe for my heart that is always too eager to please. I've gone too many years caring about what everyone else thinks, about what everyone else wants. And I don't want to care like that again.

He walks past me and I follow, enjoying the way his fresh cologne hangs in the air between us, the way his broad shoulders feel like a protective shield of sorts. Nathan wasn't small by any means, but he wasn't as broad or as muscular as Valentine so obviously is and as I'm behind him I get to enjoy it right up until the moment he turns… My brows lift, my smile feeling too wide to be natural as I mask my wayward thoughts.

He pulls open the door, his eyes not quite reaching mine as he gestures. 'After you…'

'Thank you.'

I flick the latch as I pass and keep on going. I don't trust myself not to do something foolish when I'm too close to him. Like jump his bones right on my doorstep or, worse, admit to my lack of a social circle, admit that I'm lonely, that I don't want to be tied to another, led around by another, but neither do I want to live like this.

'Do you need to lock up?' he calls after me.

'No, the latch will get it.'

He pulls the door closed and comes up behind me before I can even reach the garden gate, his arm sweeping in front of me to open it.

I smile up at him. 'Can't cope with a woman opening her own gate?'

He chuckles low in his throat. 'It's not sexist, before you say it; it's chivalrous.'

'Quite the knight in shining armour.'

'If you want to see me that way.'

We're so close now. Almost chest to chest. And that voice, it's so low, so gruff... What would it feel like to have it rumble directly over my sex-starved clit?

I swallow a squeak as my thighs clench, my exposed nether regions tingling in a swift breeze.

'You okay?' His brows lift, a smile playing about his lips. *Busted.*

'Yes,' I blurt, stepping onto the pavement. 'Where are you parked?'

But he's already gesturing to a shiny black...

No. This cannot be his car. The brand. Him. The two just don't go together.

My lips twitch. 'That's your car?'

He eyes me. 'Yes.'

'But the brand?'

'And?'

I look at him, step towards the car, look at him again. 'Do you know how many PR specialists I've met over the years, men who think their car is an extension of them, and not one of them has driven one of these?'

'No?' To my relief he smiles. I don't want to offend him, but I can't contain my surprise. Every PR specialist, every marketer, publicist, whatever, with pockets as deep as I'm sure Valentine has, drives something flash. Even at the most conservative end of the scale it's been a slick four-by-four. An expensive muscle car. But this...it's...normal.

And Valentine is far from normal.

He unlocks it. 'You going to continue staring at it, or get in?'

I laugh and pull open the door, climb inside and watch as he slips into the driver's seat beside me.

'Is this your only car, or do you have a toy for weekends? For fun?'

He shakes his head as he fastens his seatbelt and starts the engine.

'Come on, you have to admit this car is a bit… unexpected?'

He pulls out into the traffic, his laugh as deep as his voice. 'Unexpected?'

'Yes. Someone like you, working in the glitzy world of PR, it doesn't stack up.'

'So you're stereotyping me?'

I chew my lip. I guess I am.

'And I'm not being flashy enough?'

'Oh, to look at *you're* plenty flash.' And I am looking, my eyes drinking in his frown of concentration as he navigates the busy streets of London. His hair's back in pristine condition, his made-to-measure suit and Rolex watch as flash as they come. 'But your car…'

'I'll have you know this car is one of the best in its class. Safe. Reliable—'

'Boring.'

His eyes flick to me. 'Nothing wrong with that.'

'No…' I consider him long and hard, imagine him out of his suit in some casual wear, in a pub, on a beach, eating fish and chips on a street corner...no, not him. 'What do you do to wind down?'

His brows pinch together as he sends me another look. 'Wind down?'

'Yes! You know, how do you fill your spare time? What do you get up to at weekends? I know you don't drink so partying is out.'

'You can party well enough without alcohol.'

The strength of his statement is jarring, but he's right though. 'True,' I say but internally I'm filing away his reaction for future examination. 'And do you?'

His brows lift. 'Party?'

'Not just party, wind down, chill out...'

I look to the road ahead and the speed limit sign, sneak a look at the speedometer and suppress a tickled smile that he is a notch below. He drives like my late grandad with his specs and his cataracts—God rest his soul.

'I don't know.' He shrugs. 'Stuff.'

'Stuff?' Now I do laugh and it's soft with fascination. 'Sounds thrilling.'

'Just because I don't need to tear it up on a race-track, risk my life on a mountain cliff, it doesn't make me boring.'

'I didn't say you were.'

'You said boring.'

'No, I said your car was boring. But then I love my cars, so you have to forgive me that one.'

'Right.' He nods, looks out of his driver's window before going back to the road with a surprising smile on his face.

'I mean it. In fact, I think you're a bit of an enigma and I happen to find that quite interesting.'

'*I'm* the enigma?'

'Yes.'

'Funny. I thought the same about you four weeks ago…'

Four weeks. The club. DareDevils. Electra.

The very air ignites between us, the mood shifting so far away from playful as the memories send heat rushing through my core and my thighs clamp together, my lips part. Is he reliving it too?

His eyes fall to where the slit of my dress has parted over my legs, only for a split second, but it's enough for me to witness the reciprocal desire.

'And what do you think now, Valentine?' I say softly. 'Still the enigma?'

'No.' He looks away, the muscles in his jaw contracting. 'I think I know you better than you know yourself.'

And just like that his arrogance has my blood boiling and my eyes snapping to the window.

'Oh, to be all knowing like you…'

His chuckle is low. 'What can I say? It's a gift.'

And there's the cocky marketer who should be driving a flash Porsche…the cocky marketer that I want to crack.

Tonight may be about raising the profile of the charity, pushing forward with exciting political initiatives, but I have so much more in mind. I just need to play my knickerless card right and before the night is over Valentine won't be lording it over me—he'll be well and truly under me.

'Tell me again about the people we're meeting…' I ask to fill the silence in the car, the tension thrumming beneath the surface. In reality, I don't need to hear it again. I've done my research. I know what I want to ask, what I want to glean from tonight's meet-up. But I also want Valentine to relax, right up until the point we arrive, and then…

I listen as he talks me through it all, his voice measured, businesslike. His attention on the road as he drives as conservatively as his car, letting people out at junctions, maintaining the appropriate braking distance and then some, not a digit above the speed limit. My lips quiver with an amusement I can't quash. He is just so…unexpected. A fascinating contradiction.

And it makes me want to crack his exterior all the more.

By the time we arrive at the renowned fusion restaurant I am fizzing over with it, my smile impossible to dampen as he pulls open the door to the establishment. He gestures for me to precede him in and I pause alongside him, tilt my head back, lift my mouth to his ear and…

'Would now be a good time to tell you I'm not wearing any underwear?'

His eyes flare down into mine, his jaw does that little twitch thing, and I walk on in. My smile building, my hips sashaying as my heels clip against the rich wooden floor. All the while I feel his eyes burning into my behind.

Warmth pools in my lower belly, excited little flutters rising up as I clutch my bag to my front.

Gotcha!

CHAPTER EIGHT

Valentine

THE EVENING IS a blur. A successful, Olivia-dominated blur.

She's perfect. She says all the right things. Her passion lifts the conversation at the table, from the debate she sparks over the definition of homelessness and public perceptions, right down to her knowledge of the great strides Scotland has made.

As for me...I'm quiet. Frustrated. Angry.

Angry that she would stoop to that level tonight of all nights, when her focus should be wholly on the charity and what we are here to achieve, what—

'Wouldn't you say so, Valentine?' Angus, the greying politician who's made it his final job to see England follow the same path as Scotland, prompts, his thick brows drawn together as he looks to me for input.

And he's not looking for input on the knickerless state of our dinner companion to my left.

'I'm sorry?' Jesus. She's not the one off the ball. I am, but entirely thanks to her. 'What was that?'

Olivia's eyes sparkle as she looks at me, the tiny upturn to her lips telling me she knows exactly where my head is at.

'We were just discussing how important it is to change the widespread and often fatalistic and cynical view of homelessness if we are to inspire more support.'

'Yes, absolutely.'

And so the evening continues…in much the same vein. Her giving me a masterclass in what I already know—how to schmooze and develop rapport with people—while my head keeps replaying her words in the doorway.

'Would now be a good time to tell you I'm not wearing any underwear?'

She's in her element beside me, close enough that I can't break free of her scent. Close enough that I catch glimpses of the slit in her dress that rides higher and higher each time she crosses and uncrosses her legs. It was in a movie once, white dress, blonde woman being interviewed…and, just like her, Olivia knows *exactly* what she's doing. By the time the meal comes to an end and we're back in the car, just me and her, I'm wound up so tightly I worry I'll crack a tooth.

'Why so moody?' she murmurs.

I don't even glance her way. It's bad enough that she's in my peripheral vision, her exposed thigh almost glaring at me, and I grip the steering wheel tighter.

'Why would you do it?'

'What?' Her tone is pitched with innocence and it only riles me further. *Vulnerable.* I thought her vulnerable. She's not vulnerable. She's foolish. Risky. Wild.

'Pull a stunt like that.'

'Were you at the same dinner? I got the impression we—'

'You know that's not what I'm referring to.'

My eyes flit to her lap, I can't help it; it's driving me crazy. Crazy that she wanted me to know. Crazy that it was all I could think about throughout the entire evening. Crazy that I wanted nothing more than to pull her from that table and do every debauched thing that came to mind. Spanking her at the top of the list.

'I bet you're not even…' I can't finish. I can't put words to it.

Her hand sweeps over her thigh, her finger stroking at the skin between the slit. 'Knickerless?'

'*Jesus*, Olivia.'

'I'm just finishing the sentence you started.'

I shake my head, try to shift the image so eager to descend on my brain. Her, exposed, bare to my hungry gaze, her dress parted to her waist…

'Tonight was important,' I say through my teeth.

'Correction,' she sing-songs, so happy, amused at her own little game. 'It *is* important.'

I flick her a disbelieving look. 'And yet you risked it with some throwaway remark like that.'

'I wasn't risking anything. It was for your ears

only and it wasn't a throwaway remark; it was an honest declaration.'

I shake my head again, try to ignore the way my body heats, my imagination unwilling to quit.

'Are you angry because you think I was lying? That I was saying it just to tease you?'

My frown deepens, my eyes intent on the road, my mind less so. No, it hadn't occurred to me that she would lie. Was she?

'If you like, I can prove it to you, right—?'

'No.' Hell, no.

She gives a soft little huff. 'You really are no fun.'

I grit my teeth and drive, determined to ignore her, determined to get her home and get myself far away from her before I break.

She goes back to looking out of the window, quiet, still. But the damage is done; my entire body fires with it. Lust. Want. Need. An uncontrollable thirst that I know is all the more intense for four years' abstinence.

I park up outside her house, cut the engine. And we sit there. And sit there. Neither saying a word.

Outside, the streetlamps cast a soft glow over the deserted street and the only sound is that of our breathing and the odd tick from the car as it settles. It's intimate. Closed in. The air thick with this incessant tension she's so determined to provoke.

I should be telling her goodnight, I should be seeing her in and driving away, but I can't find my voice. I don't want her to go in…not without me.

A car alarm fires up in the distance and she starts.

'Okay. I guess that's it then. Thank you for this evening.'

She turns to unfasten her seatbelt and I turn with her, my hand falling to cover hers—

What are you doing?

She looks up, straight into my eyes that I know blaze with everything my body wants, and her fingers flutter beneath my hand. Her nose flares ever so slightly as her breaths shorten and her pulse beats wild in her slender throat.

Fuck.

I want this. I'm angry that I want it. I'm angry at her for making me want it.

Her eyes fall to my lips, her own parting as she leans in closer. 'Valentine?'

It's breathless, laced with desire, and my thighs tremble with the heat, the tension, the fight that I can't win.

'Why are you doing this?'

Our heads are so close now our noses almost touch.

'Because it's fun,' she whispers.

'Fun?'

She nods, her nose brushing against mine, and I lift my hand from hers, fork it through her pinned hair as my body urges me to hold her closer. 'Is it just some game to you?'

She arches her head back into my palm, lifts her lips so I can feel the air move against my own as she speaks. 'Does it matter when it feels as good as this?'

'Olivia…' It's a low growl, and I'm kissing her,

the move as aggressive as my anger, as fierce as my folly, because I can't stop now. Now that I'm tasting her, my tongue delving deep into her mouth.

She's all sweet, warm, wet and pliant, so very pliant. And I haven't done this in so long. It's familiar and yet not. Like a voyage of rediscovery and I'm losing myself in it. The sensation, the heat, the moans that fill the car, and I know they're as much mine as they are hers.

She lifts her hands to my hair, fierce, tugging, clawing. Our heads angling this way and that as our tempo ups. Our movements becoming more desperate, more impatient, eager to deepen the kiss, desperate to get enough.

'I take it back.' She scrambles across the car and into my lap, her body wedged between the steering wheel and me. 'I like your choice of car. We couldn't do this in a Porsche.'

I'm too turned on to laugh, too turned on to speak as my hands lift to her breasts, cupping, stroking. She feels so good, so needy and responsive as she grinds against me and tugs her dress to her hips. That's when I remember the underwear, the lack of… I look down, watch as she rides over my cock, long drawn-out strokes that press against her clit and massage and torment me in one.

'I want you, here, now,' she pants out between kisses, between sucked-in breaths that hardly seem enough for the emboldened grinding. 'Please, Valentine. *Please.*'

Oh, God, yes. I'm nodding into our kiss and she

breaks away, reaches over to the passenger seat to her bag. She flicks it open, her lower body still riding against me in the most hypnotic way and my hands hover at her hips, my eyes falling to the slick trail now running over my zip, to her wet and bare pussy so ready for me, and I swear there's no blood left in my brain to think. It's all straining at the head of my dick, sending me dizzy.

'Got it!' she declares, straightening on my lap and looking down at me with a triumphant smile that's all giddy, sexed-up and teasing in one. She hooks the foil packet in her teeth, her hands lowering to my trousers.

'Here?' I swallow. We can't. We're on the street. A public street. Anyone could see if they dared look close enough.

She nods and as if to punctuate her agreement she feeds the loop of my belt through, the jangle of the buckle so loud in the quiet of the car. Jesus, I haven't been this brazen since…and my brain shuts down, refusing to finish the thought. Eager to trap it with more of this crazed heat between us, I tug the packet from her teeth, yank her back to me, tonguing her deeply as I force out the past, the chill of the memories.

I want this. Right now. And we're doing it. To hell with the great outdoors beyond the rapidly steaming up glass.

'Glad you're on board.' She pulls my zip down, her hand reaching inside my briefs, tugging at my erection that's so eager it's already weeping.

I pull her mouth away, press back into the headrest as I drag in air and mentally count to ten. It's been too long, way too long. And now my biggest worry is I won't last a second.

'Olivia, I…'

How do I even say it? Where do I start?

'Olivia, you?' she says between kisses and I gulp in air. Shake my head as I try to explain. 'It's been a while.'

She smiles. 'You and me both.'

'I'm talking more than four weeks.'

'So am…' She breaks off as her eyes widen, her hand pausing around my cock as she raises her head further. 'I didn't, we didn't. Electra and me. I left when you did.'

I frown up into her open and honest expression. The fact that she wants to reassure me, that she thinks it some way important is…strange. 'It's none of my business what you did together.'

'It feels like it is.'

'Why?'

She pauses as she thinks and then she gives a soft laugh that I can't quite comprehend. 'I've no idea. Now, where were we…? Oh, that's right, putting an end to our dry spell…'

And then she's stroking me again, her mouth melding with mine, supping kisses as she drags my lower lip down, flicks her tongue over it. 'I find it hard to believe someone like you has gone without for *that* long.'

'We back to stereotyping me again?'

She chuckles low. 'I confess to being a little Elizabeth Bennet.'

It's my turn to laugh. 'Does that make me Darcy?'

'Ooh, I'm impressed.' She runs my cock down the seam of her hot, wet pussy as she coos with approval. 'A man who knows his literature too.'

My fingers bite into her thighs as I tremble with the need building. 'Am I breaking free of the mould now?'

'Perhaps.' She runs her thumb over the slit at the head of my cock, now damp with her need as well as my own, and considers me. 'So how long has it been? Weeks, months…'

'Years, try years.'

Her eyes narrow, looking for a lie that doesn't exist, but her hand still moves over me, long and slow, as my thighs continue to tremble between hers.

I wait for her to refute my confession, wait for her to laugh, or to tease, anything but the softening of her eyes. And then I fear the question that I sense coming: *Why?*

'It's okay.' She's still searching my gaze, her hand caressing. 'We'll take it slow.'

Her whispered words clutch around my heart as she kisses me and I close my eyes. They're not dirty, playful. They're considerate, caring. *Fuck.*

She's my client and I knew this wouldn't be easy, it wouldn't be straightforward, our pasts forcing us on a path to collision that I'm not sure I'm ready to meet. Do I want her to know I've been there? Experienced the same loss as her. That the reason I haven't had sex in so long stems from the same. *I don't know.* But this is messy, oh, so messy.

I kiss her harder, hold her tighter to me, open my eyes and lose myself in her heavy-lidded gaze, grateful that she doesn't probe when I know the question is still there.

She squeezes my cock and I buck as a fresh wave of heat surges south.

'This is you taking it slow?' I grind out.

She gives a coy shrug. 'Slowish.'

She's never looked more beautiful, more irresistible and I'm past caring of my performance now, too wrapped up in how she looks, how she feels. I palm her breast, roll my thumb over its stiffened peak. Listen to the whimpers trapped low in her throat. I do it more. I do it to both, concentrate on the intoxicating way she rolls her head back, bites into her lip.

I could come like this alone, feasting on her uninhibited response to my touch. I wish she was in the dress from the club, the dress with the low back that I could pull down now and gain access to her beneath the fabric, but this dress has her covered to the hip and…

'Let me…' She takes the condom from me, tears it open as my hands fall to her hips, gripping tight. She tosses the packet onto her empty seat and pumps my cock, once, twice.

'You ready?'

'What do you think?'

Her smile is to die for as she lowers the latex to my tip, rolls it over me in the most sensuous, the

most evocative way possible and then her mouth is
on mine, feasting on me as she rises up and positions me between her legs, pumps me with her hand
before she sinks over me. Surrounding my entirety
with her tight, slick heat.

My head rolls back, the pleasure unreal, and then
she's riding me, fierce, hard. Her hands tug on my
hair and the headrest, pulling me to her, her mouth
as crazy as her movements. She whimpers into my
mouth, pumping me harder, faster with her body,
too fast, too tight and the pleasure-filled tension is
ripping through my body, pulling it taut as she continues to ride, unrelenting, urgent.

'Olivia!' I cry out in some kind of warning, some
kind of helplessness and I'm gone, tipped over the
edge, pulsing into her again and again and again.
She breaks away, stares into my eyes as her climax
claims her too, and we're locked in that look, that
feeling, our bodies losing their all in the most intense
orgasm I can ever remember.

She slows above me, rides me softly and then her
fingers circle against my scalp, massaging as her
eyes stay locked on mine.

'Come in with me?'

Come in with…? I look up at her dumbly.

'The night's still young.' She rolls her hips over
me, keeps massaging my cock, her fingers still working their magic in my hair. 'And this is fun.'

She lowers a hand to my cheek and her attention
shifts, her eyes and fingers lifting to my scarred
brow. She traces the line with her fingertips and the

air catches in my lungs, my heart stutters. I don't want that memory now, here with her like this. And the more time we spend together, the closer I come to revealing it all, to opening up and exposing a side I've kept well-hidden all this time.

'Okay.' I kiss her to distract her. Kiss her to forget. Her eyes widen just enough to let me know she's surprised and then she smiles and hell, if that look doesn't gut me, so genuinely pleased as it is.

'Great.'

She lifts herself off my lap and slides back into the passenger side, shimmying her dress back down her thighs.

'And for the record…' she smooths out the creases, eyeing the fabric intently '…just in case you need it reiterating, I wholeheartedly approve of your car now that I've had the opportunity to test out its versatility.'

I come alive on a laugh, shaking my head as I slip the condom off. 'You'll hate the toy I have parked up at home then.'

'I will?'

I grin as I imagine just how much she'd actually love it.

'Now I really am intrigued.'

I reach across and open the glove compartment, pull out a rubbish bag and tuck the condom inside.

She watches me with a smile. 'Are you always so prepared?'

I raise my brows at her. 'Me? Need I remind you that you were the one with the condom.'

Now she laughs. 'So true. It seems we make a good team, Boretti.'

I pause, midway to returning to my side. Her eyes are doing that soft little thing again, her voice too, both teasing beneath the walls I've had erected for so long. I swallow, my lips curving into what feels both smile-like and serious in one. 'Does that mean I'm winning you over to my way of thinking?'

'Well, I wouldn't go that far…' She leans towards me, her hand lifting, one finger pointing to tap my nose. 'Don't be getting too big-headed on me.'

I chuckle as I ease out of the invisible hold she seems to have over me. 'I wouldn't dare.'

'So do I get any hints as to what it is?'

I frown as I right my clothing. 'To what is?'

'The toy at home.'

My smile lifts to one side. 'Play your cards right and I'll take you to see it.'

'Now?'

'Not now,' I say with a laugh. 'How about I take you back to mine after the football on Saturday?'

'Okay.' She smiles at me and I don't have time to even question the suggestion, let alone the reason why I suggested it at all as she adds, 'But now would be better.'

I laugh all the more, shake my head at her childlike impatience. 'Do you have any concept of a bedtime?'

'Sleep is full of missed opportunities; I prefer to make the most of my time.'

Whereas I wanted to sleep all the time. The

thought writes itself, frosting up the moment so completely. The sharp contrast in how we approach grief, so marked. But when I was asleep I didn't have to remember that the nightmare was real. The crash. Layla.

And there's a part of me that admires Olivia for having the courage to face it, her loss…but then, isn't hers just another form of avoidance? Distraction. Keeping herself too busy to dwell.

Isn't it the same need that led to her car accident?

'Is that why you were driving to Oxford in the middle of the night in your Bugatti?'

'Oh, don't you start.' She huffs and leans back in her seat, looks out of the window, which is so steamed up the outside lights are just a blur. 'You sound as bad as my sister, Fee.'

'I do.'

She eyes me, quiet for a moment, and then, 'So, are you coming in?'

She's trying to change the subject and as I take in her appearance, her dishevelled hair, her over-bright eyes, her nipples that still strain through her dress and bra, it would be so easy to let her distract me.

'What does your sister think of your late-night dash?'

'Pretty much what you're thinking, looking at you.'

'Which is?'

'That I was reckless, stupid, living some death wish.'

I swallow as her words cut deep.

'God, look at you! Seriously! The truth is I wanted to get away from the city, without the traffic and the noise. To take my new car on the motorway and not spend it bumper to bumper. Is that so hard to believe?'

I shrug. 'If you'd done it without coming off the road, maybe.'

'The weather was bad, the car was new and I wasn't used to it. It's as simple as that.'

'You were lucky.'

'And yeah, I've heard that a thousand times already. And, before you ask, I was breathalysed and there was zero alcohol in my system, not even a smidgen. It was enough to satisfy Fee.' She stops, looks away, raises her hand to the window and traces a small circle in the steamed-up glass. 'Well, maybe not satisfy, but it was enough to prove I wasn't being reckless on that score.'

She drags in a breath and a sudden melancholy hangs in the air between us. She turns to look at me, her eyes so sombre, so…sad. 'Happy?'

I'm not happy; I'm far from it as I take in the look in her eyes.

'If it was enough to satisfy my sister, it should be enough to satisfy you too.'

'Why?' Stupid question.

Her lips quirk, her eyes shine. Now she smiles, a big wide smile, and I curse my impulsive question. The truth is I asked because I care. I care more than I should, and now she knows it too.

'So, nightcap?'

I know nightcap is code for more. More of this. And how much more? An hour, two? A whole night?

And then what?

I know the post-orgasm chill is setting in, spurred on by a return to my senses, to sanity and the reality of the mess we're potentially walking into. Hell, we're already in that mess. Of all the people to break my celibacy with, it had to be her.

'I shouldn't. It's late.'

'It's not *that* late…and I promise to let you leave early enough for whatever it is you have to be up for in the morning.'

It appeals. It appeals so fucking much. But hell, I've already fucked up. *We've* fucked up.

'We're working together…'

'And we're working very well.'

I can't help the smile that lifts with her words.

'I don't want this getting in the way of business.'

'Which it won't.'

'How can you say that?'

She shrugs. 'Because I can easily compartmentalise the two. Or are you forgetting that I was married to my business partner for twenty years?'

How could I forget?

'Besides, I took you for a man of his word and you've already agreed to come inside, so…'

I continue to stare at her, my mind at war. I want to go with her. I want to…and yet there are so many reasons this is a bad idea.

'I'm not going to beg you if that's what you're hoping for.' She laughs as she leans forward and grabs her bag from the footwell. 'And I've had a good night; the people you introduced me to, especially Angus, they are fabulous contacts to have. So I'm grateful to you, Valentine, and I'll quite happily leave you to…whatever this is.'

She waves a hand at me, all confident and in control, and I wish I could have just an ounce of her certainty in that moment.

Fuck it. I can.

She reaches for her door handle and I reach for mine. If she can be this strong, decisive, in control…

And it's just sex. Something I've not had in an age. And if she can compartmentalise the two, then I can too.

'I'm coming.'

She eyes my trousers, her smile slow, salacious. 'Not quite yet already, but you will be, very, very soon.'

I'm out of the car quicker than my erection can stiffen and following her inside. Call it deprivation, call it acting out, call it whatever you like, I'm going in willingly because what she's offering is far more appealing than going home to my empty penthouse and staring into oblivion.

At least with her I feel…I feel more than I have in a long time.

And yes, this was supposed to be about me healing her, but being able to live again in the process… it can't be all that wrong, can it?

Damned if I know. I'm going with my gut now, or maybe it runs a bit lower than that…

She looks back at me over her shoulder, her body still swaying hypnotically as she walks along the path to her front door. She smiles, says nothing, and keeps on going and I'm right there on her tail.

Tomorrow is a new day, we can reset the boundaries, do whatever we need to in order to get back on the right track, but for now...I'm going with whatever this is.

CHAPTER NINE

Olivia

I WAKE TO shadows dancing on the ceiling, the glow from the street filtering through the trees and the open blinds I never closed. There's a hot body pressed against me, an arm slung heavily across my naked stomach. *Valentine.*

It all comes back to me. The dinner, the car, the kitchen—*oh, yes, the kitchen*—and the bedroom.

And he's still here. His breath's tickling at my ear, not quite a snore but enough to tell me he's out cold. Fast asleep.

I lie very still, angle my head just enough to see him in the low light and smile. His face is relaxed in sleep, no less chiselled but much less perfect with the dark shadow of fresh stubble and the scar through his brow that shines silver in the grey light. I want to trace its line, I want to ask him how it happened, I want to understand that tiny detail about his past.

I would have asked in the car, but I saw how he noticed my shift in focus, sensed him withdraw even before I uttered a word. And I didn't want to break the moment and scare him off, because for the first time in a year that restless energy I've been trying to kill off, the constant buzz in my veins to keep moving, felt sated.

And all because of him.

Not now though.

Now I'm awake. My usual three a.m. stint. Wide-eyed, my legs doing their whole twitch thing, my heart too loud in my ears, everything more intense and aggravating because the outside world sleeps while I can't. I snuggle in deeper, try to enjoy the heat of his body, his solidity, breathe in his scent. It's reassuring, soothing.

I close my eyes, try to calm my wayward pulse, the crawling sensation in my legs that demands I do something. Anything, other than lie here. I tell myself this is nice. Comfy. Sleep-inducing.

But it's no use. I don't know how long I lie there for, only that my body positively vibrates with the effort to keep still and I flick my eyes open in frustration, glare up at the ceiling like it's somehow to blame.

I can't stay here like this. I'll only wake him with my irritated dance, and normally I'd go for a run, but I can hardly do that and leave him sleeping. What if he wakes and wonders where I am? I can just imagine the thoughts that would race through his mind with the track record he's pinned on me.

But I need to do something…

I peel back the covers, ease out from beneath his

arm. He shifts in his sleep, a soft murmur that has me pausing beside him as he rolls away. I wait for his breathing to level out and then slip from the bed, pad across the room to my chest of drawers and open the bottom one. I pull out my swimsuit and step into it, take my robe off the back of the door and tug it on as I head downstairs to the back of the house.

I navigate the small panel beside the sliding doors that lead into the garden, switching on the pool lights and setting the cover to roll back. Vapours rise into the air from the aquamarine water, its inviting warmth a contrast to the cold night air that wraps around me as I step outside.

I pull off my robe and toss it onto a sunbed, step forward to curl my toes over the edge of the pool. A second's pause as I wait for the cover to retract fully and then I dive in.

It's an instant hit of bliss. The perfect temperature swallowing me whole, the rush against my skin, the weightlessness. I do a length along the bottom and turn, strain against the need to breathe as I enjoy the distance from the world outside. When I eventually surface, I'm smiling. This is my spot. The one thing in the entire house I designed. Swimming was my passion, not Nathan's. And it was easy for him to approve the expenditure when it gave him ample opportunity to watch me swim. He liked that I took care of myself, kept trim and toned, athletic to a degree.

I look to the empty seat beneath the glass shelter where he would have sat and feel the strange sense of my newfound freedom collide with the familiar pleasure of him watching me. His small smile of approval, the drink he would have waiting for me. Juice on a morning, coffee in the afternoon, a whisky before bed. All rituals.

And now I'm making new ones.

I dip beneath the water, swim just above the pool floor as I push the thoughts away and emerge with one thing on my mind. To swim. I don't keep track of time or the number of lengths. I just swim, cherishing the sound of the water rippling through the quiet of the night. Soothing my body that's enjoyed several hours of fun with Mr Oh-So-Perfect. I made him crack. That suave, cocky, controlled exterior obliterated under my touch, my influence…

I smile in triumph as my strokes quicken. I have no idea what the morning will bring, but right now I have no regrets, no regrets whatso—

'So, this is where you got to…'

His low rasp breaks through the night air and I look to the doors, to where his semi-naked body leans against the opening and swallow, slowing my strokes. He is so honed, his abs taut all the way down until they form a V that dips into his snug-fitting black briefs. Utterly delicious.

And now I'm hungry…all over again.

I swim to the edge, hook my arms over it and lift out just enough to rest my chin on my hands. 'Sorry, I didn't want to wake you.'

His eyes burn into mine across the distance, dark and probing… How long has he been watching me?

The way he rests against the wall, his arms folded, suggests he's settled in and been there a while. Enjoying the show…just as Nathan used to.

I swallow back the thought, mask it in a smile and wonder what he's thinking. What has his eyes slightly narrowed, his body all tense?

'No need to apologise.' He eases away from the frame and walks towards me. My eyes rake over him, feasting on every flex of muscle, and the thick bulge inside his briefs. Heat swells in my lower belly. If he's wanting to pick up where we last left off, I'm all for it…

'Do you often swim in the dead of night?'

Slowly, I tug my gaze up to his. 'Sometimes…or I run, whatever appeals.'

He chuckles, that low soft sound that tickles my insides to life. 'This all part of you making the most of your waking hours?'

'Yup.'

His brows draw together, his budding concern obvious, and I don't want his concern. I want anything but…

'You know you need sleep to function properly, right?'

'Yes, Dr Boretti, I'm fully aware. And I sleep when my body wants to sleep.'

'And not a second more?'

'Correct.'

He shakes his head and I don't want the unsettled feeling in my gut to swell, the emotion his concern is so quick to trigger. He pauses before me and I lower my gaze.

'Tell me something…' He drops down onto his haunches, flicks my chin softly to call my eyes to his. 'Were you always like this?'

He rests his arms on his thighs and studies me intently.

'Like what?'

'Like some electrically charged power tool.'

I give a shaky laugh. 'Some description!' But then… 'I'd rather be compared to a battery-powered sex toy, in which case I really could go all night.'

His mouth twitches. 'You want to reduce this to sex again?'

'Don't you?' I bite my lip, my eyes flare up into his and for the briefest second I catch his own fall to my mouth and I know he's thinking of the multitude of things I've done with it already, the things I've yet to do. But then they are back, searching mine with an intensity that scares me.

'Was Nathan like it?'

Nathan. My brows snap together. 'You want to talk about Nathan now?'

'I'm curious.'

I stare up at him, disbelieving that he can swing from wanting me to wanting to psychoanalyse me so quickly. 'You mean did he like to swim, then no. Not really. He indulged my love of it, he would happily watch me enjoy it.' My eyes flick in the direction of his chair and I can almost imagine him there right now, with that smile on his face. 'But the pool was all me, from conception to what you see now, right down to the pretty little waterfall that looks like it feeds it, only it doesn't, it's a clever little mirage.'

I wave a hand in its direction and know full well I'm deflecting. Giving the impression that I'm as rambling as the heavily scented clematis to my left. 'You like?'

'Yes.' His piercing blues don't leave me. 'But it wasn't what I meant.'

No, it wasn't, was it… I force my eyes back to his. 'Then what did you mean?'

'I want to know if he too lived every second like it was his last?'

My heart pangs inside my chest, his words cutting deep. He knows it too. I can see it in the way his eyes soften, the apology there even as he asks it.

'No.' My voice is whisper-soft now. 'Nathan wasn't like this. *I* wasn't like this. I used to be able to sleep. I used to be able to lie in my bed and enjoy just switching off.'

He nods as he listens to me and instead of finding his continued interest, concern even, aggravating, I find myself opening up. Hell, maybe it's because my muscles are appeased from the workout. Maybe it's because I feel ready to return to bed so long as he comes too. Maybe it's just that I have his undivided attention and I'm actually revelling in it. Or maybe it finally feels good just to talk about it.

'I wasn't restless, not like this. And even when I was, a run, a swim, a good book, they were all things I could enjoy. But losing him…' I shake my head.

'He was older than me, natural order says I'd outlast him, but not this soon. He was sixty-four. No age. And one minute we were together, enjoying a meal, all was fine, and the next…'

'What happened?'

I drag in a breath, lower my gaze to his arms and notice the goosebumps prickling over his skin—he's not invincible then. Or is he so focused on me he hasn't even noticed? The idea makes me shiver. 'You're cold.'

'I'm fine.'

'You're not.'

'Are you always so evasive?'

'I'm not.'

'Argumentative then?'

My lips quirk, as do his, and I see the hint of laughter in his eyes. I take another breath and think about his question, let it in and the pain too. We may have had a relationship that…that lacked in some ways. But I loved him. Loved him for a long time and he was my constant. My rock. And what happened was unexpected, frightening even. To be here one minute and the next…

He reaches down and cups my face, his thumb soft as he strokes it across my cheek and my lips tremble. That's when I realise I'm crying, that the moisture on my skin isn't all from the pool.

'You must know what happened,' I shudder out. 'The media covered it enough. It was a heart attack. Sudden. Unexpected. We were at dinner with friends. Relaxed. Happy. And then…'

'I know what the media disclosed, but you and I both know they aren't always to be believed.'

'Well, in this case they were right.'

I pull away from his touch, dip beneath the water and throw the sensation off. I've cried enough, suffered enough. And I've shared plenty. I don't owe him more. I don't really owe him what I've already disclosed.

And yet you did it anyway...

I emerge, ignoring the curious little voice inside as my eyes clash with his. 'Can we not do this right now?'

'I think it might help you to talk about it.'

'So everyone keeps telling me, but newsflash, I don't want to talk about it, not now, not tomorrow, not the day after.'

He shakes his head, looks to his feet, his voice small as he says, 'But what if I tell you that I—'

'*Please*, Valentine.' My gut rolls and I know I sound desperate, but I can't go there, I don't want to go there. I don't want to relive it. 'I'm not some child that you need to look after.'

'I didn't say you were.'

'Then let it go, let's not make this about more than it is. We're having sex, great sex. And sex doesn't warrant serious conversation. In fact, it spoils it.'

His eyes lock with mine and I sense the fight still there. A second's hesitation. Two.

'Do you really want to spoil it?'

'No.' He gives me a small smile as he rises up. 'You want some company?'

'In here?' My brows lift. 'You want to swim, in the middle of the night?'

'And you're looking at me like I'm the crazy one when you're the one doing exactly that.'

I grin, giddy with relief, and I'm about to tell him I'm ready to get out when he hooks his fingers into the waistband of his briefs.

'Unless you don't want me skinny-dipping in your pool?'

'I don't have a problem...but my neighbours might.'

He spins and scans the terraces either side of mine and I laugh because no one can see anything. I laugh because he's put me through the emotional wringer more than he can possibly know, and I'm light with the relief of being able to move on. I laugh because the truth is the garden has been well designed—by me—to provide privacy with its high walls, rambling climbers, trees and trellises.

It's fun to watch his panicked moment though, especially with his briefs now halfway down his deliciously tight arse and, more importantly, blocking my view of Nathan's seat.

'Very funny.' He shakes his head as he looks back to me and my retort dies on my lips because he's yanking the briefs off completely and tossing them aside.

He launches himself in. His long, lithe body outstretched, his form perfect, his muscles accentuated by the lights that lift off the pool. He breaks the water with barely a splash, swims beneath it and doesn't emerge until he's at the other end, turning back towards me, his eyes alive with such mischief.

My heart skips a beat, trepidation sparking. 'What? Why are you looking at me like that?'

'Payback.'

'Pay—what?'

But he's gone, under the water and coming straight for me, a dark shadow and I've nowhere to go. The pool is long and thin, designed for lengths not shifting side to side, and then his hands are on my hips, his fingers rippling, tickling and I'm wriggling, trying not to squeal. Our neighbours might not be able to see, but they'd certainly be able to hear.

I grip his arms. 'Stop it!'

Not that he can hear me; he's still submerged, and he isn't stopping either. I drop down, shake my head at him beneath the water, bubbles of protest erupting from my lips, but he's too busy grinning, his mouth sealed shut.

We burst from the water together and I suck in a breath, thrust the water at him. He shakes it off, his hair sending water everywhere as his hands close around my hips and he's pulling me to him.

'Not funny,' I blurt.

'It was a little bit funny,' he murmurs.

My response becomes a quiet squeak as his mouth covers mine and I forget why I'm mad, forget why I was laughing. All I can think is how perfect his mouth feels as he kisses me.

I lift my hands to his cheeks, palm his stubble that looks so out of place on him and comb my fingers back through his hair, clinging to him as he deepens the kiss. His cock nudges between us, hard, needy, teasing out a reciprocal beat in my core.

I moan into his mouth, giddy, high on him, on this. I wrap my legs around his waist and press my body tight against his, teasing out a growl from deep within his throat. He reaches down into the water, palms my arse as he walks us to the pool edge, not once breaking his kiss.

I feel the wall at my back, and he stops, his palm lifting to my breast, cupping, stroking. My nipple pebbles beneath his touch, sending excited little ripples straight to my throbbing clit. He does the same to my other, my legs gripping him to me as I grind against him, my hands still clinging to his hair.

'I can't get enough of you.'

His honest declaration has my insides twisting and dancing, a confusing beat of happiness and fear. I don't want to thrive on such words. I don't want to need another to make me feel this good. Especially someone like him, a temporary presence in my life, but my legs clench around him tighter, defying my internal struggle.

He urges me up his body, lowers his mouth to the sensitive pulse point beneath my ear, his stubble grazing against my skin, his fingers and thumbs working my breasts harder, more desperate.

'Yes, God, yes.' The pleasure, it's taking away all else and it's everything I need, everything I want.

His hands slide beneath the shoulder straps of my swimsuit and my clit pangs with the thrill. I lower my arms to pull them free of it and, before I can bury my hands in his hair once more, he's taking one nipple deep inside his mouth, his tongue flicking over the sensitive nub. I throw my head back, my cry guttural—

Neighbours!

I bite into my lip, thrust my hands through his hair as I stare down at his mouth surrounding me, the rippling water sloshing about us, my body half-naked as he presses me up against the pool wall. I don't feel the cool night air now; I'm on fire, desperate for him. Hungry. How is it possible to want him so much already?

'I want to taste you,' he murmurs over my breast, his eyes lifting to mine, the pool glittering in their darkened depths.

'You are...'

I arch back, nudging my breast to his mouth, and he shakes his head.

'Not enough...'

He lifts me from the water and sets me down on the pool edge, his hands lowering to tug my swimsuit down.

It's me looking to the neighbours' now, knowing we're hidden but worrying all the same. This is daring, oh-so-daring...*another tick in a box!*

He chuckles, calling my eyes back to his.

'Not so blasé now, are you?'

I smile and lift my behind so he can peel the swimsuit from me. He tosses it aside, moving back in as he pulls me towards him, spreading my legs wide to bring me up against his chest. His eyes burn into my nakedness and I lean back, relishing that look in his eyes.

Nathan was never one for oral sex but Valentine… the way he looks at me, desire tensing up his body, his eyes so dark and ravenous…he is, and he hasn't… we haven't…not yet. Anticipation twines deep within my stomach, every extremity alive as the cold air teases at the goosebumps prickling all over my skin.

He strokes his hands along my thighs, his fingers massaging, his intent blazing through his progressive touch. He reaches the apex of my thighs and his gaze lifts to mine, the pad of one thumb sliding up my seam… *Oh, God.* I grip the pool edge, feel his touch ever so slight against my clit and I clamp down on my lip, breathe through my nose.

He repeats it with his other thumb and I roll into the move. Again and again, he goes deeper each time, until my cheeks flush with heat, my hands claw into the stone, my breath pants, and then he spreads me open with his fingers, his eyes lowering to take in the sight.

He bows his head and, with one long move, flattens his tongue against me, rises up, laving my entirety until the point of his tongue flicks against the clustered nerve-endings of my clit. I buck off the ground with a cry and I have no time to recover as his tongue lashes and lashes, a dizzying dance that has my mouth hanging open, my eyes lost in the sight of him. I lift a hand to his hair, push through it as I cling to him and rock my hips as fiercely as his assault.

I lift my legs, my heels digging into his shoulder blades, my toes curling as the pleasure-filled tension starts to tighten up my limbs; my panting turns vocal, my cries desperate and still his tongue pummels me. There's no let-up, no chance to draw a full breath and suddenly I'm rolling, the fierce explosion making me scream his name as my entire body rocks with spasms so fierce I'm scared I'll crush his head between my legs.

He grasps my thighs, holds me while I shudder and shake and then he's lifting me off the side, lowering me down his body. His mouth finds mine, desperate with his own hunger, his own need, and I'm lifting my legs around him, eager to have him fill me, eager for it all.

He trembles as he pulls back, separating us, dragging in a breath. 'Condom?'

'Dammit.' I shake my head, they're all the way inside and I don't want to break this moment. But I'm no longer on birth control, why would I be, and…

He's already lifting me in his arms and heading to the stone steps built into the corner.

'You can't carry me in.'

'Wanna bet?'

I giggle like a teenager as I loop my arms around his neck and marvel at the flexing of his muscles as he carries me out. I feel safe. Really safe. And it's as reassuring as it is unsettling.

'You drop me, and I'll be thinking up a suitable punishment.'

'A punishment, hey?' He chuckles as he turns to the side and steps through the opening in the glass doors. 'Am I to take it you have your own supply of whips and chains?'

My cheeks immediately colour, my body flushes with a fresh wave of heat. I know he's referring to Electra, but…

'Perhaps.'

He stills as he eyes me, his arms tighten. 'Did Nathan…did you…?'

He doesn't quite finish and I wish I'd kept my mouth shut. It's too much, too soon. My cheeks heat all the more as my brash confession burns through me.

'I should get us some towels.'

He lowers me to the ground, and I hurry to the cupboard beside the panel that controls the pool. I switch the lights off, set the cover to roll back and pull out two towels. He doesn't move.

I toss one at him, his hand flicks out enough to catch it, but his eyes are fixed on me and I know his brain is working overtime.

'Did you?'

I take a breath, wrap a towel around me. 'Nathan liked me to…you know…'

'Be submissive?' he grinds out.

'No.' My cheeks blush further. 'He was…he was the submissive one.'

His eyes widen and my laugh shudders out of me, nervous, unsure.

'Now who's stereotyping?' I turn away to pull out

another towel and scrunch it through my hair. 'Men are just as likely to enjoy it as women, you know.'

'I know that, but…I'm surprised. He didn't come across…well, he seems to have taken control over so much in your life I can't…it just doesn't fit.'

I'm quiet at the accuracy of his deduction. I wonder whether he thought that before he met me, or whether I have given him that impression, this house, what he's seen.

'So, when you went to see Electra…?'

'I wanted to experience it from the other side.'

He swallows, his neck bobbing as his pecs ripple. 'Did you like it? Dominating him, I mean?'

I shrug. 'It wasn't something that came naturally… He dominated our life in all other areas, but in the bedroom he wanted to hand that power over to me.'

'And you relished it?'

I consider his question. 'Yes.' I surprise myself with my certainty and my honesty as I admit it out loud. 'Ultimately, I did. Over the years it became a way for me to take back control, to find some balance.'

'And you never wanted to submit to him?'

I meet his eye. 'No.'

He stares at me, the moonlight highlighting the pulse working in his jaw. He wraps the towel around his waist, tucks it in and comes towards me. 'But you want to play the submissive now?'

I straighten my shoulders against the little shiver that runs through me. A shiver that has nothing to do with the cold and everything to do with the way he looks at me, the way his gravelly voice works through me.

'Yes.'

I don't even have the brain power to analyse what it means, only that I want this. With him.

He reaches out, lifts my chin with his finger as he runs his thumb over my lower lip. I'm not even aware of the hair towel slipping from my fingers until it falls over my feet.

'Do you want to submit to me?'

Oh, God, yes.

I try to speak and my voice fails, my eyes lost in the heat of his.

'Do you want me to take control?'

I manage a nod.

'Do you want me to command you?'

'Yes.' It's breathy, a whisper, and his eyes flare at the sound, their depths glittering.

'Have you ever submitted to anyone before that night with Electra?'

'No. And we never...' a small shake of my head '...I told you, we never got further than what you saw.'

'So, I would be your first?'

I wet my lips, catch the tip of his thumb still there. 'Yes.'

'Fuck.' His curse surprises me, its severity all the more. 'Do you know how much I've thought of that night? Of you on your knees with that collar around your neck, your nipples clamped while she...while she stroked you with that thing.'

My need seeps between my legs, my clit pulsates. 'I have a thing…a crop.' Shallow breath. 'Upstairs.'

His thumb and forefinger grip my chin. 'You do?'

'I do.'

He swallows again, his hand falling away. 'Then lead the way.'

I go to walk around him.

'Without the towel.'

My lips twitch as his command makes my pulse leap, my clit pound and I loosen it from around me, let it fall to the floor.

'Very good, Little Kitten.'

CHAPTER TEN

Valentine

JESUS, I'M NOT doing this. We're not.

Only I am. The beast in me is well and truly alive now. Four years dormant and now… Now I get to unleash it with a woman as willing, as appealing as Olivia.

I tune out the voice in my head telling me to stop as I follow her through the dark house. The only sound our bare feet against the hard white tiles and every breath too loud in my ears. She turns her head enough to check I still follow, in the hall, on the stairs… When she reaches the landing she doesn't head to the room we were in earlier; she continues up to the next flight and the next. I don't even question it.

There's one door at the top and her hand pauses over the knob. She looks back to me. Says nothing. I watch her shoulders lift with a breath and then she opens it.

The room beyond is vast, even with the slope to the ceiling and the heavy wooden beams that cut through. It's swathed in moonlight from a glass wall that extends along the back, its view overlooking the rear of the house. It's a sympathetic conversion, one that blends with the street from the front, but from the inside it's something else and I realise this is the master bedroom, not the room we were in before.

This is the room she shared with her husband.

She continues to walk ahead of me, to where a bed floats in the centre covered in pure white linen. There's a roll-top bath in the corner, two more doors that I imagine lead to a toilet and a dressing room since the only furniture I can see includes a plush grey chaise longue, a wall-mounted TV and a chest of drawers. A display of artwork that even without the artist's name I can recognise as expensive and original.

She kneels before the bed, reaches beneath and pulls out a drawer. I'm too far away to see what's inside but then she's lifting out what she wants…and for a second I forget what we've come up here for. Until she turns and there it is, in her outstretched hand—a riding crop. Her other hand is still tucked behind her back.

Hell, when I thought *he* used it on *her* I freaked. When she told me it had been her using it on him I freaked even more. It wasn't what I expected. And from all I know of her, how she can hold a TV audience spellbound, a conference centre full of hundreds captivated, head a charity for years and inspire millions into supporting it… She is a woman to bow down to, to submit to, but…

She walks towards me, a fire in her eyes, a lift to the corner of her mouth as she raises it to me.

'It's actually new. I bought it in the hope…well, I'm not really sure…call it a moment of crazy and an internet shopping spree fuelled by wine.' She shrugs, all coy now, and raises her other hand. 'Same with this.'

I swear I stop breathing as I take in what else she has procured. A collar and chains. Not minutes ago, I was livid at the very idea of Nathan doing this to her, and he was with her for years and years. I've known her personally for all of five minutes… It feels like more though, so much more.

And I know jealousy is burning as bright as any other emotion. But she's not mine to be jealous over and it's freaking me out as much as turning me on that we're here like this.

'Are you okay?' She frowns a little and I give myself the mental slap I need.

'This is what you want, yes?'

She wets her lips as she looks up into my eyes. 'With you, right now, absolutely.'

Fuck. My insides clench over the rush her words trigger, and I take them from her grasp.

'Tie your hair up, Little Kitten.'

She gives me the smallest of smiles and walks to the chest of drawers, pulls open the top drawer and takes out a brush. I watch as she combs her hair through, lifts it from her nape and secures it, her eyes on her reflection in the little oval mirror above. They meet me when she's done and I smile my pleasure.

'Very good.'

Her lips lift.

'Now come and kneel before me.'

She turns slowly and my gut clenches ever tighter. I've never done this before either. I've fantasised all right, but even Layla and I…

I swallow back the memories, shutting down the voice in the depths of my brain that tells me this is going deeper than a one-night affair. Because it's not deep—it can't be. She's broken free of a husband that I believe she loved, but I also believe controlled her, kept her fixed on a path that wasn't always to her liking and now…she's free.

And this is just another step in her life plan as she relishes her freedom. Just as her free-climbing incident, her rash car purchase, her visit to Electra was, I'm just another string in her bow. Nothing more.

But as she walks towards me, her eyes fixed on mine, I feel a surge of possession so powerful I feel winded.

Get a grip and go with it. Then walk away, as she expects you to. Just as you should want to.

You're never going to tie yourself to another woman again. You've done that, been there and suffered the consequences.

She pauses before me, lowers herself to the floor and gazes up at me, acquiescent, obedient, waiting.

My grip around the riding crop flexes, the collar too. I want to keep her.

And she's not even a possession to be kept… though like this…treating her as she so desires, she is.

Maybe that's the problem, the messy avenue my brain—hell, my heart even—is too eager to explore. That she could be mine like this. Always.

'We can go downstairs if you'd rather?'

Her voice is so loud in the silence of the room and she moves to stand, her hesitation evident in the widening of her eyes. 'I should have thought. It's usually weird enough for me to be up here, but…'

'It's not that.'

'No?'

Hell, don't fuck up her fantasy just because you can't get a handle on your own feelings.

'Hold this.'

She starts as I offer her the riding crop and I know it's the way I blurt the instruction, doing my damnedest to drown out the inner critic.

And then a soft smile curves her lips, a smile that I know she's working to control. She's enjoying this.

'What shall I call you?' She takes the riding crop from me.

'Hold it behind your back…' I gesture to the crop as I frown over her question. 'Call me?'

'Yes, you know…' She chews the corner of her lip. 'Like *sir…master…*'

Lust coils tight within my gut. 'This is your fantasy—you choose.'

She breathes in deep as she ponders, her pupils so big they squeeze out the blue. 'Sir. I like sir.'

A thrill pulses through me…power, control, respect. All things I'm used to outside of these walls but none of which have ever left me feeling like this. High, drunk on lust.

'Sir, it is.' I broaden my stance. 'Now do as I told you, Little Kitten.'

'Yes, sir.'

My cock bucks beneath the towel. *Fuck*, that feels good. Too good. As does the sight of her slipping her hands behind her back, the riding crop held in her hands as her breasts thrust up towards me, their position oh, so perfect…

'Good, Little Kitten.' My voice is softer, the tension easing as I relax into the role. 'Head up.'

She lifts her chin, her eyes lowered, so very submissive and it shakes me to the core. Jesus, how the fuck am I to walk away from this when we are done?

Her eyes flick up, collide with mine, and I block out the hesitancy, the split-second panic. 'Eyes down.'

She does as I ask…of course she does… *Holy mother of…*

I look to the ceiling, a brief sanity-seeking second, and then I open up the leather collar in my hands, spy it tremble and know that's all me. I breathe, try to regulate everything—my thoughts, my body, this whole situation. I study the notches in the leather, the metal buckle.

You can do this.

Granted, I haven't done it before, but the fantasy… hell, the fantasy has been there since for ever.

I reach forward and her breath hitches audibly, her lips parting, their luscious curve drawing me in. I bow my head and kiss her, a fleeting sign of what feels too close to affection, and I break away just as quickly, concentrate instead on feeding the collar around her neck.

'Have you done this before?' she whispers.

No, I fucking haven't. And as I lock eyes with her I know I can't say it outright.

'Eyes down, Kitten,' I remind her and she obeys.

I reward her with an evasive answer. 'Not quite like this.'

Her lips quiver into a smile. 'Good.'

Good. Does that mean she'd be jealous otherwise? Or does she want us both to be new to this? Not that she's new to it…and I hate the way that makes me feel. I ignore the twist to my gut as I loop the belt through the buckle and pull until I find a notch that is tight enough.

I want to ask her if it's okay and stop myself. That's not her fantasy and I know deep down that she would tell me otherwise. Instead, her cheeks flush with the heated rush I know she's feeling. She wants this, she needs this, and I sure as hell can give it to her.

I lower myself to my knees and take up one of the clamps that dangles low down her front. She sucks in her stomach, bites into her lip, and I feel her anticipation as if it were my own. I squeeze the clamp open, brush it over one nipple, tease the tightly puckered tip and enjoy how she whimpers and sways a nanosecond before I release it. The clamp pinches into the sensitised flesh and her lips part with a sharp intake of breath, her lashes lifting as her eyes flare into mine.

I bite back the impulsive, *Are you okay?* and focus on the wanton heat in her gaze, raise the other clamp. I keep my eyes hooked on hers now as I tease the other nipple, circle it slowly and release. She rocks into the move, her eyes glazing over, her cheeks flushing deeper.

'Tighter, Little Kitten?'

She nods and I raise my brows. 'Yes, what?'

'Tighter…' She wets her lips. 'Tighter, please, sir.'

I look down her body and struggle to breathe. It's so fucking erotic, so carnal, my cock strains beneath the towel, throbbing, urgent. I raise my fingers to each screw, tightening the clamps until her eyes water and she gives me another nod. 'Enough, sir.'

I drag in a breath, look to the heavens as I stand, and then down at her.

Holy. Mother. Of. God.

She's there on her knees, her head upturned, her hands still holding the riding crop behind her back as her nipples, taut and tight, cling to the clamps I've put there. I've never felt such heat, such carnal longing, a sense of possession, and I'm scared of getting carried on a wave, of going too far. How do I know if she's truly okay? How do I know when to stop?

'Do you have a safe word?'

She swallows. 'How about I just tell you to stop, sir?'

I nod.

Nerves skitter in my gut, my erection oscillating between so hard it's painful, and softening with the unknown. I don't want her knowing that this is so far out of my comfort zone, I don't want her to get an inkling of how new this is to me. I stand tall, use my sheer size to give me the edge. I rake a hand through my hair, run my teeth over my lower lip and wrap myself in the sight of her, feel it pulse through my groin.

'You may hand me the riding crop now, Kitten.'

'Yes, sir.' She offers it out and I have to fight to hold my fingers steady as the rush threatens to consume me.

'Clasp your hands behind your back.'

'Yes, sir.'

'Don't release them until I say.'

Jesus, her obedience is like a shot of adrenaline, a shot of ecstasy, each and every time. I walk around her slowly, my eyes taking in her entirety. She starts to turn her head to follow me. 'Eyes to the front, Kitten.'

She does it and her cheeks flush anew, her breath hitches. I lower the crop to her hair, toy with it as I walk around her. She has the most perfect arse, round and ample. Her neck is slender, her skin creamy white against the black leather, save for the blush that's spreading with her arousal. It blooms on her breasts with their tiny pink hearts and the chains that hang all the way down to her navel, her pussy bare and glistening along its seam. I lower the whip to the line, following the same move as Electra, and she whimpers, the noise erupting from her nose as her nostrils flare.

'You like that, Little Kitten?'

She nods. 'Yes, sir,' she hurries out, her lashes lowered, her cheeks sinfully pink.

I rock the crop against her, press it deeper to tease at her clit and her thighs quake, her stomach fluttering with her breaths.

'You're so naughty, aren't you, Kitten?'

She whimpers.

'Aren't you?'

'Yes.'

'Yes, *what?*'

'Yes, sir.'

Fuck, my cock is seeping behind the towel, the thing's like a tent now, and I tug it from me, toss it aside.

'You know what happens to naughty Little Kittens?'

A nod. 'Yes, sir.'

'They get punished.' My cock bucks, my thoughts and body racing away with my words as I stop directly behind her.

'On your hands, Little Kitten.'

She lowers herself forward, her back arched, her arse all mine and my entire body tightens.

'I'm going to punish you, Little Kitten; is that what you want?'

'Yes.'

'I can't hear you.'

'Yes.' Louder.

'Yes?'

'Sir.'

Gently, I lower the crop to her arse, trail it along her crack, all the way down to tuck it between her legs and she rocks against it, eager to feel, but...

'No, Kitten. I told you to stay still.'

She looks at me over her shoulder, pinches her lip in her teeth as she stops. I drag the tip of the crop up her pussy, treasure the way she looks as she fights the urge to move again. I eye the leather, the moisture, her obvious arousal, and it's tipping me over. I want so many things, to try so many things. I press the tip into one soft, round mound as I stalk to her side and she watches me.

'Why am I punishing you, Little Kitten?'

'Because...because I've been bad.'

'How bad?'

'Very bad...' She rocks back against the crop, her body begging.

'I said, stay still.'

One quick flick and the leather cracks against her skin. She sucks in a breath through her nose, her fingers claw into the floor. I pause. Give her chance to tell me to stop. Instead she looks to me, all pleading, eyes hooded.

'Is this what you deserve?'

'Yes, sir.'

Fuck. I flick it down again and my cock bucks in time.

I look to her arse cheek, to where her skin is pinking up, and caress the area with the soft leather tip.

'What are you?' I say softly.

'A…a naughty Little Kitten.' It rasps out of her, husky and thick, as I bring it down on her other cheek.

'So very naughty.'

She whimpers her agreement and it's raw, carnal, filled with erotic wonder. I reach out with my palm, smooth the small welts on her skin.

'Do you want more?'

'Yes, sir. Please, sir'

I step back, fire two rapid flicks to both cheeks and realise I can't take much more of this. It's one thing to take on a role to fulfil her fantasy, another to hurt her. And there are other ways to be in control, to dominate, to keep this going…

I toss the crop aside and lower my knees either side of her bent legs, massage the marks on her skin as I caress them away. 'I think you've been punished enough. Now I want you to please me, Little Kitten.'

She murmurs, a heady desperate sound that has the blood pounding in my ears. I could fuck her like this, take her hard from behind, but her mouth, those lips that she keeps biting…

'I want you to pleasure me with that naughty

mouth of yours.' I stand up. 'Turn around on all fours, Kitten.'

She does as I ask and lifts her chin to look up at me, waiting for her next instruction, and I have to pause at the sight of her. Her eyes glisten, her cheeks are damp and flushed with longing and still I have to pause. I have to fight back the urge to ask if she's okay because I know it's not what she wants. Instead, I reach down, stroke my fingers against her cheek, comb them back through her hair. A moment's softness and then I pull away, lift her chin with my finger and grip my cock with my other hand.

'Rise up on your knees, Kitten.'

She lifts up.

'You really want to please me?'

Her eyes flash up into mine, her lips part. 'Yes, sir.'

I nod. 'Lick my cock, Little Kitten.'

She looks to me on my command, a second's hesitation and then she lowers her gaze, raises one hand to grip me and tongues me from the base up—*fuck!*

'Again.'

Her tongue twists around my length, her eyes lifting to mine, dark with desire.

'Now suck.'

She surrounds me and my eyes threaten to roll back over the pleasure and the sight. *Holy fuck.* My hands fly to her hair and she sucks me back hard.

'*Slower.*'

She obeys, lowering her mouth over me, again and again.

'*Harder.*'

She follows my every edict and my body trembles. Quakes. I want to come, but I don't. This is too good. Too intense for it to end too soon.

'*Deeper.*'

She moans around my length, her cheeks sucking in, her own arousal shining in her face and it's tipping me over. All of it. I try to ease the tension in my body, try to hold it at bay.

I loosen my hands in her hair, wrap one fist around her ponytail as I breathe through it. I want this all driven by her. Yes, she's the one on her knees, her nipples clamped, but I'm not going to force her further than she is willing to go; only my instruction will command her to do what she's already willing and as her mouth reaches the base of my cock I crumble, my thighs trembling, my release too close.

'*Enough.*'

I pull out of her mouth with a pop, and she sulks up at me. 'But...'

My eyes flash in warning but really I'm losing my all over her, and I'm not ready. I'll never be ready. And it's not all lust; it's some other emotion that comes from the trust, the power she's bestowed on me.

I lower my hand to the chains that dangle between her breasts, tug them towards me, punishing and panicking in one.

She arches back, bites into her lip, her nipples pulled taut. 'You like that, Kitten?'

She murmurs her response.

'What was that?'

'Yes.' It's a lustful whisper.

'Yes?' I yank the chains again and she moans.

'Yes. *Yes*, sir.'

Her need seeps between her legs. Her thighs glistening with it, her entire body aglow.

'Touch yourself, Little Kitten.'

She eagerly lowers her hand to her pussy, her movements frantic, her breathing rapid. Fuck, she's so close. Already. And the sight of her fingering herself at my command has my cock straining towards her lips.

'Now suck me.'

She stops, raises her hands.

'No, touch yourself while you make me come in your filthy mouth, Kitten.'

Her hand falls to her clit, her other gripping me as she sinks me in deep. *Fuck*. I want to squeeze my eyes shut as the pleasure rips through me, but I can't, not yet. I have to look like I still have this.

'Deeper.'

She takes me in so far I hit the back of her throat, my entire length pulsing inside her slick warm mouth. I have to stand taller and release the chains as I fight to delay it. Groan my pleasure as my hips buck.

'Is this what you want?'

She murmurs around me.

'Is it?' I say, plucking my cock from her sucking grasp.

'Yes, sir!'

Sir. Sir. Sir.

It's too much. All too much.

'My naughty Little Kitten, that's what you are.'

She takes me back in, her moan vibrating through me, her eyes watering as she gazes up at me, so obedient, so decadent.

'Harder.'

Her cheeks hollow out with her suck, her glistening lips stretching thin as she accommodates my lust-thickened cock. Her body trembles as she works herself faster between her legs, her head bobbing faster too, her whimpers coming in quick succession, her breaths rasping through her nose.

'That's it, naughty Little Kitten, come with me, come with me!'

Argh! My cry fills the room as I throw my head back, my hips jerking as my release spurts. It's fierce, hot, so mind-altering that it continues to shudder out of me again and again and I sense her rigidity, her movements turning stilted. I look down, see her entire body tensing, her eyes locking onto mine and then she rocks, her cry around my cock telling me she's gone. She sucks back over me, taking the last of my release, and then her body arcs away as the pleasure-filled spasms take over her head to toe.

I reach forward, palm her neck, my fingers stroking through her hair as she rides the waves and I enjoy every second of it with her.

She's a goddess. A true goddess sent to lure me out of my safe haven and turn my world on its axis.

But as I drop to my knees and press a kiss to her swollen lips I don't care. I'm too drugged up on out-of-this-world sex to care.

And that's all this is, just as she said. Great sex. It doesn't have to mean more.

Only…it feels like more. So much more.

CHAPTER ELEVEN

Olivia

I CAN'T TAKE my eyes off him. It's like I'm magnetically drawn to his very presence when my eyes should be on the football match that's underway at ground level. Not up here, across the rows of private seating that accompany the corporate box, absorbing the sight of him as he chats to an ex-player he clearly knows well.

Or at least they were chatting; now their eyes are fixed on the semi-final as the few minutes of extra time play out and Dubois' team are one nil up.

'I can't bear to look.' Adele, Dubois' wife, grimaces up at me but I barely have time to give her a sympathetic smile before her eyes go back to the pitch.

She's a bundle of nervous energy, her perfectly manicured nails caught between her teeth, her petite frame thrumming with tension. And she still manages to look utterly stunning, with the warmest of brown eyes and a smile that lights up her entire face…when she's not chewing on a nail.

'I'm sure they've got it in the bag,' I say, like I know what I'm talking about, when I don't. At all. Football just isn't my thing.

She grabs my hand, grips it with a tight nod, the act so familiar when we've only known each other a few hours. But then we bonded from the off, our shared passion and charity efforts something we could talk about for hours. I guess it was inevitable and Valentine must have anticipated that as he quickly left us to it, spending his time catching up with acquaintances that I get the sense are more like friends to him.

And it's distracting, watching him so at ease, laughing, joking, in the same room but not with me. I'm too attuned to him, to his deep gravelly voice and that laugh…oh, that laugh.

I glance in his direction now, watch as he frowns down at the pitch. I can feel myself willing him to look at me, a brief second's glance to know it's not just me that can't get the other out of their head. We've hardly seen each other since yesterday morning when he left my house after a breakfast of coffee and croissants. Nourishment that he had sourced from a local café before I'd even woken up.

And I never sleep in.

Ever.

I did then though. Too content. Too sated. Too at ease. All things I'm not accustomed to feeling, but I want more of already.

'Oh, God… Oh, God.' Adele grabs my arm and I

don't think she's even aware she's doing it. 'It's not…
it is…oh, God. I can't look.'

She turns into me, but she doesn't need to look,
the crowd are filling in. The cheers loud as the op-
position approaches the goal. It's close, real close, but
then the whistle pierces the air, and the crowd roar.

'They've won,' I say. 'They've won!'

Her head shoots up, her eyes going back to the
pitch and her grin is so wide, her eyes are tearing
up. And then I understand it; this isn't about the
football. It wasn't the match that kept distracting
her when I tried to continue our discussion about
their charity initiatives abroad. It seems she suffers
the same condition as me when her man is within
viewing distance. Not that Valentine is my man, not
at all, but as my eyes drift to his, now dancing, his
grin so broad on his handsome face as he applauds
the players on the pitch, I can't deny how the sight
of him makes me feel.

Adele gives a soft laugh. 'You'd think after all
these years of watching him play I'd be used to it,
but I swear it only gets worse.'

'I can imagine.'

'It's a little like love, I guess,' she carries on, her
eyes wistful. 'You think you'll get accustomed to
it, loving your man, but in actual fact you only ever
love them more.'

I frown as I consider her words. Nathan and I
were comfortable… I would definitely say I grew
accustomed to my feelings for him. There was never
the intense spark, the intense attraction that I feel

around Valentine, so intense it makes me feel rather *un*comfortable.

'Everything good here, ladies?'

Valentine is suddenly beside us, my thoughts preventing me from noticing his approach and now I'm unprepared, my body sizzling with awareness, with heat.

'Absolutely.' I smile at Adele, hoping I'm not as flushed as I feel. Lobster skin and a white dress. No, just no. 'We should go and get a glass of champagne to celebrate, before we're inundated by your husband and his teammates.'

She laughs and smiles up at Valentine. 'She's a treasure; I wish you'd introduced us years ago.'

She pats his chest in a very familiar gesture and I realise that they are friends too. That he hasn't just brought me to meet influential acquaintances; these are his friends. I shouldn't be surprised. But I don't know; he just seems so reserved, so measured, so controlled... *Not so much after you cracked him, though.*

'I only had the pleasure of meeting her recently myself.' He grins at me and I want to mute my brain that is talking so much gibberish as I adjust to this side of him and his life.

'You've known each other long then?'

'Oh, years and years,' Adele says, leaning into him a little. 'He used to train with Louis but a silly little stunt one night ended up screwing his right foot—*his extra-talented foot*—for good.'

'You weren't even on the scene then,' Valentine corrects her.

'No, but I know all about it! Louis dined out on that tale for years.'

'I'm so glad my misery was such a great source of entertainment.'

'Your misery?' She raises her eyebrows at him. 'Your stupidity, you mean.'

'I won the bet though.' He grins back and I absorb this extra titbit, fascinated by their easy camaraderie over something that surely must have been devastating for Valentine at the time. Even more fascinated by the surprising idea of Valentine as a stunt performing footballer.

'You used to train together? With Louis? At football?'

'Back in our teens, yeah.'

'*You* were a professional footballer?' I say, still struggling to take it in.

He nods. 'Never quite made it into the first team though.'

'No,' Adele pipes up. 'Your wild antics saw to that.'

Wild? Valentine?

Now I really do want to laugh but I manage to hold it in, not my surprise though, that's written all over my face as his eyes narrow on me.

'You could say I learned my lesson the hard way,' he says to me, like he's daring me to question any of it.

'You wouldn't change what you do now though,'

Adele says. 'It's obvious you enjoy it, and you're your own boss, none of the playing up to the fans, gruelling training sessions, competition nerves... Seriously, I keep telling Louis he's got to think about retiring soon.'

Valentine chuckles. 'Good luck with that. Now why don't I go and get those drinks...'

'I'll go.' I reach out, my hand gentle on his arm. I still need the breather and a chance to clear my head. 'Then Adele can tell me all about the wild things you got up to in your youth.'

She chuckles as I walk away and I hear Valentine grumble something I can't quite make out. But, truth is, I'd struggle to hear anything over my head that's roaring so loudly with this new version of the man I know. Was it the so-called 'stunt' that made him so... I don't want to say boring. Christ, he's anything but boring now. Thursday night drowned out that impression of the man.

And now I want to know everything. Like, did he truly learn his lesson the hard way?

Did ending his football career ruin his life's dream and create this tamer, more conservative version of him? Or was it something else?

And just how wild was he?

And how can he sit there and judge me when he's done his 'crazy' and then some?

I smile all the more, my mind puzzling over it as I obtain our drinks and wander back outside to the viewing seats and find him still with Adele, chatting animatedly about something. Even seeing him like this is different.

I offer Adele one of the glasses.

'I'm afraid I didn't grab you one, Valentine. I wasn't sure what soft drink you'd fancy, and it doesn't help me pursue my goal if you're within earshot.'

He grimaces as Adele laughs.

'I really do like this one, Valentine. Can we keep her?'

I almost spurt my drink everywhere. 'I like you too. If I'd known football attracted such like-minded women, I'd have got into it years ago.'

Valentine groans. 'What have I let myself in for? I hope they hurry up in those changing rooms; I think I'm going to need some male backup asap.'

'Surely your past can't be all that bad?' I purr, leaning one hand into his chest in what's probably too flirtatious a gesture but what can I say, Thursday has changed everything.

He chuckles beneath my palm, shakes his head at Adele, whose brows are back with the roof of the stadium.

'Right, I'm gone.' And with that he walks away.

I watch him go, my eyes caught up in his impressive frame that is encased in a light grey suit that totally suits the lightness of his mood.

'You've been all over that, haven't you?'

Jesus. I choke on the champagne I'm halfway to swallowing. 'I've what?'

I eye Adele and she just laughs, her big brown

eyes dancing, her shiny black bob swinging with the shake of her head.

'You know what I mean…' She waves her glass in his direction and my eyes flit there and back just as quick. 'You can't fool me, not with that look in your eye.'

'What look?' I sound drunk, repetitive, bumbling, but hell…

'Okay. So, maybe it's not so much you as him. I haven't seen him like this in…' she looks off into the distance as she considers it '…too long. And it's nice. It's like getting an inkling of the old Valentine.'

'The old Valentine?' I imagine we're back to the boy he was in his youth, the one who ruined his football career for a stunt.

'Oh, yeah. Seriously, you may not think it now, not with his high-flying career, the big CEO with the world-renowned PR business, but back in the day… he was trouble with a capital *T*. If anyone needed good PR it was him.'

My eyes bulge in their sockets and she laughs at me. 'Don't believe me?'

'I…well, I don't know what to say.'

'Have you never looked him up on the internet?'

'No.' My chin tucks under as I glance at her as if she's crazy. 'I'm not some weird stalker. Besides, I had no idea he would be worthy of an internet search.'

'Ah, and the truth is out.'

My laugh is awkward. 'What do you mean?'

'I mean, had you realised he was worthy of an internet search you would have done it.'

'Absolutely not.'

'Why not? I search up my husband and I know everything there is to know. Besides, it can be amusing to laugh at all the stuff the tabloids get wrong at times.'

'You got that right.'

'And better to laugh than to let it get to you.'

'True.'

We clink glasses and I sense the newfound bond between us swell. And my desire to have them front my charity arm flourishes with it. Valentine definitely called this right. And as for Valentine…

'So come on, tell me, just how much of a daredevil was he?'

'Oh, you wouldn't believe how bad he was. Thinking up crazy dares, challenging his mates to a game of chicken, ridiculous drinking games, all night parties… Seriously, if there was a party Valentine was either instigating it or at the centre of it anyway. You know the phrase, the life and soul, that was him.'

I raise my brows, hum into my glass as I take another sip. Is *that* how he got his scar?

'But the accident changed things…' She breaks off, her eyes finding him inside the bustling corporate box. 'It was understandable really. He didn't want to party. He didn't want to drink. Hell, it took us long enough to get him socialising again, and we missed him. Really missed him.'

'He was that bad? But he was only a teenager; surely they bounce back quicker than that?'

Though I feel unfair now. If he'd dreamed of being a professional footballer and he shattered that in one foolish act…

'Oh, no, he was much older.'

'He was?' Now I'm confused.

'I'm not talking about the crazy stunt he pulled busting his foot.' She lowers her voice as she leans in to me. 'I'm talking about *the* accident. You know, the one that killed Layla.'

'Layla?'

The blood drains from my face as the champagne rises in my throat.

'His wife.'

His what?

'You didn't know?' She looks at me, a frown creasing up her brow. 'Sorry, I just assumed, what with you two being so obviously close. I kind of had you pitched as friends rather than just acquaintances. The way he looks at you and how at ease you both are. And everyone who knows Valentine *knows* about it. And, oh, my God, I'm rambling. I'm so sorry. I really do need to learn to zip it.'

I'm still reeling. 'He was mar—'

'Right, ladies, gossip time is over.' His husky voice penetrates through the conversation and my eyes snap to his as he stands in the opening to the internal part of the box now.

His expression's unreadable, but I get the strange sense he knows what we were talking about. I also feel a peculiar stab in my chest. Anger. Hurt. I don't know. I just want to know why he didn't tell me he was widowed too.

'Time for us to celebrate,' he says. 'Louis is on his way up.'

'He can't have showered properly yet!' Adele grumbles. 'Can't you pull him aside and teach him how to look the part like you, Valentine?'

He chuckles as he looks at her. 'That's a battle for his wife.'

She harrumphs as she walks past him and he's looking back at me now, but I can't move. I'm still, so still, my voice and body caught up in my gut where this revelation churns and churns.

'Are you coming in?'

CHAPTER TWELVE

Valentine

'I THINK THAT went well; both Louis and Adele were clearly excited about the potential collaboration.' I sneak a look at her cool, detached form in the passenger seat and suppress a grimace. 'I reckon you've got a long-standing and very rewarding relationship building there.'

She nods. No verbal confirmation. Not even a murmur.

So much for breaking the ice…

I drum my fingers on the steering wheel and try to think of something else to say. Something that's not on the same lines as what has her so distracted. Layla. I can't even be cross at Adele for letting it slip. She has a heart of gold and her mouth has a habit of running away with itself. It only makes her more endearing, a liability for Louis at times, but nevertheless endearing.

No, it's my fault I feel like this, that we're like this. But I can't have that conversation while I'm driving.

Neither can I sit with the silence building between us, a gulf forming that I'm scared I won't be able to cross.

She hasn't said anything since we left the stadium and her mood has gone from vibrant and excited with Louis and Adele, to this: quiet, reflective, so far withdrawn from me as she watches the world go by outside her window while I drive us home—to *my* home. Something I agreed I would do on Thursday…but I'm not so sure it's wise any more.

Not that I thought it was wise on Thursday night either, but then my concern was the total annihilation of the line between business and personal. A line that has long since gone. No, my concern now is that I've hurt her. Not intentionally, but that doesn't make my non-disclosure right.

'I'm sorry you found out like that.'

Her head snaps to me, the most animated she's been since we've been alone. I flick her a brief look. Definitely hurt. Her eyes are hard, her lips pressed together like she wants to say a thousand things and is trying not to.

'I tried to tell you by the pool the other night.' I throw my attention back on the road but inside it's all on her and how I've made her feel. 'When I asked you what happened to Nathan, I wanted to tell you then.'

'You should have.'

'I know. But you didn't want to hear it; you asked me to let it go.'

'If I'd known that's what you were about to say I never would have stopped you.'

My eyes flit to her again, the truth of her words forcing me to accept that I knew that too and I let her stop me because I didn't want to ruin the moment either.

I sigh, the sound reverberating through the car. 'I know. I guess I didn't want to talk about it either.'

I feel her eyes on me, burning into me, so many questions itching to get out. 'When did she die?'

I stare straight ahead. 'Four years ago.'

'She must have been very young.'

'Twenty-five. We were the same age.'

'What happened?'

The ache in my chest is sharp, brutal. I swallow. Tell myself it's the same question I asked her and that she has every right to ask it of me. But she was an innocent party to her husband's death. Me…

My mouth dries up. I should have kept up the silence, at least until we were out of the car.

'Adele said she had an accident…?'

'*We*—we had an accident.' I lift my hand to my scar, a second's touch that's almost a subconscious gesture.

'What kind of accident?'

My stomach lurches, my knuckles glowing white as I grip the steering wheel with both hands once more and sense her eyes fall to my fists, sense her compassion building. Compassion that I don't deserve. And I can't say it. Car accident. Two simple words that are too crushing to say out loud.

Because it was my fault. All my fault.

'Valentine?'

Her voice is so quiet in the car. Or is it that my thoughts are raging so loud they drown her out?

'Yes.' It vibrates out of me, through the tension, the pain, the guilt.

'It's okay, you don't have to tell me, not if you don't want to.'

'It's not a question of want; it's more…' I break off. It's what? I don't know. The only person I've spoken to is Alan; not even the counsellors he tried to get me to see could make me open up. But Alan did and, although I found some peace through him, I'll never be entirely absolved of the guilt. That's on me.

She reaches across the car, her palm soft on my thigh. 'How long were you together?'

She's talking around it, encouraging happier memories and as my eyes flick to her and I feel the warmth of her palm permeate my skin a small smile touches my lips.

'Seven years…' I lower my hand to cover hers. 'She was the one that pulled me out of the rut when my football career was over. My friends were great but when they're all footballers too…' I shrug. 'My parents tried but you know how it is at that age.'

'Hell, yeah.' She laughs softly.

'Exactly.'

She squeezes my thigh. 'Sounds like you were very lucky to meet her when you did.'

A warm sense of nostalgia spreads in my chest, softens my voice. 'I was.'

'What was she like?'

'Blonde, curvy, a big smile.'

'Is that all you men think about? Appearances?' Her thigh squeeze is more punishing now. 'You know that's not what I meant.'

'No. I know.' I think about it. 'She was kind. Warm-hearted. Fun. She not only put up with my crazy antics, she was often the instigator of them. We were…how did Adele put it? Wild. Together. The perfect pair.'

I laugh but it's awkward as the chill starts to creep back in. The thought that always accompanies the memory taking over, that if we hadn't been so crazy, so fun-loving, maybe she'd still be here now.

'But then you changed?'

'Yes.' It's as though she's in my head, going down the same path as my thoughts. 'I realised life wasn't to be played around with. If I'd taken it more seriously, if we'd taken it more seriously, maybe she'd still be here now.'

I take my hand from hers, focus on driving and ignore the question that still persists, weighing heavy in the renewed silence: *What happened?*

Hell, all she needs to do is carry out an internet search and she'll have all the answers she seeks. But something tells me she's not the type. Bruised enough by the media herself, she knows better than to use it to research others.

And for now I've opened up enough and though she's quiet once more I sense it's gone some way to heal the wound I put there. Or is that more wishful thinking on my part?

I don't know, but as I pull into the underground car park to my apartment building and park up in the private section that serves my penthouse suite, I've never been more relieved to be getting out from behind the wheel again.

'Is that why Alan brought you in?'

Olivia

I watch as Valentine closes the car door and looks at me over the roof. I know my question has surprised him; I see it in the slight flare to his eyes, and the crease between his brows that quickly follows.

'What do you mean?'

'Why he chose *you* specifically to come in and help, the charity, the organisation… Me?'

'Does it matter?'

My shrug is subtle. 'I don't know if it matters. I just know it bothers me that I didn't know.'

'It's hardly something you just come out and mention, and like I said—'

'You were going to and I stopped you, I know. But Alan could have said something.'

'I think he was worried it would be something of a trigger for you and have you flipping out from the off.'

My brows arc. 'More than I already did?'

He rests his hand on the roof between us and studies me quietly, his blue eyes so vivid and intense as they pin me in place.

'I think he thought that with my background I would understand you better, including the backlash I'm sure he anticipated.'

'I see.' I swallow to push down the adrenaline rush his eyes have sparked. 'And does he really expect you to tame me so completely?'

His smile is slow and sexy as fuck, the rush shooting way past my control as my breasts prickle against the lace of my bra.

'I'm not sure anyone could tame you, Olivia, not completely at any rate.'

'Try at all.' My smile is ripe with challenge. 'Shall I let you in on a little secret?'

'I'm all ears.'

'I've lived my entire life confined by another. Before Nathan, it was my father, wanting to put me in a certain box and keep me there. And I'm not going back to those days. I'm living for me now and nothing and no one will change that.'

'You think that's a secret? I've already pieced that much together—not your father, but Nathan. It's obvious his mark is everywhere—in your house, in the office, in the way you act…and you told me it yourself, but what I don't get is why.'

'Why what?'

'Why did you let him take over?'

'I didn't, not intentionally at any rate.'

'But you did.'

I drag in a breath, think back to Fee's words over the years, so very much the same. 'I loved him.'

'Yes, but loving someone doesn't give them the right to control you.'

No, it doesn't. But how can I explain it to him when I can barely explain it to myself?

'Nathan was...he was an exceptional man. He pulled himself off the streets, studied hard, worked harder. He made something of himself from nothing and he spent his adult life helping others avoid what he went through.'

'I read about his past...' His eyes soften a little with understanding. 'I read about his time on the streets.'

'Then you'll understand why he lived a very safe existence; everything had to be just so. He was careful, measured about everything...' The word *boring* almost erupts and the way Valentine's eyes spark, I know he thinks the same and is comparing it to my own description of him the night of the dinner.

But I can't label Nathan in such a way; it feels disloyal, a disservice, especially when I think of his days on the streets and the reasons behind the way he was.

'He was an inspiration,' I say instead, my smile bittersweet as I think back to the early days in our relationship. 'The night I met him, he was talking at a gala dinner put on by my college and the way he spoke, of his journey and what he wanted for the future and the charity he represented...he had the whole room enthralled. We smashed our fundraising target that night and when I caught up with him to tell him how much I enjoyed his talk and expressed my interest in getting involved with the charity, told him ideas that I had, he listened to me. It didn't matter that I was young and still finding my feet in terms of what I wanted for a career.'

'Of course he would. Who wouldn't? You're clever, you're beautiful, *you're* inspiring, Olivia.'

I scoff. 'Well, when you've grown up in a house where your father believes a girl's place is in the home, it's easy to lose sight of that. To my father, I was too masculine, too driven, too clever. But Nathan, he saw me as an equal.'

'An *equal*?' He scowls at me. 'You bowed down to him.'

'No, it wasn't like that. I…I liked making him happy, I learnt from him. I wouldn't be where I am now if it wasn't for him.'

'I think you give him too much credit.'

'And you don't give him enough,' I say sharply, and bite my lip, look away. Because I don't want to argue with him over Nathan. I've done enough battling it out with my sister over the years, her conviction that I saw Nathan as a father substitute making my skin crawl even now.

'I don't know, Olivia. It seems to me that you were craving the attention your father never gave you.'

'*Jesus!*' My eyes snap to his, so many thoughts, so much emotion rolling through me in waves. How could he? How could he *and* Fee?

But then, are they not right? Don't you know that deep down? Isn't that why it affects you so much?

I shake my head. *No.*

'Just because he was so much older than me doesn't mean I loved him out of some weird daddy complex.'

'I didn't say—'

'*Look*, are you really going to do the whole counselling thing again?' I say quietly. 'Because, if so, I can just call a taxi and find my own way home.'

'No. I don't want you to go. I'm just trying to understand, that's all.'

'Understand *what*, exactly?'

He's moving now, walking around his car, and I'm a prisoner to that look in his eye, and it's not understanding or compassion or anything close. It's dark, dangerous…

'Why a woman who fought so hard to dominate her late husband in the bedroom demanded that I dominate her instead.'

My laugh catches. 'I didn't demand…'

'No?' His hand snakes around my ponytail and my insides twist up with heat; he steps so close my breasts come up against his jacket.

'You're just trying to distract me from my anger.'

He tugs gently and my head pulls back; his eyes burn down into mine. 'Are you really angry with me?'

No, I'm not. I'm hot for him, but this…

'I won't change.' I wet my lips, stare up into his

eyes with all the defiance I can muster. 'Not for anyone.'

'Good.'

And then his head bows, his lips crushing mine. I let my bag fall, fork my fingers through his hair and kiss him just as hard, every ounce of defiance burning up in the kiss. I feel like I've been starved of him since Thursday night, Friday morning, everything about me craving this—his kiss, his touch, his scent on my skin.

'This dress has teased me from the second I picked you up.' He brushes the words against my lips as his hand falls to the sedate hem of my dress, dragging it up. 'It's pristine white, so innocent and angelic. But you're none of that.'

My clit pulses with his words, my moans begging for more. More filth from his mouth, more dominance in his stance, his hold.

I want him to dominate me because he's different, because I am his true equal. He makes me feel all that and more.

'I don't want to change you, Little Kitten, but I will punish you for teasing me.'

I inhale sharply, the pang in my clit so acute as I tear my mouth away to eye him.

'Turn around.' His command is gruff. But we can't do this here, in his basement car park. Yes, his bay is enclosed but there are cameras. Surely.

'Don't disobey me, Kitten.'

His eyes flit to the upper corner of the space and I follow his glance. The security camera.

'They won't see what's happening down here...' his fingers stroke my waist '...they'll only see your face.'

'But they'll know.'

'And?'

My laugh is sultry. 'Why do I get the sense I've turned you?'

He doesn't respond, only grabs my hips and spins me to face the car. 'Hands on the roof, Little Kitten.'

I don't hesitate. The car roof is solid, reassuring, and I pin myself to it, hold myself steady as my insides tremble with the excitement of having his fingers ride my dress up, all the way to my hips, my waist. The cool air sweeps over the bare cheeks of my arse, over the damp strip of my thong that offers no protection against the chill.

'I won't change for anyone either.'

His ground-out retort denies that I've turned him, made him behave how I want. And though I hear the words, I don't believe him. I don't think the Valentine who walked into my boardroom on day one would have done this...

But then the Valentine who Adele spoke of...that's another story entirely.

Maybe it's not so much me changing him as it is me taking him back to the man he once was.

And does that mean I'm actually helping him in some way, that it's not all about him trying to help me?

He leans up against me, his body hard, his teeth

grazing my earlobe. 'You're so fucking sexy; you bring out the worst in me.'

My lips curve, my eyes flutter closed. 'And you me.'

'And you me, *sir*.'

God. The rush inside makes words impossible.

His hands lower to my bare arse, his fingers massaging my cheeks. 'Say it, Kitten.'

I'm biting my lip so hard I can't.

'You think I won't spank you here, for fear of people watching, people listening?'

I whimper; my clit is throbbing so painfully it's all I can do not to drop my hand to it.

He presses his knee between my legs, forcing them to part. Wraps his fist around my hair to drag my head back and bring my mouth to his.

'You want me to spank you?' he says against my parted lips, his hand smoothing over one arse cheek.

I wriggle into his grasp, my 'Yes' a whimper.

'I want to hear you say it.'

I stare up into his blazing blues. 'Spank me, sir, please.'

Pleasure consumes me as his hand comes down on my cheek, a short, sharp spank that has my need soaking up my thong.

'Are you wet for me, Kitten?'

'*Yes*, sir.'

'Shall I see how wet?'

'*Please*, sir.'

His fingers slip inside the dainty strip of fabric,

his 'Fuck' erupting with his breath, the groan that follows reverberating through me.

'You're so wet.' He sinks his fingers deeper, slips them up inside me, finger-fucking me as I rock into the motion. 'I want to fuck you right here.'

'*Do it*, sir.'

'No.' He withdraws his hand. 'I'm going to tease you like you teased me in this dress all day, Kitten.'

I spin in his hold. 'But I want you.'

His mouth is tight, his body rigid. He wants me as much as I want him. I can *see* he wants me, I can *feel* he wants me. 'And you can wait.'

Fuck, I love him all commanding, but Jesus. I go to tug my dress down and he grabs my wrists.

'Not yet. I've not had my fill.'

I frown at him. *Fill?*

He steps back, his eyes lowering. 'Take them off, Kitten.'

I swallow, keep my eyes locked on his and bend forward. I slip my thong down my legs, step out carefully so as not to catch it on my stiletto heels.

'Now give it to me.'

I offer it out and he takes it, slips it inside his jacket pocket in plain sight of the camera.

'Now hold your dress up, let me see you.'

Slowly, I do as he asks, watch as he steps forward once more, his hand dipping to my pussy. He slips three fingers inside me with such ease, the pad of his thumb rolling over my clit in the same motion, and my hands fly to his shoulders as my knees buckle.

'Yes!'

'So responsive to my touch, Little Kitten.' His voice is laced with approval, his skilled touch pushing me higher and higher. 'You like that?'

I try to look him in the eye, try to tell him, but my whole body is quivering, my climax building thick and fast as he thrusts in deeper, his thumb continuing to roll.

'Shall I make you come here, in front of those cameras like the naughty Little Kitten that you are? Would you like that?'

I'm whimpering incessantly now, my toes curling in my shoes, my nails digging into his jacket.

'Val—Valentine.'

He stops, his thumb and fingers pressed hard against me. 'That's not how you address me. Do I need to punish you again?'

'No. Please, sir, please—'

He pinches my clit and I buck, he does it again and again and it's no punishment. The rhythmic sensation zings through my limbs like a pulse of ecstasy each and every time. I cling to his shoulders tighter, my mouth slack, my body weightless as I rise up on a tide of pleasure and come crashing down with a surge that has my entire body collapsing against him. Wave after wave, making me cry out at him. His name on shaky repeat.

And he's not disciplining me for it now.

I drag in a breath, risk a look up into his face and the intensity of his expression has the air locked deep inside me, my eyes trapped in his.

I feel like there's something he wants to say, something he wants to hear, and all I can manage is, 'Thank you.'

He's slow to respond and when he does his voice is thick. 'Anger to gratitude; it's quite the switch.'

My smile is small. 'You have that power over me.'

He studies me a second longer and I wish so hard I could read minds. There seems to be so much going on behind those endless blues and I can't get a handle on any of it.

'You ready to see my toy?'

'Your...' I frown, jarred by his sudden shift in focus. 'I can feel your toy well enough now.'

His chuckle is low as he steps back, righting my dress for me as he does so, and I wonder at his composure, at his desire to break the connection.

Does he really think *now* is the time for showing me his *toy*?

'You don't want to go upstairs?' I eye his obvious erection, straining behind his zip. He can't seriously want to delay his own release, but he turns away from me.

'I promised you a look this evening...'

He walks over to the only other vehicle in here. It's covered in a tailormade dust sheet that's so fitted I could probably take a guess at what's beneath.

'I won't hold you to it.' I give a jittery laugh. 'In fact, I could just as easily see it in the morning...if you'll have me stay.'

'It won't take long.' I don't miss the fact that he

doesn't answer my thinly veiled request to spend the night. 'She doesn't get driven much, hence the cover.'

He hunches down to tug at the bottom corner of the sheet and I nod as I still grapple with the shift from passion to cars. And don't get me wrong, I *love* cars; it just appears I love sex with Valentine more. Dangerous territory, even for me.

'I restored her with my father in my teens. I think it was his attempt at keeping me grounded and at home a little more than football would have had me.'

I walk up to him, taking in this extra titbit while my legs tremble beneath me, all shaky from the explosive orgasm he just delivered…and swiftly seems to have forgotten.

'So…' I smooth a hand through my ponytail, seeking the same level of composure as him '…your father wasn't a football fan?'

'Not particularly.' He starts to roll back the sheet and my jaw drops at what's beneath. I was wrong; *this* I never would have guessed at. 'Cars were more his thing and it was something we could do together, you know, bond over.'

I'm listening to him, but my eyes are all for the car now as I bend forward and lightly sweep my palm along the curve that leads from the headlamp up.

'I can't believe it.'

His eyes drift to me as he continues to unveil the beauty that, even with all my motoring experience, I've never managed to see in the flesh.

'You own a Lamborghini Miura.'

He tugs the cover off the end with a grin. 'You really do know your cars.'

'I told you, they're a passion. Though for me it was an attempt at *gaining* my father's attention, rather than the other way around.'

'You really did crave his attention?'

I flinch a little. I can't help it. His far too astute observation that because my father failed to give it to me I took it from Nathan instead cuts deep. But the more I think about it, the more I know he's right. Both him and Fee. And it's worse because with my father I refused to change; with Nathan I did the opposite. Seeking to please him and keep his attention regardless of what it was I wanted or preferred.

'Yes, I did. Don't get me wrong, he was a good man, he loved me, my sister, my mother, but he was a product of his time. Girls had their place and it wasn't in the garage.'

'Hence the putting you in a certain box comment.'

'Exactly.' I flick him a look, impressed that he remembered. 'I think he was secretly disappointed he never had a boy.'

'I take it he's not around any more?'

'No. It's just Mum, my sister and me. The girls.' I smile at him. 'He made me all the more determined to succeed in a man's world though.'

'And succeed you did.'

I see the admiration in his gaze and it warms me through.

'Is your sister like you?'

I laugh and shake my head, start circling the car, taking in every angle, and feel him watching me.

'Not particularly; she loves being a home-maker, a mum, and she's great at it.'

'Not for you though, hey?'

Another shake of my head, my eyes all for the wheels as I consider his words, the old pang only subtle now. I made my peace with never being a mum long ago.

'I always thought I would have children at some point, but the time never felt right. Nathan and I were always so focused, so busy. And now...well, now it's hardly an option.'

I try the handle and it opens up. Duck down to look at the pristine beige leather interior, the gleaming dash. 'Impressive.'

'As are you.'

There's an element of awe in his voice that has my heart turning over, the warmth spreading all the more, and I try to ignore it as I rise back up. It runs too deep, sparks too much. 'What year is she?'

'1969.' He comes up behind me.

'You and your father did a great job. She's stunning.' I step away from him as fear rises up. Why do I care so much about what he thinks? I promised I would only care for my own opinion going forward. That I wouldn't fall into that trap again. I try to focus on the car; it's safer, less confusing. I take in her bright red paint, the gold sills and matching wheels that look too clean to have ever been driven and remember what he said.

'You really don't take her out much?'

He laughs. 'Not often. She's hardly safe for today's roads.'

'You want to talk safety when you have this baby under your roof?' I look at him like he's grown two heads. 'It's practically sacrilege.'

'Now you sound like my father. He's been on at me to take her on a supercar tour with him.'

'And you should.'

'Maybe.'

'Why does that sound like a *No* maybe?'

He chuckles softly. 'It's a maybe.'

And now I care that he hasn't taken her out, that he hasn't done what his dad asked of him. A request which I'm sure stems from a continued desire to bond with his son.

And I shouldn't care. This should be about sex. Pure and simple.

Sex is less messy, less complicated, and that's what we should be having.

Not sharing childhood tales, encouraging a personal connection that can never end well when the time comes for us to part ways.

I walk up to him, drink my fill of all that I find arousing about him and hook my hands in his hair. 'Will you take me out in it?'

'*Now?*'

I lower my gaze to his lips. 'Not now. Though, I have to say, your toy has been quite the turn-on…' I nudge his semi-hard cock with my body '…but I have other more pressing matters to attend to right now.'

He wraps his arms around me. 'Is that so?'

'Uh-huh.' I play with the hair at the nape of his neck. 'Maybe in the morning, after I fetch us some breakfast, it's my turn to shout for it.'

'You're on.'

My heart gives an excited leap—I'm staying over—but then the voice is back. The one telling me this is so much more than just fun and soon it will be over. That I'll have to give him up. Like an addiction you know is bad for you, but all you can do is cling to the moment and delay its end.

Though this addiction has me feeling more content than I can ever remember being and, if it feels this good, can it truly be all that bad for me?

And it isn't a relationship. It's not anything. Just some messing around while we get a job done.

Because I don't want to be in a relationship again.

I don't.

And he's so young. Close to the age I was when I married Nathan, and look where that landed me—childless and alone and missing out on so much.

'Olivia?'

'Mmm?'

'What are you thinking?'

'I'm wondering why you haven't dragged me upstairs and fucked me senseless already.'

It's not a total lie, and I know my brash language is an attempt at concealing the truth: that I'm scared I won't want to give him up, that I'm going back down the same old road, wanting to tie myself to another, sacrifice my wants and dreams for another.

His chuckle hammers over the lot, destroying the worries, the overthinking, and then his lips are on mine and my brain empties, leaving one thought remaining: *Live for the now, not the future you cannot control.*

Valentine

'Okay, so I didn't want to wake you to ask what you fancied for breakfast...'

Olivia walks into my bedroom, all light and breezy, her hair tumbling down her shoulders, her face devoid of make-up, and she's wearing— *Oh, God,* what *is* she wearing?

'So I just bought a variety.'

Her eyes lift to mine as she holds up a large paper bag and precariously balances a tower of two coffee cups in the other. She blushes and eyes her front before looking back to me with a small shrug.

'I hope you don't mind, but I didn't have a sleepover in mind when we went to the football. And your hoodie kind of works, don't you think?'

I laugh, my grin feeling too wide for my face.

'It's certainly a look.'

She wanders over with an extra sway to her hips, a strip of white just visible beneath my grey hoodie that tells me she's wearing her dress beneath. She offloads the stuff on the bedside table and turns to me, tugging on the drawstrings to the hood and looking far too cute and edible.

'What did you wear on your feet?'

She smiles. 'My heels. They're white, they go, and besides, the streets were relatively quiet and it's a glorious morning, too glorious to spend it in bed.'

I reach out for her hand and pull her to me. 'You sure about that?'

'Well…' she hums low in her throat, her hands tangling in my hair as she eyes me '…now that you come to mention it…'

I go to kiss her and she drags her mouth away. 'But you will take me out in the car…after?'

I nod against her mouth, our noses rubbing. 'I will.'

I go to kiss her again and she ducks away more. 'You promise?'

'I promise.'

I'd take her out every day in that damn car if I could just keep her…

I pull her under me, bury my hands in her hair, my mouth desperate over hers as my body comes alive, the heat rushing to my groin as my heart beats panicked, wild…

It's the same urge that struck the second I looked down into her glowing face after she lost it so completely against my hand, my car. The same urge I had when I looked down at her kneeling before me, submitting.

I want to wrap my arms around her. I want to keep her close. I want to have her always.

It's why I walked away in the parking garage, created distance, space to breathe, to think clearly. To shoot it all down before she got wind of my thoughts, because a relationship isn't what she wants. In fact, I warrant she'd run so very fast in the opposite direction if I dared hint at how I feel.

That, against all the odds and my better judgement, I'm falling in love with her.

And there isn't a damn thing I can do about it.

CHAPTER THIRTEEN

Olivia

'YOU READY FOR THIS?'

I'm buzzing, the adrenaline rush from driving these cars is comparable only to sex with the big guy next to me, who's looking a little grey. Not for the first time this morning I want to ask if he's feeling okay. But when I did so over breakfast, he quickly assured me he was fine. And I don't want to molly-coddle him, but...

'Sure.'

He doesn't look at me as he says it. His eyes are fixed on the track and the line-up of supercars, their glossy exteriors screaming power and prestige, the glorious sunshine glinting off each and every one. 'Which do you fancy first?'

He shrugs. 'It's your track day; you choose.'

I wrap an arm round my middle, grip my elbow as I touch a finger to the corner of my mouth and hum as I ponder them all.

'The McLaren?'

He nods and I turn to take him in properly, his blue jeans, his deep grey sweater, all casual, but his stance is rigid, his hands like fists inside his pockets. I can't bear it. We've spent every night together since the football and many hours in between, usually on the pretext of working, but we seem incapable of concentrating on anything but each other. And every moment has been easy, enjoyable—too enjoyable—but I'm not worrying about that right now.

I'm worrying about him.

And part of me says I shouldn't. I should push on. Because showing I'm worried shows that I care, and caring…caring just gets complicated.

But I do care…

'Are you sure you're okay?'

He turns to look at me, shakes his head. 'Sorry, yeah. Just distracted.'

'Want to talk about it?'

He reaches out, cups my cheek and his eyes… *God*, his eyes…my chest squeezes tight. 'What is it?' His lashes lower but I can't forget how they looked. Lost. Haunted. Sad.

I force a smile. 'It can't be that bad, can it? It's a beautiful day, the sun is shining, the air is crisp, and now we get to drive the track. No traffic, no city chaos.' I touch my hand over his and smile. 'It's our day.'

His eyes lift and his smile creeps into them…at last. 'You're absolutely right.'

'Hey, Liv, which one are you taking out first?'

I turn to see Harry walking towards us and Valentine's hand falls from my face, but I grasp it in mine, intertwine my fingers with his. Harry catches the move but says nothing. He knows me well enough now, and never have I brought someone to the track with me. And even though he knew I was bringing a man, I don't think he expected that someone to be more than just a business associate. Which he isn't… but he is…and now isn't the time to debate it, though the debate is cropping up more and more.

I smile over my mental ramble. 'The McLaren.'

'Sure thing.' He filters through the keys in his hands and tosses me the right one. 'And go steady, yeah, none of your usual shenanigans.'

He winks as he says it and I know he's winding me up, but I can't miss the way Valentine's fingers pulse around mine. He can't seriously still think I have some sort of death wish. Not now that he *knows* me. The real me.

'You want to drive first?' I say, trying to ignore the sting of it.

'No. It's your track day. You drive.'

'Come on then.' I tug him with me and throw a grin over my shoulder to Harry, tell myself to quit overthinking everything and being so oversensitive. 'Thanks, Harry! She's a beaut.'

'You'd know; you take her out every time. Not that you've bought her yet!'

'There's always today.'

'Yeah, yeah.' He laughs as he shakes his head and walks off into the stands.

I look back to the line-up and the adrenaline is

already pumping fast through my veins. The physical appeal of the cars all the more profound for the power beneath their bonnets, just waiting to be unleashed. 'Which one do you reckon wins on looks alone?'

I'm making conversation now, anything to put his strange mood behind us and get him involved.

'The Aston.'

I'm almost surprised he's answered me, and I smile, look at the vehicle in question. It's deep turquoise and sexy as fuck. A sheer muscle car and so very him. 'I might have guessed.'

And when I look back at him I see a spark in his eye, a spark that's been lacking all morning, and I feel better already. 'In that case, you get to drive that one…first at least…'

He meets my eye, a second's hesitation, and then, 'Okay.'

Better and better…

We walk up to the McLaren 720S, its colour a mystical blue that makes me want to smooth my hands all over it like I'm afflicted with some weird fetish, and I laugh over my own thoughts. 'You ready for this?'

He smiles and shakes his head at me, much like one would when indulging a child, and I grin back at him, pull open the door as he does the same, and climb in.

The second I'm in the seat, buckled and looking at the empty track ahead, I take a breath, calm my pulse that's working overtime.

'Here we go…' I flick him a look, start the engine and test the accelerator, let the engine roar and feel it vibrate through the car, through me. 'Nothing beats that sound!'

I sneak another look at him and the excitement swells; the spark is well and truly there now. 'Doesn't she sound amazing?'

He nods. 'She does.'

'Hold on tight.'

He promptly grips the grab handle in the door.

'I didn't quite mean literally. Jesus, Valentine!' I roll my eyes. 'Don't tell me you have a thing about women drivers?'

'No. Not at all.'

I don't believe him and his hand still gripping the grab handle proves it. The little girl in me, the one that was told she had no place under the bonnet, comes alive. Miffed. Underestimated.

Well, I'll show him.

I know this track like the back of my hand. And I've been trained to drive it as well as the best. Every corner, the preparation it takes, the split-second shift in gear, when to brake, when to accelerate…

And I go for it, loving every second. The rush, the speed, the noise…

'Okay, okay.' He waves me down. 'You've proved your point; you can ease off.'

I glance at him. 'You sure about that?'

'Yes!' he rushes out. 'In fact, I'd go as far as to say you're a better driver than me.'

I laugh, high, giddy.

'Let's see about that; it's your turn.'

I pull over and have the weirdest sense he's going to refuse, but then he undoes his seatbelt and we step out, switching sides, him at the wheel, me trusting him with it. And the fun builds. He relaxes more and more, his grin getting wider and wider, the colour returning to his cheeks, his eyes bright, and it's fun, so much fun.

We try every car several times over and by the time we test out the last one, the Aston that really is so him, he's quicker to get to it than me. Quicker around the track too.

'You know, this one does suit you,' I say as we climb out and I catch him eyeing it with what looks very much like longing.

'Is that so?'

I walk up to him and wrap my arms around his neck. 'Completely. Strong, full of muscle. Confident. And…' I run my teeth over my bottom lip '…*très sexy.*'

'Sexy?' He pockets his hands in the back of my jeans, urging me closer. 'Maybe I ought to buy one.'

'Ooh, is this a new kind of foreplay? Because if it is I'm all for it.' And then I kiss him, all the excitement of the day, the thrill of sharing it with him pouring into the kiss.

'Hey, Liv!' Harry shouts from across the stands. 'You won't believe what's just turned up!'

A phone starts vibrating between us. It's Valentine's mobile. He pulls back and slips it out of his jeans pocket as I look over at Harry.

'What is it?'

'The new Noble.'

'For real?'

'Yup.'

No way. This car isn't just new; it's still in concept territory.

'It's here for testing.'

'—don't worry, it's fine; I can talk.'

I tune into Valentine's conversation on the phone.

'You okay if I...?' I gesture to Harry and he nods. *Cool.*

'Coming, Harry.'

I blow Valentine a kiss and leg it to where Harry is grinning like it's some amazing prize. Which it is...it really is.

What a day!

Harry is letting me test drive a car that isn't even on sale yet.

And Valentine has transformed from quiet and reserved to vibrant, excited...a born-again daredevil even. The way he took those corners, the thrill in his face, he loved it every bit as much as me. The Valentine I met in my boardroom is merging with the Valentine of old and it makes me happy, so very happy.

Life really doesn't get any better than this...

Valentine

'Autumn Beckham has requested you personally. She won't speak to any of us, only you.'

I'm listening to my PA but my eyes are on Olivia.

I watch her happily skip away in her leather jacket, pale blue jeans and trainers. You'd think nothing could be sexier than how I've seen her previously, but like this, her hair in a loose ponytail, her outfit all relaxed, her face aglow…it has my body tightening even now, not to mention my heart that pulses, warm and very much alive.

'You there, Valentine? I think I've lost you, blasted mobiles…'

'No, no, I'm here. That's fine. Send me her number and I'll call her now.'

'Will do.'

I hang up and watch Olivia as she joins Harry and they walk over to the slip road that leads onto the track. She's in her element, and the truth is she's dragged me right out of the darkness and shown me the fun that can be had when you just let go again. Stop fearing the what-ifs.

And I'm all for it. Right now, I'm all for it.

Cars. Speed. Her. The works.

An engine roars in the distance and its bright orange form comes into view at the mouth of the slip road. I squint. Try to make it out. Its lines are familiar but not. I keep watching and my phone pings. The number for Autumn.

I lift it, eye the number, but find my attention drifting back to Olivia, as it seems to twenty-four-seven these days. Harry's taking over from the driver and Olivia's climbing in the passenger seat. My heart and body both lighten.

'Don't tell me you have a thing about women drivers?'

Do I? I don't think I do.

Yes, Layla was driving. But if I hadn't insisted we stay out later, if I hadn't distracted her with my antics…

My fist tightens around the phone and I swallow down the rising chill.

Let it go. Let it go and call Autumn back. Focus on work and when it's done, take Olivia home and show her just how much you've enjoyed today, be honest with her about how you feel.

I dial Autumn's number and deal with her call, her concerns, as readily as if I were a machine because I've done this so many times over. But getting to enjoy Olivia's zest for life is something so new and tantalising and I know I'm not going to be able to give her up when this job is over.

I want this to continue long past our working relationship. I want this to be official. No more blurring of lines. I want this woman to be mine and vice versa. Even now, as I talk details with Autumn, I'm planning tonight's conversation. I almost laugh. I haven't asked a girl out since I was in school. To be doing it now…

But then Olivia is fiercely independent. A point she has made to me several times over. I know it's a risk to play my hand, but what choice do I have? Say nothing and let this end with the job? Not an option. I'd rather regret telling her than walk away and always wonder.

I trace their progress on the track as I continue my conversation with Autumn. I watch as they pull into the pitstop, jumping out, a prancing Olivia racing around to the driver's seat.

She's in her element and I feel her joy across the field, feel it ease away all the stress from the morning, when I woke knowing the plans for the day and when I first laid eyes on the track and the speed at which people drive...

I speak to Autumn as I watch the car speed off, the engine rumbling through the ground beneath me, getting faster and faster. I can't even begin to guess at its speed, but it looks faster than Harry. I keep watching, every corner, every angle. Definitely faster than Harry. Definitely too fast. It's stupid.

What the hell is she trying to do? Prove a point? Show me that she's just as talented as a man again, if not more so...but seriously...?

And I get it. I get why she pushes herself so hard, stifled by the men that have come before me, but now she doesn't need to. Not for me. Not *with* me.

I start to walk towards the track as the back end of the car does a rapid wobble before righting again, but my heart is already in my mouth, my stride picking up as my vision blurs at the edges.

'Valentine—*Valentine*, are you there?'

'Yes. Yes, I'm here.' But what the hell is she doing? She's going too fast. Way too fast for that corner. She hits it and I watch as the back end slips out, but this time it doesn't recover and everything seems to slow right down—my breathing, the car, the dust building around it. Just like the night of the accident. The car spins and spins.

Fucking hell, Olivia.

I'm running, my mobile stuffed into my pocket as the car disappears amidst the cloud of dirt, the screeching tyres crippling me. It comes to a final stop, deathly quiet. No collision. No accident. But hell, it could have been, and my heart is racing, my eyes wide and unblinking as I race straight for her.

The doors open and she clambers out, laughing. She's *fucking* laughing.

'I'm so sorry, Harry!'

Fuck Harry, what about me?

'Are you okay?' My voice roars through the brake dust, overtaking her laughter, which quickly cuts.

'Of course I'm okay. I was always okay.'

My head is shaking, my body too as my mind torments me with the worst that could have happened.

I grip her upper arms. 'What the hell are you playing at?'

She looks up at me, her brows raised to the heavens. 'I beg your pardon.'

I squeeze my eyes shut, open them again. 'Can you quit playing devil's advocate with your life for just one second?'

'What on earth are you talking about? I lost control of the back end, that's all.'

I'm shaking so much my teeth are chattering and I grit them together, breathe through my nose.

'That's all? And what if you were out on the road with other drivers and you went and did the same?'

'I think you're missing the point of a track day, Valentine.' She looks to Harry, who is standing in the wings and I know his expression is one of *What the fuck?* But I don't care. All I care about is her. What if she really does have a death wish? What if those concerns truly are justified?

'I don't give a fuck about the track day, Olivia,' I say through gritted teeth. 'I give a fuck about you.'

She eyes me curiously. 'You do?'

'Yes.' It's so vehement, I'm sure she must get it. She must understand as deeply as I do that I've fallen in love with her. Watching that car spin out, feeling the old collide with the new, I know I love her.

'Then what the hell is your problem? Today's been fun. That last drive was fun.'

'That last drive?' I stare at her incredulously. 'The whole spinning out?'

'Hell, yes. Valentine, we're on a private track, only my car on the road. I was always safe.'

'Like you were in the Bugatti?'

She's shaking her head at me, her mouth slack. She can't defend her position, and neither can she convince me that this is okay.

'We're leaving. I'm taking you home.' I reach for her and she backs away. I hear my words coming back at me. *We're leaving. I'm taking you home.* It's how Nathan would have treated her. How her father would have. But it's not about that. It's about my past and the worst that can happen. It's about her safety, not about my control over her. I *have* no desire to control her. I only want to keep her safe.

'I'm not some child you can just cart off.'

'No, no, you're not, and that's not…that's not how I meant it.' *Fuck*. 'I'm sorry, I just… I panicked.'

Her eyes flicker as she frowns, her cheeks burning more. 'Fine. Let's go.'

She gives Harry a small smile. 'Thanks for today, I'll give you a call next week.'

'Sure. No probs, Liv.' He looks to me, his eyes narrowed, his smile grim. 'Good to meet you, Valentine.'

It's all I can do to nod before turning away and stalking across the stand to the car park out front. I don't turn to check she follows me. I trust that she will. She doesn't want to air any more of 'us' in public and neither do I.

It can wait until we're alone and I'm not shaking, I'm not reliving the past, I'm not brimming over with my impossible love for her…

CHAPTER FOURTEEN

Olivia

I'M SO PISSED off as I get in his car, pull the seatbelt across me and fold my arms. Stare straight ahead. I don't care if I look like a sulky teenager. He just embarrassed the hell out of me in front of Harry.

'You had no right to do that.'

He doesn't answer, only starts the engine and drives us out, his silence provoking my anger all the more.

'Did you hear me?'

His fists clench around the steering wheel and he refuses to look at me. 'I heard you.'

'Care to tell me what that was all about?'

'I told you.'

'You told me I was risking my life, which is ridiculous.'

'It's hardly ridiculous. Cars are a loaded weapon. All vehicles are in the wrong hands.'

I frown at him, my head shaking. 'Have you heard yourself? One minute you're telling me that caring for someone, *loving* someone even, doesn't give them the right to control them. The next minute, you're doing just that under the guise of giving a fuck!'

His fingers pulse around the steering wheel; there's no colour left in his face, but I can't let this go.

'You *ordered* me home, Valentine. In front of a friend, no less.'

Now he looks at me for less than a second, but it's enough to see the pain, the torment. 'I'm sorry.'

I watch his jaw pulse, his throat bob as he swallows. He looks worse than grey now. Even with his bronzed skin he looks like a ghost, his eyes too wide, his entire body tense. What the fuck is going on? This isn't just about me, this isn't about the Bugatti incident either; it goes deeper and—

Layla.

It comes to me like a slug to the stomach. The accident that killed his wife. I swallow as realisation dawns, my skin prickling up with goosebumps top to toe as I shiver. It's about her.

I want to kick myself for not working it out sooner. I should have searched the internet, pressed him for the details—anything but this.

'Is this…is this about Layla?'

His grip pulses around the wheel again, his lashes flutter as though I've struck him. I hate myself for doing this in the face of his pain, but I have to. I have to know. I have to understand.

'Yes. No.' He shakes his head. 'Yes.' Another pained swallow. 'We were in a car accident.'

His voice is hoarse with anguish and I have to suppress the urge to quit the questioning.

'Was she driving?'

He looks at me, the smallest shake of his head before he looks back to the road, the driver's side window, the road. 'She was—but it wasn't her fault.'

I'm silent, patient as I sense the rest coming.

'We were on the motorway. It was late. We'd been to a party. I was—I was drunk and fooling around, messing with the radio, teasing her…' He closes his eyes, opens them wide as he sucks in a breath. 'A lorry came across the central reservation—the driver had fallen asleep at the wheel. It all happened so fast—the motorway was empty, save for us. One second everything was fine and the next, the head-lights were straight ahead. She tried to avoid it, but at that speed…'

My stomach rolls, tears spiking as I reach out for him, my hand soft on his thigh. 'I'm so sorry.'

'If only we'd left earlier,' he carries on. I'm not even sure he's heard me. 'She was tired, she wanted to go but I—I was having too much fun and you know how the M40 can be. I figured the later we left, the less traffic there would be.'

'But it's not your fault.'

His silence speaks volumes. The guilt he still feels written in the lines that bracket his mouth and crease up his brow, the sorrow in his eyes. I think of my drive to Oxford, the same motorway. I think of his reaction, his belief that I have a death wish, that I was being reckless.

'You weren't to know,' I stress. 'Neither of you

were—it was an accident, a horrible, devastating accident.'

'It doesn't change the fact she'd still be here now if I hadn't kept us out so late.'

'You have to stop torturing yourself.' God, I wish he'd pull over. I wish I could take him in my arms and make him listen to me.

I pray my words are going in but he's so quiet, so still. I study the scar on his brow, see the scars that lie beneath the surface too, and my heart aches. I care about him too. I care too much.

I lift my fingertips to trace the bold line. 'Is that how you got this?'

He presses his lips together, bites down on them and I feel the shudder that runs through his broad frame.

'It's my daily reminder. That and my voice. Prolonged intubation can do that to you.'

I shake my head, press my palm to his cheek, my heart bleeding for what he went through and the pain he's still in. 'You need to put the past behind you. Life's too short to live it constrained by what happened. There was nothing you could do to prevent it, but you owe it to her to live your life fully again.'

His lashes flicker as the setting sun glistens in his gaze.

'You need to let go of the guilt and live your life again, Valentine.'

His laugh surprises me, the sudden brightness in his eyes too. 'Believe it or not, I'm starting to realise that. I'm not sure I can ever let go of the guilt, but the living again…' He turns to look at me, his eyes warm, his smile small. 'Thanks to you.'

My heart pulses in my chest, warmth radiating out from my core as I smile, my vision blurring with fresh tears. 'So, what you're saying is, I helped you just as much as you've helped me?'

His eyes are back on the road, but his smile grows. 'Yes, I guess I am.'

'Seems like we have quite the arrangement!'

He gives a soft laugh. 'Only I want more than just this arrangement, Olivia.'

He flicks me a look and I frown as a tiny flutter of panic erupts.

'What do you mean?'

'Isn't it obvious?'

'I…I don't know. I like what we have.'

'I like it too, a lot.'

I wet my lips, pull my hand away to grip my other in my lap. 'So why change things?'

He spies the move, his smile dying on his lips and he doesn't answer. We slip into an awkward silence punctuated by the windscreen wipers as rain begins to fall. I think back to the first day he came to my house in the torrential rain, and how different things were then. My chest aches as I realise the truth of it, that I want more too, but I can't. We can't.

He pulls up outside my place and as I turn to look at him I can't bear to say goodbye.

'Will you come in?'

'I think you should hear me out first.'

I grip my hands tighter in my lap and I want to tell him to stop but I can't find the words.

'Firstly, I'm sorry for how I spoke to you at the track. I have no desire to treat you like Nathan or your father. I would never, ever do that to you.'

'I know you wouldn't.'

'But—'

'*Please*, Valentine. We have a good thing going on. Let's not get all serious and…and ruin it.'

'It's too late for that. I already am serious about you.'

'But we're working together, we have the business—'

'And that's pretty much done and dusted. I have a few more suggestions to discuss with you and the board but I can wrap them up into a report and send it to Alan. You can take them or leave them, but our business relationship has no bearing on this now.'

I swallow down the lump wedging my throat shut. 'There might be other things you can advise on, other contracts…'

'It was never a contract in the first place; it was a favour to a friend, my mentor.'

'What?' I frown. 'What do you mean?'

'I told you Alan brought me in because of my past and he knew I would understand you.'

'But it was a job, a paid contract.'

'No. It wasn't. I didn't need money to help someone I thought was hurting.'

'You *thought* was hurting?' My frown deepens as his words sting. 'You make me sound heartless.'

'No, you're anything but that, Olivia.' His eyes soften into mine. 'If you were heartless this would be so much easier to walk away from.'

'But you don't need to walk away. Why can't we just carry on as we are? Now that I understand what happened I can be more sympathetic, I can—'

'Stop, Olivia. Just, stop. I don't want to change you. I'm trying to tell you that I'm in love with you. Just the way you are.'

I can't... He didn't... I can't be hearing him right.

'But I can't carry on like this...' He reaches for my hands, covers them with his own as his eyes search mine. 'I can't be around you without loving you. Without caring. And sometimes I'll worry, and I may overreact, and you'll have every right to bollock me for it.'

I open my mouth, close it again. *Oh, God.*

'But I...I love you. I love your zest for life, I love your spark, your intelligence, your heart.'

His words run over themselves in my head, my stomach rolls, and all the while my heart skips along like it's the best thing I've ever heard. When it's not. It can't be.

He gives a pained laugh. 'Is it really so horrifying to hear?'

'You can't love me.'

'I do.'

'But...but how? I don't get it. You hate how I live my life, the risks you believe I take.'

'None of that changes the way I feel about you.'

I remove a shaky hand from beneath his, rake it

through my hair, try to take a breath, clear my brain that's racing as fast as my pulse.

'But we would never work in a real relationship.'

'Why?'

'For the same reason you flipped out on the track! I want to live life a hundred miles an hour for as long as possible and you want to do the complete opposite. I can't live like that, not again.'

'No, and I understand that. I get it. I know why you push yourself so hard, but I also know that being loved for the person you are is the healthiest love of all. And I do love you for who you are. I don't want to change you. I want to learn to live again, with you.'

'But…but don't you see? I'm too old for you; you tie yourself to me and you will make the same sacrifices I did. You'll resent me.'

'Did you resent Nathan because he was older than you?'

I'm quiet for a beat. Two. 'No. I didn't. But…I would never want that for you.'

'Why?'

'Because I want you to start living your life again and tying yourself to me long-term won't help you do that.'

'You've done a pretty good job showing me how to live again so far.'

'Because we're fooling around, having fun. This was never a relationship. Not a serious one.'

'You may see it that way.'

'*You* should see it that way,' I throw at him, panic clambering up my throat as my feelings for him rise to the surface and terrify the hell out of me. 'If you want something serious, you should find someone your own age.'

'Now who's treating who like a child?'

I'm struck dumb. So many emotions at war inside that I can't see straight, let alone think.

'In case you haven't noticed, you don't get to choose who you fall in love with. I can't choose to stop loving you, just like I didn't choose to fall in love with you; it just happened.'

My heart pulses, my chest squeezing around it tight. 'Stop saying that.'

'What, that I love you?'

I close my ears to it, my eyes to him. 'You can get married, Valentine. Have children. Hell, you can produce enough offspring to make your own football team and I can't do that any more.'

'Now who's talking about making it serious? I'm talking about committing to this relationship. I'm not talking about marriage and kids.'

'But you will do, one day.'

'I don't know. Maybe.'

'But don't you see? That option doesn't exist with me.'

He shrugs. 'We could adopt, if it came to it, if we wanted children. There are always options.'

Tears fill my eyes anew, the future he paints so beautiful that for a split-second I lose myself in it. But it's a fantasy. Too good to be true. And I can't let that kind of hope in; I can't give him that hope either. We don't belong together. We're too different; the age gap is too much. And the longer we sit here debating it, the more it hurts.

'You're right; we can't do this any more.' I turn away, go to open the door and he reaches over to stop me, his hand gentle on my arm.

'Wait.'

I look back at him, his silent form, praying that he will release me and I can just leave, get in my house and cry until the pain of this leaves me.

'Tell me you don't have feelings for me too, and I'll let it go.'

My laugh is choked. 'You know I have feelings for you; it's because I care that I'm letting you go.'

'Don't you think I should be the one to decide that?'

'Please, Valentine, don't do this.'

'Tell me you don't love me.'

I drag in a breath, but I can't look him in the eye. 'I don't love you.'

Every syllable strikes like a physical blow to the chest. I can't love him. I can't.

I pull away from his hand and shove open the door, close it and walk away. I don't run. Running would tell him that this hurts. Running would betray my heart and belie my words.

Because I do love him.

I love him so much that I'm a quivering wreck inside, my fingers trembling as I locate my keys inside my handbag and unlock my door. I don't look back. I walk straight in and close the door behind me, breathe in the familiar scent of home, but it does nothing for me. Because it doesn't smell of him.

I hear his car pull away and sink back against my front door, my eyes squeezing shut as the tears roll down my face.

What have I done?
What have I done?
What have I done?

Valentine

I watch her go and wait for her to turn. Just one brief look and it would be enough to have me out of the car, kissing her quicker than she can refuse me again. But she doesn't.

In fact, more than that, her parting words were clear: *'I don't love you.'*

She's lying. I know she's lying. I feel it in my gut. She *has* to be.

But I won't beg. I've done enough trying to convince her. The ball's in her court and that's where it will stay.

As I drive away though, I can't ignore the crushing weight settling in my gut.

Freedom versus love.

I know which one I choose, but Olivia—wild, fun, carefree Olivia…

CHAPTER FIFTEEN

Olivia

VALENTINE KEEPS HIS WORD. He hands over to Alan and I don't see him again. It's been two weeks and not a word.

Not that I expected one. Not after all I said.

But, Christ, I miss him.

I can't focus. I can't find joy in anything. I've given up my hunt for a new car as speaking to Harry only reminds me of Valentine and our track day. The swing from fun, high-octane fun, to...to this. Emptiness. I feel as though there's a gaping hole inside that nothing can fill.

And as I stand before my sister's front door, a bottle of red in hand, and hear the chatter on the other side, the shouts from the children, even more shouts from Fee as she calls after them, a bittersweet smile lifts my lips. At least I'm not eating alone this afternoon, in my empty house that feels far too big and far too hollow with just me in it now.

The door swings open. 'What the hell are you

doing just standing there, Liv? Get in here and help me organise this rabble before I end up cremating the roast.'

My sister is already striding down the corridor back into the kitchen and I close the front door.

'Hey, Liv.' Pete, her husband, walks up to me and I hand him the bottle, kiss his cheek.

'Hi, Aunty Liv!' Billy, my four-year-old nephew, bounds up to me and grabs my leg for a hug before frowning up at his father. 'Daddy! Lucy keeps telling me to shut up.'

'Lucy, stop telling your brother to shut up!' he calls out towards the living room. 'And will you all come and say hi to your aunt Liv.'

'Hi, Aunt Liv!' comes the chorused reply, minus the bodies.

Pete gives me an apologetic grimace. 'You sure you want to eat in this mad house.'

I laugh as Billy races off again, his short blonde curls bobbing. 'Positive.'

'Can't say I'm not glad to see you. Fee's going out of her mind for some adult company. Apparently, I'm just not good enough.'

'You're plenty good enough, hubby darling,' comes her singsong retort from the kitchen. 'But I need words with my sly big sis.'

I frown at Pete and he simply shrugs. 'Damned if I know, but I'll sort you both drinks and get the kids setting the table. That ought to take her stressometer down a notch or two.'

'I heard that,' Fee calls over her shoulder as we

enter the kitchen. Steam fills the air as several pans bubble on the stove, and the smell is divine.

'You were meant to, my love.' Pete walks up to her, grips her by the hips and plants a kiss on her cheek. The gesture is so small but so sweet, and the pang in my chest returns. The same sensation I've had over and over these past two weeks, every time I see a couple holding hands, talking intimately over a dinner table, taking a walk…

'Gin and tonic, ladies?'

'Please,' we say in unison and he disappears into the dining room where the antique drinks cabinet from our old family home lives.

'Shall I open a window?' I say.

'That would be great, thanks.' I squeeze past Fee in the galley kitchen and reach over the counter to the latch on the window at the end.

'So, when were you going to tell me about Valentine Boretti?'

I almost slide down the window and faceplant on the countertop.

'What? How? What?' I turn to face her, my brows knitted together, and I know there's no colour left in my face. It's all sunk to the pit of my stomach, which is now twisted up into a tight ball.

'*Gossip Central* had a lovely little shot of you leaving a football match together a few weeks ago. I would have grilled you sooner, but you've been impossible to get hold of.' She's navigating the pots and pans but her focus is entirely on me and I'm struck still, my body awash with the pain of it, of what I've done and what a mistake I've made.

She turns away from the cooking, her eyes narrowing on me. 'Jesus, what's wrong, Liv? You look about to...'

Too late. The tears I've been fighting fall freely down my face and she's across the room in seconds, her arms around me.

'Here we go, ladies, two—*what?* What happened?'

Fee turns to Pete, my head tucked into her bosom. 'Shoo, no, leave those, then shoo.'

I hear the glasses hit the surface and the soft click of the door closing. I rise my head on a sob-cum-snort and she pulls me back into her chest.

'It's all right, honey. Whatever it is, just tell me.'

I shake my head, hiccupping as I struggle to speak, to control my voice long enough to get anything out.

'Bugger.' She quickly releases me. 'One second.'

She rushes around the kitchen, turning off the heat, pulling things out of the oven, a quick swoosh and then she's back and I'm wiping my face on my sleeve, trying to dry it even as the tears keep falling.

'I messed up, Fee.' I suck in a shaky breath. 'He told me he loved me and I...I basically told him he was ridiculous, that the idea of an *us* was ridiculous.'

'Wait. You need to back up a bit. Start from the top. Who is he to you?'

I tell her everything—how we met, minus the club detail, the boardroom visit, the fantastic strides we've made with the charity thanks to him, the people he introduced me to, the football, the week that followed and…the track day…the argument.

'So, let me get this straight…' she squints at me '…you told him that he shouldn't live his life constrained by what happened to his wife, and by what-ifs over the future, but you did the exact same thing to him.'

'I didn't.' I shake my head at her and she walks away to take up the drinks that Pete left.

'I didn't.' I repeat into her silence, only it's much weaker.

She comes back to me and passes me my drink, takes a sip of her own as she eyes me with compassion and a look that says, *You bloody did, you bloody idiot.*

'Don't look at me like that.'

'Like what?' she says over the rim of her glass.

'Like I'm an idiot.'

'You have to admit, you are a bit of an idiot. Don't you think it makes you a hypocrite?'

'A what?'

'You pushed him away because of your past, because of what you went through. *You're* letting your past dictate your future. Just as you accused him of doing.'

My gin catches in my throat. 'I— *No…*'

'Yes! And he told you he loves you, just the way you are. *Actually loves you.*' Her brows lift to the ceiling as she throws back a gulp of gin, swallows it audibly. 'And my God, sis, is he hot.'

'He's also twenty years younger than me.'

She frowns. 'I'm sure he's not.'

'Okay, sixteen, but it's just as bad.'

'It's less than the gap between you and Nathan.'

'I've done that argument to death already with myself, with him. I don't need to go over it again.'

She studies me quietly for several moments and then she places her glass down on the side, takes my hand.

'Look, Liv, I love you and heaven knows you've worried me silly this past year, but part of you had a point.'

'Part of me? How generous of you.'

She ignores my gibe as she squeezes my hand. 'Look, I know you and Nathan loved each other, but surely you must see how he changed you, how you changed yourself being with him. It wasn't healthy. You spent years trying to get Dad's approval, another two decades hanging off Nathan's. And now you have a guy telling you he loves you just the way you are…'

'*And?* What does that have to do with me having a point?'

'Correction. *Had* a point. Because it seems to me you've lost your way again. You were all about living each day to the full after Nathan passed, living for the now and making the most of the time you have.'

'And that's what I'm doing…or at least trying to.'

'No, you're not. Right now, you're cutting your nose off to spite your face, because you think some time in the future he's going to regret this, that he'll commit to you and twenty years down the line wish he'd run a mile.'

'Christ, I'll be sixty-five and he'll be forty-nine.'

'*And?* Is that really so shocking? Have you forgotten that there's fourteen years between Pete and me?'

Her words dance over my heart, a lightness lifting inside.

'Don't you think he has a right to decide on what future he wants for himself and if he wants you in it?' She cups my cheek, her eyes searching mine. 'Don't you owe it to him—*Christ*, don't you owe it to yourself to give this relationship a shot and let the future land how it may?'

'God, Fee, when did you get to be so wise?'

'Hey, I've popped out four kids, and I think they take a few brain cells with them each and every time.'

I place my glass on the side next to hers and pull her to me, squeeze her tight. 'Thank you, sis, thank you.'

'Does this mean you're actually going to listen to me for a change?'

'Yes! Yes, I am.'

'Bloody hell, look at that!'

She yanks me away from her and points to the sky through the window.

'What?'

'You missed it! There was a giant pink pig flying through the air.'

'Shut up, Fee!' But I laugh, hard, delirious almost, and it's overtaken by a child's gasp.

Billy's head is poking through a fresh gap in the doorway, his mouth agape, his blue eyes dancing.

'Daddy, Daddy…' he's already racing off '…Aunty Liv told Mum to shut up!'

Fee throws her hands in the air. '*God*, what I'd give for some privacy in this house!'

'You love it really,' I say.

She looks at me, her cheeks flushed pink, her eyes bright. 'Wouldn't change it for the world, sis. Now, you need to go and get your man.'

'It's waited two weeks; it can wait a night at least.'

'You sure about that?'

'No. Not really.'

'Go. There'll be more Sunday dinners, but something tells me there's only one Valentine Boretti.'

My smile trembles on my lips as my eyes well up again. 'Thank you, sis.'

'Any time.'

I hug her again, then head for the door. 'Sorry, Pete, kids, Aunty Liv is on a mission, but I'll see you again very soon.'

And I'm out through the door, racing to my car and to his place at a speed he would approve of, even if every second feels like an eternity. I'm desperate, so very desperate to tell him how I feel. To tell him how sorry I am that I lied. To tell him everything.

So desperate that it takes me several attempts to get my words out straight when I arrive at his apartment building and need to ask the security guard for access to the underground car park. The very same security guard that likely witnessed our extracurricular activity the other night—*oh, God, that really doesn't help.*

'I'm sorry, say that again. Who are you here to see?'

Okay, so if he did witness it, he isn't making any show of it.

I take a calming breath. 'Valentine Boretti.'

He nods. 'I think Mr Boretti is away at the moment. Let me just check for you.'

My fingers dance over the steering wheel, my entire body doing a crazy little jig in the driver's seat.

Please be home, please be home, please—

'I'm afraid there's no answer. I think he's been away a few days now.'

'Dammit!' I slap the steering wheel, startling the guard, and quickly throw him an apologetic smile. 'Any idea where he might be?'

He shakes his head, his smile sympathetic. 'I'm afraid we're not privy to that information. You could try calling him?'

'Yes, of course.'

I hardly want this conversation over the phone though and after how I treated him…there's no guarantee he'll even answer. No. I have to see him. Face to face.

I reverse back out of the entrance and think. There must be some way of finding out where he is…

Someone who will know…or at least be able to find out…

Valentine

When I decided to come to Paris and deal with Autumn Beckham directly rather than having one of my employees do it, I foolishly used it as a reason to escape London and the tempting proximity of Olivia.

It was pretty clear after Alan received my report that Olivia wasn't about to chase me down and tell me she was wrong, and I've had to accept it.

Only I haven't.

When I received a call from her office just yesterday, I had the foolish thought it would be her. The common sense telling me that she would use her mobile to call non-existent.

And I can't stop thinking about her. It's like having a fire lit inside and not being able to snuff it out, but without its instigator it continues to flare, unabating, and hell, I'm confused. Not just confused. I feel like a part of me is missing.

It's similar to losing Layla, only then I was so tormented by guilt, grief; you name it I felt it. But with Olivia…I don't know. How is it possible to feel so much for someone and have them deny it? Have them feel the opposite almost?

Damned if I know, but I was wrong, and I do have to accept it because I can't function like this. Going through life on autopilot when she's shown me what it feels like to truly live again. To actually love again.

'Thanks so much for joining me today, Valentine.'

I turn away from Autumn's balcony and the sun going down on the Eiffel Tower, the warming hues of the picture-perfect sunset doing nothing for me.

'You're welcome.' I smile to mask my thoughts and she returns it, combing her hands through her smooth black hair, shaking it out.

'I know I'm not the easiest to deal with at times—no, you can say it, it's fine.'

I merely nod.

'But having you with me, protecting my back so to speak, I appreciate it.'

'All part of the service.'

'I guess, but how about I take you to dinner, an extra thank you? I'm ravenous and you must be after that poor excuse for a lunch. I swear they think if they put out too much of a feast, us supermodels will get fat just from looking.'

I chuckle. 'It's fine, honestly.'

She pouts at me, and I recognise the little glint in her eye that's offering more than dinner. And as much as she appeals—she's funny, interesting, nowhere near the celebrity bitch the media currently have her pegged as—I can't do it.

Not when I know my mind will be elsewhere, on someone else.

'You sure I can't tempt you?' She toys with the neckline of her sheer white blouse and I shake my head.

'I'm going to call it a night. I have a few things to deal with.'

I don't, but she doesn't need to know the truth.

'Fair enough.'

She leads me to the door. 'If you change your mind, you know where I am.'

She reaches out for my arm, leans in to give me a brief peck on the cheek, her eyes searching mine for the come-on that's not there.

'Have a good night, Autumn.'

'You too, Valentine.'

I sense her eyes on me as I walk to the lift, call it and step inside. When I turn, her door is closing and I breathe a sigh of relief. To be alone. Free to be as miserable as I feel.

Though as the doors open on my floor, I contemplate turning back and going for a walk—the idea of being in my empty suite appeals even less than dinner with Autumn—but I can hear the phone ringing from inside. Strange. It's late.

Would Autumn really be so desperate to do dinner that she'd call me and ask again? Unlikely.

I let myself in just as it cuts off and I accept that they'll call back if it's important. I go to the mini-bar and pour a whisky just as it starts to ring again. I reach out for the receiver, raise it to my ear.

'*Bonsoir?*'

'*Bonsoir*, Monsieur Boretti, it is Victor from Reception. There is a lady here to see you.'

'A lady?'

'*Oui, monsieur.* Madame Olivia Carmel.'

I turn back towards my door as though I can see through it, all the way down the grand staircase to the even grander reception desk. He cannot be serious.

'*Monsieur?* Are you there?'

'I'm here.' I swallow. I can't believe it. I don't want to. To believe it would let in hope.

'Shall I send her up?'

'*Oui...merci.*'

'Very well, *monsieur.*'

The phone cuts off and I stand there, the receiver in one hand, whisky in the other, stunned still. There's only one reason she would be here... one reason alone.

But after a fortnight of nothing, would she really fly to Paris to see me? Or is it more that she's in town on business, found out I was here too, and is bored?

I stride for the door, open it and wait.

Finally, the lift doors open and there she is, breathtakingly beautiful in a pale pink sweater, jeans and trainers. No coat. She looks like she's run all the way here. Her hair has come loose from its ponytail, clinging to her flushed cheeks, her eyes overbright and glistening in the lights from the lift. But she doesn't move, doesn't react.

The lift doors start to close and she leaps forward to stop them, the sudden animation waking me up.

'What do you want, Olivia?'

It's all I can say. I don't want to let hope in, not again...

She walks towards me, her eyes wary, her hands wringing in front of her. She has no bag, nothing to suggest she's travelled here from another hotel. She wets her lips, her nervous aura not unlike that very first night I saw her in the club. And how things have changed since then...

'Can I come in, please?' She pauses before me, so close I can smell her familiar perfume and it clutches around my heart, wounds as much as warms.

Silently, I step aside.

She walks around me, her eyes lost in the view beyond the glass. 'Wow, you must have the best room in the hotel. Mine's pretty nice, but this view…'

She gestures to my private garden terrace and the Eiffel Tower beyond, all lit up in gold. But it doesn't matter how spectacular the landmark is, she's the one I'm wrapped up in, starved of her for a fortnight. I'm hungrily taking in every detail even when I shouldn't.

'Can I get you a drink?'

I raise my whisky and she eyes it with a frown.

'You drink now?'

My lips twitch at the corners as I take a swig. 'Don't worry; it's not all down to you. Though you did teach me not to be ruled by my fears any more, so maybe it is.'

Her eyes stay fixed on the drink and I see her throat move as she swallows. 'I'm good, thank you.'

'Suit yourself.'

I walk to the balcony doors, slide them open and step out, a sudden need for air that isn't tainted with her scent driving me there.

'Valentine?'

I don't turn. I can't. 'Yes.'

'I'm sorry.'

'You came all the way to Paris to tell me you're sorry?' I lift the glass to my lips, take a small sip this time as I watch the tower twinkle in the distance, the traffic below, the people. Anything but her.

'Not just that.'

I hear her trainer-clad feet against the hard floor

contending with the bustle of the Parisian streets below. 'You're here on business too, how coincidental.'

'No. I'm not here on business. I came for you.'

My pulse skips a beat, my fingers clenching around the glass as hope flutters to life inside. *It doesn't mean she loves you though. A trip to Paris is a drop in the ocean for someone as wealthy as her, money she'd willingly spend to enjoy the kind of sex we once did.*

I shake my head. Still don't turn. 'I'm sure there are many men out there willing to treat you how you so desire in the bedroom, Olivia. You don't need me for that.'

'Do you really think that's why I'm here, Valentine? For sex?'

I turn away from the view to face her, my eyes clashing with hers. 'Why else would you be here? You made it quite clear you don't love me, so tell me, Olivia, what else could you possibly want?'

Her eyes and lips tremble as she holds my gaze. 'I want to tell you face to face that I was wrong, that I lied to you…'

She walks towards me and I step back. I can't bear her being any closer without crumbling and I see the hurt that flares in her eyes at the move, feel the sight of it crushing my resolve.

'Valentine, I'm here to tell you that I love you. I loved you when I told you I didn't. I love you more than I've ever known it possible to love someone.'

The words echo through my skull, beat at my heart. Insistent. Incessant.

'Please, *please* tell me you can forgive me.' Her voice is soft with her plea, strong with her desperation. 'Tell me that you'll give me another chance, give us another chance.'

'How do I know you won't wake up tomorrow and change your mind?'

'Tomorrow I want to wake up in your bed, in your arms, and the next and the next, for as long as you'll have me. I pushed you away because I was scared. I was the one stuck in the past, fearing the what-ifs, of regrets that you may have down the line. I was being a hypocrite.'

I shake my head, the lightness spreading inside. 'Olivia Carmel, are you telling me you were wrong?'

Her lips quirk into the first hint of a smile. 'Don't let it go to your head.'

My eyes narrow. I take in all that's vibrant about her and see the love that shines so clearly in her face and I know she means it. Every word. 'What changed your mind?'

'I did. With a little help from my sister, Fee, and a dollop of encouragement from Alan. He was the one who found out where you were and reported back to me.'

'The lying devil; that was why he called. It had nothing to do with missing contact information for Louis and Adele.'

She gives me a sheepish smile.

'Olivia?'

'Yes?'

'Tell me again.'

Her smile grows, her eyes sparkle. 'I love you.'

'Again.'

She steps towards me, takes the whisky from my hand and places it on a side table. 'I love you.'

'Once more for good measure.'

Her chest brushes up against me. 'I…' she rests her palms on my shoulders '…love…' she brushes her lips against mine, her lashes fluttering closed '…you.'

Her eyes flick open. 'Sir.'

My chest expands with so much love, so much warmth, and I clutch her to me, swing her in the air. 'I should punish you for taking so long to realise it, Kitten.'

'Punish me all you like, because it won't change a thing. I am one hundred per cent besotted, head over heels in love with you, Boretti, and if you don't take me to bed right now and make good on that promise, it'll be you taking a spanking.'

My laugh fills the space, hers too. 'You're on.'

EPILOGUE

One year later
Olivia

'YOU READY?' Valentine is on my doorstep, looking model-worthy in his black sweater and jeans, his grin as excited as I feel.

'Sure am.'

He turns his head a little, eyes me sceptically. 'And you packed light?'

'Of course. I do listen to you, you know.'

'There was a time you didn't.'

I laugh. 'That's nonsense and you know it.' I step aside and show him my very modest suitcase, all packed and ready to go.

He picks it up, tests its weight with a downward smile. Impressed. 'Best get a move on; the ferry won't hang about for us.'

'Lead the way.'

The Miura is gleaming in the sunlight, ready for its very first supercar tour across Europe. 'And you're absolutely positive your father doesn't mind us going?'

'I've already told you, he'll come with us later in the year when a friend of his can join us. To be honest, he's just happy we're taking her out at all.'

He throws my tiny bag in the boot and we climb in. 'We just have to make a pit stop on route.'

'Really?' I strap myself in, watch him get in beside me. 'Why?'

'You'll see.'

'You have me intrigued.'

He simply grins, covers his dancing blues with his sunglasses and starts the engine.

'Is that really all I'm getting?'

'Yup.'

As if to illustrate his point he turns the radio on and pulls out into the traffic. I smile and shake my head, pull my own sunglasses out of my handbag and slip them on before cosying down into the seat. It's surprisingly comfortable, even with the engine vibrating through the cabin.

'You are going to let me drive at some point, aren't you?'

'Play your cards right and I will.'

'You say that a lot.'

'Because it always brings me good things.'

I laugh. 'You're insatiable.'

'You complaining, Little Kitten?'

'Hell, no.' I smooth my hand over his thigh and give it a squeeze. 'Never.'

We slip into an easy conversation, me filling him in on the latest antics of my nieces and nephews and him telling me about his parents. He also tells me about a football day he's got planned with Pete, the two of them having become firm friends over the last year. And I'm so engrossed in our talk that I don't realise where we are until a low-flying plane rattles the windows of the car.

'What the—?' I frown as I watch it land on a runway beside us. We're on a private airfield, one I've never been to before. 'What are we doing here?'

I turn to him and that grin is back on his face.

'Valentine?'

He cuts the engine. 'Come on, they're waiting for us.'

'Who's waiting?'

He doesn't answer. Just slips off his sunglasses and steps out, walks around to my door and opens it for me, offering out his hand. I take it, my head shaking, a frown still tugging at my brow.

I scan the airfield, the hangar, the people milling about with equipment and what looks an awful lot like parachutes, and my stomach gives a little flip.

'Valentine, what are we doing here?'

He turns into me, pulls me up against him. 'We, my love, are taking a leap together.'

'A leap?'

He nods and presses a kiss to the tip of my nose. 'I want to prove to you I'm ready to live again.'

'You've done plenty of that already; you don't need—'

'Shh.' He kisses me quiet, his lips turning up into a smile as he looks into my eyes. 'No more half-lives…for either of us. I want us to live it to the max.'

'By jumping out of a plane?' I say, feeling my pulse skitter nervously, my stomach doing another flip. 'You do remember that I'm scared of extreme heights?'

He chuckles. 'It's as good a time as any to face that fear.'

I shake my head. 'Why is it I feel like I could take on the world so long as you're by my side?'

'The feeling's mutual.' He strokes my hair back from my face, raises my sunglasses on my head and the look in his eyes steals my breath away. 'Which is why the jump isn't the only leap of faith I'm proposing.'

'No?'

He presses a sweet kiss to my lips just as another aircraft zips past, whipping my hair up and around us.

'No…' He lowers himself to one knee as his hand lifts and in his upturned palm is an open box with a beautiful solitaire diamond at its heart.

'Valentine?' It comes out as a whisper. He can't be. He can't.

'Olivia Carmel, I love you, I will always love you, and I want to live my life to the full with you by my side. Will you marry me?'

A sob chokes up my throat. I try to breathe, press my hand to my chest as my eyes well. 'Yes, Valentine! Oh, yes!'

I drop to my knees, uncaring of my white jeans as I grip his face in my hands and kiss him. Once. Twice.

'But, baby…' I break away, stare up into his eyes that I have come to adore so much '…there's no way I'm jumping out of a plane.'

'Wanna bet?'

* * * * *

FAST LANE

MARGOT RADCLIFFE

MILLS & BOON

To Maura and Randa.

For being the kind of people who never thought twice
about absconding with piles of Harlequin novels
from the library.

CHAPTER ONE

"BLAIR!" NATE CALLED. Blair Sandoval froze as her brother strode through the wrought-iron screen door of their family's winery tasting room clearly on a mission.

She quickly shoved the plate of artisanal cheese and imported crackers she'd liberated from the stash reserved for wine pairings (in an admittedly weak attempt to hide the fact that she'd been about to sneak off with it) behind her back so he wouldn't see it. Yes, the lunch she'd forgotten was sitting in her fridge at home, which was only a five-minute drive down the vineyard road, but Blair had priorities. One of which was to eat free cheese. That said, she'd perhaps taken a bit more cheese than was appropriate or wise, but honestly, was there such a thing as too much cheese?

Unfortunately, the overexcited smile on her brother's face coupled with the notable addition of the tall, dark-haired man beside him did not bode well for her previous plan of a lunch hour watching leaky faucet how-to videos (hers had kept her up until three in the morning) and eating roughly four times the amount of the daily recommendation of dairy. No, her brother had clearly brought her work that would obviously include that dreaded faction of humanity known as "other people." Yes, he was about to make her give the harrowing vineyard tour, which was very far down on her list of job duties as the vineyard's part owner and viticulturist.

Giving the tour was usually reserved for one of their highly decorated wine educators who excelled at public speaking, but when it was a VVIP (Vineyard Very Important Person, Nate's words) he always made her do it since she knew everything about the vineyard and was the celebrated name people associated with Sandoval Wines. Her brother, who ran the marketing side of the business (hence Blair's current torture), wasn't much for the finer scientific details of what was essentially fancy farming. People romanticized wine and the Sonoma and Napa Valleys, and with good reason since there wasn't a day she didn't love waking up and seeing her vineyard and watching people dressed in their best taste and love her wine, but when one got right down to it grape growing was just as much of an earthy and dirty business as any farm.

"Is that more cheese?" Nate barked with an annoying brotherly eye roll. "Mom would bring lunch down here for you if you asked, you know. I don't know why you always insist on eating our pairing stock."

Blair shrugged. "You know why I don't want

Mom coming down here. We're on a break at the moment." Then she glared at Nate in warning to convey that he should be quiet. A couple of months ago, Blair's world had been torn up in little itty bitty shameful pieces when she'd learned the man she'd been dating, the man she'd all but envisioned a future with, was *married*. The guilt and pit of awfulness that surrounded her now that she'd hurt another woman and her marriage was devastating. That she, Blair, who *always* followed the rules had been made to be the *other woman*. It reactivated the perpetual nausea she'd been nursing since the moment she'd found out, such that she almost reconsidered the coveted cheese. But that had been just one of the many debilitating side effects of a breakup that still had her questioning everything she'd ever done and every man she met.

So for right now while her mom was still unreachably deep in her *own* feelings about Blair's ex (as if Blair wasn't), Blair was just going to not talk about it with her anymore. The woman could not look at Blair without being reminded of her ex and what he had done to her daughter. In essence, that just made Blair feel worse, and some days lately she barely made it out of bed, let alone look herself in the mirror without feeling like a person scraped off the bottom of someone's shoe. She didn't need her mom making it worse.

She hadn't even found out from the man either. It had been her ex's wife who'd come to see Blair at a wine-making talk she was giving in Napa Valley, pleading with her to end the affair she hadn't known she was having. Her apologies hadn't been enough, obviously, but the least Blair could do was stop communicating with her husband, which she had immediately. However, she was still too sick with guilt to feel the same rage the situation inspired in her mother, so Blair was taking a step back from the family for a minute. Which wasn't exactly easy since her entire family lived on the vineyard's land, which was essentially a Sandoval compound with their respective houses only a mile or so apart from each other, but she'd been trying her best. She needed the space to heal on her own and put back the pieces of herself that had been completely obliterated by the hurt she'd caused someone else and her ex's perfidious betrayal.

Her brother turned to the man beside him who had a wide mouth, bracketed by smile lines. He looked like someone who'd had an easy, charmed life in the sun. He reminded Blair of a professional golfer, clean-cut, lean and sports chic.

"This is my sister, Blair," Nate said, introducing her. "She's complicated and a thief, but we love her anyway." A corner of the man's mouth quirked as he followed Nate's gaze to her. It gave her permission to look at him more, not that she cared what he looked like because relationships were no longer in her future. She was closer to joining a nunnery than dating again at the moment. But dressed in a mint-green golf polo and khaki shorts, a pair of black reflective sunglasses tucked into the V at his neck, she had to admit that he was attractive in that kind of bro-sports way. In his thirties, though probably a little older than her, he was tanned dark bronze that spoke of extended time spent outdoors, and the defined muscles of his thick arms were dusted with dark hair.

"Good afternoon, Blair. It's a pleasure to meet you," the man said, a thick Southern accent flowing out of his mouth like warm maple syrup. "And don't worry, I'm what you'd call labyrinthine myself, so by comparison a little complicated is practically a breath of fresh air."

Blair met his green eyes then, made even more vibrant by his matching shirt color, and smiled at him against her will because he was charming. It was a bad idea because she'd fallen for charming before and look how that had ended. But how could she not when he'd gone out of his way to defend her against her bossy older brother? He couldn't know it, but they were basically friends for life now.

So with an inner sigh of defeat, Blair set her cheese plate down on the counter of the bar that spanned nearly the length of the vineyard's currently empty tasting room. The sound of the ceramic dish hitting the solid granite was amplified in the room with its cathedral ceiling and wood floors.

"This is Cole Taggart, he was hoping for a tour," Nate informed. "He's been over at the track calling the race and I told him we'd love to give him a tasting and a look at our vines and warehouse." Nate said the words meaningfully, giving her a look as if she was supposed to have some idea of who this man was, but she had literally no clue. She knew some big racing names just by virtue of being as close to the famous Sonoma Valley Raceway as they were, but she wasn't much for driving fast, competing at things or watching people drive repeatedly around in a circle, so racing wasn't a big slice on her pie chart of subjects she was knowledgeable about.

"I'd be happy to do both of those things," she chirped, giving her brother her biggest fake smile. "As it happens, I already have the cheese ready so we won't even have to wait to get started on the tasting and pairing."

Cole himself laughed then, eyes crinkling. "Now, I don't want to put y'all out. Nate told me you were closed today but I didn't know that until after I'd already made my way out here so I'm happy to go ahead and schedule a tour during regular business hours."

Nate was already reassuring him that it was fine, but it was Blair who needed to fix this. She trusted Nate to know who she needed to entertain even if she herself didn't know. Though not a people person, keeping up the vineyard's reputation was her number one concern. She loved this land, the grapes, the people and would do anything to ensure her family's legacy. Occasional cheese pilfering aside, the vineyard was her life and she'd been the one to bring it into the future. She loved her father and grandfather, but they'd been happy owning a local vineyard. It wasn't until she came of age that the vineyard had gone to the next level to receive international acclaim.

"Mr. Taggart." Blair grinned, pulling out a bottle of their pricier wines, absolutely loving it when Nate started shaking his head. "I have in my hand a bottle so rare and special that Nate there is about to cry it's so good. I've been saving it for just the right occasion and based on your previous vocabulary, you seem like the kind of man who would appreciate indulgence. Do I have that right about you?"

A corner of his mouth kicked up, his eyes twinkling, and she was thankful he had a sense of humor. It was shocking how many people came in who didn't, as if wine made people think they had to act snooty. Maybe this afternoon wouldn't be a total wash after all. At the very least, she'd already pissed Nate off by giving Cole wine with a price tag over six thousand dollars a bottle. Definitely a day well spent.

"You have that exactly right about me, Ms. Sandoval," he drawled, then glanced down to her left hand. "Or is it missus? We in the South like to be correct in our honorifics, you know."

"I'm not married," she told him and felt Nate's eyes on her, burning into her skin with warning.

"Well," Nate finally said, backing up, "I'll leave you both to it."

"Thank you very much, Nate, and I'll catch you tomorrow on the golf course?"

Nate gave Cole a salute. "Looking forward to it." Then once he was at the door and Cole's attention was on the bottle of wine she'd opened, Nate waved a hand between her and Cole before drawing a finger across his throat indicating for her not to screw things up by getting involved with him. Blair just rolled her eyes. As if randomly hooking up with a customer was a thing she did ever. Couldn't a girl annoy her brother by giving away an obscenely expensive bottle of wine to a customer without arousing suspicion anymore?

She smiled up at Cole before setting the bottle aside. "We'll save that one for last," she told him in a hushed conspiratorial tone. "Full disclosure, most people opt to do the tour first. The tasting tends to get people a little too tipsy to traipse around the hilly vineyard afterward."

Cole grinned. "That sounds perfect," he said, leaning onto the bar. "But what I'd really like is for you to continue eating your lunch, Ms. Sandoval, like you were before I barged in here with your brother and interrupted you."

Blair was known to push the bounds of professionalism sometimes but there was no way she was going to eat lunch in front of a guest. "How about we take the tour first and I'll eat with you during the tasting?"

"Well, I don't love it because I know personally my hanger is epic, but I'm not gonna force a lady to do what she doesn't want to, so lead on to the vineyard Ms. Sandoval," he said with a tip of his head and a quirk of his lips.

"I appreciate your concern for my hanger, but I'm more of a stewing in anger type anyway, so I prom-

ise not to take anything out on you if I reach a critical hunger level."

"I won't hold you to that promise," he told her.
"And I like a mouthy woman anyhow, so I suppose
the hungrier you get the happier I'll be."

His words stopped her as they made their way to
the front door to lead him outside to the vines. "A
mouthy woman?" she repeated with a hard question
mark attached. "With all due respect, Mr. Taggart,
that sounds a little like pandering."

Cole laughed then, a deep, rich sound that resulted
in a pang of *something unwanted* in her stomach.
Something suspiciously like butterflies instead of
the petrified chrysalises that had been there previously and that she preferred.

"I'll admit that I find it a little easier to get by in
life when the woman I'm with is agreeable, but I'm
not a liar either, Ms. Sandoval." Then he paused for
a moment, as if considering whether or not saying
his next words would be wise. "But if I may say, a
different, nonmouthy, kind of woman wouldn't have
pointed out the pandering at all."

Blair struggled not to smile, having clearly been
outed as an outspoken person herself, and made her
way to the door. He beat her there, however, holding
it open for her with a knowing grin on his face. Stepping out into the bright afternoon sun, Blair waited
for him to join her before locking the door behind
her. "You're much cleverer than you look—you know
that, right?" Blair told him with her own cheeky grin.
Then immediately quit it because she was not flirt-

ing with men anymore. That was dangerous territory into which she was no longer venturing.

Cole laughed again. "Well, now, you're not the first to say so."

Giving him a small smile that was not at all flirtatious, she hopped into a golf cart with the intention of taking him to the farthest part of the vineyard first and then making their way back to the tasting room, which was the public-facing part of the operation.

Instead of taking one of the back seats like most people on the tours, Cole sat right beside her in the front seat, his massively wide and tall body taking up nearly the entire seat so she had to scoot right to the edge where the metal bar dug into her side.

"So you're a sports announcer?" she asked, initiating the obligatory small talk as she rode north of the tasting room. She had a practiced script she'd use once they reached the actual vines, but for now she could get to know Mr. Takes Up Entire Seat a little better.

"Yep, racing mostly," he said. "I announce for an American station, but I do the Formula One racing circuit all over the world. This is my first time back to the States in a couple of months."

"That sounds exciting," Blair said, even though she wasn't much of a traveler. When she'd been learning about wine she'd traveled extensively, but since she was more of a homebody it wasn't her comfort zone.

Cole just shrugged. "It can be," he said, but didn't

sound as excited about it as she might suspect someone to be with such a noteworthy job.

Blair glanced over at him, but his expression
didn't give much away and seemed focused on their
surroundings, which she couldn't blame him for.
The vineyard was beautiful if she did say so herself;
the mountains peppered with towering pine trees,
the trodden dirt paths that ran parallel to the bright
green vine rows, the cement walkway they were on
now that wound around it all like a meandering river
and the bright sun gilding it all in gold—it all felt
like someone's dream of a vineyard come to life. In
the evenings, her favorite thing to do was sit on her
porch, which overlooked the entire farm, and drink
her family's wine. It was simple, perfect and never
got boring for her.

"But you're not from here, obviously."

"Louisiana, born and bred," he grinned proudly.
"Not the bayou, mind, but Baton Rouge."

"I've only ever been to New Orleans, but to be
honest I don't remember much of it."

Cole chuckled again. "That's a pretty common
state of affairs in that town. Baton Rouge isn't as exciting, but it's certainly home. I take it you've grown
up a California girl?"

"That's me." Blair nodded, glancing at him
quickly before turning off the main trail onto another, smaller one that led to their white grape varietals. "So if you're an announcer, that means this
isn't your first time to Sonoma County?"

He shook his head. "Nah, I've been here dozens

of times. I come out to announce the Sonoma Speed
Festival at least once a year and it's turned into one
of my favorite places on my tour."

"And you're interested in starting your own winery?" she asked, steering them to why he'd come to
Sandoval Vineyard.

"I bought a house back in Baton Rouge, so I want
to invest in one around there and need to make sure I
know what the hell I'm putting my money into. Y'all
have quite a reputation wherever I go, so I thought
it would be a good place to start. Plus, I promised
my sister I'd bring back her favorite wine. She's ob-
sessed with your chardonnay."

Blair nodded, pleased. "I'm happy to hear that. I'll
give you some bottles of what I think of as our best
year when we get back to the tasting room."

Cole shifted in his seat to face her and his knee
bumped the side of her thigh and stayed there, burning a hole in her jeans. She hated that she didn't hate
it, that she, a person who didn't deserve to derive
any pleasure from another man ever, was, in fact
receiving it.

"Now, see there, that's what I want to know, what
makes one year better than another and all that. I
know what I like, I know what people tell me is good,
but I want to know that my vineyard can produce a
product that's reliable year after year."

"You're certainly in the right place," Blair said,
her fingers tingling with the prospect of talking
about the process. This was her wheelhouse and she
could talk a person's ear off about what it took to

keep grapes healthy, soil science, weather management, the works. "And I'm happy to answer anything you'd like. But while there are a lot of factors in the differences in wine from year to year, the largest one is simply weather. If it's cooler with low sun, grapes are slower to grow, which is good for some grapes but not as good for others like cabernet, which needs more heat to ripen fully. That's why our cabernet sauvignon grapes are planted where there is full sunlight as opposed to sauvignon blanc, which you want to ripen slowly to retain a more refreshing taste."

A lot of people would be bored by just that small amount of grape information, but she saw that Cole was making notes on his phone. "This is great. Do you know what kind of grapes grow best in Louisiana?"

Blair looked at him. "I'd say the climate in Louisiana is too hot and humid for a profitable winery based on wine grapes and that anyone who told you otherwise is either a liar or a not very well-researched person."

Cole looked at her doubtfully. "Well, now, I've been to wineries there before so I know they have to be growing something."

Blair shrugged. "My guess would be they were fruit wines or made from grapes like muscadines or something. I'm not saying it's impossible, but the varietals that could work there aren't popular or especially hardy, which just makes grape growing, something that's already challenging, even more so. And honestly, you probably wouldn't be getting a return on your investment. Another practice is that wineries are making wine with grapes they've had shipped in from somewhere else. If we have a surplus harvest, for instance, we sell our grapes to other wineries."

Cole stared at her. "Well, now, I'm again going to go back to my earlier statement about mouthy women. A nicer lady would have tried to break all that news to me gently like before trashing my hopes and dreams, but you just let it loose."

"I'm just trying to be factual with you. Muscadines are the only variety of grapes that grow well in southern climates and there's not a large market for that wine. There are some vineyards that live by it, but it's a type of wine that hasn't really caught on to the rest of the country, so if you're wanting to invest in a vineyard, it wouldn't be my first pick. I can give you the names of a lot of operations I think your money would be better spent on, but that's entirely up to you."

"Wouldn't there be more competition if I went with a place that used traditional grapes? At least there aren't a lot of muscadine producers in the first place."

Blair shrugged. "That's a better question for Nate. I just know most people don't have a palate for muscadine wine." She glanced over at him with a grin. "But then again, I'm a snob with a vested interest in people not drinking wines we don't sell so you'll have to take that into consideration."

Cole snorted and leaned back into his seat. "I like

you, Blair Sandoval, but you've clearly never had a sweet muscadine wine on a hot day while relaxing on a riverboat. I've traveled around the world and I'm here to tell you that there's not much better in life."

"Sounds like you miss home more than the wine."

A deep "hmm" came from Cole this time. "You may be right about that." His gaze wandered out to his right, down the hill into the valley of the vineyard, and he seemed to get lost in thought for a moment. "But you know what they say, you can't go home again."

Blair finally stopped the golf cart next to the field of sauvignon blanc vines. She got out and looked over the grapes she'd had a hand in growing and tried to imagine not being a part of this vineyard but simply couldn't. From the moment her grandfather could feed her a grape, she'd been in love with the vineyard. "This has always been home for me," she told Cole, plucking off a grape. The grapes were still a little over a month away from harvest, but they were coming along well enough. "We Sandovals bleed wine."

"I hope it's the red kind," Cole quipped, meeting her at the row of grapevines.

Blair gave him a bland look. "Maybe." Then she handed over a grape for him to try. "They're small but mighty."

He took the grape from her and popped it into his mouth, his face immediately puckering.

"Now that's what someone might call a textbook illustration of someone eating sour grapes," Blair laughed. "They're not ripe yet," she explained. "But they're getting there."

"You're an ornery woman," Cole said, moving closer to her as he inspected the grapevine. For what she didn't know, but he was very large and his scent was in her nose again, piney and fresh and masculine. She wanted to bury her nose in the soft cotton of his shirt, but also the idea made her want to vomit. As had been her habit since her unfortunate ex, she looked down at Cole's empty ring finger trying to spot a tan line, but she couldn't discern one. Though that didn't exactly make him single.

Not that she was looking.

Instead she imagined her future room at the nunnery and put to rest any lascivious thoughts she might be having about Cole.

Until, that is, he leaned close to whisper in her ear, his warm breath like a feather's kiss on the shell of her ear.

"I might as well mention that I like that in a woman too."

Blair's eyes slowly closed and she mentally said about a thousand Hail Mary prayers even though she'd never been much of a church person, because just being near Cole Taggart made that nunnery seem about as far away as the moon.

CHAPTER TWO

COLE HADN'T INTENDED on being attracted to his favorite vineyard's viticulturist, but then, there'd never been any rhyme or reason for who he'd been attracted to in the past. For a lot of years when he was racing overseas, discriminating wasn't exactly a term that described how he'd chosen a bed partner, so it wasn't totally out of character for him to be blatantly flirting with a woman he'd just met. What was notable was the fact that for the past two years he hadn't felt remotely interested in sleeping with anyone. He hadn't felt much of anything, in fact, in a long time.

It helped that Blair Sandoval smelled good, like imported vanilla and laundry soap, and it'd made him hard the moment she'd scooted by him out the door of the tasting room. It was actually a relief that he wanted her, and yet at the same time, the ever-present guilt wasn't far behind, the memory of the crash rising to the forefront of his mind the moment he made any attempt to move on or forget that he'd killed his own brother. An accident, people said, but Cole knew the truth. If he'd only listened to his brother. If they'd retired from racing when he'd wanted to, the crash would have never happened. His brother would still be alive right now. Being able to flirt as shamelessly with a lovely woman as Cole was. It was ironic then, that his wish to reconnect with his family was why he was at the vineyard in the first place and it had quickly turned into where, instead, he betrayed his brother even further by being attracted to the vineyard owner. He was hoping to set up a business that his family could work on together thinking that it might fill the hole Scott's death had left in all their lives, absolving him of his guilt. Yet here he was, flirting with the woman he needed to do that. It was classic him.

"It sounds as if you like a lot of things about women," Blair observed, moving away from him down the row of grapevines. He couldn't blame her for creating space, his flirting was unprofessional at best, but he didn't want to stop. Not when it had been so damned long.

"That would be an accurate observation," he joked, running a hand over the shiny green leaves, fascinated with the process of wine making already. He understood what people loved about wine country, had let the rolling farmland quiet his racing thoughts for a moment on their way here. He'd been searching for that kind of peace.

"Well, just so we can get this out of the way, I'm not interested in men at the moment so you're wel-

come to continue flirting with me but you'll probably be disappointed in the results."

"Are you telling me you're with a woman?" It
was possible, but he knew she found him attractive.

"No," she said. "Just that I'm off the market and
I hope all men die together in an enormous fire so
that the entire sex can start over from scratch and
maybe get it right this time."

He laughed, frankly, a little longer than he
should have at the prospect of his own demise. "Bad
breakup?"

That earned him a pointed glare with a well of
heartache behind it that she tried to hide, but he recognized the look of someone in pain. "And general
observation."

Shoving his hands in his pockets, he watched as
she rearranged some of the grapevines that were
too close together. He was curious about wine but
he was finding that he was more curious about her.
Her jeans were frayed at the bottom and worn white
at the knees and her cropped purple plaid button-
down looked soft and well loved. She looked like
what he would have imagined a female farmer to
look like, capable and tough but warm. Or maybe
he was just projecting what he wanted to see. He'd
known her for all of a half hour, but he had an increasingly insistent need to touch her, to see if her
skin was as soft as it looked. "You going to tell me
about him or do I just assume that he's a dog who
cheated on you?"

A shadow passed over her face and he hated that

apparently likely scenario for her. He'd never been exclusive with a woman to be able to cheat on her and that look was exactly the reason why.

She met his eyes, hers amber in the bright sun, matching the auburn of her hair. "Technically, no, he didn't cheat on me actually."

"Did he steal a secret family wine recipe?" Cole asked, trying to keep things light but also not willing to let the subject go. "Kick a dog?" he added. Then, to further rib her, "You found out he was actually a felon?"

A dark eyebrow rose. "A felon?"

Cole shrugged. "Yeah, I imagine that would be a deal breaker for you."

Blair just rolled her eyes. Pulling off a withered and brown grape and throwing it on the ground a little too hard if he did say so himself, she met his eyes straight on. "A felon would have been a blessing." Then she sighed with disgust, eyes sliding away, clearly not willing to give him the real answer. "I would draw the line at kicking a dog, though." She tore off another dead grape from the vine and threw it out into the field.

She turned to him then, her sneaker crunching on the sandy pebbles beneath her feet. "But I will say that I can never date again because I've proven that I'm epically inept at picking men, which means I'll probably just die alone in this field someday."

Cole opened his mouth to laugh, and also point out that she was too beautiful to be alone forever. Out here in the sun, she looked like a kind of earth goddess with her dark hair pulled up in a ponytail and escaped tendrils blowing in the gentle breeze. He'd never had a fantasy about having sex in the dirt, but if she was willing he wouldn't say no. However, something about her tone, made him not want to make a joke of it. He wanted to know the real reason for how she'd been so hurt that she'd sworn off men for life. He had an ill-advised urge to tell her to make an allowance for him because he wanted very badly to touch her and it was a real hardship imagining that he'd never have the chance.

"That seems like a harsh punishment for men everywhere," Cole finally settled on.

"Trust me," she told him, "I'll never get over the shame of what happened so it's best for everyone that I opt out of love from here on out." Blair let out a breath. Then she pointed in the general direction of the grapes to continue her lecture. "These are the sauvignon blanc grapes. For a wine grape varietal they're fairly easy to grow but need at least six feet of space between the vines, ideally a loamy soil, which is abundant in the Sonoma and Napa Valleys, and unlike a lot of grapevines you don't want to plant these too deeply into the soil. Also, you don't want them to get overripe or else what is meant to be a light, dry wine will become too sweet."

Cole had been staring at her during her half-hearted instructional session because he definitely had some follow-up questions. "I suspect, Ms. Sandoval, that regardless of what you might have done that you're a good person." He stepped closer to her, expecting her to move farther down the vineyard row like she'd done before, but she stayed where she was. "Hell, I've done some shit I'm not proud of, but even a tainted soul like mine is redeemable, so I hope you'll find it in you to forgive yourself one day," he told her, locking eyes with her, wishing he actually believed he deserved redemption.

She shrugged his sentiment aside. "We'll see, but it'll be quite some time." Then she blew out an annoyed breath. "I can't believe I'm even talking about this with a total stranger. Please don't tell my brother I mentioned it, okay? In his own words, I should only be allowed to make decisions about wine."

Cole walked a ways down the dusty dirt path, considering how to proceed and also wondering why he was so interested in a stranger's love life. "Well, while I just hate the thought of you being alone indefinitely," he said, "I agree that time does heal all wounds." He was still waiting, of course, for his to close, but people did often say that. "Doesn't mean that while you're waiting you can't have a little fun."

He could hear Blair's footsteps behind him stop, but he kept going, enjoying a walk in the outdoors. This place, though vastly different from Louisiana in a multitude of ways, starting with the uppity people, reminded him of home and of goofing off outside when he was a kid. But as usual, he couldn't think of home without thinking of his brother so he forced his thoughts back to the matter at hand.

"Is that an invitation?" Blair joked, obviously thinking he'd be scandalized by her forwardness.

Cole turned to face her. "If I had an invitation to issue, I'd probably be less subtle about it, Ms. Sandoval, but in this case, I'd be willing to make an exception."

Blair stared at him, her expression blank.

Cole wasn't sure what he was doing, but he felt her angst on a soul-deep level and he was drawn to her, period. He still had about a million questions about her breakup but figured he didn't have a real right to ask them and it certainly wasn't his business anyway. But it was obvious that whatever it was was eating Blair up inside, which was a state of affairs he was all too familiar with.

She looked up at him, eyes wide. "I'm a smart person, Mr. Taggart."

"Please, sweetheart, call me Cole." Her eyes narrowed at the unearned endearment. "I know it's forward to call you sweetheart, Ms. Sandoval, but perhaps under the circumstances you'll allow me some liberties. I usually don't make friends this quickly, but we seem to have stumbled into a kinship, you and I."

Blair shook her head but didn't argue the point.

"And I can tell you're smart as a whip, just as you say," he continued. "A genius is what people tend to say in relation to how you make wine, in fact."

Blair accepted the compliment with a raised eyebrow. "What I mean is that I consider myself a smart person and I'd be throwing away everything I learned from my previous breakup by turning around and jumping into another relationship. So I won't be doing that."

The finality of the words grated. He'd just found her, felt the spark of possibility, and she was already closing the door in his face. He knew it wasn't personal, but it sure felt that way.

"Men are pigs," Cole offered in commiseration. He'd been in the mud most of his life, after all. "But you'll find a good one, one of these days."

Blair snorted. "Doubtful." Then she was trudging back to the golf cart.

"Not exactly a positive attitude," Cole laughed, following her. "Where are we off to now?"

He levered up into the cart again, this time sitting even closer to her on the seat. Instead of her pressing herself so tightly up against the opposite side of the golf cart, however, she stayed where she was, their bodies fully touching from knee to hip. Heat collected on his skin, a prickling reminder of what it felt like to want someone. It was just his luck that after two years the only woman to catch his interest wanted nothing to do with the whole of men.

The rest of the tour continued with him taking notes every now and then because what she was saying was extremely interesting and educational. However, he did occasionally get caught up in the way the sun glinted red off her hair, the way she'd squint and hold her hand up against the sun as she spoke instead of wearing her pair of sunglasses forgotten in the golf cart, and the way she talked about wine in general. She'd been right before when she'd said she bled wine and he wasn't too proud to say that he was under her spell. He was still marveling over the fact that she'd moved him at all when the last two years of his life had been a barren wasteland, devoid of happiness or fun.

By the time they made it back to the tasting room, Cole needed a drink to stop from touching Blair. But, smartly, she flew behind the bar, which impeded him from doing something stupid like that. He resented the barrier; wanted to return to the golf cart where they'd been wedged together and he could see the thin sheen of sweat on her neck. Christ, was he seriously fantasizing about licking sweat from a virtual stranger's neck?

Blair slid him a glass of water to start the tasting as well as a rectangular piece of black slate piled with crusty white bread that she'd deftly sliced thin with a serrated knife. "Eat and drink that first while I get the wine ready." After pulling out a couple of bottles from a cabinet below her, she snagged a piece of cheese from her previously abandoned plate and popped it into her mouth with a sigh. Giving him a sheepish look, she confided, "It's better now that it's warm anyway."

He grinned and munched on a piece of bread before washing it down with the cool water, just what he needed on a day in the mideighties.

Cole took in the rest of the room while she worked. High ceilings with wooden beams and a skylight that ran the entire length of the room let the

natural light shine down on the rows of clear sparkling wineglasses on display in custom-made racks.
The furniture was polished leather, with big stuffed
couches in corners and alcoves with modern glass
tables and lived-in wingback chairs. One wall was
made of smooth stone where old wine bottles and
oak barrels served as the decor. It felt understated
and expensive, much like Blair herself.

"So," she began, gently placing several differently
sized glasses in front of him and one in front of herself. "Why us? Out of all the wines in the world, why
did you choose Sandoval Wines today?"

Grinning, he ate another piece of bread, realizing that he was starving. "About three years ago at
the raceway, your wines were served at the after-
party," he explained. "I've never been much of a
wine guy—I like a cold beer generally, but I had your
2014 cabernet and thought, well, hell, if this is what
wine's all about maybe I need to try more of it. So
I started drinking a ton of different stuff but nothing quite measured up to that cab, so I started buying just your wines and loved 'em all. So I figured I
should come see what it was all about."

Blair smiled and it was one of the first full ones
he'd seen today and he had a fleeting thought that
he'd like to see them more, be the one who put them
on her face. "2014 is my favorite year for our cabernet as well. You have excellent taste!"

He smiled then too. "Well, I don't know about all
that, I just know what I like."

"And that's what wine is about really," she allowed. "But, we all know that Sandoval wines are the best." With a playful wink, she pushed one of the flutes of sparkling wine toward him and kept one in front of her. "We'll start light with the sparkling. This is only our second year for it and I love it." She took a quick sip, giving a little shrug. "Tell me what you think."

Cole took his own sip, letting the fizziness float over his tongue. "I like it, but I don't know that I'm a sparkling kind of person."

She pushed the bread toward him again. "I'd say you're very sparkly," she disagreed, pointing out the cheese he should eat with the next wine.

"I don't know if that's a compliment," he told her, popping a piece of bread into his mouth, "but I'm going to take it as one."

"As you will," she said as she poured sauvignon blanc into their glasses and gave him a small plate of goat cheese and pine nuts. She wasn't skimping on the pours either, which meant he needed to slow things down if he intended on walking out of here upright. "Now, you will want to swirl this one around in your glass for a second then give it a little sniff. Nothing too intense, you just want to enhance the flavor of it before you drink it." He watched as she swirled, sniffed and sipped, eyes riveted to how her lush lips closed over the delicate rim of the wineglass. He never would have thought a wine tasting would be downright erotic but he was being proven completely wrong.

"Are you sure I shouldn't spit it out?"

Blair shrugged. "You can if you'd like. Plenty of people do, but—" she leaned in conspiratorially to whisper "—why would you want to do that when drinking it is so much more fun?"

Then she slid another piece of cheese into her mouth, those white teeth smiling as she did it and he fought the urge to vault over the blasted bar and taste her for himself.

But instead he swirled the wine, sniffed it, then took a sip himself, enjoying the ritual. Then he watched as she spread goat cheese on a piece of bread and he did the same, finally sitting down in one of the tall chairs instead of standing.

"Well, we've established you have excellent taste in wine, but what has inspired you to want to invest in a vineyard?"

His pointer and middle finger drew the bottom of the wineglass around in a circle as he contemplated how he would answer her question. "The truth is I'm getting sick of all the traveling I do for my job," he said, then told the whole truth with his next words. "And what's more, I hate racing in general now, so I thought while I was transitioning out of one career, I could get the ball rolling on a new one. Louisiana is short on wine and I thought I'm the kind of guy who might be able to make something happen." He left out the part about his family because it would inevitably bring up his brother and just for one day, he wanted to be with someone who didn't know that about him. To just be Cole Taggart, a man who hadn't killed his brother and ruined his family.

Blair pulled out another bottle of wine, setting it down in front of her as she met his eyes. "You hate racing? That seems odd for an announcer."

"I wasn't always an announcer," he informed her. "I raced professionally up until two years ago when I retired, but the more I'm around it the more I realize I've outgrown the life. I don't want to party with women I barely know after a race or hang out with a bunch of guys afterward who just want to talk about how many of those women they've slept with."

"But you used to like to do that?" she said dryly.

He shrugged. "You do what you think will make you happy until you find what actually does." Taking another bite of his bread, followed by the wine, he closed his eyes in pleasure. It was a simple thing, wine and cheese and bread, but there was just something about being here in this vast California country that kept bringing him, unexpectedly, a little bit of peace. "I did a lot of dumb stuff when I was younger but I'm more than ready to give it all up."

Blair smiled. "Well, if you want to bottle wine in Louisiana, you can talk to Nate about the price of our grapes."

Cole returned Blair's smile and leaned over the bar, catching a whiff of vanilla again. "Or he could loan me your expertise for a few months while I get things up and running."

He laughed at the look of shock on her face, eyes big and mouth hanging open.

"I'm just trying to rile you up, Ms. Sandoval," he

admitted, although the idea wasn't without its appeal. "I don't see you slogging through the swamp any more than you'd see me reading a book about soil science."

She still looked skeptical as he swallowed the last of his glass and the first tingles of tipsiness flowed through his veins.

CHAPTER THREE

"IF SWAMPS DIDN'T have alligators, it probably wouldn't be so bad," Blair told him, cutting up the fontina cheese and prosciutto for the next wine sample. He was taking his time with drinking, though, and she found that she didn't mind it. The tour had lasted nearly two hours already and she didn't want to poke his eye out, which was, frankly, unusual for her. Most people on tours tended to either try to impress her with their own wine knowledge or get bored by the second grape variety.

"Aw, they're sweet little guys at heart," Cole said, that already familiar ornery twinkle in his eye.

Blair snorted. "I do know people who could help you get started on something, though, if that's what you're really looking for."

Cole shrugged. "That might be good. Can I give you my contact information and you can just send me some names?"

Blair nodded, a few names already in her head. "Sure." When he finished the last of the sauvignon blanc, she rinsed his glass in the small sink in the bar, wiping it out as he watched her.

"You know, that wine sure was better than the grape of the same name that you tried to poison me with back in the vineyard."

"That would have certainly taken a lot of planning," Blair mused, somehow already used to his nonsense.

"Yeah, but you're a wily one," he went on, "I can tell. And you've got a murderous turn of mind."

Blair found herself laughing again and she might have laughed more in one day than she had since her breakup scandal. It felt really lovely and was endearing him to her so quickly she'd be a little worried if he lived in Sonoma and wasn't off traveling the world.

"You are making outlandish claims against my character, Mr. Taggart," Blair told him, sitting back down in the cafe chair behind the bar. "Are you saying you feel unsafe in my presence?"

Cole met her eyes and his green ones seared into hers. "Well, I'd be lying if I wasn't on the lookout for a firepit for you to throw me in."

Blair chuckled at her previous declaration. "Yeah, but don't you think you have some sins to atone for anyway? It could be a good opportunity for you to be reborn."

A shadow darkened his eyes for a moment and he broke eye contact, his expression serious. "I have a whole hell of a lot to atone for, as a matter of fact," he said, his voice suddenly low and quiet. "But burnin'

me ain't gonna help. To tell you the truth, Ms. Sandoval, a lot of days it feels like I'm already in hell
anyway."

After dropping that grenade, he tore off a piece of
bread with his teeth to clear his palate and washed
it down with water. "Didn't see that one coming,
didja?" He laughed when Blair still hadn't responded.
But then how could she? He'd gotten serious so fast
when they'd previously been joking around and she
hadn't shifted gears fast enough. "I've been known
to be a drama queen every now and again, so go
ahead and pour me what's next and we'll get back
to the flirting you don't want to do because you're
done with men."

Blair's eyebrows rose and he laughed. "Yes, I realize that you probably didn't think threatening to
throw me in a fire was flirting, but surprise, I warned
you at the beginning I was a complicated type of
person."

"I don't know that complicated is the word I would
choose," Blair said, her tone as dry as her mouth had
gone when he'd mentioned flirting. Had she truly
been flirting with Cole? She certainly hadn't meant
to, but either way, it was good news. In that she was
still able to, that after enough time and her complete
shutdown of all things sexual, that the muscle memory still existed. It was unwelcome as well, sure, because it would be a waste at the nunnery, but still.

As for the other, where he felt like he was in hell,
she'd defer asking about that for now, taking it at face

value that he was dramatic. Everyone was entitled to their own secrets and she had her own to keep.

"You know, I kind of hate being on the other side of this bar," he said, leaning over the top to see what she was doing. "I'd rather be back there helping you out."

Without waiting for an answer, he vaulted over the narrow stone surface, landing beside her on the other side.

She stared at him.

"What are you doing?"

"Offering my assistance," he said, taking the knife from her hand. "I can't help but notice that you're going a little slowly cutting up some of this cheese, and my mother wouldn't have it if she thought I was just letting you do all the work while I just sat and did nothing."

"This is my literal job," Blair told him, wondering how to retrieve the knife without cutting herself, realizing it was impossible, and then just unearthing another one from a drawer.

"I know your job isn't cutting up cheese for people, Ms. Sandoval," he said. "From the way you rattled on about pH levels and loam and whatever the hell out there at the vines, you're a scientist, not a wine taster."

"Our wine educators that normally do these tastings may not have as many college degrees as I do, but they're certified in the field of wine and have a diploma in wine and spirits training from a global academy with the most rigorous of programs. It's not a downgrade for me to do their job."

"I wasn't trying to downgrade anyone," Cole said, slyly taking the new knife from her hand as well before she knew what he was doing. "I was just trying to say that I don't love that your brother made you do this and I'm trying to make up for it, okay? So can you let a man cut his own cheese?"

Blair rolled her eyes at his lame joke, but waved a hand out in defeat. "Go ahead, but if you tell Nate about this you'd better be even more vigilant in looking out for a firepit."

Cole laughed and started cutting up the different blocks of cheese and assorted meats himself. "I'll keep an eye out, but now can you eat your lunch, please, so I can put a damper on my self-flagellation and guilt that you're starving. I heard your stomach growl so loudly on the cart I thought we were being chased by Bigfoot."

Giving him another bland look, she took a few bites of cheese and crackers from the plate she'd made earlier. "Happy now?" she asked, her mouth overstuffed.

"Very hot," he confirmed. "You'll have no trouble finding another boyfriend when you're ready." He cut another hunk from one of the wheels on her platter and put it on one of the crackers, nudging it to her. "In fact, probably more cheese in your mouth when you talk would be even better."

Blair swallowed and took a drink out of her water bottle. "This tasting has really gotten unprofessional very fast, hasn't it?" she joked before grabbing his glass from the other side of the bar and placing it back in front of him. "This is our pinot grigio. A new grape for us in the past couple of years but I think we've got an interesting flavor profile, you'll probably get some ginger in there as well as kiwi."

"These are the grapes that were purple even though the wine is white?"

Blair grinned. "I bet you were a straight-A student, Mr. Taggart."

Cole snorted. "I'd say the opposite." Then he took a drink of the wine, watching her as he did so, which was unnerving. A lot of things about him were unnerving. For instance, the way he got closer to her without her being aware of it. Just like in the golf cart, they were side-by-side now where she could feel the heat of his massive body again, warming the space around him like a portable heat lamp. "I just remember it since all the other white wines have white skin."

"Yes, and with some exceptions, most grapes actually have clear juice. It's the skin that gives red wine its color."

"Now that's what I call a fun fact," Cole said, tipping his glass to her before taking a sip. "May I ask what your preferred wine is or is that a violation of vintner code or something?"

"I like all wine, of course, but my favorite usually depends on the time of day or year or mood," she told him, but saw immediately by his raised eyebrow that he wasn't satisfied with that wishy-washy answer.

"But if you're asking me what wine I'll drink when all things are equal, I'd have to go with the cabernet sauvignon. It's bold, it's big and it doesn't make apologies for any of it."

That had him smiling again and she was finding it increasingly difficult to resist that peek of a dimple in his right cheek. If he didn't clearly know how attractive he was she might be in danger, but he was obviously well accustomed to women falling all over him. And yet every time he lifted the glass to his mouth the cords of muscles in his bare arms twisted, and when he chewed, his cheeks went concave and his jaw got tight and she had *serious thoughts*. She'd never in her life examined how a man ate before, but she'd been watching Cole Taggart for twenty minutes now as if he were a new release at the movie theater.

"Now that's a woman after my own heart," he said, giving her a wink.

"Cabs are very popular, but that means you run across a lot of mediocre ones as well." Since he'd taken over the cheese, she poured herself a glass of the pinot grigio. It was clear that this wasn't a normal tasting and she hadn't had much of the current year's wines yet. "This, though," she said after a sip of the white wine, "this is great."

"I've liked all the whites so far and I didn't think I would," Cole admitted, moving on to put a piece of salami into his mouth.

"Whites are perfect on a hot summer day," Blair said. "And actually," she continued, crouching down into the fridge for some fruit, "it's better with fruit even though we usually stick to the meat, cheese and bread for tastings." She cut off a hunk of a juicy peach, then a pear and set them on his plate. "But since this particular tasting has already gone so far off the rails, what's another detour, right?"

He ate the peach first, a drop of juice remaining in the corner of his mouth before his tongue came out to grab it. She averted her eyes, but it was already too late because the visions of other things that tongue could do were already in her head. Then before she knew it, she was imagining his big body over hers, which was highly inadvisable. And even when she tried to conjure up mental images of the nunnery all she saw were Cole's bare forearms rippling as he cut a hunk of Havarti.

"I'd give a lot of money for those thoughts," Cole cut in, his voice gravelly and a little wistful.

Blair shook herself out of the sex trance because she wasn't going to have sex with Cole ever. "Sorry, got lost in thought there."

"I'll say." He grinned. "I'd be willing to bet I'd like that particular detour as well." He grabbed another slice of peach from the plate and slid it into his mouth. "You were right about the fruit too, it really does something to the wine, makes it come alive or something. I don't know, I'm not a writer or a wine-maker so I don't know how to describe it, but I sure like it a lot."

"You're doing just fine," Blair assured him, ignoring the rest of his flirtatiousness. "Let me know when you're ready to move on to the chardonnay."

"You trying to get me out of here?" Cole demanded, giving her a fake pout. "I thought we were having a good time."

She looked up at him, her own slice of pear in hand. "I'd never. I just don't want you to think I'm being lax in my tasting duties by letting you simmer on one for too long. We're off book now so I'm just trying to make sure you're happy."

"It might be *because* you're overserving me, but I think you're doing a great job. Don't worry about little old Cole here, I'd be fine if you poured me unsweetened tea and served dirt all day just as long as you keep smiling at me like you mean it."

Blair met his eyes, having been caught off guard by his candor for about the tenth time today. He was definitely the most charming man she'd ever met, but he was hiding pain just like she was. She recognized the same self-loathing in him she'd been carrying around.

"Have I smiled at you?" Blair asked, skeptically even as her cheeks hurt from months of disuse. "I don't recall that. Maybe you should talk to your doctor about glasses. It would probably help with your job too, for all viewers know you're just out there calling out random names of racers who don't exist."

Cole chuckled, sidling even closer to her as he lifted a slice of pear from his plate. "If I admit I'm attracted to you first, will you feel safe to do the same?"

"It doesn't matter if I'm attracted to you or not,"

Blair told him honestly. "I'm not going to sleep with you because I'm done with men." She pulled his empty glass over and poured the chardonnay, then put some aged cheddar on his plate along with an apple slice to join the peaches and pears.

"So you are attracted to me then?" he persisted, ignoring the wine refill to focus on her.

"Of course," she admitted. "You're an attractive person, but," she warned, lifting a fork in between them as a mock weapon, "I'm not interested, which means you should take your big self and step back at least a good foot or so."

Grinning wildly, he took a large step back. "Like this?"

She gave him a sarcastic thumbs-up. "And just stay there."

"But I can't smell you from here," he complained. "And my wine is too far away now."

She slid the wine down on the counter and looked at him pointedly.

"Did you bake sugar cookies earlier or something? You smell like vanilla."

Blair's eyes rolled heavenward. "I don't bake. I leave that for my friend Greta who is so deep into her cottagecore lifestyle I've had to purchase a separate wardrobe for all the knitted sweaters she's gifted me. Now quit smelling me. It's weird. You're here to smell wine only."

His nose crinkled adorably in displeasure, but he remained where he was. "Okay, but do you have any cookies then?"

She just shook her head. "If you don't behave yourself, I'm going to have to end this tasting early."

"That would be fine if you'd agree to come to dinner with me instead."

"You know that's a bad idea."

"I do not know that," he argued, his eyes locking on hers. "I've had plenty of bad ideas in my life, some that would make your hair curl, but I don't think this is one of them."

"When do you leave town?" she asked.

"Two days from now."

She just raised an eyebrow. "I'm not sleeping with you, Mr. Taggart."

"Now you're just doing that to irritate me and pretend we're not fast friends. I asked you to call me Cole but you won't."

"You're a customer and you've been calling me Miz Sandoval this entire time. I was just returning the courtesy."

He took a drink of his chardonnay and regarded her. "I want to get back to the matter at hand, but I think you might have just made me a white wine convert."

Blair laughed and nodded to the cheddar and apple. "Try those together and then take a taste of the wine."

He followed her directions and both his eyebrows rose. "Now that's good living." Then before Blair realized what he was doing, he'd reached out and grabbed her hand, pulling her slowly toward him.

"What are you doing?" she exclaimed, trying to

dig her feet in. It probably would have worked, too, if she'd actually been serious about it.

"You told me I had to stay away, you didn't say anything about you coming closer." He grinned, but he did let her hand go, which meant she could get away if she wanted to. But her feet didn't move. He took a deep breath and said, "That's better."

"You are not right," she told him and moved a step away to pour herself her own glass of the chardonnay. The cheddar had breathed and was warm and sharp in her mouth along with the sweet tart apple so that when she finally took a sip of the chardonnay her eyes drifted closed in pleasure. She wasn't a wine snob like a lot of the viticulturists in wine country, but there was little better than a light meal of charcuterie and wine after a day in the sun.

"You're making it really difficult for me not to one, flirt with you, and two, touch you, Blair," Cole admonished, his eyes adorably beseeching. "So if you could throw me a bone and stop also eating and drinking so sexy-ish I'd surely appreciate it."

"I've done no such thing," she told him, offended, crossing her arms over her chest.

He huffed a laugh. "You know exactly what you're doing. Do you eat like that in front of all your customers?" He proceeded to do an exaggerated impression of her eating, his lips smacking, eyelashes fluttering, topped off with an obscene sigh of pleasure.

Ignoring his display and instead taking his empty glass, she poured in a good bit of rosé. "You don't deserve this wine, but if you like this then we'll know you've been fully converted." As he swirled it, she said, "You can pair this with goat or cheddar cheese and strawberries or blackberries." She pushed over the bowl of berries to him as well. He ate again, which was a mistake, as he watched her the entire time. But she wasn't going to give in again. Flirting time was over. Even if he was cute and fun and nice. And lovely and attractive and a gentleman.

Blair didn't trust herself to pick a good and honest man anymore. And one who'd already admitted to sleeping with women he never called again and who went from country to country for his job and could have four different families for all she knew? Nope, that was the definition of a bad idea.

Her gaze drifted back to his left hand where there, again, was absolutely no trace of a tan line. Maybe he *was* an actual decent person, though.

But no, that line of thinking was madness and she wasn't even over being mad about her last breakup. She couldn't go throwing herself into a meaningless affair with a stranger. No matter how much she might want to.

Then he ate a strawberry, his straight white teeth slowly piercing the lush red flesh and she felt herself melting a little. He was so dangerous.

"So what's the verdict on the rosé?" she asked.

A corner of his wide mouth kicked up. "Oh, I definitely like it too." He popped another strawberry into his mouth before bringing the glass to his lips again. "But I guess we'll see what happens

during the rest of the tasting if I go back to prefer-
ring reds."

"I guess so," she agreed, organizing the bottles
of red they used for sampling as well as the special
bottle she'd opened earlier, which she poured into
a decanter. She was saving it for last so that would
be more than enough time for it to fully aerate and
any sediment to drop to the bottom. It was an older
bottle of wine, from one of their very best years and
she was practically giddy to drink it.

"Now that I've dutifully gone along with your
subject change and not flirted with you for at least
five minutes," Cole said, resting his glass on the
counter and hijacking her attention, "let's talk about
that dinner."

Blair took a long drink of the rosé. She'd been
wrong earlier, because this was obviously going to
be the longest wine tasting of her life.

CHAPTER FOUR

"I THOUGHT I had you beat earlier," Nate told Cole, laughing as he took a canapé from a passing tray. "Gotta work on my putting game some more but it's hard to get away from here on the weekends."

"You weren't so bad," Cole laughed, giving him a friendly slap on the back, "for someone with a thousand handicap." Cole had even taken it easy on the guy because he genuinely liked Nate, but the guy was not a master golfer.

Nate chuckled and Cole grabbed a couple of the crostini slices from the next waiter and popped them into his mouth. Normally, he'd never come to a party at a winery with a bunch of hoity-toity people he didn't know, but the possibility of spending more time with Blair before he took off again had been too appealing. She'd firmly refused to have dinner with him yesterday after the tasting and he'd had little recourse other than to show up at the party, hoping he'd see her again and get her to admit there was something between them. Because despite his best efforts he hadn't stopped thinking about her whatsoever.

"Do you want me to introduce you to some other winery owners? I know a couple who would love to give you more information on opening up your own," Nate mentioned. "We inherited this from our parents so we can't really speak to the start-up, but there are plenty of newbies here who are already doing well that could provide that kind of insight for you."

"Thanks, man, I appreciate that. Maybe shoot me their email addresses," Cole suggested. "To be honest I'm more interested in talking to your sister at the moment. She knows a shit-ton about growing and it made me realize just how much goes into it. I still have some more questions from yesterday. Does she happen to be here somewhere?"

Nate rolled his eyes just like an older brother. "I doubt it," he griped. "She was around earlier but she normally makes an obligatory appearance at these things and then she's out of here as soon as possible."

Well, that was information that would have been helpful before he'd shown up an hour later than the start time, having been held up doing some last-minute voice-overs at the track.

"She lives just right up the road, though, if it's important. I can call her back," Nate offered, his look saying he'd clearly love the opportunity to annoy his sister. "You're not the first person to ask about her. She's become the name and face associated with the company so people generally like to pick her brain, but lately she's been keeping a low profile."

The why of that was still a story he wanted to know. "You know what, why don't I just go ahead over to her place? She mentioned that she had a bottle of pinot noir she thought I would like, and after that fantastic tasting yesterday I'd love to get my hands on it before I head out of town."

Nate opened his mouth, probably to say that they were currently in the winery full of all the wine Cole could possibly need, but he got the message fairly easily. "She's up the main road and take the first left until you get to the white farmhouse."

Cole nodded. "I appreciate it, man."

Nate's eyes narrowed in speculation before he dropped his own hand on Cole's shoulder. An echo of what Cole had done earlier yet not quite as friendly and heading more into warning territory. "I understand that my sister is an adult but I'll be damned if anyone else messes with her. She's going through a rough time right now and I wouldn't be doing my brotherly duty if I didn't tell you to proceed with caution."

Cole nodded, strangely pleased Nate had his sister's back. He'd do the same for his own sister if she'd been in Blair's position. He also wondered more about the rough time and if it was about the breakup she'd mentioned yesterday.

"I'm not that guy anymore," Cole told him, referring to the fact that two years ago he wouldn't be caught dead at a fancy winery party mostly because he would have been at the nearest bar getting shit-faced before sleeping with whoever wanted to come back to his hotel. But his old life seemed like something that happened to another person at this point. His entire existence was divided into before and after the crash. "And she'd bust my balls if I tried anything anyway," Cole said with a laugh.

Nate grinned. "Well, you've gotten to know her then at least."

"She's a singular woman, your sister," Cole told him. "I'll let her know her presence was missed."

Nate just shook his head as Cole turned to the exit. "I'm sure that'll go over well."

In his car, Cole wondered just what the hell he was doing by going to Blair's house, what endgame was he hurtling toward exactly? If something happened with Blair, it couldn't go anywhere. Maybe that was what was driving him now, the fact that he'd never see her again after tonight. But the reasons why this was probably a bad idea didn't seem to matter as he came upon the cute two-story white modern farmhouse with twinkle lights draped around the length of the wide wraparound porch.

He'd no sooner opened the door and emerged than he heard, "You weren't invited." He could make her figure out, sitting on one of the cushioned loveseats under a wide picture window.

"You promised me a bottle of special pinot noir and I'm here to collect," he called back, leaving his car doors unlocked like he'd seen Nate do yesterday at the tasting room. The casual trust around the winery reminded him of home. The Sandovals were open and honest people, something he'd missed over the years working the races and being in constant competition with damn near every person he met. Here on the vineyard, that life didn't matter and he found some of the tension he carried fade away.

All that mattered to his body, in fact, was that Blair was close, and it wanted to say hello. Intimately.

"Nate could have given it to you at the winery."

Cole stopped at the bottom of the stairs and looked up at her. She was lovely sitting on her porch with her feet drawn up beside her and her white linen skirt floating over her legs and a loose-fitting sky-blue tunic on top. "Nate also wanted me to check on you," he lied. "He seemed pretty upset that you decided to shirk your hosting duties."

Blair snorted. "He can go kick rocks. He knows exactly why I left and why it was necessary."

"You scared of meeting your competition?" Cole taunted mildly, thinking of Nate's offer to introduce him to other winery owners. Though he got the point that she must have seen someone there associated with her ex.

He could see her roll her eyes even in the low light. "Trust me, they're far more scared of me than the other way around."

"I take it you've told them about your whole men in a firepit idea as well?"

She met his eyes then. Their little game was over. "I told you I didn't want to go to dinner with you."

"Yeah, but this isn't dinner." This was what he wanted anyway, time with her one-on-one and the closer they were to a bed seemed to just better the odds that they might end up there.

As he watched her, he wondered if she'd ever give him clearance to join her on the porch, but at her next words he wasn't sure he wanted to. "I did an internet search on you today."

He knew it was inevitable and it wasn't as if he hadn't done one on her as well. He didn't find much besides write-ups about the winery, her awards for craftsmanship, articles about how she was an innovative and badass female grower in an industry dominated by men. All stuff that basically intrigued him more and which had ultimately driven him to where he was currently standing. A search on him, on the other hand, well, that was a different thing altogether.

She stood and walked down the steps, eventually stopping on the last one so that they were the same height.

"You lost your brother," she said quietly. Then she laid a hand on his shoulder, the first time she'd purposely touched him, and despite the fact that it was purely out of pity, it set his body on fire. "I'm sorry about that, Cole."

He nodded mechanically, used to the sympathy by now. The long googly-eyed looks from people who barely knew him but wanted him to know just how much they felt for his loss, the awkward claps on the back from men he used to party with who were now uncomfortable in his presence, the silence from his family who were even more devastated than he was. Those simple words from her brought all of it back.

"No reason for you to be sorry," Cole assured her, swimming hard upstream to not get dragged into the past. "Racing is a dangerous sport. You don't do it without knowing the possible consequences."

Her eyes locked on his then, the twinkle lights turning hers a golden amber. From this close, he also spotted a few pale freckles on the bridge of her nose. She was as adorable as she was fierce and being with her felt like he was seeing himself again for the first time since his brother's death. He could get addicted to it if he wasn't careful. Except that, of course, he would be careful because he owed it to his brother to be gone tomorrow.

"You don't have to talk about it," she said, giving his shoulder a squeeze before her hand drifted off. At the last second, he caught it in his, lacing their fingers together. He looked down at their joined hands trying to figure out when the last time was he'd held hands with a woman and coming up completely blank. Worse, the answer might actually be never. She gave their hands a glance and a raised eyebrow when her gaze returned to his, but she didn't try to remove hers. "You can tell me instead how you got the nickname *Easy Rider.*"

A corner of her mouth quirked up and she continued, "Because I think there's probably a double meaning behind it."

He shook his head. "I won a lot of races," he explained. "Easily."

She smiled. "What are you really doing here?"

"I liked hanging out with you and I thought you

liked hanging out with me too." He gave her hand a squeeze, her soft fingers warm in his. "And your brother beat me at golf today and was being insufferable about it. I had to get out of there."

"Now I know you're lying," she laughed. "Golf is the only thing my brother isn't good at."

"I'm not much for parties anymore," he tried instead, "and especially ones where I don't know anyone and where everyone there wears a watch worth more than the house I grew up in."

"Why did you go to the party at all then?"

He raised an eyebrow. They both knew why he'd gone.

She sighed then, seeming to have made a decision. Then she let go of his hand, climbed the stairs and disappeared into her house, the squeak of the screen door loud in the quiet evening. Cole wasn't sure if he was meant to follow her, but just as he was about to call her name, she reappeared with a wineglass, another bottle of wine and a very large bowl of popcorn.

Tilting her head for him to join her, he noticed an open bottle and half-full wineglass already on the wicker table in front of her. There were several seats he could take but he opted to sit next to her on the two-seater.

"What are we drinking?" he asked, peering down to read the label.

"It's next year's first bottling of zinfandel."

"And?" he asked, interested in how she felt about her own wine and excited to try something no one else had had yet. It felt like a secret they were sharing together here on a world-class vineyard where people would kill to be in his place.

"It's pretty lovely. Lots of cherry, lots of pepper but it feels balanced." She gave her glass a swirl and he decided he could watch her drink wine for hours.

She poured him a glass and watched as he drank. "I like it," he eventually said. "Definitely less intense than the one we had in the pairing yesterday, but I liked that one too."

Laughing, Blair dug into the bowl of popcorn. "Yeah, that's how most people feel. People take all that sniffing and flavors so seriously. The truth is that it's just fun to see what all you can taste in a single sip of wine but ultimately you'll have fun drinking it either way."

She pushed the bowl of popcorn toward him and he took a handful, mostly to be polite and to have something else to do with his hands besides touch her, which he was already missing.

"So you quit racing after the accident?" she asked, meeting his eyes.

He nodded, reluctant to share but finding that he didn't feel as reticent as he usually did. He wasn't worried that Blair would go tell the press what he said or hold anything against him. He didn't know if he'd ever find the absolution he'd been searching for, but after two years he couldn't say he was picky. Most days he'd give anything to wake up without the gnawing pit of guilt and sadness the loss of his brother and the resulting rift between him and his family had left in his life. One that up until now he'd had little hope of ever filling. But for whatever reason, the moment he'd stepped into that winery and seen Blair trying to hide a plate of cheese, a light had turned on inside him, giving him hope that maybe one day he'd see himself out of the darkness. Then learning she had her own demons to contend with, he just felt more comfortable with her than even his old friends.

"I quit racing after the accident," he acknowledged. "I don't know how much you know about Formula One racing but it's different than NASCAR. Two drivers from each team drive together during a round. So my brother and I were basically partners, both trying to nudge the other up in the ranks to get more points for the team as a whole. He wanted to retire that year but I made him keep going." He met her eyes, wanting to see her face free of judgment before he told her the whole ugly truth of himself. "And then he died on the track all because I wasn't ready to give up the lifestyle."

A corner of Blair's mouth tugged downward and he steeled against his own disappointment. But then she said, "You're too smart to blame yourself for your brother's death, Cole." His heart beat again. "But I can tell you do and while I have wished death by fire upon you, I have to say that if your brother was anything like you, if he'd wanted something badly enough he would have done it, not let you push him into continuing to race instead."

Cole opened his mouth to disagree except that

she was probably right about that. But it didn't mean anything because Cole had been seriously persuasive when Scott had brought up retiring, and like Cole himself would have done for him, Scott would have done anything for Cole. Which had ultimately led to his own death and left Cole picking up the pieces of his life, while trying to rebuild his broken family.

"Yeah, well, the rest of my family doesn't seem to think so," he said wryly, taking a hefty drink of wine. "So maybe you could shoot them a friendly email for me and plead my case."

Blair's eyes widened. "What do you mean? They don't talk to you?"

"They do, they do," Cole assured, not wanting her to get the wrong idea or paint himself as too much of a martyr. He was, after all, the villain of his own life. At least as far as his family was concerned. "I was always the outcast of the family. So when they knew Scott wanted to retire and come back home to Louisiana they were thrilled, but then when I talked him out of it they were already upset that I'd committed us to another year of traveling nonstop. Then when it ultimately resulted in his death, you can imagine how they felt."

Blair took his hand then and he felt guilty for liking it so much. Guilty that he was getting the thing that he wanted all because he was sharing the story of his shame. "But you want to open a winery at home," Blair said, thoughtful. "So you're trying to mend fences with them."

Cole scrubbed at the back of his neck, uncomfortable with all the talk about his life. "They're not mad. Things just aren't the same. Like, they love me like they always did, but for my parents it's clouded by the loss of their son, and for my sister, her brother. Time is what it'll take to heal, but I intend to do what I can to smooth it along so we can be a happy family again." He'd already bought his parents and his sister new houses, new cars, beach vacations—anything he thought might make amends, but even after two years things just didn't feel the same. The truth was without Scott, things would always be different, Cole just hoped that one day it wouldn't feel like his fault anymore. "I thought maybe I'd start a winery as a way to move home and try to rebuild the family."

"Well, if you need hands-on help, I'm happy to send Nate with you to Louisiana. I could really use a vacation from him around here," she said, thankfully lightening the mood. "Last week he made me post an informational video on fermentation on social media. As if that's what I want to be doing with my time." She rolled her eyes and he smiled. "Creating content."

"I'd love to see you talk about fermentation."

Blair rolled her eyes. "I don't know how you made that sound perverted, but you really have a gift for that kind of thing."

"You won't be surprised to hear that I've heard that before too," he said, giving her hand a squeeze and at the same time pulling her forward a little. She raised an eyebrow, knowing what he was up to, but letting him get away with it. "Thank you for offering me your brother. I think after dealing with you he'd be counting his blessings to have me as a sibling."

"You're probably right," she admitted, holding back laughter.

They were close now. He could feel her breath on the side of his neck and he wanted to lean forward and kiss her but thought better of it. The anticipation was good for now—let her think nothing was going to happen.

She reached out and took another sip of the wine and when she started to put the glass back on the table he took it from her hand instead, turned the glass to where the print of her lipstick was and drank from the same place. Watching her the entire time, he saw her eyes grow darker and then her frown appear. It was clear she was going to fight him to the end.

He placed the glass back on the table with a gentle click. "I know you don't want to get involved, but I'm leaving tomorrow and who knows when I'll be back. So honestly, what's the harm in having a little fun, Blair?" Taking her other hand in his, he continued, "After all you've had to deal with, don't you think you deserve some no-strings-attached fun for once?"

The look she gave him was bland and he knew he was laying it on thick, but now that the idea had taken root he was loath to let it go. Two years of celibacy did that to a person. This was the most he'd felt around a woman since his brother's death. He'd tried to get back in the saddle, so to speak, even had taken women back to his hotel room before ultimately realizing that he couldn't do it and sending them away. Maybe it was because Blair was so unlike the party girls who followed racing and looked at him with just a little bit of pity for his loss or how his family looked at him, like he was the person responsible for his brother's death. Blair already made him feel like he had a purpose other than being a race car driver and that maybe just he, Cole, was enough to interest someone.

Which is why he laid all his cards on the table.

"I haven't told anyone that my brother wanted to retire but I told you because—" he shrugged, unable to articulate the feeling of ease he'd felt with her instantly "—I guess I trust you." He took a deep breath. "So I might also go ahead and admit that I haven't slept with anyone for two years. And not because I haven't had the opportunity, but because I haven't been interested."

Their eyes met but he had absolutely no idea how to read the expression on her face. He nearly grinned at the fact that he was working so hard to get a woman in bed. Past him would be laughing his fucking ass off. Present him, however, was too focused on, if nothing else, her joining him in a little fun where they could both forget all their shitty problems, whatever hers were, and enjoy each other. Future him, that poor bastard, was the one who needed to worry because if he looked too closely into why he was breaking his extended celibacy after all this time, he might have to admit that he might be interested in Blair for more than sex.

"And it's as much of a shock to me as anything, but I'm into you, Blair. A lot." He sighed, his gaze drifting away from hers before returning as he said, "After two years, it's you."

CHAPTER FIVE

BLAIR WASN'T AN exceptionally chatty person on the best of days, so while it wasn't shocking that she didn't respond to Cole right away, she did have to admit that she *wanted* to say something to him after he'd revealed his not sleeping with anyone for two years. And that she was the one who had finally compelled him to want to do so.

That was a lot of responsibility for one taciturn viticulturist to handle. The mountain of expectations that would accompany sleeping with someone after such a long dry spell was crushing! But the expectations weren't the problem. Not really. The problem was her and the fact that she was probably still a little broken. If she'd thought she was improving, she had only to look to tonight and the fact that she'd had to bail on the party because she'd seen a mutual acquaintance of her ex and hadn't been able to bear the brunt of the shame. Had the man known her ex was married and thought Blair was fine with betraying another woman? She didn't know and she hadn't been about to stick around and find out.

"I'm sorry, what?" she eventually got out. She thought of the pages and pages of Google images of Cole with different women on his arm and was still astounded by two years of celibacy. Taking his previous playboy lifestyle into account, this was a man who had taken himself off the market in a very serious way.

A corner of his wide mouth quirked and she liked that he was always so quick to smile even though she knew now it hid so much. For knowing a person for only two days she already felt closer to him than to people she'd known for years, knew what it was like to loathe oneself.

"I haven't felt like it," Cole said with a shrug. "It's just not something I've wanted to do, but I like you, Blair. I don't know how chemistry works but we definitely have it and I'd say that's pretty rare."

"So you want to sleep together, leave tomorrow and never see each other again?" she clarified for posterity's sake.

His eyes widened, shocked that she'd put it so bluntly, she guessed. "It doesn't mean that we won't ever see each other again, but I'm on the road a lot so I couldn't be certain about when the next time would be."

As a rule, Blair wasn't really a one-night stand type of person, but she had to admit it had crossed her mind yesterday. And today she'd woken up wondering why she hadn't just agreed to dinner with him. She'd had *fun* yesterday and in trying to remember if she'd ever had that much fun with anyone she'd dated, she'd come up empty. She didn't deserve it, probably, but it didn't mean she didn't want it.

One thing would stop things dead in their tracks, however. "How can I be sure you're not married?"

The way Cole's head shot back so quickly was comical and she thought he'd given himself a mild case of whiplash, but then he choked out, "Trust me, I am not married. I have never been married, and at the rate I was going before, I'll never *be* married."

Not exactly a good attitude for a life partner, but a fine one for someone she'd never have to see again. In that respect, Cole was ideal. They could hook up and there'd be no awkward run-ins at the grocery store, no gossip circulating to the other vintners in the area, no expectation of seeing each other again. And bonus, if the sex was awful, he was leaving and she wouldn't have to pretend to let him down easy.

Except she was pretty positive sex with Cole would be anything but awful.

But apparently he had more to say. "Nor, if I was married, by the way, would I cheat on my partner, which is another reason I haven't gotten married. However, if you'd like to be sure, you can check the marriage records. You won't find my name in their database."

Blair wasn't unmoved by his speech and the earnestness in which it had been delivered, but she wasn't going to be fooled again so she did a quick search on her phone as he watched in amusement.

"Darling, you can search the marriage records for all fifty states and the world, but you're not going to find my name anywhere. Plus, you could do a general internet search for me and marriage and still come up empty. And that's how you really know. You'd better believe if I went to the trouble of getting married, I'd blast that news all over the tabloids and beyond. Cole Taggart Finally Loses His Mind, the headlines would say, and the picture would just be me with a white veil tied around my neck like a noose."

Blair rolled her eyes at his nonsense, but he did have a good point. Someone in the public eye as he was would have definitely made the news with a marriage. Nevertheless, she did a couple more marriage record searches as well as a couple of Google searches to be sure and came up with nothing. Meanwhile, he continued to munch on popcorn and drink wine, his eyes never leaving her.

"I pity the woman you do finally end up marrying," she told him, her tone beyond bland. "Not only will she have to deal with you but you'll also just keep reminding her every five minutes how much of a favor you're doing her."

"I suppose if I ever meet a woman with enough bolts loose to agree to marry me, I'll do my best to shape up. My parents are still happily married, after all. Thirty-seven years and still counting. So if I thought my life could ever settle down I might consider it."

"I'll believe that you're not married but how do I know you don't have a girlfriend or fiancée somewhere?" Admittedly, Blair felt embarrassingly paranoid asking but she absolutely *would not* do that to another woman again. She'd learned that it was on her to check the men she slept with. Relying on males to tell the whole truth when the possibility of sex was on the table was like asking a kid to put a cookie back once their hand was already in the jar.

Cole reached for her hand. "Blair, I know you have no reason to believe me, but I haven't had sex and/or even laid a hand on a woman since the day my brother died."

Blair sighed. Maybe it was enough that she'd done her due diligence, contacting family members sounded a step too far. After all, at some point she'd need to trust her instincts again.

"I believe you," she finally said. "And yesterday after you cried when I refused to have dinner with you, my search on you was pretty extensive and there wasn't a mention of marriage."

"I'm a lot of things, but I'm not a liar," he said. Cole took her hand in his and her eyes fluttered, wanting to close at the heated contact. He was just so big and warm and there and like a breath of fresh, uncomplicated air in a life that had gotten far *too* complicated. "Look, I know something shitty happened with an ex, but I promise you that I would never try to screw over the person I've had the most fun with in a long damned time."

"I had fun too," she admitted with a wry smile. "Despite my better judgment."

"Well, that's not the first time someone has liked me in spite of knowing better," Cole laughed. "But why don't you think of me as the loaf of bread you made me eat between wines yesterday. A good palate cleanser before you start your next serious relationship. I'm a carb, which means I'm delicious to eat but too much of a good thing isn't smart, but singularly perfect for a one-night indulgence."

Blair laughed because how could she not? The man was charming and he would be as good as the freshly baked bread they had delivered to the winery every day that she made herself not eat.

But she deserved bread, damn it. Everyone deserved bread sometimes, in fact!

She probably should just go ahead and stuff her face. Yes, she'd regret it a little tomorrow but not enough to stop her from having it again in the future.

"Drink the rest of your wine," she ordered, because they did not waste wine on this vineyard. Except in the spit buckets, but even then it hurt her a little because she'd grown those grapes, lovingly watched over them and the soil beneath, saw them through the fermentation process, all the way to the uncorking. It was necessary to spit sometimes, but the pragmatist in her was too strong not to feel a tinge of regret.

"Yes, ma'am," Cole said, leaning back on the loveseat and putting his feet up. "Now, I feel honor bound to tell you before any of this gets started that I am not an easy fellow in the sheets."

"Of course not, I wouldn't expect you to be a completely different person in bed than you are in life."

That comment was rewarded with a huge grin. "Hell, Blair, you're a treasure."

While a joke, it felt like a compliment to Blair, who for one reason or another had been known to be a challenging person herself. She hadn't grown their wine to worldwide success by being easy, after all. It was probably why she'd accepted so little from the relationships in her life—she'd just been thankful someone found her tolerable.

His arm came around the back of her seat and it felt like a line had been crossed and there was no going back. The bounds of politeness had been breached. They were touching and she liked it, and yes, her body wanted very much more of it.

"Where are you going after this?" she asked, bringing things back to the ordinary.

"Spain," he said. "Barcelona to be precise."

"Do you like announcing?"

He gazed out into the dark vineyard beyond, the butter-colored dirt standing out in relief against the darker rows of vines. "I like it well enough but not so much that I want to keep traveling to do it much longer. Hence the winery."

"Sounds like you've got a plan," she said, wondering idly what she'd be doing if she couldn't make wine and literally coming up with nothing. Could one eat cheese professionally? Seemed improbable. "So I know why you hate racing now, but don't you miss it a little?"

Cole's head shook immediately, but then he blew out an audible breath. "How the hell should I know? I'd never let myself race again regardless, but I do love to drive fast."

"I have a car and there are roads on our property no one drives on, you could show me just how fast you are."

That arm behind her, resting innocently against her back, curled in as he moved forward and before she could blink, she was being hauled into his lap looking down at his satisfied face. "That's how fast I am, sweetheart."

From her new vantage point, lots of things were suddenly very clear to her. First, he was larger than he looked. Two, straddling him was erotic and he liked it too. And three, there was no stopping this now because her body would revolt if she tried to move. His thighs were thick and strong against hers, his chest was unmoving as her hands pressed against it, and his eyes held hers when she might have looked away.

"I have an idea," he said, "to make this fun and so we don't get too serious and fall in love with each other."

Her eyebrow rose. "I wouldn't worry about that." Cole huffed another laugh. "Yeah, well, do it for my poor little old heart then, Blair. You've nearly got me on my knees for one night with you, who knows what two nights might bring."

A good compliment that had her asking, "What's your proposal then?"

He met her eyes, a dark brow winging upward in challenge. "A game of truth or dare."

Blair, who had been preoccupied with the flex of his thigh muscles under her own and not giving his words too much attention, sat up straight and choked, "Pardon me?"

"You know," he said, "like truth or dare. We'll go back and forth and choose truth or dare until one of us wins."

"How do you win truth or dare?"

Cole's eyes waggled. "I think we both know how you win this particular game of truth or dare." At Blair's groan, his hand came around the back of her neck and drew her gaze down to his. "You win when the other person won't answer your question or complete your dare."

"What's the prize for winning?" Blair asked, still skeptical and ready for another lewd reference to having sex with him being the prize.

But to her surprise, he just shrugged. "I promise not to bother you afterward."

"A big sacrifice for you, I'm sure."

His thumb started caressing the back of her neck and suddenly Blair found it difficult to think. "You never know," he said, staring at her mouth, "we could fall in love right here on this porch and I'd be unable to ever contact you again. A lost love for the ages."

Blair snorted but found herself scooting closer to him, wanting to feel the rest of his body against hers. "I'll go first," she declared. "I choose dare."

"That's my girl." Cole grinned, meeting her eyes again. "As you know I like a daring woman."

Blair just stared at him, not condoning his ill-conceived flattery. "The semi-insulting word you used earlier was mouthy," she reminded.

He leaned in, his mouth so close to hers, and she waited for the kiss, her body primed and ready to go. Except his lips never fell and instead she heard him whisper, "I dare you to pour me another glass of wine."

Blair's nostrils flared. "You know you're the worst, right?"

Cole's shoulders were shaking in laughter and his hand drifted down her back. "Yeah, I'm well aware. Does your irritation mean you're refusing to complete the dare?"

Instead of answering, Blair reached over and opened the additional bottle of wine she'd brought out earlier, poured it and then handed it to him. "I really hope you don't choke."

She'd heard Cole lightly chuckle before and he was always quick with a grin, but when he threw his head back with laughter she grinned too, enjoying the rich sound echo into the night beyond them. They were all alone on her porch with no one around, only the fireflies to see them, and it felt cozy yet also somehow illicit to be outside about to do who knows what in the outdoors.

Sobering slowly, he took a drink of the wine, making a big deal to swallow without incident and when he was finished, she said patronizingly, "Good job."

He was still grinning when he said, "Your turn. I choose dare."

It would be sweet justice to torture him the way he'd done to her and it was all part of the game anyway, the anticipation, the one-upmanship. "I dare you to take your clothes off and run down one of the rows of grapes out there." Then she added out of consideration for his safety, "You can keep your shoes on."

He met her eyes, his green ones dark in the dim light of the porch. "I'll need a good reward for that, princess."

Blair's eyes closed at the goofy endearment. She'd already figured out that he put on that Southern act when he wanted to annoy her. Incidentally, it worked.

Rising from his lap she stepped back and hoisted herself up on the porch railing to watch the upcoming show.

Holding her eyes, he unbuttoned his crisp blue shirt, the light glinting off his silver watch. Once that was on the ground, he reached behind him and pulled off his T-shirt and she just shook her head.

"That shirt move is so obvious," she taunted. "Absolutely shameless."

Undeterred but amused, he dropped the shirt on the floor with the first and she found her gaze riveted to what he'd revealed, the hard pecs, the dark hair covering his chest and arrowing down beneath his pressed gray pants. He looked effortlessly expensive and athletic and hard in all the right places.

"You know, people complain about stuff being obvious, but you eat apples, don't you? Those are delicious and I don't see anyone complaining about how they're over apples because everyone eats them."

"Deep thoughts, Cole," Blair said, nodding. "Maybe you should write a philosophy book sometime. But for now, why don't you take your pants off instead?"

"Hell, Blair, can't a guy ease into nudity?" He scratched the back of his head like he was embarrassed. "I'm ready to get things rolling but it sure would be easier if you'd take a little something off too."

She shook her head. "You had your chance to get me out of my clothes," she reminded him. "Instead you chose to aggravate me and have me pour you a glass of wine. Seems like you got yourself into quite a pickle."

Then she nodded in the direction of his pants and pointed down to the ground with her finger. His eyes alight, he gave her one last look of disbelief before unbuckling his black leather belt, way more slowly than was necessary, before dropping it on the love-seat behind him. That finished, as if his fingers were broken, he played with the button of his pants, seemingly trying and failing to get the button through the hole multiple times before it poked through.

Then, obviously, the zipper was temperamental, a full minute passing as he struggled to get it unstuck.

"Have you used clothes before?" she asked, arms crossed over her chest now. "I hope you don't plan to become a male erotic dancer anytime soon because I'm not sure it's the career for you."

The final rasp of his zipper sounded and her eyes zoomed back to his crotch, seeing that he was already stiff behind his pants. It crossed Blair's mind that he might actually be truly embarrassed or shy.

But then she was reminded of the wealth of pictures of him on the internet where he'd been partying flagrantly seminude and decided he was more probably just messing with her.

Achingly slowly, he pushed down his pants, finessing them over his tobacco wingtips before dropping them on top of his shirts and belt. Their eyes met as his hands played with the elastic of his blue boxer briefs, the final piece of clothing and indisputably the most important.

"You're sure I'm not going to run into something out there that will maim me?"

Blair thought of the vines. Most of them were strung up with wire but she couldn't truly be sure something wouldn't slap him. It would be difficult to see in the dark and it felt cruel to make him venture out there. She was a hard-ass, but she wasn't without mercy.

"You can leave those on too."

"You're a good woman, Blair Sandoval," he breathed in relief, giving her a salute of gratitude. Then he made his way off the porch, and Blair had never considered herself someone interested in the male form before, but leave it to Cole to prove her wrong. Even his back had muscles, and really nice ones.

"I thought you drove cars and talked for a living. Where'd you get so built?"

"A gym, Blair," he said to her as if she were a child. "The place where people exercise. I have a trainer and everything." Then that grin again. "Incidentally, she likes my ass too."

Blair just pressed her lips together and watched him as he made his way toward one of the vine rows. "Do you want a flashlight?" she called.

"Nah, the moon is bright enough," he said, then turned around to face her on the porch. "You gonna signal the horn or should I go anytime?"

She made a hooting sound and started laughing the moment he began running, a string of curses floating behind him as he went.

"I hate this!" she heard him yell as his footsteps grew fainter the farther away he got.

Just as she took a drink of her wine, she heard, "Oh, shit! I need help!"

Blair didn't believe him for one second. He was one hundred percent just trying to get her out into the dark with him. "Did you find another woman out there to annoy or what?"

A pause. "Blair! Please, I need your help!"

The tone of his voice was one she'd never heard before and she immediately became alarmed.

"Are you okay, Cole?"

"No, woman, I AM STUCK!" he shouted urgently.

Then, for what had to be a record number of times for her in a single evening, she went against her better judgment and went to help him.

CHAPTER SIX

COLE KNEW HE was probably going to hell for tricking Blair, but, by god, if the little troublemaker didn't deserve it. He'd started easy on her by giving her the wine as a dare only for her to command he get completely nude right out of the gate? No way was she getting away with it, no matter how cute she looked checking out his ass.

She took her time about coming to help him, however, and it felt like forever before she appeared at the end of the row, peering down it to see him. "You look okay to me," she called.

"I am not okay," he returned, pretending to unsuccessfully pull his leg out of a small dip in the ground that he hoped looked like a hole from far away in the dark. "And honestly, I'd say by the looks of this hole you have yourself a gopher problem."

Blair snorted. "If you knew just how big of a problem that would really be, you wouldn't joke about it."

The comment got her moving, though, and while he probably should have come up with a plan before she was halfway down the row, he wondered what he should do when she finally got to him besides the thing he wanted to do—which was tackle her to the ground and get to some dirty naked business.

"I don't even know what you expect me to do that you can't," Blair told him, her tone dripping with suspicion. "If you're stuck in a hole, just dig yourself out. I suspect you've had practice in that."

Didn't he know it. "It's a weird angle," he lied. He watched as she finally stopped in front of him, looked down to his foot that was clearly not stuck in a hole, glanced at his face, then bowed her head with a put-upon sigh.

"You just can't not be this way, can you?" she asked, her head shaking at the silliness.

He laughed at her exasperation. "I mean, I thought we could enjoy the night sky together from here."

"You're just trying to get me off balance," she disagreed, crossing her arms over her chest. "And besides, we could see the stars from the porch."

"Yeah, but this is a more romantic setting for our first kiss, wouldn't you say?" he asked. "Under the stars amongst the very grapes you grow. You should be thanking me for being so thoughtful. I'm creating a *moment*, Blair. Enjoy it."

So saying, he tugged on her arm, pulling her closer. She didn't rush into his arms, but she also didn't resist so it felt like a win. "Now it's your turn, truth or dare."

She looked him straight in the eyes, a mischievous twinkle there that signaled to him that she definitely was going to choose truth because she knew he'd dare her to kiss him. And as he'd suspected, she said, "Truth."

"Truth it is." He grinned, wishing he wasn't such a crafty person, but enjoying every second of it. "Now, remember, while you're not quite under oath in a court of law, you are bound by the sheer magnitude of personal ethics that comes with a game like truth or dare, a game that has been operating since the dawn of time on the very rigid presumption that those who choose truth will, in fact, hold themselves to the high standard of honor that precedes the game by telling the absolute truth."

A bland stare before she gave him a sarcastic salute. "I get it."

"All right," he drawled, "if you're super sure you don't want to choose dare."

Then he took his foot out of the imaginary hole and stood up straight, giving her a once-over that took his cock from resting hard to actively growing, but he could tell she was into it too, because by the time his gaze had touched every part of her, there was heat in her eyes.

"I'm sure I don't want dare," she told him, eyes pinned to him in challenge.

"Truth it is then," he declared. Then, "Do you want to kiss me right now?"

Her nostrils flared at the question because he'd still gotten her. And he would have his kiss with her under the moonlight in a vineyard. He wasn't much of a reader or a poet but he was still a romantic at heart, and he really was ready to let a little bit of whimsy into his life after two years of drudgery. He didn't know why or how it had happened on this particular trip, at this particular vineyard, with this particular woman, but he wasn't a man to question happiness when it came along. Not when he knew now how fleeting and rare happiness could be.

Blair opened her mouth immediately and he could tell by the look on her face that she was going to say no, so he held up a hand to halt her. "Remember now, if you lie, you're challenging the venerable legacy of truth or dare. Imagine if young children weren't taught to respect a code, where we'd be as a nation, nay, as a civilization?"

Blair's eyes fluttered closed before they opened again so she could openly glare at him. "Fine," she bit off. "I want to kiss you."

He brought her closer then, could feel the heat of her body against his bare skin, the soft brush of clean cotton fabric. She looked like an angry bohemian angel in her flowy skirt and tunic, her long, wavy hair a messy curtain down her back. He let go of one of her hands, letting his own drift up her arm until he hooked it gently around the back of her neck, his thumb running over her bottom lip. She was so soft and he could smell the sweet scent of vanilla on her, bringing to mind ice cream on a summer day.

Then he leaned his head down until their lips were mere breaths apart and whispered, "It's my turn." With a quirk of his lips, he continued, "I choose truth."

He watched with delight as her eyes flared again

and she took a spiteful step back. While he regretted the fact that she'd created physical space between them he simply could not stop riling her up if he tried.

"Why me? Why after two years of celibacy are you choosing me to sleep with?"

Well, shit. His girl knew how to play too. He wanted to lie, of course he did, and maybe if he hadn't goaded her into telling the truth earlier he would have, but she'd pounced on the opportunity like the smart-ass she was.

"And remember, don't sully the spirit and integrity of truth or dare," she tsked when he continued to hesitate.

"I wish I had a straight answer for you, sweetheart, but after my brother died I didn't feel like talking to anyone, let alone having someone in my bed. Then as time went on, it didn't feel right to be living like I had before he died, like I needed to honor his memory by not wasting my life fucking everything that breathed. But then I came here and you didn't know anything about my brother and talked to me like a normal human being. It was nice." Then he met her eyes straight on. "And the fact that you're sexy as hell doesn't hurt. You're just making it seem okay again, and since I'm not a man to overthink things I've made the decision to go with it. Also, the calluses on my hand need a break, if you know what I mean."

She raised an eyebrow. "Kind of sucks for me, though, right? For you to be so out of practice? I assume I'll be having to teach you how it works again."

Cole grinned and couldn't believe how much he was enjoying himself and not having sex at the same time. And yet, here he was virtually naked himself in the middle of a field of grapes extending the conversation to see just how long he could go without picking her up in his arms and running the both of them straight to her bedroom because he was having so much damn fun.

At the realization, the guilt crept in, weaving around in his gut like an old houseguest who wouldn't leave. The inclination to indulge himself was strong, but the remembrance of the pain he'd caused his family had his smile slowly fading. This was a just a one-night stand like any other and it was all he that he deserved.

"That sounds like a dare for me to prove you wrong," he said. "But I told you the truth, which makes it your turn. So go on and choose while I mentally revisit how sex works so you won't have to break out the instruction manual later."

"Dare," she said, taking another step back from him.

Finally. "Kiss me."

The look of surprise on her face was a treat. She'd expected him to mess with her some more and while that would certainly be entertaining, he'd reached his limit. He *needed* to touch her, to have her fully in his arms with every inch of her pressed up against him. His entire body was begging him to grab her and never let go.

When she hesitated, he lifted a brow. "If you'd

like some direction, I'd be happy to give you step-by-step instructions."

Her lips thinned then and she marched the two steps back to him, lifting her chin. "One last time, if I learn that you're secretly married I will find where you live and burn your house down."

"Your continued and now-localized threat of arson has been noted." Taking her hand in his, he gave it a reassuring squeeze. "Blair, cross my heart and hope to die, I am not married."

She shook her head, then with a small smile, she leaned up and gave him a quick peck on the cheek instead of the real kiss they both wanted, and he kind of wanted to haul her against him and simply do it, but he respected her move too much.

"Your turn," she told him, settling back down on her feet.

"Dare," he said, his eyes never leaving hers. And the word held a double meaning because he was also daring her to let them do what they both wanted.

Her own eyes grew serious, and she said, "Kiss me."

He didn't waste a millisecond before pulling her back into his arms. "It's about fucking time," he growled before setting his lips on hers.

The game was over because the moment he felt her soft lips against his he was lost. Their tongues met in a hurried crash of teeth that wasn't awkward exactly but completely devoid of finesse. Whatever savvy he might have learned over the years had flown out the window with his extended celibacy and the fact that they'd been teasing each other for over an hour now, waiting for just this moment. She arched against him, trying to get closer, while he thrust against the soft pad of her stomach, his dick becoming increasingly insistent that he find it a nice, warm place to go.

When it wasn't enough, he grabbed hold of her upper thighs and hoisted her up into his arms, her legs wrapping around his back to keep hold.

"Truth or dare," he asked her as he walked them back down the row toward her house.

She ignored him at first, her breath hot against his neck as her lips traveled down, pressing against his skin and driving him fucking nuts. Finally she answered, "Truth."

"Where's your bedroom?"

Her head came up and her genuine smile, one that wasn't exasperated or begrudging, was a true gift, her eyes bright, smile wide, unguarded and fully in it with him. "You're really great, you know that, right?"

"This feels like a really sneaky way of throwing me off by complimenting me so you won't have to answer the truth."

"My bedroom is on the second floor, down the hall, last door on the right." She proceeded to kiss her way down the other side of his neck. "It sounds to me like I've stumbled upon the fact that you're uncomfortable with compliments. So if it makes you feel better, considering the aforementioned poor performance I'm expecting from you, that will probably be the last one I issue."

A corner of his mouth lifted and he thought he was probably gazing at her with affection in his eyes. "You're a woman of grace and circumspection to think of my little old feelings that way, Blair."

She bowed her head. "It's my pleasure," she said, then leaned in to touch her lips to his again, her hands climbing up into the back of his hair, sifting through the strands and then gripping with authority.

He took over then, his tongue full-on invading her mouth, the earthy taste of wine lingering on them both. She made a sound of pleasure that reverberated in his ears and he'd reached the limit. Striding toward the house with her in his arms, he didn't stop the kiss, loved, in fact, that his eyes were open while hers were closed and he could see what she looked like while they kissed.

When he reached the steps, however, he had to break the kiss and appeal for her to open the front door for him since his hands were currently occupied with lush female.

They crossed the threshold of her house into a handsome foyer lit with an old brass chandelier and a burning candle that smelled like fresh herbs he couldn't quite place. While he couldn't be bothered to look at anything too closely, it felt like Blair as soon as he walked in. He climbed the curved wooden staircase up to the second floor and followed the rest of her directions, her hands playing with his hair and dropping idle kisses on his collarbone as he pushed in the cracked door of her bedroom.

It smelled a little sweeter in this room, like the

same vanilla scent of her skin and it only amped up his need. Not wasting any time, he dropped her gently down on the edge of the bed before stepping back.

"Ask me truth or dare," he told her. When she did, he said, staring straight into her eyes, "Dare."

"Take off my clothes."

He gave her a full smile then. "You are so good at this game."

They both laughed then. "You're not bad yourself," she told him as he pulled her off the bed so she was standing in front of him. His hands at her waist, he played with the drawstring holding up her skirt for only a moment before pulling at it and helping the wispy fabric fall to the ground. They both glanced at it for a second before their eyes met and she arched an eyebrow in question. "Bottoms first," she said, "that's an interesting choice."

He shrugged. "I thought I'd waited long enough to get to the good stuff."

"Truth or dare," he told her.

"Dare," she said, again without any hesitation.

"Take those little undergarments off then, my fingers are already tired."

He took a step back so he could watch. Her fingertips, stained faintly purple from the grapes, which was a little detail that had his dick jerking, dragged down a pair of nude, barely-there underwear. The scrap of fabric hit the floor along with his knees. One thing he hadn't forgotten in his sex sabbatical was the natural order of things.

Smiling at her intake of breath as his fingers landed on her thighs, he let them travel downward instead of up like they both wanted, but it was enough to smell her arousal. Soon enough he'd bury himself in her but now he had some stuff to take care of, namely driving her so out of her mind she could barely stand for want of his mouth on her.

"Truth or dare?" she asked, her voice low.

"Dare," he said, his eyes snapping to hers.

"Keep going," she told him.

"Oh, I'd say you couldn't stop me if you tried but I do respond to a verbal negative," he said, running a finger over the back of her knee. Then he hoisted it up over his shoulder so her legs were spread and the heart of her was exposed to his gaze. "Now that's been worth the wait."

And with no other warning than that, he went in. Spreading her apart with his thumbs, he licked up either side of her, tasting her, learning her as her fingers tightened in his hair. He loved it, and responding to her tugs, he lightly licked over the slick nub, applying more pressure when she bucked against him. Finally suckling it as he slid a single finger inside her wet heat, her cry of pleasure nearly undoing him. His own blood was rushing in from his ears straight into his throbbing cock. He was beyond impressed that he'd already lasted this long without exploding. Between the erotic truth or dare and simply the pleasure of having all that silkiness under his tongue as she got closer to climax, it was a wonder he was still hanging on.

When he added two fingers, brushing up against that rough patch of skin inside her, her head fell backward, as if she'd given herself up to the pleasure. They'd both forgotten the game and were now simply committed to giving each other what they needed. And he needed so damn much from her.

"It's your turn," he reminded her, though, because this was the game and for them both to win, they needed to keep playing. He added a third finger and she gasped. "Truth or dare?" he prodded.

"Dare," she choked out, looking down at him from above with a spark of challenge in her eyes.

He stopped the movement of his thumb on her clit, then sped it up again before he commanded, "Come now."

He pumped his fingers in and out of her as he sucked the slippery clit into his mouth again, licking and licking until she finally cried out, her come soaking his fingers. He felt his cock jerk against his abdomen and watching her head thrown back in ecstasy, her harsh cry of release, was triggering a need in him so deep it was already too far gone to control.

Rising, he shifted her back on the bed, pulling off her shirt and bra in record time. "Condoms?" he asked, licking some of her off his hand. He was like a rabid animal—he had to have her.

Eyes darkening, she nodded to her bedside drawer and a flicker of annoyance hit him at the open box that signaled she'd used the absent condoms on her loser ex. But he couldn't care about that now. He pulled one out and tossed it on the bed beside her as he climbed on top of her. His gaze raked her body.

"Is the game over?" she asked. "Because I think you know what my next dare will be."

He only nodded and lowered his head to take a beaded pale peach nipple into his mouth. Taking the other breast in his hand, he squeezed and conformed his hand to her size, testing the weight of her. She wasn't big but she was perfect against his palm, the warm velvet a weird balm to his raging erection while at the same time keeping it at a steady arousal.

"Game was over when you invited me onto your porch, but then I think we both enjoy playing," he murmured, giving her nipple a deep suck until she whimpered and he let go, giving her other breast the same attention.

No longer able to wait, he ripped open the condom and slid it on his waiting cock in record time.

At her disappointed look, he raised an eyebrow.

She shrugged against the pale yellow duvet. "You didn't let me play with you." Her gaze lowered meaningfully to his cock.

"Oh, don't worry," he promised, "that's my very favorite game and I wouldn't deprive you of the pleasure."

He hitched himself to her slit, right where he needed to go, the warmth already traveling down the length of his oversensitive dick.

"But right now, sweetheart, if it's all the same to you, I'd like you to tell me that my time away from the sport hasn't diminished my skill so that I can finally slide into you and give us both what we want."

Tonight certainly hadn't been his best performance, but he'd make it up to her later. Right now, his mind was literally mush.

"High marks," she managed as he couldn't help but enter her, just an inch. "No extra tutoring necessary."

"I take back everything I've said about you, Ms. Sandoval, you are a very good woman, indeed."

And then he proceeded in doing his best to make them both very bad.

CHAPTER SEVEN

COLE PUSHED INSIDE HER, his big body covering hers as
he did and Blair could barely breathe for the roiling
emotions inside her. She hadn't anticipated that she'd
like Cole so much and that when he came fully inside of her that she might already be sad that he'd be
leaving in the morning. But those thoughts were just
as quickly lost to her as he started thrusting, gently
at first, but then eventually rearing back and giving
it his all, their grunts and sighs and the creaking of
her bed the only sounds in the room, the game put
away for less intense times.

"Fuck, Blair," Cole gritted in her ear. "You feel so
good. I can't—" He trailed off and reached down to
rub her with his thumb, taking her closer to the edge.

"You can't what?" she breathed, writhing against
him. He was large, which was probably one of the
reasons he was so damn full of himself, and he honestly barely fit, but she was so revved up, so ready
for him after he'd made her come that the friction
between them was easy yet still intense. More than
anything she could sense his desperation, that he

was struggling to hang on. Two years was an extremely long time to not have sex and she wanted it to be amazing for him.

"I can't take it anymore," he told her, his thumb flying over her clit and in seconds she came again, crying out as his mouth came down to slide openmouthed kisses down her neck.

He came then too, stiffening against her, his breath hot against the burning skin of her neck.

When he was finished, his head came up and he pinned her with his gaze. "That wasn't my finest performance, Ms. Sandoval, and I do vow next time we'll take our time with it, but if I could just extend my sincerest and deepest gratitude for that which has just transpired, I'd surely appreciate it."

Blair nearly laughed that the man who'd just given her two orgasms was asking for her permission to thank her. He was a peculiar type of person but she liked it.

"I'm happy to break your celibacy streak," she told him, running a hand down his back, then wondering if she should. It felt weird to make such an intimate gesture now that the sex was finished between them. But he seemed to like it, dropping a light kiss on her nose before pulling out of her and asking for directions to the bathroom.

When he was gone, she went to one of the guest bathrooms to clean up herself and when she returned to her bedroom he was lying back on her pillows examining one of the grape cultivation manuals she had on her nightstand.

"This looks old," he observed, holding the book up to her.

"The original was written in the 1800s."

His eyes widened. "You trying to study up on old techniques?"

Blair shrugged. "Yeah, I think it's important to look at the history of growing. As regional climates change we know we constantly have to be thinking about how it affects our grapes. And it's also interesting to see just how much *hasn't* changed. For all the new machinery and automated bottling, winemaking is one of those things that has kind of stood the test of time."

Cole's grin was huge. "This has got to be the sexiest afterglow conversation I've ever had." He pulled the covers back. "Now get in here because the night is young and I was previously promised a blow job."

With a wry smile, she opened her drawer to get an oversize T-shirt and a pair of boy shorts before climbing into bed with Cole. Once there, Cole put his arm out and pulled her into his crook. She settled in with an inward sigh as the smell of him, piney again with a side of fresh laundry, permeated her brain.

"I like this room, you know."

"I'm glad it meets your standards," she said dryly.

"This bed, especially, was sturdier than it looked for a man my size." He nodded at the long wooden, somewhat spindly, posters. "I'd like to see how those fare as well, you know what I mean?"

"No, I don't actually know what you mean," she

said, certain whatever he said was going to be mildly perverted.

"Oh, just that they give a man visions of tying your hands to the top and screwing your brains out against them."

Blair cleared her throat. "Well, that is certainly one idea."

Cole laughed. "Oh, don't you worry, I am full of ideas. And unfortunately for you, I'm like a bull that's just been let out of the cage, sweetheart. Now that I'm loose, it's gonna take all night to wear me out so I hope you're prepared."

"I'll believe it when I see it," Blair teased, plucking playfully at his small nipple. "You're a big talker, after all. For all I know you're going to fall asleep in a couple of minutes and not wake up until morning."

Cole squeezed her against him. "Blair, darling, I'm a big everything, if you know what I mean."

Blair struggled not to laugh because the last thing she wanted to do was encourage this kind of behavior.

"Just do it," he whispered in her ear, his tongue coming out to trace the shell of her ear. With just that little contact, her body was ready to go again. "Let yourself laugh at me. I like it."

Then he nibbled her earlobe and there was very little reason to laugh.

"I won't laugh at you because you're already too full of yourself."

He let her earlobe go and raised a lascivious eyebrow. "And you'd like to be full of me instead? Is that the problem? Because I'm working my way around to doing that again as we speak. So don't you worry about it, Miz Blair, Cole is gonna make it better."

"Dear god," she muttered, shoulders shaking as he returned his attention to her ear. "I don't know whether to be disgusted or amused."

"I don't think they're mutually exclusive emotions, but if you're dead set on picking just one my vote is for amused." He lifted his head up again. "Although, now that I think about it, being amused while you're full of me doesn't help my poor neglected ego. You know I've gone two years without a woman screaming my name and telling me just how big I am. One tends to forget."

Blair rolled her eyes and ran a finger down his abs, following the shallow cutouts. "I'm too much of a lady to comment on a man's size." Her hand dropped lower and she circled his hardening cock with her hand. "But I can tell you with some confidence that you're very pretty."

He apparently didn't have anything to say to that and when she looked up, she was stunned to see that he was blushing. His cheeks were flushed and he averted his eyes as soon as she met them.

Lifting up to her elbow to make him meet her gaze, she laughed. "Are you embarrassed right now?"

"Nah," he said, still not able to meet her gaze.

"Oh, my gosh, you totally are," she exclaimed, releasing him from her hand and straddling him so he couldn't avoid her gaze. "Is it because you don't know you have a good-looking penis or because you've heard it so many times before."

A heavy shoulder shrugged and while he turned his face forward he still wasn't looking at her eyes. "No one's ever come right out and said something like that, no."

"And why are you embarrassed by it?"

"You know, you're all of a sudden real interested in me, aren't you?" he asked, trying to change the subject, his hands drifting up her thighs until he was lightly gripping her ass. "When before you wouldn't even laugh at my legendary wit and charm."

"Yeah, because that was boring and rehearsed, but now you just got interesting."

That got a smile out of him. "I'm a man—it's weird for me to hear shit like that."

Blair rolled her eyes. "Compliments about your appearance? You do that all the time to me."

"Yeah, and you don't take it too well either." He ran a thumb over the crease of her ass and tendrils of anticipation floated throughout her body.

"Because I know you're saying that stuff just to sleep with me."

"Doesn't mean it's not true," he pointed out.

Blair drifted her thumbnails over his nipples down to the undersides of his pecs, playing around just like he was, stoking the embers for their next round. "So why are you embarrassed again?"

Cole's eyes met hers then, the green suddenly intense. "I don't know why. Just that I guess you're different from other women I've slept with and you're not exactly issuing out compliments." He sighed hugely. "It's been a little bit since someone's seen it, so I guess—" his eyes slid away and then back again "—it was nice to hear and I liked it probably more than I should."

The guilt was apparent in his voice, that he didn't think he deserved happiness after his brother died. A pang of sadness gripped Blair. She couldn't imagine losing Nate, but then feeling as if it was her fault as well? Cole had been through it the past two years and she felt good that she'd been able to make him smile a little. Guilt was definitely something she understood, still struggling under the weight of her shame. Even if she was innocent in the damage she'd caused, that naivete didn't help her sleep at night. She was the very worst kind of woman and she didn't deserve the man currently beneath her, but at least she'd been able to alleviate some of Cole's misplaced guilt as well.

She leaned down to drop a kiss on his lips and his hand came up around her neck and held her there, taking the kiss from a sweet tap to an instant conflagration. Pulling back for a moment, she managed, "I think you should enjoy it however much you want."

Then she kissed him again, tongue exploring his straight white teeth, the plush inside of his lip. Tugging on his lower lip and eventually letting it go, she sat back up and started kissing her way down his body. His skin was like an inferno, radiating serious waves of heat into the air around him. She slid a wide tongue over his nipple, sucking and nipping until his grip on her ass became tight, his big fingers digging into her flesh. Dropping more kisses down his chest, she didn't waste much more time getting where she wanted to go.

Looking up, she met his eyes. "So is this something you've done in the past two years?"

He shook his head. "No one's touched me but you, sweetheart."

It shouldn't have pleased her, but it did. For once, *she* was the one who'd been chosen. She wasn't just some side woman someone was using to spice up their boring life or because cheating on their wife was some kink of theirs. Cole wanted *her*. He could have slept with anyone tonight or in the past two years and yet she was the one in bed with him now, seeing him naked, making him blush with the most casual of compliments. It shouldn't matter at all, shouldn't signify in her life, but she couldn't help but feel warmed from the inside out. Out of nowhere, maybe it was possible that she'd unexpectedly found the friend she'd needed. Someone who didn't know her or her history of epic shame. In two days, knowing Cole had done more to pull her out of her funk than all her family and friends hovering with concern, her mother's vengeful musings and her father's sad puppy eyes full of pity every time he saw her.

In this bed, she was finally allowed to be fully Blair. Mouthy, powerful and kind, and that was enough. It was such a huge relief to know she was *enough* for someone else.

* * *

Blair wrapped her hand around his length, the thick vein pulsing heavily against her hand and Cole thought he'd died and gone to heaven. He crossed his arms behind his head and gave her a heated look, intending to enjoy himself while she worked, which was pretty fucking phenomenal because he loved seeing her enjoy him. It was the first time someone (else) had touched him like this in too long and to know that she was having such a good time with it, he was barely hanging on.

She stroked him a couple of times, his hips rolling of their own volition, his eyes locking on hers, as his body soaked up every single bit of her touch. Nothing had compared to how he felt with her hands on him, the banked reverence and curiosity was killing him more than the maelstrom of sexual need she was stoking as she stroked him. She adjusted her position so she could take him into her mouth, but he scooted back from her amazing hands and stood up instead.

"Let's just do this right, shall we?" He proceeded to throw a pillow on the floor at his feet because he had truly waited long enough for a decent blow job and he wanted it how he wanted it.

Blair understood immediately and sank to her knees in front of him, taking a quick intake of breath when his hand sifted through her hair and to the back of the skull.

"Just so you know, sweetheart, I'm a little demanding." He ran a thumb gently over her cheek and adjusted her head so he could see her face because he wanted her to see how much he was loving what she was doing. "But you've proven yourself a hard-working woman so I think we'll be all right."

Then he guided her to his waiting cock, feeling the wetness of her mouth and nearly losing his shit. She made a whimper of need and his ass clenched knowing she wanted him. Her mouth opened wide as the tip of him hit her lips, a drop of liquid there for her to lick, which she did. His intake of breath was audible as her tongue shot out to taste him before he eased himself into her mouth. Inch by inch he made progress, her jaw widening as he went to accommodate him until eventually he hit the soft back of her throat with a ravaged groan.

"Holy hell, Blair," he gritted, his thumb brushing over her cheek again. "You are fucking amazing."

She kept going, her tongue sweeping across the sensitive skin of his cock as she took him in and out of her mouth. His hips thrust against her and he could feel him grow even harder in her mouth as she whimpered around his mouth again. The depth of feeling stunned him as he watched her take him, that she cared to do it, that she didn't find him disgusting or unworthy considering she now knew about his role in his brother's death. It felt like water in the desert.

"If you don't stop I'm going to go before we get to have some more fun," he warned.

But she ignored him, sucked him in harder, her hand coming up to grip the thick base of him as she shuttled him in and out of her mouth, her lips swollen with the friction.

"Damn it, Blair," Cole gritted, his hips thrusting. He was no longer in control at all. "You just can't let a man be a gentleman, can you?"

She shook her head the slightest bit and he gripped the back of her head so that he could see her eyes. He brushed the hair out of her face and sighed in glorious defeat. "Well, go ahead and take me, sunshine." Their eyes locked, she brushed against his tightened sack and then he was letting go. His eyes narrowed as she swallowed the thick spurts of hot liquid. With a final groan that he felt in his toes, she milked him, licking him clean before finally dropping a small kiss on his hipbone and rising to her feet.

"This was worth all the fucking wait," he growled, then picked her up in his arms and placed her on the bed on all fours with her ass in the air. He ran a hand down her left cheek. "But you shouldn't have taken me all the way. Now we're both going to have to wait until I'm inside you again and that's a damn shame, Blair."

He gently opened her up to him from behind, setting his mouth on her, his tongue sliding into her, deep and erotic and wet from this angle, and he feasted like it was a banquet. After she was all but shuddering against him, he pulled back, his breath hot on her skin. "I get why you took me all the way now," he said, drawing a finger down her entire, drenched slit, "you were getting just as turned on, weren't you?"

He spread her thighs wider apart, then held her open and so she could feel his gaze on her. "Ms. Sandoval likes to suck my cock," he mused, running his thumb down the side of her lip, possessive, because he was staking his claim on her vagina, exploring but also planting a flag there for everyone else to see. Because no one had ever paid so much attention to him before, clearly enjoying the learning of him like she would a particular variety of grape. He was under her spell completely. "I think that's good news because I fucking love returning the favor, sweetheart."

And then he was on her, his tongue sliding forward to work over her clit while his fingers stretched her inside, two fingers, then three, pumping as if he were already inside her. She was gasping already, so close to coming yet he was as relentless as she'd been with him. He wanted to make sure she never forgot this night—never forgot him, maybe, even though they had only tonight. Every time her hips found a rhythm and she was building toward release, he pulled back, gentling his touch, removing his hands and tongue. Right now he was blowing on her oversensitized clit like an animal trainer cooing to a trapped animal. He wanted her out of her fucking mind with need. Wanted all other men to pale in comparison to him. It was an insane thing to want, but he wasn't really in a position to examine the emotion at the moment.

She was at the edge and tried to change positions and take control, take him inside of her to get it done but he held her with an iron grip, essentially bolting her to the spot as he proceeded to suck and nibble and caress.

"I hate you right now," she choked out as the pressure built again and she finally, *finally*, came. She cried out her release, the wave of relief and pleasure and sensation taking her under as his tongue slid over her clit.

He laughed at her ire before he slid her arms out from under her until her face was on the bed, and hoisted her hips higher into the air. Then he breached her entrance in one long, demanding thrust, burying himself to the hilt with a wickedly low growl.

"Fucking hell," he gritted, letting them both get used to the new turn of events. "I can still feel your muscles clenching."

She tried to buck up against him but he held her still, dropping a kiss in the middle of her spine.

"You want more of me here, Blair?" he asked. "Because if you're feeling too tender, you know I'll stop."

She shook her head immediately, and breathed out a raspy, "Keep going."

He did, too. Slow at first, dragging every single long inch of him through her on-fire inner walls. She was slick and ready and lush and he felt it everywhere.

"Too slow," she choked out, her fists clenching in her silky duvet.

He laughed again, loving how demanding she

was. Instead of obeying her demands, he slid out of her and picked her up instead, making a quick detour to pick up the discarded scarf he'd seen on her dresser. Then true to his word, he stood her in front of one of her bed posters and proceeded to use it to tie her hands to the top of the wooden pole.

Then he hoisted her up, threw a leg over the footboard and put the other one around his waist and thrust into her again. He couldn't go as deep in this position but he could see her eyes now as he worked himself inside her again and nearly lost his mind.

He almost grinned when she tried to move her arms but found that she was well and truly stuck. "Now normally I like a handsy woman, but I have to admit that I like you being all tied up too." Then he drew a nipple into his mouth and sucked until she yelped with the tiniest bit of pain.

"Cole, please," she begged, her body flushed red with need.

He grinned. "Well, since you asked so nicely."

Then he gave her want she wanted. Hard, fast, messy, a rhythm that existed for only a few thrusts at a time before he changed his position to deliver more and more pleasure until finally she was breaking all around him, her untethered cries urging him on and making him wild.

With a guttural roar, he let go as well, taking her mouth as he did so, wringing every last bit of connection from her that he could as he untied her.

Both breathing hard, they clung to each other.

Two years had led him here, to a vineyard in California, and to a woman who was as uninterested in a real connection as he was, and yet, as he was about to fall into the best night of sleep he'd had since Scott's death, he wondered if she'd nudged awake something else inside him along with his libido.

CHAPTER EIGHT

SIX DAYS HAD passed since Cole had left Sonoma. He'd been gone when Blair had woken up the morning after the party, a short note from him on her pillow, and she hadn't heard from him since. It was her most successful one-night stand ever. Most importantly, her crisis of conscience had been averted. She'd had a single night with a man as a palate cleanser and now she'd return to no men all the time. He was a celebrity who wasn't married or in a relationship, so there were no secret repercussions to further mire her in self-loathing.

Except there was a different problem altogether.

It was that she couldn't stop *thinking* about him. And if she were being honest, she *missed* him. Found herself hanging out in the tasting room more than she ever had just on the off chance he would walk in one day again with that goofy smile, even though she knew very well he was on an entirely different continent. Since the breakup, Cole had been the only person to tempt her into more than perfunctory small talk.

Instead, most evenings she'd found herself internet searching, reading more about his career and life,
and finally taking a deeper dive into his brother's
death. As she scrolled through the photos of him on
the side of the track that day staring at his brother's
mangled car her heart ached for him. She found well-
wishers from all over the globe who had started fan
websites dedicated to the brothers and who mourned
Scott right along with Cole. It looked as if Cole had
retired immediately after that race and resurfaced
six months later as an announcer.

Nate appeared at the threshold of her office, reminding her exactly why this newfound preoccupa-
tion with Cole was misguided. So what if they'd had
a good time together? So had she and her ex and look
how that turned out. It was better that it had only
been one night and that was it. She didn't have the
emotional bandwidth for anything else.

"So are you going to tell me what happened with
Cole Taggart?" Nate asked, his arms crossing as he
regarded her.

"I took him on a tour, just like you demanded,"
she said pointedly, having already answered this
question three times this week from her meddling
troublemaker brother who just wanted to needle her
and was the reigning gold medalist of the Annoy
Blair Olympics.

"Why did he want to go to your house?"

"How do you know who he is, by the way? He
doesn't even race for NASCAR."

"You didn't answer my question."

She shrugged and gave him a haughty sister look. "Neither did you."

Her brother snorted and threw himself into the only other seat in the room, an elaborately carved dining chair from two tasting room redesigns ago. "Just tell me you didn't sleep with him. The guy is a massive player and you're not exactly batting a thousand with men."

Blair's lips thinned as her brother's constant drudging up of the past threatened her newfound state of semi-hope for the future. But now with the mention of her epic fail of a love life, the image of her ex's *wife's* tear-streaked face was right back in the forefront of her mind. The woman's heartfelt plea for her to stop seeing her husband was burned into her soul and Blair would never forget it. She'd give anything to fast-forward time and not have the memory of that woman's misery in such sharp focus.

"I'm not batting with men at all," Blair declared for the umpteenth time. "Which is why I didn't sleep with Cole Taggart. As I've informed you at least a dozen times by now, I had a bottle of a 2015 pinot noir there that we'd talked about that I forgot to give to him so he came to get it."

Nate looked skeptical, and she imagined that since they resembled each other with the same russet hair and eyes, that it was very similar to her own expression as she stared at him right back. "Just take care of yourself this time, B. I don't want to see you hurt again and guys like Cole are just as bad as the ex who we are not allowed to name. He might be open about the fact that he screws around, but he still, in fact, screws around."

"And how do you know him again?"

"I'm trying to tell you. His reputation with women is *legendary*. So much so that I know about it from all the guys over at the raceway. On the Formula One off-season, he'd work as a color correspondent for the American races and made quite an impression on a group of guys known for partying, Blair. I'm just trying to look out for you."

Blair had a flashback to him tying her to her bedpost and warmth flooded her face. Legendary, indeed. But he'd also been so sweetly vulnerable that Blair knew his brother's death had changed him. Maybe now that he'd broken his self-imposed celibacy he'd return to his former rock star lifestyle, but either way it certainly wasn't any of her business.

"So thankful for your concern, big brother, but I'm not going to date Cole Taggart," she assured. "I highly doubt I'll ever see him again."

The sound of throat being cleared sounded from the doorway and both her and Nate's heads swiveled to her office door where Cole Taggart was standing, looking the same as he had when she'd first met him. In a pair of charcoal pants, a pale lemon polo shirt with familiar aviators tucked into the open V-neck, he looked fresh if not a little worn around the eyes.

"Well, now, you know I don't like to be contrary, Ms. Sandoval, but I'd say your doubt is misplaced."

Blair's insides twisted and about a million questions were on the tip of her tongue. And yet the only words that left her lips were, "You're here."

A corner of his wide mouth kicked up. "I, uh," he said, nodding a greeting Nate, "well, turns out I needed to be in the area for some other business and thought I'd come by to thank you again for your hospitality and illuminating education about wine-making."

Nate stood and held out his hand to Cole, pulling him in for one of those guy things where they patted each other on the back. Blair gave a side-eye to essentially no one but couldn't hold it in.

"Glad to have you back," Nate told him, then looked at Blair. "It's good to know my sister, despite her general displeasure in giving tours, was able to provide you with such excellent service."

Cole's eyes strayed to hers for just a millisecond before he smiled at Nate. "I'd say it was unequivocally *the* best service I've ever received."

Nate's eyebrows rose and Blair felt her face heat to volcanic levels of embarrassment.

Her brother cleared his throat. "Well, I can't tell you how happy I am that she exceeded your expectations." Then he pinned Blair with a look. "Glad to know she's finally putting some effort in with the customers."

"A whole lot of effort," Cole agreed. "She probably needs a raise."

Nate snorted at that and Blair knew why. She was the driving force behind Sandoval Wines' explosion into the upper echelon of wines. If she wanted a raise, she could get one, but the truth was that she didn't even bother drawing a viticulturist salary because the company profits were so large. That wasn't even taking into consideration her booking fee to go speak or teach people about wine was only going up as her reputation grew.

"I'll let our parents know of your regard," Nate said, giving Blair another look, only this one had her rising from the chair in alarm.

"I don't think that's necessary, Nate," she warned. "They're far too busy with the upcoming harvest. I'll just put Mr. Taggart's compliment in my file for my next review." She neither had an employee file nor a yearly performance review but it was the only thing she could think of. What she wanted to do was grab her brother by the collar and shake him until he promised not to mention anything to her parents, particularly her mother, who had already called her twice today to "check up on her," aka make sure Blair had made it to work and wasn't lying in bed overdosing on liquor-filled truffles and gory horror flicks like she had when she'd first found out she inhabited the lowest rung of humanity.

Nate scratched the back of his head. "I don't know, sis, you know how they like to be informed about the winery's performance."

Cole, whose gaze had been bouncing between them both, finally spoke. "I can see my compliment has caused a bit of commotion here, but I just wanted Ms. Sandoval to know that she made a lasting impression on me."

Nate gave Blair a withering look, then did an about-face and spoke to Cole with an easy smile. "Don't you worry about us—we're just playing around. I'm always happy to have a return customer." Then with another shake and pat on the back, Nate promised he'd see Cole after his meeting, and left the room, closing the door behind him.

"Well, I guess your brother knows we slept together."

Blair snorted. "He only suspects."

"And he has a problem with it?"

"I don't know or care," Blair told him, meeting his eyes and trying to stop the butterflies from beating her insides to shreds. Her palms were suddenly sweaty and was her mouth drier than normal? Did she need to see her dentist or doctor about this sudden new ailment where it felt difficult to open her mouth and speak words? As if her tongue was glued to the roof of her mouth?

"What are you doing here?" she finally managed.

Cole's head tilted and his gaze lingered over her torn and wine-stained jeans and then the faded California Redwood National Park T-shirt before landing on her face. "I had some time off and I had a lot of fun with you," he said, shoving his hands into his pockets, looking almost irritated with himself.

Blair bit the inside of her lip. "Well, it's nice to see you." She nearly rolled her eyes at herself. Brilliant, Blair, nice to see you? Like he was an acquaintance in a grocery store instead of the man she'd reimagined having sex with every night since he'd left.

He smiled, that roguish dimple appearing in just the one cheek. "It's nice to see you too, Ms. Sandoval."

"Did you want some more wine?"

"I'd love some more wine," he said. "But I can see that I've interrupted you so I'm happy to come back after you're finished with work for the day."

Blair glanced at the clock. She lived to work, but maybe after months of burying herself in it she'd quit at a normal time.

"I just brought up our newest year of wines that will hit shelves soon and need to try them. Would you have a problem doing another tasting?"

Cole's eyes gleamed. "I'd have absolutely no problem with that at all, in fact." He then obediently followed her to the tasting building and into the private room where she'd already set everything up for the tasting she'd intended to do with her brother this afternoon before Cole showed up.

She pointed to one of the cafe chairs for him to sit in and set herself up behind the bar again, much like the first time they'd met only now they were in a small enclosed room instead of the larger public hall.

Handing him a glass, their fingers touched as he took it and she couldn't hide her shiver. "So how long are you in town?" she asked, trying to be super casual but undoubtedly not succeeding considering her palms were now full-on swimming pools after just a paltry brush of his hand.

"Two days," he told her.

"Where do you go after that?"

"Hungary."

She met his eyes, surprised. "So you were in Spain and decided to fly back here for only two days before flying back to Hungary?"

Cole nodded, his eyes opaque and unreadable.

"And why did you do that?"

His gaze locked on hers, the meaning in his clear as the answer hit her in the chest. He'd come to see her. He'd flown halfway across the world to see *her* for two days. Breathing was now an issue.

"What's your other business in the area?" she asked, just making sure she had the right of it considering just how often she'd had it wrong with guys before.

"I don't have other business in the area, Blair," he said. "I came to see you."

Her mind completely blown, Blair found herself nodding repeatedly and way too much. "Okay," she finally said, the real master of words that she was. "Well, I'm touched that you would do all that to see me."

"Yeah, well, I told myself that I'd done far stupider things for a woman, that just hopping on a flight to see one was actually a normal thing to do." He sighed. "Though I can tell by your expression that it's not, so we can just call this what it is—damn Looney Tunes, Blair."

She laughed then, happy that someone said what she was thinking. "Maybe a little," she agreed, her eyes drifting away from his for a moment.

He threw his head back, shoulders shaking in laughter, eyes dancing when they met hers again.

"Yeah, I'd say that's the understatement of the century." He shook his head, blowing out a breath as he got himself together. "I guess the thing I also need to ask is if you're okay with me being here? I know it's fucked up that I am. I'm jet-lagged as all hell—I honestly couldn't tell you what day it is—but I've been thinking about you since I left your house and I just couldn't stay away. But I'll go if that's not how you feel too."

It probably shouldn't be okay that he was here. Having a long-distance affair with a man who led a completely separate life was *exactly* the thing she'd sworn not to do. It was how her ex had sold her on the lie, after all. He'd come into town for a few weeks at a time, wine and dine her, and then leave for his home and she thought that was the whole story. But it hadn't been. He'd had an entirely separate life in a different part of California. She was just some side candy he was keeping because he was awful and had made her awful, too, with his perfidy. The only reason he'd been caught was because his wife had found texts from her on a phone she didn't recognize as his and she'd told Blair immediately. And ever since, Blair had wondered how she could have missed the signs? But she sure as hell wouldn't again.

Which was why she'd all but taken out an FBI report on Cole so she knew he was fair game. And this was just sex anyway so it was fine. She'd allow herself this as part of the healing process and then look into the nunnery again to obtain her future penitence and salvation.

She poured them the first of the wines, the newest sauvignon blanc, before assuring him, "Yes, it's okay that you're here."

Cole blew out a long, relieved breath. "Thank god, because it's a hell of a long way to travel to get a no, thank you, sir."

A corner of Blair's mouth kicked up. "A text probably would have saved you the trouble."

"Yeah, but you know me, I like a little drama. Shakes life up a little in a good way."

Blair shook her head but realized that was a fact she knew about him already. It was a new experience for her to feel so tuned in to someone so fast. Normally it took at least five dates for her to really get a true read on a person's personality and even then she obviously wasn't great at it, and she couldn't let his easy personality fool her into thinking something real could be between them. Just because they got along didn't mean she could trust him. Or herself. But that he didn't know about the affair and wasn't concerned about her was the biggest gift. When she was with him, she was just Blair again. Not other woman Blair, not the pitiful daughter who couldn't find an unmarried man to be with Blair, and not the dummy sister whose older brother had to watch out for her because she was so inept with men Blair.

With Cole, she was back to her outspoken and seminerdy self. It was such a damn relief to know she still existed somewhere.

"Well, flying across the world just to see me and have wine and maybe not have sex again certainly is dramatic," she said, swirling her wine and nodding for him to do the same. "Are you hungry? I've got the snacks back here as well."

"You know I am, sweetheart, plus I should probably tell you that watching you eat cheese is one of the most erotic things I've ever seen. It got me so hot last time now I get hard just glancing at a wheel of brie."

A responding thrill that he'd thought of her assaulted her against her will. "You did grocery shopping in Spain?" she asked skeptically.

"Nah, but there were cheese plates at all the race events. Trays and trays," he lamented. "I nearly went out of my mind."

"You're nuts," Blair laughed, leaning down to grab the plates she'd had the tasting room staff prepare for her and Nate. "But I'm happy to feed you. Just don't be disappointed if I don't eat much, I like to do these new year tastings with a fresh palate."

"But you'll have some afterward?"

She nodded as he scooped up some of the goat cheese with a cracker. "You remembered that goat goes with sauvignon blanc." She grinned. "What a good student you are."

Cole's eyes flared. "I do remember and took diligent notes, if you'll recall. But mostly I remember that you had a little piece of cheese on your thumb and licked it off. It was a close one there for me. I'm only a man—I barely survived it."

Blair didn't further indulge him in his melodrama but met his eyes. "Thank you for coming back to see me. I might have thought about you a time or two as well."

Cole reached over and took her hand in his, the contact, the feel of the rough, cracked skin of his palm reigniting all the memories of his hands sliding over her skin, of them inside her giving no mercy as he'd played her like a world-class pianist, had her breath catching in her throat. His eyes drifted shut for a moment as well, the touch clearly affecting him too, which made her feel better. She wasn't alone in this madness.

Desire was burning in his eyes when they opened and riveted to hers, pinning her in stillness, every part of her body on pause for what he was about to say and do. Ideally, it would be her vision of him sweeping all the wine and cheese plates off the bar that separated them and throwing her down on it.

"I can't tell you how relieved I am to hear that, Blair," he said, swallowing. "Because in the interest of full disclosure, I sure as hell have left a lot of bedrooms in the morning, but I've never wanted to be back in one as badly as I want to be back in yours."

The words rang warning bells again in Blair, especially considering the conversation she'd just had with her brother, but she knew the racing schedule, knew that he traveled more than half the year for his job and that the season wouldn't end for months. It meant that there was no way they could ever have an actual relationship. Whatever happened between them had an expiration date and it settled her nerves. The idea that maybe she, Blair Sandoval, who on most days found dirt and crusted wine beneath her fingernails as well as sticks and leaves from the vineyard in her hair, that this same person could inspire a man into a torrid and passionate international affair, well, sorry good sense, she simply was not going to pass it up. The fact that for once she wouldn't be "the other woman" for someone, that just her was enough for him to fly to California for two days was far too much of an enticement.

And if he was offering another guilt-free weekend where she didn't have to think about her personal humiliation and ex, a part of her desperately needed it.

"Well, it makes sense to me," she said, feeling her lips curve up in a sly smile. "I did splurge on a top-of-the-line mattress. You won't find better comfort anywhere—the salesman guaranteed it."

Cole smiled too, and they just stayed like that for a moment, grinning stupidly at each other before finally he broke the moment by popping a grape into his mouth. "Yeah, I'd say you hit the nail on the head there. I had the best night's sleep of my life on that thing."

CHAPTER NINE

COLE SHOULD HAVE been in Spain. But then besides the death of his brother, he wasn't really a man who particularly dealt in recriminations. He'd left Blair the morning after they'd spent an incredible night in bed and literally thought of nothing since. But the sex hadn't been all he'd thought about—it had been this too—the easy way they'd found together so quickly. That's what had truly drawn him back to Sonoma, and that for the first time since the accident he'd felt like his old self.

He'd never considered himself a particularly deep or thoughtful person, but something had happened to him after that night with Blair. In the morning, he'd followed the routine he'd used for years and left before she got up and was gone before having to say an awkward goodbye.

And yet, he'd flown across the globe for another night with her.

It was fucking nuts, but just looking at her made some of the pain go away. He didn't know why or how, but being here around her family, around

Blair, who was carrying around pain herself—they'd formed a kinship of sorts. And being *with her*...he'd had a lot of sex, but it'd never felt as unbelievable as it had with Blair.

And when he thought about how long it would be until he had a significant portion of time off to come see her, realizing that it would be months and she could be with some other loser by then—he'd made the decision. Seeing her smile at him told him it had been the right one. But he knew, too, that this had to be the last time. He couldn't lead her on into thinking this could ever be something. Because it couldn't. For a lot of simple logistical reasons, but mostly because he didn't deserve to be happy with a woman. Not when his brother was cold in the ground and would never know the joy of a wife and family and home. The very thing he'd wanted to quit racing to find, and that first Cole had taken away and then racing had irrevocably.

"How did you find me anyway?" Blair asked, bringing him back from the edge of the gripping despair he'd battled since the accident.

He cleared his throat. "You weren't in the tasting room but I saw your car out front and reckoned you'd be back here making wine or playing with dirt, whatever it is you do all day to create grape-y masterpieces. I just followed lights and sounds until I found you."

Blair raised her eyebrow. "Grape-y masterpieces?"

"The wine," he told her, slowly, as if she were a child.

"I'm not going to engage," she muttered, shaking her head at him. "How do you like this wine?"

"As you know, I'm not huge on whites but to be honest with you, Ms. Sandoval, I think I liked whatever you gave me the last time better."

"Yeah, definitely a better year," she told him, taking another sip from her glass. "But this isn't bad."

"Hell no, not bad at all," Cole agreed even though his opinion on wine didn't count for diddly. But he'd already learned a lot from Blair, especially in just the way she tasted the wine. Not like the uppity wine guys on television. She simply looked like she was studying and enjoying it. Every once in a while, her eyes would close in pleasure and he'd feel an answering twitch in his cock but other than that he wasn't sure what he was adding to her current research quest. He was more than happy to be part of it, however. "You've really got the job of dreams, don't you? Just tasting wine all day and calling it work? I'll be damned if I didn't go into the wrong career."

"People say that but I'm mostly a farmer and businessperson. Ninety percent of my work is making sure the fields are fruitful and that the grapes are healthy. Which I do love so you're right that it probably isn't a job to me." That satisfied smile appeared again, tugging up a corner of her mouth as her amber eyes twinkled. "But yeah, you're right, I do like that drinking on the job is not only encouraged but actually *is* my job."

She held up her glass for a cheers and he indulged

her. "So are you gonna let me take you out to dinner tonight? Like on a date?"

She paused, her drink holding still in the air below her lips. "Today?"

"Well, darling, I'm not here for that long so today would be nice. But maybe tomorrow night is better?"

She swallowed. "Okay," she said. "If we think that's wise."

"We've gotta eat sometime, and to be honest, Blair, unless you've got pressing plans I think I'm already so addicted to that mattress of yours I don't foresee myself doing much of anything else."

He watched her eyes heat at his words and then just as quickly she tried to bank the desire. He felt the same. It was almost unwanted by him too. He'd made peace with his celibacy, had settled into his guilt and his life without his brother, and now all of that stuff he'd remembered about life was roaring back, reminding him how sweet it was and how much he enjoyed living it.

So if this was going to be the last time he saw her, he might as well take all the pleasure he could get.

He held up his wineglass. "I'm ready for the next one."

She raised an eyebrow and poured a pinot grigio.

"What did you think about that last one, by the way?" he asked.

"It was decent. I got a little lime and some peach. Not as complex as the one we had the first time, but definitely drinkable."

"Do you ever had a really bad year and do discounts on your wine?" Cole asked, remembering perhaps belatedly that he was interested in starting a winery in Louisiana. He and his financial guy had run the numbers and the wine economy was still in an upswing so it made sense for him. He'd floated the idea by his family on their weekly phone chats and they'd seemed interested in running an operation like that with him so it felt like progress.

Blair shook her head. "No, our discounts generally only take place on something we're not moving fast enough and that's mostly dependent upon the market. Some wines hit a quick trend. Pinot grigio now outsells our sauvignon blanc, for example, when that wasn't always the case. But as far as the quality of the wine, if it's so below par that we'd have to offer a discount, we just don't sell it that year. We don't offer our customers something inferior—my grandfather would rather die."

"So what happens if you don't sell a whole type of wine for a year?" he asked. "That has to put a dent in your bottom line."

"It's only happened once and that was early eighties, before I was born, when there was a major drought. Dad and my grandfather just said they sold more of the other wines." She shrugged. "Nate has a contingency plan if something like that happens again, but to be honest, a large part of my job has been preparing for those kinds of inevitabilities. When you're at the mercy of the weather you set realistic goals so you can meet them, and with any luck the years you exceed them will make up for years you come up short."

Cole nodded, having been impressed with their operation on more than one occasion. Blair Sandoval was a wine superstar, her name spoken with reverence at every vineyard he'd ever visited. Her knowledge and care for wine garnered respect amongst billionaires and other international wine growers alike and he found himself falling under her spell again, just like he had last weekend. She was seducing him with alcohol, research and a visible passion for her work. "I'd like to meet your grandfather. You have to be a certain type of person to start and build something from the ground up into such a successful business."

Blair snorted. "You can meet him, but he's not exactly a people person."

"I'm starting to understand why Nate is the face of this thing." Cole chuckled. "He's apparently the only one who likes people."

"My mom does too," Blair told him. "She was head of public-facing operations but is kind of in a state of semiretirement now where she only works whenever she decides something is happening that she doesn't like." Blair held up her glass to cheer him again. He didn't know why but he liked that maybe they were celebrating the fact that he was back. "But that is, of course, her prerogative, however. Plus, I love watching Nate get annoyed. Mom might poke her nose into my personal life but she doesn't bug me about my job, whereas Nate gets it in both areas.

It's a pretty sweet karma for all the grief he gives me on a daily basis."

Cole wanted to laugh at Blair's gentle teasing of her brother, but the story only got him thinking about his own brother and how their easy affection and ribbing had been completely taken from Cole's own life. He loved his sister more than anything, but they'd never been as close as Cole and Scott.

Blair must have sensed his shift in mood, despite the smile he still had plastered on his face, and reached out to give his hand a squeeze. "Hey, I'm sorry. That was insensitive of me to go on about how much I love my brother," she said with a wry smile. She'd been upbraiding her brother, but she was right, that was love. "I wasn't thinking."

Cole returned the squeeze and pulled her out from around the small bar so that she was standing in front of him. "I think a kiss would make it better," he said, smarmy and opportunistic individual that he was. "I've been waiting with bated breath for one for well-nigh an hour now. I didn't get quite the reception I was hoping for." He wrapped an arm around her waist, drawing her closer. "Hell, woman, I flew halfway around the damn world for you. It's the least you could do."

Blair shook her head at his continued and insistent theatrics, but her arms rose and clasped behind his neck. She was so close and Cole could smell her again, vanilla and sun and earthy wine. He understood alcoholics now because he was addicted to her smell, the feel of her warmth against him, as if she was waking up his body. Just a week ago he'd been grumbling about having to fly back to the States for the Sonoma Speed Festival and now here he was back again of his own volition.

Her face lifted and she met his eyes. "I guess that probably does deserve a kiss," she allowed, leaning in to drop a kiss on his cheek. "Even though I didn't ask you here and technically you just showing up unannounced when you could have texted me does border on the creepy."

"I will have you know that I weighed the potential creepiness against the thrill of the surprise and surprise won handily," he admitted. "But I hear you"

"That's okay," she told him, pressing a delicately soft kiss on his other cheek. "I like surprises."

So saying, she moved away from him, clearly intending for those barely-there smooches to count as kisses, but Cole wasn't having it. He pulled her back against him and stood, locking his eyes on hers.

"Well, here's a surprise for you if you think that's an acceptable kiss for a man who has imagined kissing you again since the moment he left your bed." And then he pulled her fully into his arms, his eyes closing to savor the sweet moment he'd been imagining for days as their bodies connected again. She fit right into him, standing between his thighs.

She looked up and he took her chin in his hand, thumbing her bottom lip. "I'll show you the kind of welcome I've been expecting."

Then his head dropped and he took her mouth, her arms tightening around his neck as the contact intensified. She was just as hungry as he was, their lips and tongues tangling together in a wet, hot joining. A whimper escaped her and absolutely inflamed him. He picked her straight up off the ground and into his lap, her legs wrapped around his waist and her warm center up against his already-throbbing cock.

"Is there anywhere we can go?" he murmured against her lips as he thrust against her. "For privacy."

She nodded but didn't say anything, just set her lips to his again, caught up in the kiss. So he went with it; he wasn't picky, and quite frankly, if she didn't have a problem with it he'd take her on the floor, on top of the bar or right in this chair with every single winery employee looking in if that's what it took to have her again.

Finally, she pulled back, her hand sliding down to his chest, a finger running down the V of his shirt. "There's a storage room down the hall that doesn't have a window," she told him, her voice breathy.

"Thank god," he whispered, lifting her in his arms. "Do you care if people see you like this?"

She shook her head against his neck. "No one is really around right now anyway."

"Well, I guess that means you can scream your little heart out," he said.

"You wish," she told him, setting her lips to his neck and sucking.

"You gonna leave a mark on me, Blair?"

When she continued to suck, he supposed he got his answer and it drove him fucking nuts. No, he

hadn't had a hickey since high school but he damn
sure wanted her to mark him. The thought of being
claimed by a woman even in a small, transient way
should have had him shaking in his boots, but instead
it was nearly causing him to lose his fucking mind.
The thought that anyone would want him after all
he'd done was a drug he hadn't expected. The anti-
dote to two years in an emotional desert.

"Did you do it?" he asked when she finally lifted
her head to point to a door at the end of a long hallway.

She slid her thumb across his neck, the wetness
cool on his skin. "Yeah."

"Christ," he muttered as he booted open the door
to the room she pointed out. There wasn't much, in
what was clearly an old storage room, in the way of
a bed but he couldn't care less. There was a table
similar to the ones he'd seen in the tasting room
that would do nicely. He set her down on it, standing before her.

"You want everyone I see to know this was
yours?" he asked, pointing to his neck.

Blair looked away, embarrassed now that they
were face-to-face.

He lifted her chin. "Don't be that way. I like it. I
want everyone to know I'm taken," he told her, even
though that was a major leap forward in a relationship that was not a relationship at all but instead a
one-night stand that they were now stretching out to
include a brief afternoon interlude in a storage room.

Something like possession flared in Blair's eyes,

replaced almost immediately by uncertainty. He felt the same because he wanted to take things faster than was advisable.

Her gaze drifted to the mark and back up to his face. "It's too small, I think."

That got him laughing and he took her mouth again before saying, "Well, you've got two days to iron out the details."

Then he pulled off his shirt, watched her do the same as he unbuttoned his shorts and kicked them away before helping her do the same with her jeans. He held the soft jean material in his hands for a moment. "I like these, you know?" he mused, running the fabric in between his fingers. "They suit you. Lived in but stylish, clean but rough around the edges." He kissed her again, tugging at her bottom lip until she whimpered. "And I like it when you're dirty, Blair. So fucking dirty."

Crouching down to her newly bare pussy, his eyes fell closed as he breathed in her arousal. "You're just as hot for me as I am for you, aren't you?"

She nodded, eyes wide. He'd already figured out that she responded to dirty talk and he was more than happy to oblige her.

He drew a finger down the top of her slit, the moisture already pooling around his finger. "You're extremely wet down here. Does that mean you want me?"

A harsh intake of breath as his finger kept sliding downward before stopping, poised at her entrance. "Are you planning to answer me?" he asked. "Unfortunately, I'm not a mind reader and making assumptions about a person's needs in bed is generally frowned upon."

She exhaled loudly through her nose. "Yes, I want you."

A corner of his mouth quirked at the begrudging way she'd said it. It was okay—he did understand that people didn't like to be prodded into doing things. It was just that he excelled at prodding and she was so cute when she was exasperated.

"That's a good girl," he cooed, knowing the patronizing words would send her through the roof.

As he suspected, her eyes narrowed and nostrils flared. Leaning back on the table, her legs came up to cross behind his neck, inching him closer to her center, which was just the place he wanted to be. With a raised eyebrow, she said, "Maybe it's time for you to use that mouth the way I want."

"That would certainly be both our pleasures," he readily agreed, meeting her eyes. His thumbs opened her as their gazes locked and with his eyes still on hers he licked her in one slow lick from bottom to top, dragging his tongue wide across her slick clit. She shivered and he smiled. "I guess you like just about anything my mouth does?"

He played at her entrance, tucking his tongue inside her, eager to taste more of her. Pulling back he waited, looking at her expectantly. "Are you going to answer my question?"

That spark of danger flared in her eyes. "I would, but I don't think you're going to like the answer."

Suppressing a grin at her refusal, he fastened his lips right on that growing bud, his tongue feathering over it again and again and again. When she was right on the precipice, writhing against him, he pulled away. "So you don't like it when my mouth does that?"

"I do like it," she choked sitting up to guide his head back to where she wanted him.

"Uh-uh," he told her, resisting. "You still haven't answered."

She groaned. "Oh, my god, I don't like it when you talk, okay? That's the whole joke. Just, please."

Cole wanted nothing more than to settle in between her thighs and never come out, but he couldn't do it just yet. He also liked waiting, prolonging things until they were out of their goddamned minds. Some might call him a masochist, but he just liked to have a little fun.

"So let me get this straight," he said. "You don't like it when I say I want to eat your pussy so hard that my lips go numb?"

Her hips twitched and he raised an eyebrow.

"And I guess that also means you don't like it when I say I want to take you over into that tasting room in front of all those fine wine enthusiasts, bend you over the bar and fuck your brains out."

She was outright glaring at him now but he could see her getting wetter, the light glistening off her as he held her open to his view. But she still didn't retract her statement.

"So then I can only assume you also don't like it

when I tell you how much I want to ride you bare and come so hard inside of you that you have trouble standing the next day?"

She snorted and he grinned. "Too far?" he asked.

She just shook her head because of course he'd gone too far. *They* were going too far and it was exactly what they both wanted even as they both knew it couldn't last.

"I love everything your mouth does, okay, Cole?" she finally said, thumping the table with her hand for emphasis. "Everything!"

"Aw, sweetheart," he murmured, his fingers sliding inside of her. "That's so nice of you to say, but I know you do. You didn't have to tell me."

CHAPTER TEN

BLAIR MIGHT KILL COLE. What had been a small possibility earlier was now a full-blown certainty as he drove her closer and closer to the edge of insanity.

His fingers were thick and clever and relentless and his tongue twice so, and as much as his words infuriated and inflamed her, what he was doing to her physically was far more difficult to handle. He *played* her, like she was his vehicle and he was easing her into each turn gently and then throttling down the straightaways going for the gold or whatever they won in racing, she had no idea.

She arched back, her body undone in the attempt to try to contain the pleasure and heat and lust raining down over it, from fingertips to her toes, her nerve endings were lighting up small fireworks of sensation. She *wanted* in a way she never had before. This virtual stranger had been holding a secret key to her own sexuality, letting her explore uncharted waters of desire.

He sucked on her clit again, hard, and just like that she came against his mouth, his irreverent, demanding and downright sinful fucking mouth. He tongued her through all of it, the crest and all the residual little earthquakes she felt as her body slowly returned to normal again.

"Thing is," Cole murmured, licking his lips in the filthiest way possible before giving a regretful sigh. "I was in such a damn hurry to get here I did not pass go or collect two hundred dollars, which in this case would be condoms. Though right about now I'd pay a billion dollars for that magical slice of latex, because I'd like nothing more than to flip you over and fuck you, but I don't think it's going to happen right now."

The words echoed in her head like a doom gong, *no condom, no condom, no condom* until she could barely think straight for the avalanche of disappointment. But then, a light bulb appeared. What was the saying, necessity was the mother of invention? Well, the possibility of having Cole inside her again was going to turn her into the next Thomas Edison. "Nate's office!"

"Well, now, I don't know that defiling your brother's space is the answer to our contraceptive problem," Cole said, scrubbing a hand over the back of his head.

"No," she grumbled, shoving at his shoulder so he'd let her up. "I think there might be a slim chance that he has condoms in there."

Understanding dawning, Cole moved back and scooped up her clothes, handing them to her to put on. When she was at the door, he called out, "I hope you're coming back and this isn't just some elaborate plot to avoid giving me a reciprocal blow job!"

Blair shook her head. "Why would I do that?" she asked. "I love having you in my mouth." Heaving open the door, she grinned and had one more thing to say. "It's one of the only times I can get you to shut up."

Blair heard Cole's bark of laughter through the door as she rushed down the hall to her brother's empty office. After flying through all the drawers, there, in the very bottom one, inside a brown paper bag shoved in the back, was an open box of condoms. She had hit the jackpot.

Running back to the storage room, an errant giggle erupted in her throat because she'd never even dreamed of having sex in the winery before and yet she was doing exactly that without any second thoughts whatsoever. She, Blair Sandoval, was someone a man like Cole Taggart wanted so badly they couldn't even have waited until they were finished with the tasting to go back to her place. It was hard to believe, and yet, wonderful. To be so caught up in another person was heady and something out of a movie that she'd envied but never thought would happen to her. And she reciprocated the sentiment.

She dashed back into the storeroom, the door banging against the wall as her nerves and excitement got the better of her. Cole's eyes were riveted to hers, caring not at all about the commotion, or the responding thump of the door closing behind her. He stood against the table, hand on his cock, an eyebrow raised. He'd also managed to take his tobacco-leather loafers off, which meant he was completely naked, stroking himself as he waited for her. A flood of desire hit her hard.

She lifted the condom up in the air so he could see. His responding grin was huge. Then he growled, "Clothes off and get the fuck over here."

She stripped in record time, her clothes making a scattered trail on the ground as she went to him. As soon as she was in range, he grabbed the condom, lifted her into his arms and spun her around, leaning her face down over the table.

She heard the rip of the condom package, a brief pause, and then he was kicking her legs apart, and a sound of need escaped her lips.

"Holy fuck, Blair," he gritted, hitching himself against her, right where she wanted him to be. "I was about to lose my fucking mind." He thrust inside, the stretch fast and delicious, and their simultaneous groans bouncing off the walls. He pulled out and thrust again. Another deep thrust that bottomed out and had her whimpering. "I will do any fucking thing you ask to be right here where I am."

She was sliding the table backward, the force of his entry inching the table across the cement floor with a resounding squeak, but he just kept going, stepping forward, keeping the pace. Her cries were loud and frenzied as her muscles clenched around him, accommodating, stretching, gripping him as if she never wanted to let go. Waves of wonderful and explicit pleasure tore through her and she feared she'd never feel so good again. Cole was taking her, using her, bringing them both to some higher plane of sensation and all she could do was accept it in this position. He was in total control and she'd never had a better master.

"Fuck," he growled again, grinding against her ass, his cock pushing up against her cervix.

"Cole," she gasped, swallowing hard, needing release, needing him to touch her where she wanted it most.

"I love it when you say my name like that," he gritted, shuttling in with short, staccato strokes, keeping them both on the edge, but far from where she wanted to be.

"Cole, please," she begged, her voice cracking. "I need—"

His hands gripped her ass and squeezed, spreading her for his gaze and she felt more vulnerable than she ever had in her life. "You've got a pretty little ass, Blair," he told her, his voice rumbly with the same need speeding through her veins like a freight train. "I'll take that too, if you want. Anything you want."

"Touch me, please," she croaked, so close to the edge after his allusion to anal sex, something she probably wouldn't try, but in the moment felt incredibly provocative. She wanted to push the boundaries with Cole, felt wild and liberated with him.

"Now, darling, I know you want me to, but the thing is," he ground out, back to those short, maddening thrusts, "I don't want to stop fucking you, and the minute I touch that slick little clit of yours, you're gonna milk my cock so hard I'll come right then. But this feels too good to end that quickly."

He gave her a big wind-up push then, taking both their breaths away. "Being inside of you is just too damn good." But when she moaned again he lost it, pounding into her like he was a man on the brink of delirium, finally reaching around at the last second to run his finger over where she needed him, his rhythm fast and hot. Her cries as he invaded her rang out, he held her down tight against the table, his hand gripping her hair, pulling just the slightest bit and that little slice of pain sent her right over the edge.

"Fuck me," he growled, stilling against her back and letting go himself, his fingers digging into her hips.

After several loaded moments, their breathing heavy in the quiet room, he gently pulled out of her. He smoothed a hand over where his fingers had indented her skin before pulling her up and turning her around. Their eyes met, the marvel she felt reflected back at her in his eyes. His kiss was ravenous as he crushed her to him, their lust banked but the emotions that they'd evoked in each other still raging out of control, the vulnerability of that need on full display. Clinging to him, she brushed his tongue with hers as he went deep, not able to lose the connection they'd just forged between them. It felt special and extraordinary but also so tenuous because she knew it couldn't last, that two days were all they had together.

The kiss ended slowly, reluctantly, with small

kisses along her jaw until he eventually sighed and dropped his forehead to hers.

"I know I have a habit of being overdramatic, but trust me when I say this, Blair. I'd like to die doing that."

She gave him a quick peck, taking a deep breath to try to get her own self under control. It was not possible that she was falling for a man she just met, but the way he held her, his smell, the corner of his mouth that always seemed to curve upward, like he was either about to say something outrageous or simply thinking it—she liked it. Liked all of it. A lot. Maybe instant connections like this did exist. Maybe all her other relationships had been forced. Either way, she felt more alive and valued in a way past boyfriends had never made her feel. Even the way he was holding her now, close and tight, a hand playing with her hair, was *nice*, casually luxurious in that it felt like he cared about *her*, that she meant something to him. That was what she'd been missing before. Her most recent ex aside, she'd had semi-successful relationships with men who were her equals and treated her well, but no one had been madly in love with her. She didn't really think she was the kind of person men went bonkers for, and yet, Cole had proven her wrong and she wasn't going to be able to let that feeling go easily.

"Maybe we're already dead," she murmured against his lips. "And this is us floating to our reward."

She felt his shoulders shake against her right before he lifted her up into his arms, as if she were nothing instead of a fully grown woman with a bad cheese habit. "If there's a better reward than that, I don't want it," he told her, nipping gently at her lips before setting her down on the table.

With a sigh, his gaze slid over her sitting there before he turned around to collect her clothing. When he returned he slid the bra up her arms.

"What are you doing?" she asked, trying to take the bra from him so she could do it herself.

"I'm just trying to help you out," he said innocently, even though he was full of mischief. "I know you're finding it difficult to stand up and your muscles must be complete jelly, so I thought I'd come in with the assist. You know, since I have rendered your body useless, stunned it into shock with my superior lovemaking skills."

She stared at him blandly but let him put on her bra even though she was sure he'd screw it up. But of course, he surprised her. "You're good at that."

He adjusted the silky sage-green strap on her shoulder. "Full disclosure, I'm better at taking them off, but as I'm sure you're already aware, I'm a man of many talents."

Blair snorted, even though her body was still very much aware of those other talents and she did feel slightly delirious and sleepy from what they'd just done. And in her family's winery for heaven's sake. Old Blair would never.

She tried to pick up her T-shirt and put it on but he snatched it out of her hands. "Now, I hate covering you up, but unfortunately, I don't think we can live in this storage room." Then he opened the neck of the shirt and slid it over her head. "Arms in," he directed and she glared at him.

He ignored her ire completely, picked her up and put her on the ground. With her panties in his hand, he seemed to mull something over. "You know," he told her, as if he was coming to some kind of long-sought-out conclusion, "I think I'll keep these if you don't mind."

"I do mind," Blair squeaked. "What am I supposed to do all day without underwear?"

"I'll give you mine, if you'd like," he told her, as if that was a thing women wanted. Just piles of used male underwear in a shoebox in their closet.

"No!" she exclaimed. "Give me my underwear back!"

Cole's head tilted and his eyes met hers. "We'll talk about it later."

And then he proceeded to pull her pants on, lifting her leg when she remained stolidly recalcitrant and refused to do so on her own. She watched as he zipped up the fly of her jeans, his eyes meeting hers as he pulled her T-shirt down over her hips. They shared a moment of something she couldn't quite name, but he'd done her a service, one she didn't particularly need or want, but it seemed to be important to him.

Quickly, he dressed himself and held up the panties. "What if I say pretty please? Would you let me hang on to these, so I have something of you during my long, lonely nights of traveling? I promise I won't share them with the other announcers even though anyone would like to get their hands on these."

"You're an animal," she groaned, but she didn't want to argue with him.

His head tilted as he shrugged. "That seems mostly accurate." Then he added, "With the caveat that I'd be a nice animal, like a polar bear or a horse."

Blair didn't bother to respond to his nice animal thread. Instead she inspected the room, dragging the table back to its original spot just in case anyone got any ideas about why it was moved. It was a pointless endeavor because no one ever came in this room for anything—it was just where extra furniture for events was kept—but now that Cole was no longer touching her reality had begun to filter back in. Blair Sandoval, a mild-mannered viticulturist who had, until very recently, never experienced the sort of mind-altering passion with a man and had been laboring under the assumption that she simply was not a very sexual person, had fucked a stranger right under what was kind of her parents' roof and her place of work.

She'd flat out lost her mind. So she scanned the rest of the area, looking for anything, a random button, a piece of ripped clothing fabric because who knew what they'd done in their rush to disrobe, some loose change that didn't belong in the room. Blair didn't know exactly what she was looking for, but if anything was here she'd find it and make sure no one had any clue what they'd done.

"You okay there, Ms. Sandoval?" Cole asked, peering at her strangely.

"Why do you sometimes call me that?" Blair asked, her head snapping up from its search for the condom wrapper she'd realized she needed to find. "But other times call me Blair?"

"I don't know," Cole said, shoving his hands into his pocket. "But if I had to guess I'd say it's because I'm from the South and we stand on a little ceremony as a rule." His eyebrow lifted. "But it doesn't seem appropriate when I'm inside you to call you that."

"Okay," Blair said, holding up a hand. "How about we make a rule then, when we're in situations that you find it more appropriate to call me Ms. Sandoval, we don't talk about sex and stuff."

Cole grinned. "You got it, Ms. Sandoval, no sex and stuff will be asked about."

"I mean, this is, like, my grandfather's house in a way," she went on, lifting up an old yellowing tablecloth to look for the condom wrapper. "I just had sex in my grandfather's house. That's weird. I'm a sex weirdo now."

"I don't know that *sex weirdo* is a medical term, but then again, I assume I am one so maybe there's something to it," Cole mused. Blair could tell he was smiling but she couldn't look at him at the moment. His face reminded her of what they'd done and what she would do again with one word from him. Hence the reason for her keeping busy and not touching him. Good grief, would this just be her life now, finding ways to keep busy so she didn't throw herself at a man who didn't even live in the country for most of the year? She was going to have to take up a new hobby. Maybe something like lumberjacking, not exactly earth friendly, but definitely physically exhausting.

"Do you want to tell me what it is you're looking for?" Cole asked. "Or would you like to continue freaking out in silence?"

She pulled up to her full height, hands on hips. "I am not freaking out."

He raised that infuriating dark eyebrow again. "Granted, we haven't known each other for that long, so I'm not accustomed to your moods, Blair, but I'm not blind either. You're tearing through this storage room like a starved raccoon in a dumpster."

Blair moved a chair back onto the stack she'd pulled it from and turned to face him. "I'm fine." The words were said but even she could tell she'd delivered them from a place on the fringes of hysteria.

"Of course you are," Cole placated. "*Dandy* is a word I'd use to describe your present state of mind, in fact. So do you think you might at least tell me what you're looking for?"

"I'm looking for the condom wrapper. I don't want people to find it."

Pulling his hand out of his pocket, he held up the torn and empty blue-foil wrapper. "I wouldn't leave any evidence for the public to find." He'd also wrapped up the used condom in a paper towel he'd apparently found, ready to dispose of it as soon as they left.

Blair pulled in a deep breath and let it out. Okay, so maybe she was freaking out a little. Because the quick palate-cleansing affair with an international racing star wasn't supposed to be so good. *She* wasn't supposed to feel anything for him, but she did. And it was a problem. A big one.

"Is this about the fact that I want your undergarments?" Cole asked, meeting her eyes. "Or is it about the sex?"

She shook her head. "I don't know," she admitted, not sophisticated enough not to just blurt out her feelings. "I—" she stopped, then started again "—I've just never felt this way before about sex with someone."

Cole's head tilted, eyes melty, and he started toward her, pulling her into his arms. Her pulse slowed remarkably as she relaxed into his hold, the strong, solid body of a man who wasn't afraid to show affection. "Yeah, it's pretty fucking good with us," he told her, dropping a gentle kiss on her lips.

Blair's heart was beating in her chest because it was good with Cole. It was really super amazing with Cole and even though she knew it wasn't going anywhere and they lived two completely separate lives, she knew she was in danger. The sex wasn't just about sex anymore for her.

She must have telegraphed her worry because Cole peered down at her, eyebrows furrowed. "Hey," he said, tapping a finger gently on her head, "what's going on in there?"

Blair took a deep breath because she didn't want

to say what she was going to say, but she needed him to know. For reasons great and small, but mostly because she wanted him to have all the information before he flew all the way back here again thinking that she was a good person, someone he might think he could be with for real. Because she wasn't. She wasn't the person he thought she was, and the moment he learned her secret he'd know it too, and it would end their fun. It would be the end of the happy Blair she'd been able to be with him.

"My ex was married," she admitted on a whisper. She avoided looking directly in his eyes at first, but then made herself do it, made herself see how disgusted he was with her. "That's why I think all men should burn in a firepit."

Cole's head tilted, gaze considering. "Did you know?"

Blair shook her head, then said, "Of course not, but it hardly changes the facts, right? I ruined a marriage." She lifted her hands up and then dropped them back down to her sides with a dejected thump. "I'm a homewrecker. The other woman. The evil villain. And I don't deserve to be happy." She pointed a finger at his chest. "I don't deserve this great sex with you."

A moment of loaded silence filled the room wherein she kicked herself for trusting Cole with the truth, but resigned herself to the fact that now he'd leave and this would end just like it should.

What she hadn't expected was that Cole would start laughing, but that's exactly what he did. He was full-out laughing at the gnawing guilt and unworthiness she'd been feeling since it happened.

"You're not a villain, sweetheart," Cole said authoritatively, running a hand over her hair. The hand came to rest on her shoulder, giving her a firm squeeze so she'd meet his eyes again. "You got played, but a man cheating on his wife is the person at fault here, not you."

"That's not what his wife said," Blair informed him, a little annoyed by the fact that he was brushing over it, as if what had happened wasn't a big deal at all. She might not feel responsible for someone's death, but she'd hurt someone. Badly. And one didn't just get over it or brush it aside. It wouldn't be fair to the person she'd destroyed.

Cole's eyebrow rose and Blair nodded. "She found messages from me on his phone and then tracked me down at a talk I was giving. Told me they'd been married ten years and how dare I try to break them up. They have children." Blair got lost again in the memory of that day, the pain and betrayal and anger. "I understand that it's not my fault, but it doesn't take the guilt away—and how in the world could I be so dumb?"

"So that's what's got you all nervous?" Cole asked. "You think this is some good sex we're having and are trying to find a way out of it?"

Blair stared at him. "No, I'm just telling you what kind of person you're sleeping with."

Taking her shoulders in his hands, Cole crouched down to look in her eyes, fire burning in his. "Blair

Sandoval, I can almost see the gears turning in your head. It has been really fucking good between us. Maybe we'll never see each other again after today, I don't know, but by the time I leave this weekend I want you to believe that you are not at fault for that shit. You ran into a hurt woman who was looking for someone else to blame, but she got it wrong."

"It doesn't make me feel any less guilty," Blair sighed, "knowing that it wasn't my fault. I thought he loved me, Cole. I just don't know how I could have gotten it so wrong. I don't trust myself anymore."

"I'd say that you're right to distrust people, Blair. Let that be your guide in the future," Cole advised, brushing a thumb over her jaw, making her shiver.

His easy acceptance made Blair uncomfortable because it felt a little like absolution, the thing she'd been waiting for for so long, and she wondered warily now that she had a little bit of it, how was she going to let Cole go when he was the one providing it?

He smiled at that and pulled her into his arms, holding her so tight. "You're a good woman, Blair Sandoval. A mouthy one too, but a good one nonetheless. Don't ever doubt it."

Then he gave her such a sweet kiss, one that was simply meant to soothe, and she decided she'd probably let him have all her underwear if he wanted.

CHAPTER ELEVEN

TWO WEEKS LATER Cole disembarked from the airplane in California kicking himself for the fact that he hadn't been able to stay away. He should have stayed away.

Instead the day after he'd arrived, he'd followed Blair to Napa Valley, this time, to a different winery tasting room only to wait while she had a meeting with the owner. He sat inside a large room with high ceilings, gold-and-crystal chandeliers in a row down the rectangular space, the light reflecting and refracting off the building-length picture windows overlooking the vineyard itself. He'd traveled the world and met some wealthy people, but Napa Valley seemed to be the upper echelon of wealth, and the full effect of just who Blair was was hitting home to him. She might hide cheese and wear dusty jeans to work, but she was a wine star and the very definition of a coastal elite. In comparison, he was just some retired race car driver who killed his brother.

He should have stayed in Europe and left her alone.

"Sorry about this," Blair told him, her eyes worried as she approached him. "I would have canceled if I'd known you were coming."

It wasn't an admonishment, but Cole only smiled and assured her that it was fine. And it was. She had a fucking life, unlike him who was just flying around the world for a glimpse of her.

On their way back to her place, Cole chastised himself for being ridiculous. So what if he'd flown back; she was the one who'd gotten him out of his sexual slump—it stood to reason he'd be interested in more. But that's all it was; he didn't need to worry about her getting the wrong idea. He'd just explain when he left this time that it would be the last time. Then he'd leave her alone and they could both get on with their lives.

He kept up his end of the small talk just fine, but it wasn't until they were sitting on her porch, the midday sun shining down and a bottle of chardonnay on ice on the table between them, that Blair seemed to sense his mood.

"You don't like it?" she asked, nodding to the salad she'd made that he was currently not eating.

He shoveled a huge bite into his mouth. It was a good salad as far as salads went, with crunchy apples and candied walnuts, and a vinaigrette he'd watched her make while standing in her huge kitchen with glossy white shiplap walls, wide-slatted wood floor and top-of-the-line appliances. "Of course I like it," he told her, eating more of it. "I'd eat just about anything you gave me. My mom would have my head if she thought I'd refused someone's hospitality."

Blair's eyes narrowed. "So...you don't like it."

Cole wasn't exactly in full command of his senses, which might be the reason this conversation was getting away from him. Having flown all night and most of the next day, sleeping fitfully on the plane, he'd arrived at Blair's in the middle of the night and they'd been on each other, making desperate love into the dawn when they'd finally fallen asleep. Needless to say, his body and mind were not firing on all cylinders.

"Blair," he said, eyes beseeching. "I can't say I love salads as much as I love a heaping plate of my grandmother's gumbo, but this one is excellent."

The tension leaked out of Blair's body. "I know, I'm sorry," she said. "I don't know why I'm so on edge. I just know you're tired and I feel guilty that you flew all the way here again just to see me and all I'm feeding you is this stupid salad."

The uneasiness he'd been battling since stepping off the plane took a deeper hold because honestly what the fuck was he doing here? He was making an uncomplicated one-night stand into something else entirely. Blair sure as hell wasn't traveling overseas to see his ass.

But the four-day stretch he would have had between races had seemed endless and being with Blair was the only thing that put a stop to the recriminations and sense of loneliness and loss that creeped in every time he had a moment of free time. Since the accident, Cole had made sure he was busy all the time, hoping for the day he'd wake up and the hurt would be gone. But a year in, he'd come to the realization that the pain was *never* going to go away. He was always going to miss his brother like he would a limb and he accepted that, but seeing Blair had become like a drug, for the time he was with her the pain faded into the background.

But that didn't mean they were or could enter into in a relationship. Nothing had changed and he still didn't deserve her and the happiness she brought.

He set his bowl aside and took her hands in his, only letting himself enjoy knowing that him being here was important to her for a moment. "First of all, there's no 'just to see me' involved here. I get to see you, you understand me?" he asserted, making sure she got the point. He hated her asshole ex for ever shaking her confidence. Regardless of how things would eventually end with the two of them, he never wanted her thinking he didn't find her amazing in every way. "Second of all, you're right, the travel is ravaging my body, but even so, I still think I made a pretty good showing of it last night, so why don't we quit worrying about little old me and enjoy the afternoon?"

"You're right," Blair said, leaning back in her chair. "I'm sorry I tried to torpedo our afternoon."

"Sweetheart, you couldn't if you tried," he assured her. And it was the truth. He was so happy to see her he doubted even her punching him in the face could dim the happiness he felt at being near her again. He'd never truly adjusted to not having a home for the better part of a year, knew his brother, Scott, never had either. But that aimlessness was part of the reason why Cole had spent most of his time partying and carousing at all hours of the day and night. He'd missed home and since he generally had trouble looking his family in the eye, this was the closest thing he'd felt to home in far too long.

"Do you live in a swamp?" Blair asked, curious, idly crunching on an apple slice.

"No," he laughed. "But there is a small pond on my land. I own just a regular old house. Nothing too fancy. Probably the size of this farmhouse."

Blair nodded. "This used to be a small place, but I've added a couple thousand square feet since I've been here."

"I bought a big house because I figured before long I'd want a couple of kids running around. It's a great set-up for a family."

"So you'd want to settle in Louisiana?"

He shrugged. He'd thought that's where he'd end up eventually but he'd never had any real plans in place. He hoped the vineyard business would bring his family back together, though. "It was just the thought I had when I bought a place, looking toward what might fit my future. That's about as far as it went."

He had an errant vision of Blair in his house with dark-haired kids running around and it stopped him cold. Being with Blair, or anyone, wasn't in his future. He'd been busy the past couple of weeks, putting in the transfer to American announcing soon as well as buying a local winery to begin putting his family back together, but those plans didn't include a mouthy viticulturist who lived all the way in California. Hell, he wasn't sure he'd ever let anyone close to him again. All he wanted was to make sure his remaining family was happy and safe, and with the winery, he'd be creating an income stream they could always rely on even if he wasn't around, as well as a reason to always be around each other. Not like now when they could avoid him as much as they wanted.

"I didn't think I'd ever have kids," Blair admitted, taking a sip of wine. Her gaze traveled idly over her land before meeting his again. "My mom is always nagging me and Nate to have them so someone will take over the vineyard." She shrugged. "But it's not like I would make my kids do something they didn't want to anyway, and what if they didn't want to grow grapes or sell wine? We'd still need to find someone to run this operation."

"Have you always wanted to work here?"

"Yeah," she said. "Maybe that's boring but I spent my childhood running through these fields and eating warm grapes so juicy and sweet that finally piercing through the thick skin of a wine grape was like a special surprise. All that fruit bursting in your mouth."

Cole warmed at the image of Blair as a kid, was struck by the idea of his own children doing the same thing in a vineyard that he owned.

"Leaving never really occurred to me," she continued. "I travel a lot for speaking engagements. I lived in France and Spain and Australia in my twenties just to study and learn what I could about different types of wine making. Staying here never felt like a sacrifice because I love what I do. I think Nate feels the same way."

"There's never any shame in doing what you love." He held up his wineglass to toast. Though announcing wasn't his dream, he'd sacrificed a lot to race, especially overseas, and he knew what it was to love what you were doing. The sacrifices were worth it up until they weren't.

"Where are you flying when you leave here?"

He wanted to sigh. Hated to even think of the travel. "Germany."

Blair took a sip of her wine. "Ah, the land of Riesling. That was my favorite wine when I first started an actual position in the vineyard. We had a tall bottle, nearly up to my waist, and I'd stared at it for years because even though I lived on a vineyard I had to spit every time I tried something up until I was nearly twenty-one." Blair rolled her eyes at this and Cole just found himself smiling stupidly. It was like that whenever she talked, him soaking up every word to take with him when he left.

"In my limited wine experience, I've come to understand that sweet wines aren't as well regarded."

"Well, the sweetness, which can be cloying and so overpowering to the palate that you can't taste any of the other flavors, is the problem, but I never felt that way about a Riesling. There are different varieties anyway that are drier." Blair shrugged.

"I tell you what," Cole said, having eaten the rest of his salad and kicked his legs up on the chair beside him. Damn if he didn't feel relaxed. "You're sexy as hell when you're talking about wine."

Her cheeks reddened in an adorable blush that matched the pink wine in his hand. "You're the worst, you know?" she complained, trying to pretend he hadn't embarrassed her with the very real truth.

Cole wasn't much of a person for school, he probably would have failed out if not for some very helpful girlfriends who'd taken pity on him and tutored and maybe done his homework for him a time or two.

"Oh, come on now," he cajoled with a lecherous grin. "Give me some more vitification tutorials. I'm loving it. Only this time, why not take off your shirt too? I think that would really work as a memorization tool. You know, like word association or something. I'll think of a breast and remember concrete fermentation tank."

Blair rolled her eyes. "Get out of here."

When his laughter died down, he took a deep breath, letting the slow breeze sweep over him. He felt great and if some small part of him felt guilty about it, he was making the executive decision to ignore that part.

"You do have a nice setup out here," he observed, taking in the rows and rows of grape vines. She lived just beyond the cabernet grapes field, the deep indigo bunches nestled into the green leaves.

Blair leaned back in her chair with her glass of wine. "Yeah, it's not so bad." Taking a sip, she continued, "Sometimes I wonder if I should at least move off the vineyard, though. Even now it's kind of like I'm staring at work. I can't really get a break."

Cole nodded. He understood that. "Well, when you come work at my winery you can live in my big house far from any grapes." He smiled, waggling his eyebrows in a suggestive manner. He was joking, but then maybe not totally. What the hell did he know anymore? He knew she'd never move to Louisiana, but he had to admit that he didn't mind the image.

She just rolled her eyes, but he continued. "Doesn't that interest you, though? Starting your own vineyard from scratch instead of inheriting one?"

Shrugging, she said, "Maybe, but my grandfather and father would pour epoxy on my tongue so I couldn't taste anymore before they'd let me off this farm." She smiled ruefully. "Obviously I'm just kidding."

"Obviously," he said. But he understood what she was saying to him, that their future didn't go beyond this farm. And despite the good talking to he'd been giving himself all day to remind him of just that, hearing it from her lips rankled. He wasn't asking for her to sacrifice anything but maybe showing him that this was something for her, too, might be nice. He'd been happy to fly back to California, but she hadn't even made mention of traveling to him. So *some* kind of effort or mention of the future would be nice, but instead she'd gone out of her way to make sure he knew that she was firm on staying at the vineyard. The message had been received.

"I wish you didn't have to go back so soon," she said with a sigh and all the unfavorable thoughts that had been rattling around his big dumb noggin vanished. She was enjoying the moment—he was the one getting too serious with it even after he'd vowed this would be their last time together. "This is so nice. Usually Nate or my friend Serena are always trying to get me to *do* stuff, like blind dates or paint and sips thinking that they're helping me get over the breakup. It's like they don't understand the quiet sanctity of a glass of wine on a porch in summer."

Cole huffed a small laugh because who knew how many times he'd thought today how often he could sit on this porch with her and do not much of anything. It was as if he'd entered into some kind of meditative state of bliss.

"Well, I enjoy a good sit myself but most importantly, where are these paint and sip creations? I definitely need to see your art, Blair."

She snorted. "Art is not the appropriate term. And I don't have any of them, I gave them away as holiday gifts to people I don't like very much."

Cole laughed then, the sound busting out of him unexpectedly. "Blair Sandoval, are you being serious?"

She shrugged. "What? They received a personalized piece of art. That's nice."

"Well, how do I get on this list of people you

don't like, because I'd kill to get my hands on an original work."

"Oh, it's easy," she told him. "You could keep up with this line of questioning, for instance, and you'll get your very own canvas, signed and everything."

He was laughing again but couldn't hold back his desire to touch her so he turned his chair to face her and then lifted her out of hers and into his lap.

With a surprised squeak, she squirmed in his lap. "What are you doing?"

"I'm sorry, Blair," he said, dropping a kiss on her neck. "But you're too adorable for me not to touch right now."

He heard her sigh and brushed his nose against her ear, his lips traveling to the soft line of her jaw. "You're not a normal man," she claimed, but her head fell to the side, exposing her neck for him as his lips ventured farther down. He drew in a deep breath, her scent strongest there, sugar cookies and earth and sun. He licked the dip in her throat wondering if there was a chance in hell he'd be able to convince her to let him take her on her porch in the bright sunshine of the afternoon where any old person could come driving up the dusty lane and see them.

"I've heard that before," he told her. "But I've never had much cause to be normal." He slid the remnants of their lunch to the side, ceramic clanking. Then he leaned her back onto the table and picked up his glass of rosé. "Besides, would a normal man do this?" He proceeded to pour a thin stream of the pale blush wine over the tip of her breast, staining the pristine white satin of her shirt the same color as her skin.

"What the hell are you doing?" she asked, watching as he poured more wine over her collarbone and leaned down to lick it up with his tongue. He sucked on a nipple, loved that it beaded underneath the fabric. He undid the clasp and pulled the bra off, taking a long look at her pale breasts in the afternoon, sun-kissed and golden before pulling one wet nipple into his mouth.

Letting her go, he met her eyes with a grin. "I just thought I'd try my own version of a wine pairing." He sampled the other nipple, tasting the sweet wine with her faintly salty skin before returning his gaze to her.

Blair's head shook and he watched her plop it back down onto the wooden table with a dull thud.

"I give up."

He laughed, getting back to the hard work of tasting her. "I knew I'd wear you down eventually."

But as he stripped the rest of her bare in the sun, he was very worried that in the process he'd be the one who couldn't let go.

CHAPTER TWELVE

BLAIR STOOD IN front of Cole's door in Louisiana, her heart pounding so furiously hard in her chest that she thought she might faint. This was probably a mistake. Just another crash and burn in Blair's history of epic relationship fails.

But something had changed between them on Cole's last visit because for the first time in their acquaintance, he'd been downright taciturn, which was totally unlike him. And it turned out, the why of it wouldn't leave her alone. Why, in fact, did he keep coming back to see her? It couldn't just be about the sex because although incredible, he could find anyone. Which meant that the idea that he wanted her specifically had taken hold and wouldn't let go even as she knew she was heading straight into folly. Hope, apparently, wasn't done having its way with her.

So with a silent prayer and a deep breath, she knocked on Cole's front door in Baton Rouge.

His sat house by a pond just like he'd said. It was a gorgeous French Creole house with double front doors, thick columns that started on the bottom floor and thinned out on the second, surrounded an enormous wraparound porch she'd had to climb a wide staircase to reach. Towering old oak trees with limbs as long as school buses had shaded the white pebble driveway as she'd ridden in with her rental car.

He hadn't been able to come to California on this trip because of an obligation at home, but he'd invited her. She'd declined, thinking that this would be the break they needed. Their growing attachment was risky and she knew it was time to do something because she'd been racked with disappointment at the thought of not seeing him this week.

But then her ex had reappeared in her life like a bad dream. Like his wife had done, he'd tracked her down at one of her speaking engagements. And because she'd blocked his number and email address before she'd even left the hotel bar that day with his wife, they'd never had a real breakup, nor had he known why she'd stopped returning all his communication full stop.

Well, they'd had a real breakup now.

Seeing his face had brought everything roaring back, but this time, her anger and guilt were finally directed toward whom it belonged—that lying, cheating, unworthy jerk. After his pitiful barrage of excuses and bullshit explanations and lies about how he was divorced now and had been planning to do it the entire time they were together (aka the cheater's refrain), she'd unleashed a torrent of rage on him that had left her stunned. She'd been holding in so much angst, she hadn't known how deep it went.

Then she'd direct messaged his wife on social media about the incident because she was no longer a party to his grossness.

The whole ordeal had left her shaken and still angry. But also a little liberated. *He* was so clearly to blame and seeing his guilty face had only driven the point home. And immediately afterward, despite her mom making sure she was okay and the threats to enact physical harm on him from Nate, the only person she'd wanted to see was Cole.

So she'd taken what was probably an foolish leap of faith and bought a plane ticket.

The waffling she'd done between then and now would win awards in the Museum of Indecision because as much as she wanted to see Cole, this was not in their plan. The plan was that this was *not* the plan.

Once on the plane, the decision had come with its own set of personal horrors. Namely the fear of admitting that she had actual feelings for Cole, a man who was a one-night stand and did not fit into her life in any way, shape or form. Definite and unwanted and epically terrifying *feelings* for Cole. It wasn't smart for her to pretend there could be something between them, but as the weeks stretched on with only phone calls between them, she'd *ached* to see him again.

It was as if finally letting go of her past had let her see that there could be a real future with Cole. It was like standing on the edge of a cliff with her

arms outstretched just basically waiting for someone to push her off.

When his front door didn't immediately open,
bolts of anxiety attacked her. What if he didn't want
to see her? What if he'd been lying the entire time
and his wife answered the door instead? These were
the types of thoughts that had plagued her in the
week following the encounter with her ex.

The nervousness dragged out as she waited,
the time stretching interminably. Her fingers were
sweaty and maybe so were her ears? Her entire body
felt like she'd only recently been allowed to remove
her finger from an electrical socket.

She told herself she'd ring the bell only one more
time, then go get herself a room in a hotel. However, as soon as her hand lifted to press the button
for the last time, the door flew open, revealing a wet
Cole with a towel swung carelessly around his waist.
"Good lord, I don't want any—"

The words stuck in his throat when he saw her
standing there, his head jutting forward, mouth open
in shock. "Blair?" he whispered, as if not quite wanting to believe she was there, as if something louder
might scare her away.

"Sorry I didn't call," she told him. "I thought I'd
try my own Cole-size surprise."

He looked at her from head to toe, his smile growing obscenely large when he met her eyes again.
"You flew here to see me?" he asked.

"Well, yeah, you invited me," she reminded him.
"And you've been doing it for me."

That silly grin warned her that he was about to say something ridiculous, and she found that she couldn't wait. "I'm a man and sex was involved. Frankly, I've done more for less."

When she returned his comment with an extremely bland look, he only laughed and pulled her into his house. It was lovely inside, an old rambling country house with bare wooden floors in a houndstooth pattern, and massive room-sized rugs in the dining room and sitting rooms that were off to the sides of the foyer. But she barely had time to even look at the rest before he swept her into his arms and carried her up a grand staircase. His room had a large king bed with a fluffy white duvet and carved antique furniture—an open door to a steaming bathroom spoke to the fact that she'd interrupted his shower.

He dropped her unceremoniously onto his bed and pulled off his towel before climbing over her.

"My bag is downstairs," she pointed out.

Cole sighed. "Good Christ, Blair, do you need it right now? I'm dying here," he muttered, then he stopped in his tracks. "Did you bring condoms?"

"That's why I need my bag," she said, and he let out a relieved breath.

"I take it all back, sweetheart," he said, bounding off the bed to put on his towel. Then he was out the door and with a second alone, Blair allowed herself to smile. She was glad she'd come, and before she knew it he was tugging her bag into his room while stripping himself of the white terry cloth once again.

"Where?"

"In my toiletry bag," she instructed. "And you're welcome." He all but leaped back on the bed once he'd found what he was looking for, perching on all fours as he looked down at her. "I can't believe you're here and that you're so goddamn smart that you thought to bring protection."

Then he finally, *finally*, brought his lips to hers, the kiss she'd been imagining since she'd booked her plane ticket. If this was all they did it would still be worth it. "I must be legendary in bed for you to do all that."

Blair shook her head. "Sure, you'll go down in the books, but do you think I might be able to take these gross clothes off now? I've been traveling all day to get here."

"Well, hell," Cole said, lifting up from the bed. "Why didn't you just say so? I had to hop out of the shower to come to the door anyway so I've got no problem finishing up with you."

So saying, he didn't even let her sit up on her own, as if he couldn't bear not to be touching her. He stripped off her shoes and clothes and carried her to the shower.

"You know I can walk, don't you?" she asked, laughing.

"I'm just not ready to believe you aren't really here," he admitted, giving her a shy smile. "I figure if I keep hold of you, you won't disappear on me."

Blair wasn't a romantic, at least she hadn't been for a long time, but the words touched something inside of her she hadn't known was still there and she found herself batting back tears. Tightening her hold around his neck, she kissed him, letting everything she felt flow into it, the anxiety, the excitement, the affection, the gratitude that he'd helped bring her back to life. He was a man worth traveling for and she hoped if nothing else came out of their time together that he'd at least accepted that he was worthy again as well.

"I'm going to put you down now but wait over there so you don't get a blast of cold water," he instructed, pointing to the shower's vestibule. She did as she was told, watching as he played with the tap and tested the water before crooking his finger for her to join him.

"I was real torn up that I wasn't going to be able to make it back to California this time and that you didn't want to come with me to Louisiana," Cole admitted, pushing back her hair as the water dampened it. "But I understood, and I'm thankful as hell that you changed your mind."

He kissed her again, his tongue running along hers, widening her mouth so he could deepen the contact, explore and take over her mouth. His arms wrapped around her, like tight bands of steel unwilling to let her go.

"How long?" he asked when they finally came up for air.

She shrugged. "The whole week if you want me here," she admitted.

Cole shook his head. "I want you here."

Then his hands were all over her, caressing her

nipples as the rain shower fell over them, water racing down her skin. His already-hard cock bobbed against her slick skin—the deprivation she'd been subjected to in his absence resulting in the pounding need inside her body.

Grabbing the soap and washcloth, Cole began to systematically clean her off, letting her stand fully in the spray of water.

"We're gonna have a hell of a time," he promised, wiping the last of the soap from her chest before pumping the shampoo from the handy dispenser and lathering it up in his hands first. "Can you imagine just what we could get up to without a clock counting down our time together? Now just close your eyes and quit glaring at me so I can clean this filthy mop of yours."

She did as he instructed, which meant she had to resort to crossing her arms over her chest to communicate her displeasure at his antics. Not that it ever did any good and not that she wanted it to. She liked Cole just as he was.

So she suffered through her rising lust as he carefully cleaned her hair, his blunt fingertips gently massaging her scalp and lathering her hair down to the ends that reached the middle of her back before giving her a rinse. He let her do the conditioner as he scrubbed himself the rest of the way clean from when she'd interrupted him, but then before she'd fully rinsed he was pulling her against him again, kissing her like he'd never stop.

"Blair," he murmured against her lips, "I've fucking missed the shit out of you." His hand clasped the back of her head as his other dropped to her waist, pulling her in closer to him until not even a piece of paper could fit between their bodies.

"I couldn't stay away," she told him honestly, reaching back to grab the condom he'd brought into the shower. Her skin was scalding hot and not from the water either. She was burning for him, arousal lighting up every nerve ending. Just the thought of him worked her up and the two weeks they'd been apart had simply compounded it, drawn out the anticipation and wanting until it was a living, breathing thing of its own.

Out of the direct spray, he took the condom wrapper she'd already opened and slid the condom onto his waiting cock. "Have you been thinking about me when you get off?" he growled, rubbing the callused skin of his thumb against her engorged clit.

She nodded, head falling back as he moved over her, increasing the speed and pressure with her every sigh of pleasure.

"What did you think about?" he asked, adding a finger inside of her. "Fuck, you're wet, Blair."

Blair felt the blush climb up her neck and over her face, but didn't care much either since she could barely think of anything when he touched her like this. He was so cocky, so sure of his ability to give her pleasure, but always somehow so amazed when he was presented with evidence of it. It was a strangely endearing quality that just made Cole a singularly complex human.

She brought her gaze up to meet his again, his eyes dark and hooded and suddenly no-nonsense, as he awaited her answer. "I thought about exactly what you're doing now," she admitted. Then went further. "I thought about you in my mouth."

Blair started to kneel down to make that vision a reality but Cole shook his head. "Not this time, sweetheart, I'm too wound up," he said, stroking a hand over his dark, straining cock. "Why don't you turn around for me, hands on the wall, ass out."

Combusting with the need to have him inside of her, she complied readily, a rush of liquid at her core as he kicked her legs wider apart. His warm, wet body was at her back, the smell of his own fresh and masculine body wash lingering in the steam as he positioned himself at her opening. They were both out of the water now and the droplets were chilling on her skin but the steam was trapped inside the shower, warming her along with his body.

And finally, he slid into her with a tortured groan.

"Thank god," he whispered in her ear, his voice choked. "Thank fucking god you came."

She nodded, her breath already coming fast as her inner muscles clenched around him.

"Oh yeah, Blair, milk my cock. I love that," he gritted, his rhythm catching. After a few preliminary thrusts, he took her arms and lifted them up the sides of the tiled shower so that they were spread like her legs. He was in complete control of her body, his hands gliding back down her arms, raising goose bumps as he went, his mouth buried in the crook of her neck, his hands perching on her waist.

He repeatedly thrust into her, grinding against her ass to go deep. Gripping her ass cheeks he angled her better so he could reach that spot inside her that drove her over the edge. He hit it again and again until she was wild against him, squirming and crying for release. Then he was pulling her back and bending her over the shower bench, barely pausing before crashing into her again, her hoarse cries echoing in the glass-enclosed shower.

With a thrust that would have had her losing purchase had it not been for him holding her up, she came on a long wail of release, quickly followed by him stiffening behind her and gasping out his own.

"Sweet Lord," Cole muttered, carefully setting her to rights on the slippery shower floor, letting the spray wash away the evidence of what they'd just done. "You oughta come visit more often, Blair," he said. "That was the best surprise I've ever gotten."

Blair grinned as he handed her a towel. "The orgasm or the visit?"

"Both," he said, grinning back. He gave her his robe to wear while he pulled on a pair of worn-out boxers. "You want dinner or a nap?"

"Nap," she said, feeling lethargic and sated.

Cole threw back the covers and followed her into the bed, dimming the lights and turning on some music as he did so. This was part of the habit they'd gotten into. He'd visit, they'd fall on each other, ravenous, then veg out in bed or in front of the television. When Blair woke up again it was still dark out but she felt rested enough.

She looked over to see Cole propped up on the bed doing a crossword puzzle, of all things. "I didn't sleep too long, did I?"

He shook his head, leaning down to give her a gentle wake-up kiss. "Nope, just an hour. You want something to eat? It's slim pickings around here so I ordered Chinese."

"Whatever is fine," she told him, just as her stomach growled. Blair watched as Cole set his book aside and disappeared downstairs, her heart clenching in her chest. No one had ever bothered to dote on her the way Cole did, and when he appeared back at the bed with a plate of food and some wine, tears sprang to her eyes. And she almost hated her brother for it. For ever bringing Cole Taggart into the tasting room that day and showing her the kind of man she could never have.

"I like watching you eat," Cole said idly, climbing back into bed with her, his bare chest golden in the dim light of the bedside lamp. "Makes me horny and hungry, two of my favorite things."

Blair just shook her head. "One day you're going to say these things to the wrong woman and it's not going to be good for you."

A corner of Cole's mouth lifted in a wry smile. "I don't see myself saying that to another woman, in fact, Blair. You're a very unique case."

"I hope you're right, I'd hate to read about your

loss of a certain appendage on the internet in the future."

Cole burst out laughing then, the sound warm and lovely and what she'd flown to Louisiana to hear. "You missed the point entirely, as usual, Ms. Sandoval, but I sure do appreciate the concern." Then he proceeded to steal an eggroll from her plate.

CHAPTER THIRTEEN

"Now are you gonna tell me how I did?" Cole asked Blair, the soles of their shoes crunching over the gravel as they headed to his car. Two days into Blair's visit they'd decided to actually leave his house. He'd thought it'd be nice to show Blair around his hometown, take her to the winery he wanted to buy and try to gauge her interest in her helping him with it. From the moment she'd shown up at his doorstep, he knew he wanted to keep her there.

"It was really lovely, Cole." Blair peered up at him, a cute smile on her face. "But you didn't have to tell them who I was." She moved away from him to the passenger's side of the car, peering over the hood of his silver Mercedes.

Cole shook his head. "They were excited to meet you, Blair. You're a superstar. I think that's pretty darn cool."

"Okay, it was nice," she admitted, giving him a quelling look before opening the door and ducking into the car.

"We'll go back to the house and change for dinner?" he asked when he'd settled in beside her. "All the times we plan to go out during my visits seem to be waylaid by your aggressive sexual appetite."

He didn't need to see her to know she was glaring at him.

"And then tomorrow you'll meet my family?" he asked again, making sure she was on board for what came next. Knowing it was a big step in their relationship.

Blair buckled her seat belt and smiled the soft, almost shy smile she'd been giving him lately that he hoped meant that she was beginning to feel the way about him that he felt about her, which was to say a hell of a lot. When he'd opened his front door and seen her there the happiness had been so intense, the rush of pleasure so overwhelming it had nearly broken him. And for the first time since Scott's death he hadn't been completely wrecked being at home. This, more than anything, felt like maybe he could *finally* move on with his life and find some measure of closure.

The trip back to his house was spent talking about anything under the sun, but mostly the wine tasting and tour they'd just finished, what Blair had been doing on the vineyard since he'd last left and how he'd been faring on the road (bad because every time he left California, he seemed to miss her more). He didn't say the last part but he wanted to, had been crushed when she'd declined visiting him here when he'd asked. But he knew theirs was an impossible situation. He still had three months of traveling abroad left and she lived half a country away from where he'd made his home.

Back at his place, they showered again and got ready for dinner, maybe other stuff too that he couldn't help doing, but he'd been hungry and needed an appetizer, namely her. When they were back in the car, he was instantly surrounded by her vanilla scent, which somehow transported him back to that California vineyard tasting room with all its glamour and chic and cachet, but Blair in the middle of it being solid and strong and Blair.

They were dining at a cozy place in downtown Baton Rouge. As for himself, he was excited to be with her in public, almost giddy to have her on his arm and have people see that they were together and refer to them as a couple. He'd never been in an adult relationship before so it surprised him just how much he liked being so obviously tied to someone, to belong to someone, in fact. The wait staff, some of whom he'd known forever were pleased to see him, but also surprised to see him take a woman to dinner. All of his usual dates took place either overseas or after hours, and as a rule, he usually never fooled around with anyone in his hometown. That was certain to get too messy and he liked his life simple.

Seated at a small table in the corner, they ordered— though in truth, he'd paid very little attention to the menu. Blair was sitting across from him wrapped in the tightest little navy blue dress that covered nearly all of her, stopping right above the knees, but the way the fabric accented her curves had his mouth watering for more than his dinner.

"You have to stop staring at me like that," Blair hissed, placing the white cloth napkin over her lap. "You look depraved."

Cole leaned over and met her eyes. "I *am* depraved, Blair," he told her. "And to be honest, I kind of feel like that's on you at this point. I've shown you exactly who I am."

"Yes, I know you're a deviant in private but we're in public right now," she reminded him.

"If you'd like me to behave, just say so," he said, teasing her.

"I just—" she began, but then just shook her head. "Never mind, you're the worst."

He chuckled and took her hand, running his thumb over the top. "I'm sorry, I still kind of can't believe you're here."

Blair looked at him, her eyes uncertain, which gripped him in the gut. "I didn't think I would be, but my ex tracked me down."

"Oh, shit, sweetheart," Cole said, giving her hand a reassuring squeeze. "What did that asshole do now?"

Blair shook her head. "Nothing, it was good actually," she said, pulling in a deep breath. "He tried to give me all these excuses about how they were unhappy and he'd been planning on a divorce, just lies really, and I finally understood that it was his fault."

"Fuck yeah, it's all his fault, Blair." He swore to god if he ever met the guy he'd punch him right in his face. That he'd gotten to be with Blair alone meant he had it coming, but then to treat her so shabbily, Cole wasn't having it. "You've been beating yourself up when someone should be beating him up."

A corner of her mouth lifted. "I know that now, I think," she said.

"Good," he said, feeling better for her, thinking that she was less guarded now, wondering what that meant for them. Wondering if it meant she'd accept what he was already feeling for her now.

"It took seeing him to really understand that my guilt was misplaced. I mean, I do still feel guilty for the wife because it was terrible what happened to her, but after talking to him I can forgive myself. I really let him have it and afterward, I realized that's who my anger should have been directed at the whole time, only I'd been arrowing it inward."

"Because you're a good person who cares about people. That's admirable."

"Well, I finally forgave myself."

"Good for you, Blair," he said emphatically, giving her hand a kiss before finally releasing it.

The rest of the meal was good. They chatted, but even though Cole enjoyed himself he was mostly counting down the minutes until they could go back to his house, and more specifically, to bed. Her finally being free of her ex had also broken open something inside of him and he felt charged up and excited. As if a whole world of possibilities had just opened up to him and he had only to reach out and choose one.

"Dinner was delicious," Blair told him as they entered his house. "Thank you again for taking me."

Cole held the door open for her, tingling as her shoulder brushed his chest as she passed through. "Anytime," he promised. "One day maybe we won't have to travel to do it either."

Cole tugged at his tie, dropping it on the floor. He couldn't wait to get his hands on her.

"That would be nice," Blair told him, watching him with interest as he shrugged out of his shirt.

He strode to her, laying his hands on her shoulders, knowing he was about to possibly change the course of their future. He only hoped it wasn't a leap of faith that ended with his face smashed at the bottom of a ravine. "Truth is, Blair, if you'd have me, I'd end this tour right now and come live with you on the vineyard."

Her eyes widened and he panicked a little. "Or," he continued before she could list all the ways that would be preposterous, "I could get my own place in the area and we could be in a regular relationship and see how that goes. No pressure."

Blair's dark brows furrowed, but she wasn't immediately dismissing the idea so that gave him hope that he wasn't going completely insane. "What about your job? And opening the winery here to spend more time rebuilding your family?"

Cole shrugged. "I've talked to the station and they're willing to put me on a couple of American racing slots for announcing, but it's not like I can't do other jobs, Blair. For instance, maybe I'll invest in a competing vineyard or something, keep things between us spicy. As for my family, I can still do the winery for part of the year."

"You're nuts," Blair told him, her eyes still strangely wide.

"Yeah," he agreed. "I am. But you love it and I love you, Blair. So why don't we do this for real?"

All the air went out of the room as Blair's entire body became as stiff as a board.

She tilted her head as if she didn't hear the words. "Um, what did you say?"

He smiled and ran his hands down her arms to take her hands into his. "I love you, Blair," he said. "I know it's sudden and totally unexpected, but I'm pretty sure I do. I'm not an expert or anything, so there is, admittedly, some margin for error, but I mean, I know I've never felt this way about anyone before and being apart from you is pretty fucking awful and the thought of you ever being with some other guy feels like someone's repeatedly driving a car over my face, so yeah, I guess maybe that's love?"

Blair's eyes were wide and rimmed with tears as she struggled to not laugh. "I didn't know that's what we were doing," she finally managed. "You said we were just sleeping together."

He squeezed her hands, willing her to feel the same way he did. "Maybe that's what it was at first, but it hasn't been just that for me for a while."

"I—" She stopped, still mystified, and he felt suspended in time, elated and jittery that his own feelings were out there and at the same time terrified of what hers might be. Wanting anything to believe that he'd made her as happy knowing how he felt as she made him simply by existing.

Her head fell onto his chest and he experienced a very real moment of sheer terror, his heart beating inside his chest like a jackhammer. So he tried to steel himself against what was coming, that she didn't have any interest in dating a foul-mouthed television announcer from the Louisiana swamps and that he was good enough to fuck but she was looking for a sophisticated gentleman to marry and raise wine-drinking children who discussed viscosity and taste structure at the dinner table together.

But then her head rose, her eyes bright as she met his. "I love you too, Cole," she said, slowly and deliberately, so he was sure to hear the words. As if he would miss them.

"You do?" he asked, his voice cracking embarrassingly.

She nodded, giving him a gentle swat on the chest. "Of course I do," she admonished with a little smile. "It's against my better judgment, obviously, but I'm here, aren't I? Basically in the middle of the busiest part of the year for me because I couldn't stay away. My family is probably forming a spreadsheet of possible therapists to send me to when I get back they were so concerned I was flying off to meet another heartbreak."

Cole laughed and picked her up into his arms. "Well, we all could probably use a little therapy but not because of this, not because of us," he promised. He kissed her then, already missing the connection even though they'd just been apart for the length of dinner.

"I can't believe this has happened," Blair murmured against his lips, her breath sweet from the bowl of lemon sorbet they'd shared. "It doesn't feel real."

"It's definitely real," he told her, already unzipping her dress, dying to touch her bare skin again. Dying to simply have her. "The realest thing I've ever been in." Her dress came undone and he helped it slide to the floor as she stepped out of it and her heels. She was shorter now, her head barely glancing the bottom of his chin.

"So we'll work out the details," he prodded before hoisting her up into his arms and carrying her to the bed. "I'll probably have to finish out the tour until the my contract ends, in three months. We were still in negotiations for a new one, but that can change."

"Are you sure they'll let you switch to America?"

He laid her down on the bed, his eyes sweeping her from head to toe, taking in the curve of her peach-tipped breasts, the bold slope of her hips, the smooth flesh of her thigh. He loved it all. Starting from her foot, he kissed her ankle, her kneecap before answering her question. "Yeah, my agent says it looks good. I know it doesn't register much with you, but I'm pretty popular in the racing world. Like, probably the most popular because of my stunning wit and general sparkling personality."

Blair rolled her eyes, but he ignored her and continued his journey up her leg, licking and sucking wherever he felt like it. He wasn't going to leave one millimeter of her unexplored and unloved. He intended to drug her with adoration until she basically was the physical pile of mush that was currently his insides.

"Well, there's no accounting for taste," Blair managed, but he could tell that her heart wasn't in the insult because her voice was breathy and strained.

He laughed softly, licking his way up the jut of her hipbone. "With all due, sweetheart, I think you just insulted yourself since you've just effectively tied yourself to the classless heathen currently about to eat your pussy so good you'll forget your name."

Blair's intake of breath was sharp and had him grinning. He loved putting her off balance. He lifted his head to look at her. "Unless, of course, you'd rather I not."

She glared at him and he laughed. "Right, I get it, I'm just the lowly race car driver allowed to service you."

Blair growled and pushed up onto her elbows, then shoved him onto his back. "I don't have time for this," she muttered, unbuttoning his gray pants and hopping off the bed to pull them down his legs. "You're the most maddening person on the planet. Revving me up for the past two hours, then telling me you love me, and then that dirty talk," she muttered, climbing back onto the bed and straddling his hips. "I'm just one woman, Cole, how much am I expected to take?"

She leaned over and grabbed a condom from the nightstand. Her fist clasped over his cock and his hips jerked up. She hadn't been the only one he'd been taunting at dinner; he'd imagined fucking her on the restaurant table a least a thousand times in their short time there. She was savvy, stroked him with just enough pressure to drive him mad.

"Fuck me," Cole gritted. "Just do it, Blair."

A sly smile appeared on her face and he knew payback was going to be a bitch. "Don't worry," she told him, brushing a soft kiss on his lips, "I'll take care of you."

Then she had him in her mouth, her wet, soft, insanely skilled mouth. Sucking and licking and squeezing. She palmed his balls, fisted him in her hand, pulling him into her mouth until he thought he'd die. "I'm going to come, Blair," he choked, his hands buried helplessly in her hair. "Have some mercy."

She laughed and then rose back up onto her knees, ripping the condom wrapper open and slowly sliding the latex down his shaft, his body jumping at the contact on the ultrasensitive skin. "You said you wanted to talk about the details?" she said, referring to the earlier conversation.

She rose, poised right on top of his waiting dick, but made no move to take him into her as she waited for him to return to the conversation thread he'd derailed. "I'll downsize the house in Baton Rouge," he gasped, because this was a power play on her part, but he didn't fucking care. He'd do anything to get her to lower herself on his throbbing cock. Literally any fucking thing. He was about to fuck the woman he was in love with and he was mad to do it, to finally experience it. "I'd like to keep a small residence here because family is important to me, but I know you can't leave Sandoval Wines, so I'll tell my assistant to start looking for houses in Sonoma first thing tomorrow morning."

Looking at her expectantly, he thought he might expire from lust, simply die right there in the bed with her above him. "I love you, Blair, ever since the moment you hid your cheese and the second you opened that sweet, dirty, snarky mouth. I'll live with you anywhere, just let me live, please, because you're killing me!"

She relented, lowering down onto him, the head of his dick breaching inside her a mere inch before she stopped again. "So you're for sure being honest when you say you're not married."

He groaned so loudly the neighbors probably heard him. "Blair!" he shouted and she giggled.

"Okay, okay," she said, lowering onto him with a gasp.

His head fell back onto the pillow in relief. "Son of a bitch," he gritted as she began to move. Slowly at first because she was an evil woman, but then faster. His hands gripped her hips, guiding her even as she set the pace. Her sighs and moans filled the air as he watched her work him. She was sexy as hell above him, her dark hair falling in sheets over her breasts, the dark peach nipples poking out as she moved, her breasts swaying as she bucked. White teeth bit into her puffy pink bottom lip as she concentrated on bringing them both to pleasure.

"You like it?" Blair asked, breathless, her hands coming to rest on his chest for purchase as her pace quickened.

"You know I do, Blair," he told her, his hand coming around to her front to play with her clit. He was rewarded with a desperate cry. "I like everything you do, so I wouldn't worry overmuch about this. You're always guaranteed to make me come considering just the thought of you a million miles away gets me so hard I have to stay inside the hotel on my free days and get off."

Blair moaned again as his thumb sped up over her slick nub, her inner muscles clenching over him. A low, thundering pulse began in his lower back, signaling that he was close. Blood thundered through his body and in his ears. "You deserve to be loved, Cole," she gasped as he took her over, her muscles spasming around him as she came. Eyes closed as she came back to herself, "I hope you finally know that."

The words, so softly delivered as she came hit his heart like an anvil. He levered up and flipped her over and hammered into her, trying like hell to accept them, wanting to be able to more than anything, but fearing she would take them back at any moment. They both came again together and he was murmuring his love and devotion and promising wild things like horses and children and rainbows as he exploded, his whole previous world crumbling around him as they built a new one together.

When he'd returned to himself, he pulled her into his crook, their breathing the only sounds in the room as they fell into a lazy state of bliss. He caressed Blair's back—her soft puffs of breath glanced his chest as she fell asleep.

Almost asleep himself, he realized his phone was buzzing in his pants on the floor. Able to reach down to get them, he pulled out the phone and checked his incoming message.

At the words printed across the screen, his entire body froze.

Then before the sun rose in the morning, he was gone.

CHAPTER FOURTEEN

BLAIR WASN'T FIT for relationships, she knew that now. The jury was in, no more surveys needed, no additional mistakes left to be made, she shouldn't be allowed to make serious decisions about her love life without certified counsel.

Back in the vineyard, Nate stared at her as she hunked off a small piece of cake and put it on a serving plate before taking the rest of the dessert back with her to her office.

"Are you going to tell us what happened?" Nate asked for the fifty millionth time. "You know you should tell me first so I can at least give Mom something. She's been worried sick since you threw her out of your house last week when she came by with a care package."

Blair rolled her eyes. "I did not throw her out of my house," she said, again, for the fifty-one millionth time. "But she was already plotting to send Thou Who Shall Not be Named Part Two a poisoned pie, Nate. She's literally gone zero dark thirty and only force will get through to her."

Nate nearly argued but even he had to agree that Cole, though a maiming would be the *very* appropriate punishment for what he'd done to her—checking out of Louisiana and leaving her completely by herself without so much as a word—deserved a more appropriate punishment than death.

Well, excuse her, he had also left a note on the pillow before he'd left. A hasty scrawl of, "I'm sorry. Be well." And that was all she wrote from the man who was a river of words on any given day. His assistant had shown up after she'd woken up with a curt explanation that Cole had other business and had left Louisiana. She'd gone back home, but texted and called for a full three days until she finally got the message that he was finished with her.

And fine, Cole was an asshole who she was never going to see again and Blair *was fine*. So extremely fine she didn't know just when she'd been more fine. She was going to eat this cake, keep her mother from murdering another one of her failed exes, lock herself in the winery offices and never come out. There was enough wine in there to numb her for the rest of her life. No big deal. Hey, at least this one wasn't married!

And if she continued to be assaulted by memories of his face as he told her he loved her, the gentle way he touched her and his crafty mouth, luckily she made wine so she had enough alcohol available to make her forget.

"Okay," Nate relented. "You're right, she probably needs some firm boundaries, but I know something happened with you and Cole." He glanced point-edly at her platter of cake. "Maybe you should talk about it."

"There's nothing to talk about, Nate," she told him. "Cole and I didn't work out, not that I ever ex-pected us to, but we didn't and breakups happen to the best of us, so I'm just going to eat this cake and in a little bit I will be just great. There's no need for you to worry. I've got this." Her rage would guide her through it this time. Because unlike last time she hadn't hurt anyone else, didn't have the gnawing guilt of breaking up a marriage to con-tend with. No, now she was simply mad and she was done keeping it in. Done pretending as if her feelings didn't matter, that people could treat her shabbily and somehow it would be her fault. Nope, sorry, not anymore.

So maybe she should thank Cole because she was never going to let herself be taken advantage of again and she felt empowered by that. He'd also taught her to trust in herself and her instincts be-cause she'd known he was trouble the moment he'd walked in the tasting room door and she should have run away from him as fast as she possibly could. Which, okay, was not very fast as she was not an athlete, but still.

Only two weeks had passed since she'd flown back to California alone, her hopes and dreams for the future drowned like the sediment in the bottom of a wine barrel. After a couple of days of pure rage and denial that she'd let such a thing happen to her *again*, the internet searches were what finally brought her to terms with it and had her investing in self-renewal. It was as she originally suspected, men were awful and she was wonderful, therefore she no longer needed them to be happy.

Articles abounded of Cole with countless girls on his arm in Italy and then France. In fact, just moments ago she'd seen one today of him in Brazil with a chipper-looking blonde on his arm looking at him like he was the cake Blair was currently carrying and she a starving child at a birthday party. So apparently, he'd extended his international contract with the station so he could gallivant across the world sleeping with all the women he wanted.

He'd gotten one whiff of commitment with her and that had been enough for him to realize that he preferred his regular carefree life. She'd done the work to awaken his libido after his brother's death and now that he was recovered and his guilt assuaged, he'd returned to his freewheeling ways posthaste.

God, she'd been so unbearably naive. Every single thing he'd said to her had been a lie and like a lovesick dummy, she'd believed it, had imagined a future with him here in California but also in Baton Rouge. It was ludicrous.

"He's called me, you know," Nate said carefully. "Wanting to know if you were okay."

Blair's jaw locked. "How considerate of him," she gritted, thinking of how patronizing that was. As if

she was so fragile and susceptible to heartbreak that
he'd broken her.

Well, sorry, buddy, Blair Sandoval was not broken, nor would she ever be.

Which was why when Cole Taggart came walking into the tasting room just like he'd done all those
months ago, she didn't even bother to acknowledge
him even though said unbroken heart was busting.

"Looks like you have a customer," she sneered to
Nate before swanning out of the building.

Then she dropped the cake.

She didn't mean to drop the cake, but she dropped
the cake.

Cursing at the loss, but not letting it stop her sprint
to her car, she hopped in and drove back to her house.
There was absolutely no way she was going to stay
in the same building or vicinity as Cole. She didn't
care what explanations he might have or how the
very sight of him, tall and strong jawed, made her
yearn to forgive him.

No, thank you. She was staying strong and maybe
she'd make a panic room out of her closet and wait
there until he left again to some exotic foreign country to sensually liaise with a bevy of models.

Pulling into her garage so he wouldn't see her car,
she flew up the stairs to her house, stopping abruptly
on the landing when she realized that this was the
first place he'd look after he discovered she wasn't
at the winery.

"Fuck," she cursed, irritated all over again that
she'd let herself get in this position. All she'd ever

wanted was a simple life on the vineyard with a man who liked her and wasn't married or an international philanderer, and yet, here she was again even after being so careful to not fall in love with a man she shouldn't. To a man so clearly damaged that he couldn't accept her love when she'd given it.

Well, he could crawl on his knees to her house from the winery for all she cared because she was not going to be fooled again.

Except when she raced back down the stairs to go back outside and drive somewhere off the vineyard she saw a black sedan already gliding at a fast clip down her drive, swinging at the last moment to block the road entirely so she couldn't get out.

A growl bubbled up in her throat. But news flash for Cole: she had a four-wheeler in the garage that she used to travel around the vineyard as well and it could go anywhere. So she made a beeline for the outbuilding even as he unfolded his big body from the car and tracked her.

Wearing a pair of charcoal shorts and a white polo, he shouldn't look so normal and so clean after annihilating her heart, but that's what awful people did. They didn't care who they hurt—it gave them strength or something. Cole had been feeding so long on women's regard he was practically aging backward.

"Blair!" he called. His voice was hoarse. She could tell that even from a distance.

But that wasn't her problem. Her problem was getting to the four-wheeler before he caught up to her, which with how quickly he moved and his stupidly long legs, he was gaining a lot of ground. She'd reached the door and was unlocking it when he appeared in her peripheral vision.

"Blair, will you please hear me out?" Cole choked out, desperate to get to her before she did something like run him down with her car.

She didn't answer, just sped away from him like her feet were on fire. He deserved whatever she was going to throw at him, but he did need her to, in fact, throw it, not just leave the way he had. Like a fucking coward.

He tracked her as she went inside the garage and walked in through the large door she opened. She was sitting on a four-wheeler, prepared to start it up and get the hell out of Dodge, but Cole wasn't having it and stood right in front of it. On her other side was a golf cart without a key so the only way for her to leave was to plow right over him. He was only half sure that she wouldn't do just that. Hell, he'd do it to himself.

He might get his wish too, because she twisted the key in the ignition, eyes glinting as she revved the engine with her foot on the brake.

"You're going to have to get through me first, Blair," Cole warned. "And I'm not going anywhere ever again."

He'd learned a lot of lessons real quick the moment he'd gotten on the plane and back to Europe, leaving her alone in his home. As he'd stood on the side of the same track his brother had died on, he'd seen the rest of his life flash before his eyes. Was he really going to continue living half of one forever? Scott wouldn't have wanted that. And if their places had been reversed, Cole sure as hell wouldn't want his brother wandering around like a fucking zombie. He'd want him to be happy.

So here Cole was, trying to take back his happiness.

Except it sure as hell wasn't gonna be easy.

"Yeah, well, I've heard that before," she bit off bitterly, letting the ATV inch closer to him.

His big hands wrapped around the handlebars and he braced himself. "I'm sorry, Blair, okay? But please let me explain."

"Unless the explanation is amnesia and you suddenly woke up in bed and forgot who I was, I'd say I wouldn't bother."

Cole took a deep breath, his eyes closing because he was in a fight for his life and he was battered. He watched as her gaze locked on his face, cataloging his sallow and pale skin, dark circles under his eyes and red rims around them as well. His stubble was untrimmed, left to grow wild and unkempt and to top it off, there was a big stain on his shirt just off to the side of his abdomen. He'd spilled coffee on the plane and hadn't bothered to change.

"I forgot the anniversary of Scott's death," he said, his voice low and still tortured. He met her eyes, for the first time letting his pain show to someone. He might be taking back hold of his life, but he'd still

carry the loss with him too. "You and I had that incredible day together, you fell asleep in my arms,
then I got a text from my sister saying that I'd forgotten to meet them at the gravesite earlier in the day
and I lost it, Blair." He felt the tears in his eyes. "I had
such a good time with you that I'd allowed myself
to forget him when I'm the last person who should
find happiness, let alone so much that I actually for
one fucking day forgot that I killed my own brother."

The words were choked and broken and tears fell
down his cheeks and he let them go. She was worth
it. *They* were worth it.

Finally, she flipped off the ignition to the four-
wheeler and went to him, her arms circling his stomach as he got hold of himself. For the first time in
weeks, with her arms around him, he was able to
take a full breath.

"Like I told you before," Blair said, her voice firm
and matter-of-fact. "You did not kill your brother,
Cole, it was an accident."

"I should have remembered the anniversary," he
said stubbornly, not willing to let himself off the
hook for that at least. "They didn't even text to ask
where I was because they know that I'm a shitty
brother and a shitty son. And now I'm a shitty boyfriend because I've fucked things up with the only
woman I've ever loved."

Blair gave him a wry grin and released herself
from his embrace. "That's probably true, but I have
to admit that it's gratifying to see you brought down
a level, doubting yourself."

The look he gave her was miserable, but just like when he'd first met her, she was already shaking him out of the guilt trap he'd been in for the past two weeks.

"Say to me that you didn't kill your brother," Blair demanded, pointing a stern finger at him.

His lips stayed sealed and she flicked him in the chest. "You have a lot to apologize for, Cole," she reminded him, "but the death of your brother is not one of those things." She stood firm. "Say it." Jaw tight, Cole stared at her, unmoving because it was his fault, but he'd forgiven himself and been able to make it up to his family. "If you don't say it, I'm going to run you over with this four-wheeler and it will be the last time you'll ever see me."

"Because you'll be in jail," Cole muttered under his breath.

"I can hear you!" Blair called from where she'd returned to her perch on the ATV and he held back a smile. Damn, he was doing the right thing here. Against all odds, he'd found the right woman to bring him back from the dead all on some chance visit to a vineyard on his day off. That was the type of serendipity a man had to marvel at.

So he grabbed his future with both hands. "I didn't kill my brother."

"One more time," she ordered, ruthless.

"I did not kill my brother," Cole gritted out, because it still wasn't easy to say. It probably never would be.

"Good," Blair told him briskly. "And maybe you'll

let yourself be happy now and not drag other unsuspecting nice people into your world of pain." With that, she started the ignition again. "Now get out of my way."

Cole's hands came down on the handlebars again and he glared at her. "No," he declared, his eyes boring into hers, as if he could make her stay with just a look.

"It doesn't matter what you say, Cole, I'll never trust you again," she told him. "Those photos with women alone would have done it."

That was a hit and he flinched, but refused to back down. "I get that, Blair, and I deserve it, but those photos in the articles were old. I would *never* do that to you. Nor would I even want to sleep with anyone else. You're the only person for me. The only one who I would still love even as she threatened to run me over with a recreational vehicle. I'll take whatever you need to give me, pay whatever penance I need for you to trust me again. But I am asking for at least a chance."

She was unmoved.

But it didn't matter because he had more to say. "I got the transfer to America, I've already bought a house about twenty miles from here, right on the Russian River, so we can take things as slow or as fast as you want. I'd settle for one hour a week of your time, to just see your face and hear your voice." His voice broke on the last. "I've missed you so much, Blair, and I'm so sorry. I just panicked because I should remember him. He was my best friend and brother and being with you is so good that I didn't even honor the fucking memory of his death. I could barely look at myself in the eye, let alone let you be in love with someone like me. You deserve better, Blair. That's just the truth and I know it."

Something must have gotten through to her because there were tears on her cheeks and his chest had loosened. Maybe he hadn't lost her after all.

Blair had never experienced the kind of loss Cole had and his words touched her. She'd finally had the courage to trust her heart and it had led her to Cole, but she wasn't the only one his actions had broken. Maybe it was up to her to overcome the fear of failure that gripped her every time she thought about putting her own heart on the line, because he'd just done it for her and it felt glorious. Like an oasis in a long journey through the desert.

"I don't deserve better than you, Cole," Blair finally said, letting go of the fear. Her whole body felt light, the weight of denying her heart lifting. "Because you are pretty wonderful."

His eyes widened at her about-face. And for the first time since she'd woken up to that note on her pillow, Blair felt powerful. No longer running or plotting revenge, she was going to do this right and give them a real chance. Cole wasn't getting away from her again. Unless, of course, he truly wanted to break up with her—she wasn't a person smuggler, but what she meant was that she had a part in this too. She was no longer the side girl in someone's life where someone could take her out and play with her when they wanted while she accepted it because that's all *she* expected from someone. She was going to be in Cole's life for real. All in, cards on the table, future on the line, with an emotionally misguided man with a mouth that never shut up. He was hers and she was going to work at it no matter how much cutting her losses might be easier.

"You are the kindest, silliest, smartest, hottest and just plain perfect man I've ever met," she told him. "And I'm just not going to let you go again, so decide now if this is a situation you're okay with because the next time you leave me somewhere will be the last time you see me."

He swallowed. "I understand," he said, quietly, his voice serious. "I don't ever want to."

"And I decide what I do and don't deserve," she reminded him. "Do you understand that too?"

He nodded, looking appropriately chastised.

"Good," she said. "So now what?" Smiling, she continued, "I've never been in love before so I don't know what happens now."

Cole's shoulders shook. "I love you so much," he said, lifting her straight off the vehicle and into his arms, some of the color back in his face. She was glad for it. "I don't know what happens exactly at this moment, but I can tell you that we're gonna make our way up to that bedroom of yours so I can show you just how sorry I am. Twelve unreciprocated orgasms, at least, are coming your way. Pun definitely intended."

She shook her head, but then he grew serious as his forehead met hers. His smell, his warmth, the firm way he held her against him all felt new and familiar because this time she was in the arms of the man she planned to spend the rest of her life with. These were her arms now.

"Can you forgive me?" he whispered, anguish still in his voice. "Like honestly forgive me, Blair? I asked my manager to keep records of my time on the road, he'll verify that I never left my room at night. Those pictures of me with women only surfaced again because of the anniversary of Scott's death." He took a deep breath. "I wanted to call and reassure you, but after what I did, I honestly didn't think you'd care."

The last part of Blair, the scared and hurt part she'd let rule her life for so long wanted to see the proof that he hadn't been out, but she was either in this thing with Cole or out and whatever this was, a relationship or a marriage, their future together started with trust.

"I forgive you, Cole," she assured him, finally letting her lips find his. He held on, squeezing her against him.

"I love you so much," he rasped, clearly overwhelmed by the exoneration. "I'd still be miserable and hopeless without you, Blair. You gave me my life back."

Blair smiled, unable to stop kissing him. "You brought me back too, Cole," she told him. "For the first time I finally found someone who wants me for me." He kissed her then, nearly suffocating her as he held her tight, their tongues and teeth bumping in a rush of exploding, uncontainable emotions.

She pulled back so she could see his face and grinned at him. "I should have known from the moment you shared my love of cheese that we were meant to be."

Cole looked uncertain for a moment, cringing as he avoided her eyes. "Yeah, so the thing is…" he hedged, scratching the back of his head. "I actually don't love cheese at all. In fact, I'm lactose intolerant. I just ate it to spend time with you."

Blair laughed at first but it soon gave way to an uncontrollable giggle as she kissed him all over his face. "Well, what can I say," Blair finally said, "I've always said there's no accounting for taste."

He lifted her into his arms and kissed her forehead. "Fair," he agreed, "but then that would explain why I love *you* so much."

Ignoring her playful glare, he kissed her again, and Blair knew she was loved.

* * * * *

MILLS & BOON

THE HEART OF ROMANCE

A ROMANCE FOR EVERY READER

MODERN

Prepare to be swept off your feet by sophisticated, sexy and seductive heroes, in some of the world's most glamourous and roman locations, where power and passion collide.

HISTORICAL

Escape with historical heroes from time gone by. Whether your passio for wicked Regency Rakes, muscled Vikings or rugged Highlanders, a the romance of the past.

MEDICAL

Set your pulse racing with dedicated, delectable doctors in the high-pr sure world of medicine, where emotions run high and passion, comfo love are the best medicine.

True Love

Celebrate true love with tender stories of heartfelt romance, from the rush of falling in love to the joy a new baby can bring, and a focus on emotional heart of a relationship.

Desire

Indulge in secrets and scandal, intense drama and plenty of sizzling he action with powerful and passionate heroes who have it all: wealth, sta good looks…everything but the right woman.

HEROES

Experience all the excitement of a gripping thriller, with an intense ro mance at its heart. Resourceful, true-to-life women and strong, fearles face danger and desire - a killer combination!

To see which titles are coming soon, please visit

millsandboon.co.uk/nextmonth